WHISTLING
WOMEN

WHISTLING WOMEN

KELLY ROMO

LAKE UNION
PUBLISHING

This is a work of fiction. Names, characters, organizations, places, events, and incidents are either products of the author's imagination or are used fictitiously. The principal characters, as well as the workers' camp, contained within it are pure inventions. Any similarities to anyone living or deceased are merely coincidental. Even though this is a work of fiction, the famous figures, exhibits, and key events associated with the 1935 California Pacific International Exposition are based on facts and rendered to the best of my ability, with some creative liberties to help the narrative flow.

Published by Lake Union Publishing, Seattle

www.apub.com

Amazon, the Amazon logo, and Lake Union Publishing are trademarks of Amazon.com, Inc., or its affiliates.

ISBN-13: 9781503950887 (hardcover)

ISBN-10: 1503950883 (hardcover)

ISBN-13: 9781503948785 (paperback)

ISBN-13: 1503948781 (paperback)

Cover design by Mumtaz Mustafa

Printed in the United States of America

For my children: Brittany, Brennan, and Ryan
You never stopped believing in me

"A whistling woman and a crowing hen always come to some bad end."

—proverb

CHAPTER ONE
ADDIE

Sleepy Valley Nudist Colony
Northern California
May 22, 1935

Addie arrived at the exercise grounds the same way she always did—naked. Bits of mowed grass clung to her feet and ankles as she and the other goosefleshed nudists hopped about, trying to keep warm, waiting for the morning sun to break through the chill or for Elsa to start beating on the tom-toms. Every morning began with exercise, a swim, and then breakfast. Stimulate the blood, then feed the body. Heinrich ran Sleepy Valley like a German clock, precise and on time. The routine suited Addie. She always knew where to be and what Heinrich expected of her; she knew when she'd eat, when she'd sleep, when she'd clean, and when she'd exercise, and she never felt guilty about lounging around in the sun or floating in the lake, because Heinrich made time for that too. Some of the other nudists resented his schedule, itching to get away from any hint of a rule or obligation, but since Heinrich controlled who came in the gates and who he threw out of them, they all toed the line—for the most part.

Elsa began beating an aboriginal rhythm on the tom-toms. Addie moved into her place—front row, far left. She noticed that Daisy's normal spot—third row, second column—was empty and so was Eleanor's. Daisy hadn't been in her bed when Addie awoke, either. Addie glanced back at Yvette, who shrugged and shifted, filling Daisy's place and causing the rest of the residents to reposition. Heinrich didn't tolerate gaps. Addie and the other nudists mirrored Frieda's movements, reaching to the left, to the right, and touching their toes. They all moved in perfect synchronicity, except for the guests in the back—flushed in various shades of brown, white, and newly sunburned, they moved one beat behind the residents.

Two new guests, a man and a woman, lingered on the outskirts of the exercise grounds, shrunken in their nakedness and trying to get up enough nerve to join in. The man had the markings of a laborer, a white torso with a tanned face, neck, and forearms. With his red hair and brown-and-white skin, he reminded Addie of Neapolitan ice cream. His wife, slim and wispy, cowered, with her arms shielding her breasts. Even at thirty-two years old and with fifteen years at the colony, Addie still wasn't comfortable with the newcomers. Through their eyes, she remembered her own shock the first time she saw people cavorting about the outdoors naked and exposed. So much flesh. And on the exercise grounds, oh, the exercise grounds, with breasts and johnsons bouncing, bodies bending and perspiring in the sun. The normally unseen effects of gravity and momentum had undulated before her eyes. New people made Addie wonder if her butt jiggled as much as Clara's did or if they judged her as brazen or debased because of her willingness to be unclothed.

Many guests and residents commented about the freedom of nudity, the feeling of the wind and the sun on their bodies, and how it offered an escape from the rigors and drudgery of everyday life, but to

Addie, you could strip off every shred of clothing and still be bound. Real freedom was freedom of the spirit. It was not what covered your flesh or did not cover your flesh, it was the tethers of sin on your soul.

The beat quickened and they all followed Frieda, running, leaping, swinging, arching, and bending their bodies like amateur contortionists, naked and bronze from the sun. Even though most of the permanent residents were young, tanned, and toned, Addie had come to love the sight of regular guests like Mr. and Mrs. Thurman, gray haired and exercising out of step with abbreviated movements, and Mrs. Thurman always wearing her white pearl choker with a cameo clasped around her neck, making her—even in the nude—appear dignified and refined. Or the Harrisons with their brood of seven children, like stepping-stones, each one an increasingly smaller chip off the old block of Mr. Harrison's massive form and Mrs. Harrison's weary child-bearing body.

Every time Addie twisted to the left, she caught glimpses of the newcomers backed up against a hedge of oleanders. She judged them to be what Addie called *experimental nudists*, here to have a new experience. She imagined the man coming home with some brochure he'd found and selling the idea to his wife, working on her for months until she relented and they finally came—only to hunker in a bush like Adam and Eve after the apple.

Addie glanced around at the familiar bodies, perspiring and bending and reaching in near-perfect cadence and harmony. She and all the other permanent residents were scheduled to leave in the morning, and for the first time, Addie had decided to stay behind. She hadn't had the nerve to tell anyone yet, but she wasn't going. The cars would arrive at six forty-five to cart the residents off to the ferry, and from there, across the bay to San Francisco, where they'd catch a train to the world's fair in San Diego. Another world's fair. More police supervision and strict policies of decorum from fair directors. More outraged bluestockings picketing for removal of the colony, and outraged nudists from other colonies calling them exhibitionists and sellouts. A different place, a new routine. For the past two summers they'd lounged around naked at the Century of Progress in Chicago, sightseers gawking or taunting them, as if they were no better than caged monkeys in a zoo, while others watched silently, shocked at the indecency or fulfilling their own perversions.

Heinrich, like a devoted missionary, schlepped his family of nudists around the country to spread his own religion of *Nacktkultur*—nakedness and vegetarianism—to the United States. Unfortunately, because the attitudes of most Americans differed greatly from those in his native country of Germany, Heinrich's message wasn't received in the way he intended and they ended up in the category of girly and peep shows. Most people considered them lewd, indecent, immoral, and shameless. Even though Heinrich rarely received any converts, he did earn enough money at the fairs to keep Sleepy Valley going as an affordable pleasure resort.

One less disciple in the road show shouldn't make too much of a difference. Addie knew that the expectation was that she go, and she would—if it were anywhere but San Diego. That part of her life had been slammed shut for seventeen years, and she didn't know if she had it in her to crack it open.

Addie figured she'd better tell Daisy first or she'd blow a gasket. She had planned on telling her right after morning gymnastics, but Daisy had obviously played hooky. After thirty minutes of vigorous exercise, Addie took the short path to the lake. Lining her toes up at the edge of the wooden dock, she stretched her arms straight above her head and plunged into the emerald depths, diving with her eyes open, as she did every morning. Rain or shine. The cold water snapped every pore to life. Rays of sunlight penetrated the water, as if, even beneath the surface, God could see her. No matter how much time had passed or how long she'd laid low at the colony, God knew her sins. Addie surfaced and filled her lungs with air and then floated facedown. The voices around her mingled into a single hum of unintelligible babble. She wished she could drift there forever, suspended, separate from the life playing out around her. Addie imagined her hair forming a golden halo around her head—a naked and fallen angel.

Afterward, with her hair still dripping strings of cool water down her back and breasts, she searched the oak savanna for Daisy but found only five naked adolescents on the rope swings, three girls with newly budding breasts and two boys, one still round faced and the other lean and gangly. The two boys looked like Harrisons—they had the tell-tale ruddy complexion and dark wavy hair. Even in their nakedness, the children seemed healthy and innocent. The boys and girls laughed together, flirting, but none of them grabbing one another or aroused. None of them hid or acted ashamed when they noticed her presence. The gangly boy, with a buzz cut and fresh sunburn, gently pushed a girl who stood on a wooden board knotted at the base of a rope. The other boy worked the tip of his pocketknife into the bark of a tree. These youngsters appeared at ease with one another, no shame about their bodies or embarrassment about exposing themselves. Much different than when she was young and in the orphan asylum, where girls would pull your hair if they thought you looked at them while changing, and boys peeked through keyholes at the girls dressing or dropped their britches, just for the shock of it.

The bell clanged from the *landhaus.*

"Breakfast," the girl on the rope swing yelled, jumping off and falling flat on her butt. She sprang up before the boy had a chance to help her, brushed the dirt and bits of leaves off her bare bottom, and hightailed it toward the *landhaus.*

Addie joined the throng of people emerging from the exercise grounds, the lake, the forest paths, the cottages, and the showers, all crossing over the rolling lawns toward the German manor house where she and the other permanent residents lived. Addie breathed in deep, taking in the smells of spring—sweet, damp, and earthy.

Three times a day, the dinner bell sounded, causing a mass migration of people of every shape and size—anywhere between golden brown or sunburned from head to toe. Some were tall and thin, spindly or muscular. Others had doughy flesh or pear-shaped bodies. Flat or round bottoms. Thick waists or long waists, short legs or long legs, perky or drooping breasts, stocky or athletic. Some moved with grace and ease, and others stepped flatfooted or lumbering. For some reason she could not explain, Addie felt a sense of unity with the variety of people. Most of them were unknown to her or only casual acquaintances, but all were headed in the same direction, with the same needs, and on the same schedule. They gathered together around long wooden tables laden with oats, breads, jams, bowls overflowing with oranges and grapefruit, baked sweet potatoes, and pitchers of water and orange juice. Some were shy and others outgoing or boisterous, some irritating, others humorous, but everyone worked together, passing the food and napkins, sharing stories or personal histories.

Daisy wasn't at breakfast, either. Addie grabbed an orange and a slice of bread before climbing up the two flights of stairs to the bedroom she and Daisy shared. How she longed for bacon, a chicken leg, or a single slice of ham. Heinrich enforced his third golden rule of no meat as strictly as the other two: no alcohol and no tobacco. That said, Addie frequently found guests ducking behind the brush on the nature trails to sneak cigarettes, and one time, while walking along a path, she caught a man crouched behind a coyote bush, tipping a flask into his juice cup. Addie pretended not to notice. Live and let live. She had to admire how he snuck the flask out there in the first place, given that nudists have no pockets.

Addie tried to push her bedroom door open, but it banged into Daisy's trunk. The noise startled Hobbs, Daisy's miserable red-and-green macaw, causing him to squawk and beat his wings against the cage.

"Why's the door blocked?" Addie asked through the gap.

Addie could see Daisy lying on her bed, with a plume of cigarette smoke rising above her, but she didn't answer. Addie leaned into the door, scraping Daisy's trunk across the hardwood until she could squeeze through. Hobbs shuffled back and forth on his perch, like an old man with a hunchback, moaning and watching Addie with his yellow eyes. A haze of smoke clung to the ceiling, and the curtains fluttered out the open window as if trying to lap up fresh air.

"Where'd you get the cigarettes?"

Daisy took a long drag and exhaled a gray cloud. "None of your business."

Daisy and Addie were the same age, but Daisy had never managed to shake the *ward of the state* look with her mop of short brown hair and *I dare you to cross me* glare.

"Can I have a drag?"

Daisy sighed but held it up to Addie. From the looks of it, she'd smoked nearly a whole pack. A trail of ashes dusted Daisy's breasts and her stomach and peppered the white bedspread.

Addie reached for the cigarette, but Daisy pulled it back. "Just a drag." Daisy offered it again and Addie closed her lips around it. She hadn't had a smoke since last summer in Chicago.

"You're not packed," Daisy said.

Addie's trunk lay open at the end of her bed, exposing the pink fabric inside. "You opened my trunk?"

"Sal came for it and said it felt awfully light, so, yeah, I opened it." Daisy reached beneath her pillow and pulled out a silver flask with a hummingbird engraved on it. With a few twists, the cap dropped to her stomach, then wobbled onto the bed.

"And where'd you get that?"

"Lay off the third degree." Daisy took a swig. "Why aren't you packed?"

"I'm not going."

"You being thrown out too?"

"Too?" Addie lowered herself onto the edge of her own bed, the chenille spread cool and bumpy on her bottom.

"Heinrich's throwing Eleanor out. As soon as we leave for San Diego—to avoid a scene." Daisy took another sip. "Gettin' too old to hang around for free."

"Can't she stay in one of the guest cabins?"

"How's she gonna pay for it? With her good looks?" Daisy let out a fake laugh, then pushed herself up and swung her legs to the side of the bed. The ashes fluttered onto her lap, dusting her pubic hair. "That's what *we're* doin', Addie, paying with our good looks. And guess what?"

Daisy aimed the flask at Addie and she took it. With the cigarette still burning between Daisy's fingers, she scooped up her breasts, boosting them practically to her collarbone. "These aren't what they used to be, and neither are yours. We're next."

"Can't Eleanor help out in the kitchen or clean the *landhaus*?"

"Wise up. Heinrich's a businessman, and old nudists just aren't good business."

"But what about his dream of helping men on relief?"

"Eleanor's not a man. What good is she to him? What could she do that Frieda's not already providing?"

Addie hadn't thought much about where she'd go when Heinrich didn't need her any longer. In fact, she'd never planned any part of her life at all. Someone either took her away, shipped her out, or she just ran off, ending up wherever she ended up and making do. It had never occurred to Addie that one day she might be too old to make do. With Eleanor gone, that left her and Daisy as the colony's oldest permanent residents. Except for Elsa, but she was Heinrich's sister. Addie couldn't imagine leaving Sleepy Valley.

"Just like Eleanor," Daisy said, "you and me, soon we'll be no good to Heinrich and his grand plan."

"At least you have Sal," Addie said. No matter what, Daisy had her son. Addie had nobody.

"Thank God I do." Daisy reached out, demanding the flask back. "But Sal's only seventeen. He can't support me yet."

Daisy sucked in the rest of the cigarette, stubbed it out on the flask, and pointed the butt of it at Addie's empty trunk. "So?"

"I'm not going."

"Why the hell not?"

"My sister lives in San Diego."

Daisy flicked her cigarette at Addie. It bounced off her shoulder and dropped to the floor. "Listen, I've known you all these goddamned years and you've never mentioned a sister?"

Addie knew she shouldn't have flapped her trap. It had never done her any good to tell her business. "My sister disowned me a long time ago," Addie said.

"Oh, wah, wah, wah. So what? You won't step foot in the entire city?" Daisy took another swig. "If you don't go, you might as well pack your bags and live in some shantytown with Eleanor. Heinrich won't put up with it."

"Mother?" Sal poked his head into the room, and Daisy waved him in. "Hello, Addie," he said, kissing her cheek.

"What am I? Chopped liver?" Daisy asked.

Sal frowned at the flask in his mother's hand. "You alright?"

"Just swell," Daisy said.

"Heinrich's looking for you."

After an exaggerated salute, Daisy held out her hand. Sal's thin muscles tightened as he helped her up. Even after fifteen years at the colony, seeing mother and almost-grown son, both completely naked and oblivious of it, astonished Addie.

Daisy waved the flask at Addie. "To the end." She took another swig. "To the *bitter* end."

Addie hoped Daisy could pull herself together and not get close enough for Heinrich to smell her breath. Before leaving the room, Daisy set the flask on the windowsill and put a dab of perfume on each of her butt cheeks. "Just in case Heinrich wants to kiss my ass," she said.

"You gonna be packed soon?" Sal asked Addie. "We're sending the trunks on ahead and Heinrich's been on me. Yours and Mother's are the last two."

Addie closed her eyes and took in a deep breath. She'd never gone against Heinrich's wishes, but why did it have to be San Diego? She knew Daisy was right and she'd better not cross Heinrich. "I'll have it packed and ready in an hour."

"Thanks, I'll come back for it then."

"Sal," Addie said, causing him to pause in the doorway. "It's hard to believe you're so grown-up. Sometimes I still think of you as a toddler or the eight-year-old boy who used to catch frogs and hide them in my bed."

"I only did it because I was sweet on you." He winked, then shifted his mother's trunk onto a dolly and rolled it out of the room.

The inside of Addie's trunk smelled of mothballs—the scent of leaving, of train rides and strange places, of strange people and long fretful nights. Her one print dress and tweed suit dangled from their hangers on the wardrobe bar in her trunk, with her navy pumps and bedroom slippers in the shoe box below. A pair of cotton gloves, a handkerchief, a pink chemise with lace, and a corset with boning, which she'd never worn, all floated around in the top drawer. The other two drawers held her training suit, nightgown, and robe, and the only books she owned, *Among the Nudists* and *On Going Naked*, given to her by Heinrich when she'd first arrived at the colony, and the detestable book she should've burned long ago, *How to Be a Lady: A Book for Girls, Containing Useful Hints on the Formation of Character*. She felt as if she'd forgotten something, but her drawers, closet, and the space beneath her bed were empty.

Addie felt like a child about to play dress-up and venture away from home. Away from the security of her own bed, her own routine, and her own comfortable night sounds. Addie's white crepe dress, silk stockings, and garter belt hung over the footboard of her bed, ready for the train trip the next morning. Standing before the vanity mirror, Addie held the dress against her bare body. Clothed Addie. And took it away. Nude Addie. As she put it back, the fabric brushed against her skin. She dreaded sliding her legs into stockings.

Hobbs's cage waited by the door, an iron prison in the shape of the Taj Mahal. Addie wondered if he'd be packed in with all the luggage on the train or if they had a special compartment for animals. He shuffled around inside, complaining and cracking his sunflower seeds. A dingy macaw in his Taj Mahal. Daisy should've named him Taj Macaw.

The lace curtains breathed in and out of the open window, still lapping at the fresh air. Daisy had left her bed rumpled and dusted with ash, and her flask still sat on the windowsill.

The cigar box. She'd forgotten the cigar box. Addie dragged the vanity stool to the closet and stepped onto the cushion with her bare feet. Even then, she could scarcely reach the back shelf. People had always teased her about her height, calling her small fry, half pint, Thumbelina, little bit, pip-squeak, elf, canary, or anything small. She used to tell people she was still growing, but now at thirty-two, she could no longer sell that bridge. Addie scooted the old wooden box forward with her fingertips until she could grab it. The label, thin and worn, still showed the little robin redbreast perched on a woman's finger under the red "Bellefair" banner. Addie hesitated, then raised it to her nose. She didn't know whether it was only her imagination, but she caught the slight scent of Ty's cigars still lingering inside. Memories of the little house with the chicken coop, the eggs in various shades of brown, the red-splotched oleanders, and the cigar smoke that clouded the rooms and seeped under her closed bedroom door pricked their way in, bringing that familiar feeling, as if stitch by stitch, her throat were being sewn shut and she couldn't breathe.

If she could only stay at the colony, away from San Diego. Addie ran her fingers over the top of the cigar box. She hadn't looked through the contents for years. She occasionally cracked the lid to slide in a postcard, but she couldn't bring herself to hold it open and stir up all those old memories.

She could still unpack and refuse to go. But if Heinrich kicked her out, what would she do? A middle-aged woman with no other skills than canning, weeding a vegetable garden, hanging laundry on a line, and tramping around the outdoors in her birthday suit didn't have many options.

The head of the little robin redbreast on the lid of the cigar box was tipped to the side, innocently staring up at her, as if he had no idea of the painful memories buried beneath him. Addie sat down on her chenille bedspread, with the box on her lap. She ran her finger over the worn image of the woman, who'd always reminded her of her sister, and lifted the lid. Postcards from the 1934 Chicago Century of Progress, San Francisco's Fisherman's Wharf, and Chinatown lay on top like a colorful window-covering on a funeral parlor, not fooling anyone about what lay behind them. She lifted the postcards off, uncovering her father's old pocket watch and a lock of Mary's baby hair. Mary must be eighteen by now, but to Addie, she remained a golden-haired toddler, standing at the bars of her crib and waking her with gibberish.

She set the lock of hair and pocket watch on the bedspread, and continued removing her past, layer by layer, unearthing the artifacts of her ruined life. The onionskin page of the Ten Commandments, which she'd torn from a Bible—another sin, no doubt—crinkled as she lifted it out. *Thou shalt not kill. Thou shalt not commit adultery. Thou shalt not steal.* She set it aside, on top of Mary's baby hair. Then, finally, on the bottom layer, the eight yellowed envelopes she'd sent to her sister a lifetime ago, which were never opened. Wavey had scrawled "Return to Sender" across each one, and they had all come back over the years, like pathetic and bone-weary homing pigeons with their undelivered messages, until Addie had finally stopped sending them. Addie drew one out and tipped it toward the light. The postmark read "December 20, 1918," the first one she'd sent. Addie didn't need to break the seal; she knew what it said. What they all said.

Addie had nothing left of Daniel's, though, no baby hair or christening gown. His life so short that it had never amounted to anything. Ashes to ashes. She remembered that morning fifteen years earlier, waking from the sun and not from Daniel's hungry cries. How long had the room been silent? Something in her had tried to keep her from looking into the cradle. But she did. And found a tiny blue body in the shape of her baby. God had not finished punishing her. She and Daniel had barely survived his birth. Addie had thought both she and her baby would die during the long labor—just like her mother and baby brother had—as the doctor tore Daniel from between her thighs. In her case, it would have been well deserved. An eye for an eye. But they had both survived—at least long enough to make losing Daniel all the more painful.

They'd buried Daniel in a crooked wooden box, wrapped in only a thin blanket made from scraps of Uncle Henry's old farm shirts; her sweet baby boy lay shrunken like a rag doll only half filled with sawdust.

The preacher's worn-out voice had faded in and out of her awareness that morning as they stood at the family graveyard behind the farmhouse. "O God, whose beloved Son."

Everyone averted their eyes from her, shunning and shaming. They knew that God had punished her for having a bastard child—and that she deserved it.

"We beseech thee, to entrust this child, Daniel, to thy never-failing care."

But they didn't know all of it. If they had, they would've never given her sanctuary in their home—family or not. Harboring a fallen woman with a bastard child was one thing, but a murderess would have been inconceivable. Even if Uncle Henry didn't know, God knew. And He had punished her. Again.

"Thou hast set our misdeeds before thee, and our secret sins in the light of thy countenance."

Uncle Henry and the preacher lowered Daniel's woeful little coffin into the hole.

"And we commit Daniel's body to the ground, earth to earth, ashes to ashes, dust to dust."

Addie piled everything back into the cigar box and shut the lid.

Four shiny black Buicks, all chrome grills and whitewalls, caravanned up the oak-lined drive toward the Landhaus Verhoven, where Addie, Daisy, and twelve other newly clothed nudists waited, looking like a line of Russian nesting dolls—biggest to smallest, with Heinrich at the head and Addie at the heel. Addie imagined that at any moment they would all be swallowed up by Heinrich, tucked in one at a time, with Addie buried in the deepest core. They always stood in order, aesthetically pleasing to the eye, even if those eyes were only those of the drivers of the rented cars hired to take them to Sausalito. In Sausalito, they'd catch the ferry across the bay and then drive to the train terminal in San Francisco. They loaded into the cars in order, only Frieda stepping out of line to ride in the same car as her husband.

The ferry cut through the wind-chopped waters of San Francisco Bay, where seabirds dipped and dove through the early morning chill and only a thin gauze of fog blurred the surface. Heinrich could hardly contain himself at the appearance of the two gigantic steel towers, one on either side of the Golden Gate Strait. The last time they'd passed, on their way home from Chicago, only the north tower had been erected. Heinrich gave a long soliloquy on how the new bridge meant economic growth and easy access in a motorcar from San Francisco to Sleepy Valley—a continuous flow of guests to and fro. He'd returned from a visit to his homeland of Germany four years earlier—the trip from which he'd come back with Frieda, his young bride, and armloads of German nudist magazines and pamphlets—with a grand plan. In Heinrich's vision, the out-of-work men of San Francisco would camp in the woods of Sleepy Valley. And just like in Germany, the destitute men could stay clean and bronze and healthy by throwing off their dirty and bedraggled clothing to work in the sun. A free exchange of labor for health and hygiene. Other than money, which the trips to the world fairs were intended to solve, the two main kinks in his plan were the long ferry lines across the bay and trying to convince hard-working men who liked their drink to come frolic naked and sober in the woods. At least one of Heinrich's obstacles would be eliminated with the construction of the Golden Gate Bridge.

In contrast to the new bridge, Alcatraz Island rose out of the bay like a rocky and desolate lump of coal. The prison made her shudder, since she knew that she could very well be shut away behind iron bars. Addie wondered if the men of Alcatraz could see the bridge from their cells and yard, only able to watch the world being built and connected around them, knowing they could never touch or step foot upon it. She wondered if it drove them mad.

The rented cars carried them like royalty, shuttling them through streets littered with hordes of grim-faced men squatting against walls or perching upon empty food crates. Women and children wandered around, looking dazed and bewildered. On one sidewalk, men in dark suits waited in a thick line, the front of which disappeared into the open doorway of the Salvation Army. The only thing between Addie and the shantytown of old crates and cardboard and malnourished children was Heinrich's generosity. She pictured these same beaten-down men at the colony and agreed with Heinrich's vision. Without their soiled clothing and unwashed skin, and with a few weeks in the sun and some food in their bellies, they'd be indistinguishable from anyone else. Addie wondered if Eleanor would become one of them or if she'd head into the valley, looking for work picking cantaloupes or apricots. She wondered if Heinrich could bring himself to look out the car window at this chaos of humanity with no sense of order or hygiene, or did he avert his eyes and focus on their traveling papers, neat and crisp in their leather folio?

At the station, police and railroad detectives monitored the terminal, cars, and tracks, keeping them free of vagrants. Once on the train, Addie took a window seat, flabbergasted that she was on her way to San Diego. Everything in her told her to escape. To jump off the train and run down the platform—find a way back to the colony and spend the summer lost in Sleepy Valley, exercising, swimming, and sunning with the guests. She stared out the window at the travelers on the platform—at the bustle of purpose and direction, everyone all buttoned-up in stiff and binding fabrics. A stern man in a black suit walked in front of a woman trailing three children, all linked hand in hand and followed by a porter with an overloaded cart of trunks. Many glum-looking businessmen strode past with newspapers tucked beneath their arms and clutching briefcases. A scrawny girl limped by, as if her shiny new shoes were scraping the skin off her heels. She tried to keep pace with a heavyset woman in spectacles, who demonstrated no motherly tenderness for the girl trailing behind her. By the cropped hair and freshly scrubbed red skin, Addie guessed the girl to be an orphan on her way to a new home, the girl imagining that all her troubles had ended and a bright new life awaited her. Eighteen years earlier, Addie had been that girl, with the same fanciful, but completely misguided, expectation.

Logsdon Orphan Asylum and Home for Friendless Children
Logsdon, Kansas
February 1917

Addie had read the letter so many times that the creases of the paper had worn thin and fibrous. Wavey's familiar tight-looped script slanted to the left in the most delightful words. It had been almost an entire year since the last letter, and Addie had thought something terrible had happened to her sister or that Wavey had given up on her. But now, here it was, the most wonderful letter she'd ever received.

> *My Dearest Addie,*
>
> *Please forgive my lapse in correspondence. I've married a man named Tyrone Fulton Briggs. Imagine me, married. Mrs. Wavey Rose Briggs. Mrs. Wavey Rose Briggs. Mrs. Wavey Rose Briggs. I love the sound of it. Isn't it lovely? On top of that great news, I've been working some time to convince the courts to release you to me, and they have done it. I want you to come and live with us. I hadn't contacted you earlier because I didn't know how long it would take and didn't want to get your hopes up, but it is done. The arrangements are being made, and you will come to live with us in California. It is sunny here year*

*round. Can you believe a winter without snow? But that
is how it is here in San Diego.*

Your beloved sister,
Mrs. Wavey Rose Briggs

Addie tried to imagine her wild-haired sister all grown-up, with a
husband and her very own house, but all that came to mind was the last
time she'd seen her, kicking and screaming at their Uncle Henry as the
agent took Addie away and Aunt May tried to reason with her. Aunt
May couldn't manage both of them, and Addie was just too darned
puny to be of any help on the farm. If only Aunt May could see her
working for farmers now. She might still be tiny, but she could haul
water for animals, milk cows, or husk and shell corn. The orphan home
contracted her and the other children out to the farmers for pious rea-
sons. God himself said in the Bible that anyone who is not willing to
work should not eat. At every complaint from the children, Mr. Hayes
would remind them that *without hard work, nothing but weeds will grow*
and *the only thing that vanquishes hard luck is hard work*—and, boy, if
anyone had hard luck it was a friendless orphan child.

Addie's schoolteacher, Miss Adkins, had a child's picture book of Los
Angeles. It wasn't San Diego, but Miss Adkins said they were close
enough, so she let Addie take it home to the orphan asylum for the
night. Addie, Rose, Anna, Hazel, Pearl, and Victoria paged through it
for hours, marveling over the pictures showing palm trees and oranges
and flowering gardens, while Harriet sat on her own bed, knitting a
malformed mitten and making a point of ignoring them. Harriet used
to be more cordial, but ever since Harriet and Rodney had been caught
playing naughty, the other boys taunted and bedeviled her and the

girls treated her as if she had the smallpox. Addie felt sorry for her, but Harriet wouldn't accept sympathy or compassion, especially from the likes of Addie. The children like Harriet, Rodney, and Carl, who were placed in the orphan home by the courts for delinquency or criminal acts, always seemed to have nastier temperaments than the rest of them.

Los Angeles had motorcars, trolleys, and tall buildings. The girls counted one building with nine stories and couldn't imagine how anyone could have enough to fill it. Los Angeles had beaches and a pier that stretched into the ocean, where people could walk out over the waves without getting a tiny bit wet. The biggest surprise in the book was a pigeon farm and an alligator farm. The girls had no idea that people ate those things and wondered what the farmers fed to the alligators and how they caught them to butcher them.

Addie imagined taking sunbaths on the beach with her sister and plucking an orange from a tree any time she had the notion. She would no longer be contracted out to work on farms and would no longer have to avoid the farmers and their sons—their taunts or rough and calloused hands that hit or grabbed her by the arm so hard it bruised her bones. She wouldn't miss waxing the banister or scrubbing the floors at the orphan asylum, either, or feeding the chickens, or setting and clearing the tables and scrubbing the dishes for twenty-two children and four adults. She'd help her sister with one family home and maybe even have a bedroom all to herself. She would no longer be a friendless orphan child.

The night before she left, Mrs. Hayes had a special going-away supper for Addie, with corned beef au gratin and baked tomatoes. The little ones even got to come back into the dining room with the big kids to have steamed fig pudding. Mr. and Mrs. Hayes presented Addie with a brand-new pair of boots that had never been worn by anyone else, two brand-new store-bought dresses, and a valise to carry it all in. Addie wondered if the gifts were from the goodness of Mr. and Mrs. Hayes' own hearts, the graciousness of the courts, or from money sent by her very own beloved sister; but since Mr. and Mrs. Hayes accepted her thanks, she assumed it came from them.

In the middle of the night, unable to sleep for the excitement of it all, she heard the bedroom door creak open and the sound of someone sneaking across the room as quiet as a shadow. She hadn't heard any of the girls go out to use the outhouse, but maybe she had dozed off for a bit. As the footsteps crept closer, she wished she had kept her valise in the bed with her. Maybe someone had come to steal her things like a thief in the night. She flinched when a deep and moist voice whispered close to her ear, "I want to show you something." It was Wallace.

"Damn you, Wallace, you scared the bejesus out of me." Addie knew the type of thing Wallace liked to show the girls, and she'd already seen it. "You shouldn't be in here."

"I need to talk to you."

Addie knew she shouldn't, but she didn't want any of the girls to wake up and call for Mr. Hayes, tattling on Wallace. Mr. Hayes had never laid a hand or a switch to any of the girls, but when he got mad, he stared at you like a stone statue and you knew Mrs. Hayes would be coming in to smack your knuckles with the ruler, and then you'd be doing extra chores to give you time to think about whatever you'd done wrong. But the boys were another story altogether. Mr. Hayes called them slack-jawed imbeciles and gave it to them upside the head anytime they broke the rules or did anything sinful, trying to knock the sense into them right through their ears. And for really bad transgressions, they got taken to the woodshed and given the switch. Wallace had told Addie that Mr. Hayes gave them the whipping with their britches down and it stung like hellfire. One time, Wallace even showed Addie the welts; they were all red and crisscrossed his backside. Almost any chance he got, Wallace lowered his trousers in front of the girls to send them shrieking. But it never worked on Addie. She thought his ding-a-ling rather curious and wiggly. She wanted a longer look but knew better or she'd get her knuckles whacked for being naughty.

Addie wrapped her blanket around herself and followed Wallace down the staircase and into the parlor. She decided that if Wallace dropped his britches, she'd get in a good long look, being that everyone else was fast asleep and she'd be leaving in the morning anyway. What was there to lose? Without the fire, the parlor was cold and dark like in one of *The Campfire Girls* mysteries. She peeked out the curtain, half expecting to see a shadow lurking behind the walnut tree, but saw nothing except the moon making the new dusting of snow sparkle on the empty street.

"Come and sit with me," Wallace said from the corner of the sofa, patting the spot next to him.

Addie plopped herself down in Mr. Hayes's wingback chair, which nobody was allowed to sit in, not even Mrs. Hayes. Wallace's eyes popped open in surprise, but then he smiled. "Guess they can't do much to you at this point."

"Guess they can't," Addie said, opening the top of Mr. Hayes's smoking table and rummaging around through his tins of tobacco, matches, rolling papers, and his pipe. "I'm dog tired. What do you want?"

Wallace sat there, twisting his finger up in the cuff of his nightshirt, unable to speak.

"If you don't have nothing to say, I'm going up to bed."

Wallace dropped to his knees before her. "I want you to marry me." It burst from his mouth like a backfire from Mr. Underwood's internal combustion tractor. Addie stared at him, waiting for the cloud of black smoke to cough out from his pipes. When she didn't respond, he continued—his words picking up steam into the ping, ping, ping of what sounded like a practiced oratory. "I know how to repair machines.

Irrigate crops. Cut firewood. Herd cattle. Hunt rabbits. Plant fence posts. Carpentry. Plow. Plant. Harvest. Hoe. Rake. Drag. Feed."

"Stop," Addie said, causing him to choke on the word still left in his mouth. "I'm only fourteen."

"Don't you think I know that? I'd planned on waiting until you were sixteen or seventeen and I had a chance to buy me a place and to get it ready for you. But you're leaving."

"There ain't no way in hell that I'm gonna stay here," Addie said. "I get to be with my sister."

Wallace plunged his hand into his pocket, clamping something in his fist. When he pulled it out, Addie suspected that it held a worm or beetle that he'd toss at her, like the boys always did. Instead, he opened his fist to a paper cigar band.

"Can you make me a promise then?" He held the band out between his thumb and forefinger. "Give me your finger. This can be our promise. I'll work hard and get me a place, and you can come back when you're old enough and marry me."

Addie clenched her fist and held it in Wallace's face. "You're not going to trap me here. You think I'm gonna be a poor man's wife doing nothing but have children and work her fingers to the bones? And what makes you think that you're not gonna be called up to fight in the war? And then what? I'd be sitting here in Kansas while you're getting your legs blown off in Germany just like Quentin Myers?"

He did not budge or speak, just knelt there round eyed in his nightshirt. Addie pulled her blanket tight around her and pushed past him. She ran back to her bed, where she lay staring at the dark ceiling and feeling sorry for what she'd said to Wallace, but damned if he'd keep her tied down in Kansas.

***

Everyone gathered on the porch to say good-bye. Lionel and Rodney had just finished clearing the walkway and stood with their shovels by their sides, just like the soldiers in Mr. Hayes's *Literary Digest*. Ever since the Great War started, those two boys tackled their chores with honor, saluted at every command, and ducked behind bushes with stolen broom handles. Victoria and Hazel had little Rosalie and Helen balanced on their hips, all the girls in identical white dresses and the boys in brown suits. Addie counted only twenty children, Mr. and Mrs. Hayes, and Mrs. Jennings. Mrs. Bishop was probably in the kitchen, as usual. The only child missing was Harriet. Addie glanced up at the window to the girls' room and saw her glaring out. When their eyes met, Harriet's face disappeared and the curtains swung shut. Wallace stood far from the rest, in the corner of the porch, leaning against the house with his hands in his pockets and his hat pulled low over his eyes.

Mrs. Hayes had followed Addie to the sled that had come all the way from Topeka and waited like a coach in a fairy tale to take her to a sunny land with oranges and sandy beaches. A bundled-up man with a cigar in his mouth sat in the front, holding on to the reins. A woman in a pretty hat trimmed with ribbon and tiny pink roses, a high-collared white shirt with ruffles, and a wool coat sat in the back with a fur blanket across her lap.

"You must be the agent from the court," Mrs. Hayes said.

"Yes, I'm Miss Stanley. Pleased to meet you. This must be Addie."

The plan was for Miss Stanley to escort Addie to San Diego, then hand her off to her sister, Wavey. Addie felt like the package in a game of Pass the Parcel. The agent looked fine, not too old or pinched up like she'd imagined. She sat bone straight, obviously in a corset. She'd introduced herself as *Miss*, still young but not young enough to be unmarried. Addie blamed Miss Stanley's lack of matrimony on her long nose and high forehead. She looked back up at Wallace. He'd pulled his hat even lower over his eyes, but she knew he was watching, maybe hoping she'd change her mind at the last minute and come running into his arms.

"Now, you listen to Miss Stanley," Mrs. Hayes said to Addie after she'd climbed into the sled. Her words formed a fog that rose from her mouth and dissolved into the icy air. Harold handed her valise up, then backed away, standing next to Lionel and Rodney, with their shovels at the ready. Mrs. Hayes handed a book to Addie. "This will serve you well as you become a woman. Please write to us and let us know how you are doing."

Addie imagined everyone in the parlor, gathered around the fireplace, Mr. Hayes smoking his pipe as Mrs. Hayes read Addie's letters to the children. As she took the book from Mrs. Hayes, Addie promised she'd write.

"I'm sure Miss Stanley will be more than happy to read it with you on your long journey." She turned to the woman. "Won't you, Miss Stanley?"

"Of course we will. It's a long journey and it will give us something to occupy our time."

Addie looked down at the book, old, with ratty edges, and probably from one of the church donations the orphan home received. Tipping the spine up so she could read the title, Addie's heart sank when she read *How to Be a Lady: A Book for Girls, Containing Useful Hints on the Formation of Character*. She'd hoped it was one of *The Campfire Girls* mysteries or a *Dorothy* book.

"Thank you," Addie said, dropping it into her valise.

"Good morning," Mrs. Hayes said to the driver. He mumbled something, nodded, bit down on his cigar, and flicked the reins. The sled lurched forward and they glided away.

"He's not one for sentiment and wants to be on our way," Miss Stanley said.

Addie turned around and waved to everyone gathered on the porch and walkway. Wallace hurtled himself over the porch railing, dropped into the snow, and disappeared around the back of the house. Addie felt bad for hurting him, but she wouldn't miss the opportunity to live with her sister in California. Especially not for a boy she didn't love.

By the time they arrived at the train station in Topeka, Addie already felt her new boots pinching her feet. She felt pretty, though, in her new tan dress with blue trimmings and forty-two tiny cloth buttons just for decoration, even if her heavy wool coat hid most of it.

A porter tried taking Addie's valise, but she wasn't giving it up to him, not with her other new dress inside it. On the train, their seats faced backward, making them sit knee to knee with a man and a boy they had never met. Who'd have thought that she'd be traveling to California, going backward the entire way? The man and the boy both wore dark suit coats and had their hair parted and slicked down, all greasy-like. The man's mustache grew over his jowls, making him look like a bulldog. Other passengers stomped the snow from their shoes and removed their coats before settling onto their seats, making the inside of the train smell of oil, leather, and musty wool. As they waited to pull out of the station, the man across from her shuffled a deck of playing cards and fanned them out for the boy to pick one. After he did, he glanced at it, replaced the card, and the man reshuffled. Magically, the boy's card popped up from the deck of its own accord. The trick amazed Addie but seemed tiresome to the boy. Maybe he'd seen it a million times or maybe city boys needed better amusement. Mr. Hayes's only tricks were his stone-statue stares and the smoke rings he blew from his pipe, but he wasn't a real father to anyone.

"Might as well take a look at that book," Miss Stanley said.

Addie pretended not to hear her, looking instead out the window at women on the platform. Many wore feathered turbans and narrow-brimmed hats decorated with flowers and bows. She imagined herself the daughter of one of those women and wondered if they fussed over their girls, buying them beautiful dresses and hair ribbons.

"Let's not start out on the wrong foot, now. It's not polite to ignore someone who's talking to you."

"Oh, I'm sorry. I was daydreaming." Addie wondered how Miss Stanley came to be an agent of the court. She wondered if she got paid or if she volunteered as an act of Christian charity. They got a lot of charity at the orphan home. It seemed to make people feel good about themselves. "Your hat's pretty."

Miss Stanley touched her fingers to it, as if she'd forgotten she had it on. "Why, thank you. I just had new ribbon and trimmings put on it."

"My dress and shoes are new."

"I can see that, and you look mighty pretty. How old are you? I'd guess you're ten?"

"Fourteen. I'm small for my age." Somehow, the home had stunted her growth. Some of the farmers referred to Addie as *the runt of the litter*. She had been growing normally until they dragged her to the orphan asylum. Then even her hair had stopped growing. When Addie had arrived, they'd chopped off her waist-length hair, and since then, it never grew past her shoulders. Mrs. Hayes always puzzled over it, even having the doctor check Addie, but he couldn't find a cause. Addie's chart listed her height at four foot one inch the day she arrived and four foot four inches the day she left. Three inches in six years. It just wasn't normal.

Miss Stanley eyed her suspiciously, as if she thought Addie were lying about her age.

"You can check my papers." Addie looked down at the large envelope in Miss Stanley's lap.

"I'm sure it's in there. I must have missed it."

The orphan asylum was filled with liars, but Addie wasn't one of them.

Many well-dressed people and a few ordinary ones boarded the train. An old sailor with a gray beard and beanie hobbled past them, steadying himself by grabbing the top of the seats. Addie checked as he passed by. No peg leg, just a limp. The man across from them lit a cigar, and the boy stuck his finger up his own nose. When the man noticed, he slapped the boy's hand and passed him a handkerchief. A bell clanged, the train hissed, and the conductor called, "All aboooooooard."

"Addie, dear," Miss Stanley said, sounding annoyed, "I asked to see your book."

Addie opened her valise and handed over the book. Miss Stanley turned to the table of contents, counted the chapters, and then extracted a map from the big envelope. She unfolded it on her lap and ran her finger along a dark black line, pausing at every dot. "We have twenty-seven stops and there are thirty chapters. We will read one chapter between each stop, but we will need to double up three of the shorter chapters to get through them all."

"We're doing the whole book?"

"Indolence is not becoming. You should be grateful for the instruction. Young ladies need to work hard on their character."

Addie glanced at the man across from them. He closed his lips around the cigar, suppressing a smile.

As the train pulled from the station, Miss Stanley began to read, "'Chapter One, On Childhood and Youth. In one sense, very young persons are apt to think too much of themselves—in another, not enough. When they think they know more than their parents and teachers, or other elderly people, and so set up to be *bold* and *smart*, then they think too much of themselves.'"

The lessons continued the entire trip. Almost as grueling as when Dr. Paul had extracted her tooth. Addie watched miles and miles of cold and dry land flash by as Miss Stanley read to her. Between the Florence and Newton stations, Addie learned about piety, but she wanted nothing more than to walk from car to car along the length of the train, exploring every inch of it, seeing the people on board, and imagining herself in their shoes. Miss Stanley let Addie out of her seat only to use the ladies' room and then straight back again.

When the man and the boy left for the dining car, Miss Stanley and Addie stayed put and ate boiled eggs and salami from Miss Stanley's valise. Probably another reason she wasn't married. Addie imagined company coming to call on Miss Stanley and her serving them sausages from her valise. Smiling at the thought, Addie did have to admit that she'd be a handy guest at picnics.

Between Peach Springs and Blake, Addie learned the pitfalls of inquisitiveness, then behavior at school and at the dinner table. That night, they slept in berths, Addie's directly above Miss Stanley's, which prevented her from sliding out of bed and exploring the other cars. Trying to fall asleep, Addie thought of Wavey, seashells, orange trees, and tall palms. No more lessons on morality or scrubbing laundry or ironing dresses, bloomers, or sheets. Addie fell asleep to the rocking of the train. As they moved through the night, she dreamt of her sister hugging her and kissing the top of her head.

The next morning, Miss Stanley woke Addie, and they headed right back to their seats for a breakfast of hard bread, again from her valise, smeared with a thin layer of peach preserves, plus another hard-boiled egg. The water from the train tasted of metal and didn't quench Addie's thirst, making her saliva feel thick and pasty. Miss Stanley continued the lessons as they traveled through mountains and canyons and deserts. Between Winslow and Canyon Diablo, she read, "'Character is formed under a great variety of influences. Among these influences, none are more direct and powerful than that exerted upon us by the companions with whom we associate, for we insensibly fall into their habits.'"

"Do you believe that to be the truth, Miss Stanley?" Addie asked.

"Of course I do. Other than family, friends are one's greatest influence. We need to choose wisely."

After hundreds of miles of lessons, Addie couldn't hold her tongue for another minute. "Then why would they put orphans like me, girls who've never committed a single crime, into an orphan asylum and into the same room with *condemned* and *delinquent* girls sent there from the court?"

The man across from them couldn't hide his smile any longer and arched his eyebrows at Miss Stanley.

"I'm sure there's more to it than that," Miss Stanley said, but instead of continuing the lesson, she closed the book and placed it on the seat between them.

The train finally groaned to a stop in Los Angeles, and Addie had time to clean up and rinse the taste of hard-boiled eggs from her mouth before they changed lines. Their new train chugged past palm trees and citrus groves so close it felt almost as if Addie could reach her arm out the window and pluck an orange right off a branch. The train turned alongside the ocean, with cliffs on one side and nothing but water on the other. Addie squinted real hard, trying to see if she could spot China on the horizon. They used to sing, "My father went to sea, sea, sea, to see what he could see, see, see," at the asylum, clapping each other's hands faster and faster, "but all that he could see, see, see, was the bottom of the deep blue sea, sea, sea."

Only a few hours out of Los Angeles, the train hissed and steamed as it squealed to a stop alongside the looping Spanish arches of the San Diego station. Addie had never seen so many men in straw hats and white jackets and women in white lace dresses or sailor dresses and frilly white parasols. Nobody wore heavy coats or muffs. Addie's eyes dashed from face to face until she caught sight of Wavey, almost not recognizing her with her hair twisted up into a bun like a grown-up woman. Addie pressed her hand to the glass, trying to get Wavey's attention.

Wavey's eyes skipped from window to window. Spotting Addie, she lit into a smile. Nobody had eyes like Wavey—sky blue, but fractured like cracked ice. The man at Wavey's side wore a lamp-black suit with a fedora cocked sideways on his head, just like a fancy man in a magazine. His eyes followed Wavey's gaze, but he didn't smile.

Addie tried to push past Miss Stanley and rush for the door, but Miss Stanley took hold of her elbow. "Young ladies do not dash about causing mayhem to those around them."

When they finally disembarked, Addie ignored Miss Stanley's admonitions and raced into Wavey's arms, but Wavey's stomach pushed back.

"A baby?" Addie asked.

"I wanted to surprise you." Wavey lifted Addie's hand and placed it on her belly, round and firm.

"Wavey!" the man said. "Not in public."

"Sorry." Wavey dropped her head like a scorned child.

"Introductions would be polite," he said.

"Of course." Wavey looped her arm around Addie's. "Ty, I'd like to introduce you to my sister, Addie."

Addie felt Miss Stanley's presence directly behind her, so she curtsied and said, "Pleased to meet you."

"We're glad to have you here," Ty said. "Wavey could use some help, now that the baby's coming."

Addie introduced Miss Stanley. Ty thanked her for accompanying Addie on such a long trip. It seemed as if he expected Miss Stanley to turn right around and hop back on the train.

"I won't bother you for long," Miss Stanley said. "I just need to inspect your home and have you sign a few papers, then I'll let you be. I have a reservation at a hotel for tonight, then I'll catch an early train back to Topeka."

He looked annoyed, but said, "Well then, as soon as they unload Addie's trunk, we'll be on our way."

Addie held up her valise. "This is all I have."

Ty didn't look happy about that, either. They all followed him through the terminal—a huge vaulted room ribbed with bone-colored arches. It felt like walking through the stomach of a giant whale. Addie glanced over at Wavey and down at her stomach. A knot formed in her throat. What if the baby wouldn't come out? What if she died just like their mother had? The image of their dead baby brother lying on their mother's chest with her arms crossed over him flashed into Addie's head. And the sound of her hard soles on the hardwood floor reminded her of Father hammering the lid on the coffin.

Addie said a silent prayer, hoping that God could hear her through the loud cavern of the train terminal. *God, please don't take Wavey away from me again.* If God could hear Jonah all the way beneath the deep blue sea, he should be able to hear her in California.

On the streetcar, Wavey and Addie sat side by side, across from Ty and Miss Stanley. This time, they all traveled sideways, on the bench seats along the walls of the car. The conductor rang the bell, and the wheels began to rumble. They rode in silence, swaying, as light poles and palm trees bobbed by the windows. The city had stores and restaurants and movie houses. They rumbled past brick buildings so tall that Addie had to tip up her head against the window to see how high they reached. A city. A real city. She couldn't wait to go to the department stores with Wavey. Maybe she'd be able to watch one of the flickers.

"They have elevator service too," Wavey said. "Have you ever rode in an elevator?"

Addie shook her head.

"Have you ever ridden," Ty said, correcting Wavey's grammar.

Addie waited for her sister to lash out and tell him to mind his own business or make a face at him, but she never did. Maybe Wavey knew to play proper lady for Miss Stanley, afraid she wouldn't leave Addie in her care if she didn't. Addie looked down at her feet or out the window, anywhere but at Ty. She felt his eyes bore into her, as if looking for fault, for one single reason to ship her back. Ty drummed his fingers, as thick and dry as hickory sticks, on his knees. Addie would bet a nickel they were rough and calloused, just like the hands of the Kansas farmers.

"You have a good trip?" Ty asked.

Addie glanced up at him. "Yes, sir."

"I'm your brother-in-law, not your father or schoolmaster. Call me Ty."

Miss Stanley stiffened, silently admonishing Addie about calling an adult anything but mister or missus.

Wavey reached over and patted Addie's hand, just like their mother used to do to let them know that everything would be fine. Once off the streetcar, Wavey and Addie followed Ty, with Miss Stanley trailing behind, down streets lined with palm trees, tropical plants, and flowering bushes. Addie's new shoes rubbed against her heel, opening up a blister as they all turned up the walkway toward a little white house with fruit trees and a porch swing.

Surf Line, Santa Fe Railway
May 23, 1935

Addie sat alone, her forehead bumping against the train window. The landscape blurred past, unfocused—a smear of greens and browns against a blue backdrop. She wondered what had become of Wallace. She never did write to the orphan home, completely shutting it out of her life the moment the agent of the court turned her back, leaving her in her sister's care. Wavey's house had been brand spanking new with push-button lights, hot- and cold-water spigots, a gas stove, and their very own Victor Victrola, with at least half a dozen phonograph records. The first week in her new home, Addie went in and out of rooms just so she could push the light buttons. The same week she arrived, Ty had a brand-new, gas-powered Maytag clothes-washing machine delivered right to the house on the back of a delivery truck. That thing had driven the neighbor, Miss Mabel, to fits every time Ty pulled it out of the garden shed and into the yard. The motor on it hummed and popped, filling the neighborhood with "confounded noise," as Miss Mabel liked to say.

Daisy slid into the empty seat beside Addie, with two open Coca-Colas in her hand. "Penny for your thoughts." She held one of the bottles out and Addie took it, surprised that Daisy was talking to her again.

Addie wasn't about to confide anything in Daisy, especially after the whole cigarette-flicking incident. "Thanks."

When Daisy lost her temper or her patience, she never apologized. Days of angry silence would pass, then she'd do something nice—take it or leave it. Sometimes she'd appear with a handful of wildflowers or a giant pink grapefruit she'd pilfered from the kitchen as her peace offering. Addie took a sip of the Coca-Cola, surprised but not shocked to find it spiked with whiskey.

"Bottoms up." Daisy tipped her bottle.

"I see you survived your meeting with Heinrich."

"Heinrich can go to hell in a handbasket. He gave me some cock-and-bull story about why Eleanor couldn't come. Guess he figured we don't talk to each other."

"What'd he say?"

"Doesn't matter. The bottom line is that Eleanor was our acid test."

The train rocked back and forth; it seemed almost at a standstill now, with nothing but ocean out the window. Addie ran her finger through the condensation on the soda bottle and took another swig. The colony had been Addie's home for the past fifteen years. She'd never thought about it ending, never imagined that Heinrich would kick any of them out. She should've known it wouldn't last. Nothing ever did.

"Here's to Eleanor," Addie said, making a toast. The bottles made a dull clink and they both took a swig.

"I know you're not asking for my opinion," Daisy said, "but if you were, I'd tell you to contact your sister. Blood's thicker than water, and pretty soon, you'll have nowhere to go. If she won't take you, you need to get yourself a man."

Daisy never tired of attempting to pair Addie up with someone. She always introduced her to single men who showed up at the colony—single, as defined by Daisy, only meant they came without their wives or girlfriends—and then, only the ones Daisy wasn't interested in. But maybe the time had come for Addie to face her sister. If Wavey could finally forgive her, then just maybe she could begin to forgive herself.

***

When the train finally pulled into the station in San Diego, Addie couldn't help but give every woman on the platform the once-over. She knew Wavey wouldn't be there, but just maybe, by coincidence or twist of fate, she would be. But she saw only strangers in print dresses, white gloves, and flirty hats glancing into the windows, none of them familiar and none of them with the fractured blue eyes of her sister.

Daisy leaned over Addie, pressing her face to the window. "Goddamn, not again."

Toward the end of the platform, right in front of the terminal, a group of women armed with picket signs guarded the doors. Addie couldn't read them from that angle, but she knew what was up.

Sal bent over their seats and whispered, "Operation Bluestockings." Before either Addie or Daisy had time to respond, he made his way down the aisle to the next set of women from the colony and whispered the same two words. *Operation Bluestockings*, code for *split up and look normal*. As long as they didn't travel in a pack, who could spot a nudist in clothing?

Sal appeared next to their seats again, extending his elbow toward Daisy. "Mother," he said, "may I?"

Daisy slipped her arm through his and handed him her valise.

"After you." He bowed, allowing Addie to step in front of them.

Behind them, Joe, the self-appointed pastor of the colony and theological-school dropout, began quoting scripture, murmuring, "'You shall bring out to your gates that man or woman who has committed that wicked thing, and shall stone to death that man or woman.'"

Everyone from the colony disembarked from the train in twos and threes, pretending not to know each other. A dozen prim and matronly bluestockings, draped in layers of clothing and fine jewelry, formed a blockade in front of the terminal with placards that read "Nudists, Go Home," "Don't Soil Our Garden," "Public Nudity Is a Sin," and to top them all, "May God Forgive You." Addie decided to take that placard as a premonition, hoping there would be forgiveness for her in San Diego. The women peered around Daisy, Sal, and Addie, craning their necks and scanning the passengers for nudists. Next to the bluestockings, two police officers stood as straight as rails, all stuffed tight in their uniforms.

Addie took a deep breath as they passed by the group of women, none of whom had probably ever had a day of trouble in their lives. Behind her, she noticed Joe striking up a conversation with several of the women. "Good afternoon, sister. I see you are out here doing the Lord's work for the good citizens of this great city. Well, God bless you, sister." Joe might not be good for much, but he sure had a knack for biblical sarcasm.

Stepping through one of the Spanish arches, Addie entered the terminal with the same bone-colored arches, like the ribs of a giant whale, that she remembered from so long ago. Addie glanced from face to face, hoping to spot her sister's blue eyes. If only Wavey could give her another chance, maybe this time, Addie could make things right.

Joe passed by them, gazing up at the arches and quoting Jonah, "'For You have cast me into the deep, into the heart of the seas, and the floods surrounded me; All Your billows and Your waves passed over me. Then I said: I have been cast out of Your sight.'"

In her mind, Addie recited, "'I will pay what I have vowed. Salvation is of the Lord.'"

CHAPTER TWO

RUMOR

Palmetto Court Bungalows
San Diego, California
May 1935

Mother was still out, gallivanting around and dancing with strange men. Rumor imagined her mother's crumpled-up body stuffed under some bush on the side of the road, one red heel dangling from her lifeless foot, the other still lying on the floorboards of some man's motorcar as it sped away. Mary, without a care in her head, lay asleep on her side of the bed making a slight wheezing sound as her tiny breasts rose and fell under her nightgown. She never snored, just wheezed—whether it came from her nose or her lungs, who knew. On her head she wore a peculiar-looking wave cap to hold her pin curls in place, making Mary resemble a synchronized swimmer who had been put under some sort of hypnosis. Rumor shimmied the window open just enough to poke her head out.

"Rumor?" Mary asked, dreamy and half-asleep.

The curtains billowed in like two full sails, and the smell of gardenias drifted in with the onshore breeze.

"Please shut the window. It's frightfully cold." Mary sat up, pulling the blanket up to her chin.

"I want to listen for Mother." Peeking out, Rumor saw nothing but the silhouettes of telephone poles and palm trees, tilting lower and lower all the way down the hill, until they finally collapsed into the harbor. Occasional yellow lights blinked at intersections. The deck lights of the battleships and destroyers moored in the harbor created new constellations across the pearled bay, then darkness—the ocean meeting the night sky where Scorpio sat on the horizon, its tail arched and ready to sting. Somewhere close by a radio played "It's Only a Paper Moon."

"Why do you torture yourself? She's only out dancing and she always comes home, darling."

Ever since Mary had found out she got the job at the Cabrillo Theater as a candy and cigarette girl, she acted as if she lived in a motion picture, saying "darling" this and "dreadful" that. And ever since Mary had turned eighteen, she acted as if God himself had given her permission to start bossing Rumor around.

"Close the window and go to sleep."

"You're not my mother." Rumor left it open and scooted back beneath the covers. Mary might be older than her by two years, but as far as height and intelligence were concerned, Rumor felt that she had the upper hand.

"Mother won't be home until one at the earliest. I don't want some dreadful tramp climbing in to molest us."

Knowing she had the protection of a knife tucked between the mattresses, Rumor ignored Mary until she gave up and lay back down. Over the years, Rumor had honed her ability to listen to the night. She'd learned to breathe so slightly she could hear every tick of the clock and chirp of the crickets outside. When their mother first started leaving them alone, Rumor's breathing whooshed so loud in her ears that she couldn't hear the noises around her. Now she could tell if someone walking up the street was a man or woman, whether they were drunk and meandering or in a rush. She knew when neighbors clicked their door latches at night and when they opened or closed their windows. Rumor heard which neighbors argued and when Little Benny woke up crying. She knew that Mr. Harrington snuck home late every Friday night, slowing his pace the closer he got to the courtyard and tiptoeing the last few feet before he reached his bungalow next door. Even cars made different sounds as they rumbled, ticked, sputtered, or coughed down the street. Sometimes she could hear the mournful bleat of the foghorn coming from Point Loma. Between her intensified hearing and the knife, Rumor didn't worry about tramps or hobos.

Rumor must have nodded off, because she woke up to female giggles floating in the window. Peeking out, she saw two women walking arm in arm toward their bungalow. Staggering in high heels, their moon-washed shapes seemed formed of water, loose and flowing in their dresses and silk stockings. Handbags dangled from their wrists as Ruth and Mother supported each other, both completely soused. Rumor counted with the ticking of the clock in the living room. It usually took her mother from forty-three to sixty-seven seconds to walk around the bungalows, through the courtyard, and finally fumble with the door lock—depending on how drunk she was. Sixty-one, sixty-two, sixty-three. The key. One, two, three, four, she opened the door. Five, six, shut the door. Stepping across the floor, seven, eight, nine, ten. The figurines on the end table clattered, sounding as if they'd all toppled over. "Ow," Mother said in the loud whisper of a drunk trying to be quiet. When their bedroom door finally squeaked open, Rumor closed her eyes.

Her mother's warm breast squashed against Rumor's shoulder as she bent and kissed her forehead with her oily lipstick and booze-breath, slurring, "Good night, sweetheart," into Rumor's hair. Then she stood and click-clacked to the other side of the bed to do the same thing to Mary.

Mother had no particular skills or good looks. She was a waitress with a long chin, scrawny legs, and curly brown hair cropped just below her jawbones. The only thing remarkable about her were her eyes—a kaleidoscope of blue. But even Rumor knew that kaleidoscopes were only reflections of cheap bits of colored glass.

The door to Mother's room banged shut and Rumor pictured her flat on her bed, face-first and fully dressed. Rumor used to creep in behind her mother to remove her shoes and pull the covers over her, but not anymore.

Rumor smelled the burnt toast on Mary's breath and knew that she'd been up for a while. "Rise and shine, Rumor. I thought we'd go to the First Methodist Church today. You know, the one with the spice cookies and apple juice?"

At the clink of a bread plate on her nightstand, Rumor sat up. Mary always made her toast just the way she liked it, usually pressing in a happy face before browning it and spreading a thin, even layer of butter over the entire slice—unlike the toast her mother made, which had no happy face and usually a chunk of half-melted butter right in the center.

Rumor and Mary went to a different church every Sunday. If they stayed at one too long, the questions invariably started coming.

"Where are your parents, sweetheart?"

"You new to the area?"

"You poor things, havin' to go to church all by yourselves."

"Well, bless your hearts."

Some Sundays they worshiped as Catholics, others as Episcopalians or Lutherans. One time, they'd stumbled into a gospel church—two white faces in a jamboree of black Praise-the-Lord Baptists.

Mary brushed Rumor's bushy hair, clump by clump, into long ringlets. A year ago, just before Rumor had turned fifteen, she'd refused to let her mother comb her hair anymore. Mother used to rip the brush through the tangles, calling Rumor a *wild jungle girl* and whacking her in the head if she squealed or moved. Rumor and Mary couldn't have been more different. Rumor had long brown hair while Mary's was short and blond. Rumor's hair was curly and thick, Mary's straight and fine.

Rumor asked Mother if she wanted to come to church, but as usual, she just raised her head—last night's makeup all smeared and her hair flattened on one side. Mother mumbled in her sleep that they should go on without her, promising to join them the next time. Mother frequently claimed that the biggest problem with church on Sunday morning was that it came after Saturday night. Her mother waved her finger in the direction of her handbag, and Rumor fetched it, digging around in it until she unearthed the change purse. Mother twisted open the clasp, pulled out two nickels, and pressed them into Rumor's palm. Five cents for the church offering and five cents to get themselves a refreshment. Rumor didn't know how Mother could afford to give them ten cents every Sunday when most people struggled to pay their bills and bums waited in lines for a bit of food. Maybe Mother was trying to buy her way into heaven, with Mary and Rumor depositing the dues for her. Little did Mother know that they didn't put the nickel in the offering at all. Instead, after services, they used both the nickels to take the streetcar to Mission Beach to see Papa Jack. If Mother intended to buy her way into heaven with all those nickels, Rumor and Mary were sending her straight to hell.

Rumor wished the First Methodist smelled more like St. Joseph's. The exotic scent of ashes, candles, cloves, and myrrh made it feel more sacred, more holy. Instead, the First Methodist smelled of coffee, talcum powder, and Aqua Velva.

An electrified current seemed to run through the church that morning. Women in ribbon-trimmed hats darted across aisles, slipping into pews next to other women. It looked like a game of telephone. A woman would start at the end of a pew and whisper something, then that woman would tell it to the woman next to her, and so on. Rumor wondered how the message changed as it went. It may have started as *We're having donuts in the hall after the sermon* and ended up *Mrs. Hall ate donuts with a serviceman.* The men seemed uninterested in the game, sitting stoically or leaning back so the women could gossip over their laps. Rumor picked out words like *morality, decency, garden, boycott, picket,* and *protest.* Heads shook, fingers pointed, and white-gloved hands covered prim mouths.

"Did you hear?"

Rumor's heart leapt at the sudden voice in her ear. She turned to see the giant face of Mildred Stucky, the junior class secretary from her high school and volunteer for the League of Women Voters, which Rumor knew was only an honorary title for the highest-ranking envelope licker.

"Did you see the paper this morning?"

Without giving Rumor time to answer, Mildred continued, "A nudist colony will be at the fair. They've already arrived."

"I'm sure they'll be clothed," Mary said. "We have laws about things like that, darling."

"Not to visit," Mildred said. "They're an exhibit at the fair. Completely naked. I was looking forward to the world's fair coming here, but now my parents said I can't go if there's a nudist colony."

"That's hard to believe," Rumor said.

"I saw the headlines myself. My mother nearly choked on her oatmeal. Said she wouldn't stand for it."

The pipe organ belched, silencing the congregation and causing Mildred and all the other messengers to scamper back to their own pews. Mildred plunked down next to a large, straight-backed amazon woman, obviously her mother.

A door to the left side of the stage opened, and the pastor stepped through, wearing a black robe with a long stole draped around his neck. Some pastors wore dark suits with neckties, and others dressed in collarless shirts with a white band around their throats. This pastor approached the pulpit in the usual church-stride. One step at a time, slow and dignified, no smiling or gesturing, just like a bride walks up the aisle. It was the same at all churches. They all did it. Pastors, priests, altar boys, organists, the choir, even the line of people waiting for Holy Communion.

The organist began again and the congregation sang "A Mighty Fortress Is Our God." Rumor loved to sing, she truly did, but not in public. Mary had once told her that their vacuum cleaner had better pitch than her, so she only mouthed the words next to Mary, who sang like an angel. Sometimes Rumor felt sinful for faking it, so she tried to feel the joy in her heart as her lips moved silently with the music.

The pastor's bald head already glistened with sweat. He blessed the congregation, then jabbed the open Bible with his finger. "In First John, two-sixteen, it says, 'For all that is in the world—the lust of the flesh, the lust of the eyes, and the pride of life—is not of the Father but is of the world.' The good citizens of San Diego must stand up against the approaching tide of evil. Humans are not only capable of good but also of the immoral exploitation of their fellow beings. Christians must avoid the temptations of the world, for Satan is the head of its system."

Mildred wasn't lying. Rumor glanced over at Mildred, who looked back at her with pursed lips and an *I told you so* expression.

The pastor took a breath and paused, looking out over the congregation as if trying to spot an exploiter. "Major industries profit by satisfying the lust of the flesh."

Would nudists walk through the Exposition wearing nothing but what God gave them? Rumor imagined them in a parade of bare skin, strolling down the Avenue of Palaces, tossing flowers to the crowd. Mary posed like a prim and proper saint next to her, her hands crossed in her lap, appearing to nod at the pastor's words but more likely to some song trapped in her head. If Mary squealed to Mother about the nudists, they might not be allowed to go to the world's fair, either. Rumor would wring Mary's neck if that happened. Rumor felt guilty for not wanting to stand up against sin, but she wasn't about to miss the world's fair because of one exhibit. Would she see a naked man there? Rumor's undersides started to tingle, and the church became so stuffy, she fanned herself with the hymnal. She couldn't bear to sit in the house of God with those visions flickering through her head. Rumor slipped out of the pew as the pastor's voice droned on.

"Where are you going?" Mary whispered.

Rumor felt everyone's eyes on her. Maybe they'd think she was a nudist and the pastor's words drove her from the church, but she didn't care. She walked straight out the heavy white double doors.

Mary must have followed her, because from the top of the church steps, she heard her pleading, "We need to stay for the cookies. I want to bring some to Papa Jack."

With their two nickels, Rumor headed straight for Third and Broadway to catch the Number 16 Streetcar.

"Rumor, wait. What's the hurry?" Mary panted behind her. "Slow down, I'm going to be an awful mess by the time we see Papa."

Mary caught up and slid her arm through Rumor's. Cars, buses, and streetcars rumbled past them. Electric trolley lines stretched down the center of the street, crisscrossing the intersections like a drift net. As they passed by the Owl Drug Company, Mary slowed, entranced by the window display of perfumes and cosmetics. The vanity cases drew her to the window like a moth, but Rumor pulled her forward, eager to get to Mission Beach. Bellmen stood sentry outside the U.S. Grant Hotel, waiting to pounce on the luggage of arriving guests. Rumor wondered where the nudists would stay and how much luggage they would even need. A gray ocean fog flowed over the city, washing out the tops of the tallest buildings and promising a chilly morning at the beach.

Rumor and Mary waited in the plaza for the Number 16 Streetcar. The trip usually took forty minutes each way, hopefully enough time for Rumor to convince Mary to keep tight-lipped about the nudist colony. When the streetcar arrived, they climbed aboard and found two seats behind the motorman, on the polished wooden bench. Mary smoothed down her white Sunday dress with little blue flowers and two rows of matching ribbon at the bottom. She looked like one of the blue-and-white peacocks on Mother's china plates. The streetcar lurched and jostled down the center of Broadway, passenger cars coasting by on either side.

"We probably shouldn't tell Mother or Papa Jack." Rumor wondered if she should threaten Mary with bodily harm or itching powder in her cold cream.

"Tell them what?"

"About the nudist colony."

Mary leaned in close and whispered, "Darling, I'd have to be half mad to tell Mother anything about naked people." Instantly changing the conversation to her favorite subject, Mary said, "I get my uniform next week. And Mother's going to take me to get a corset with garters and my own silk stockings to wear with it. Isn't it thrilling?"

Sometimes Rumor wished she could live in the clouds like Mary, not worrying about Mother or always trying to fix things. Mary crossed her legs, showing off the new shiny black patent-leather heels that Mother had bought her for her eighteenth birthday. Rumor looked down at her own feet, at the leather uppers with Goodyear rubber soles and ankle socks. She pulled them back, stowing them beneath the wooden seat.

It seemed as if every person on the streetcar had a newspaper. Swabbed in big black letters across the front pages, the headlines read,

"Real Nudists Slip into City" and "The Bare Truth." There'd be no hiding it from Mother.

When they stopped at the main gate of the US Marines base, three uniformed new recruits with fresh haircuts and bright red sunburns boarded. Mary gave them a coy little smile, and the dark-haired one winked at her. Always at her.

The tracks turned northwest, across a meadow filled with a sea of purple and gold wildflowers. They approached the tidal marsh just before the Ocean Beach Junction, where the motorman disconnected them from the Number 14. The streetcars always traveled in tandem until the switch at Ocean Beach Junction. There, the motormen unhitched them and sent them their separate ways—one north and one south, just like Mother and Papa Jack, dislocated, divided, divorced.

Their streetcar crossed over the Mission Bay Bridge. Men, many wearing ragged trousers, lined the sides with their fishing poles dipped in salute to the bay, their sons balanced on upturned pails so they could see over the railing.

When the breakers and beach came into view, Rumor squeezed Mary's arm. "We're almost to Papa." The fog had already begun to burn off and only a slight haze dulled the sun.

Mary and Mother loved the city, but Papa and Rumor loved the sea. When she was little, Papa had read her stories about the sea. *The Little Mermaid*, *Robinson Crusoe*, *The Rime of the Ancient Mariner*, and her all-time favorite, *20,000 Leagues Under the Sea*. Rumor grew up imagining herself a castaway, a sailor, or living beneath the surface in a monstrous submarine. As she got older, she dreamt of being a naturalist, just like Pierre Aronnax, studying and classifying marine life. But when Papa moved out, Mother told Rumor to stop filling her head with such fantasies, because she was a girl, and girls did not go to sea.

***

Papa always joked around, calling Mission Beach the Isle of Despair, saying that some bad judgment had marooned him there—just like Robinson Crusoe. But Rumor knew the truth. A tempest had shipwrecked him, and her name was Wavey Rose Donnelly, aka Mother.

Mission Beach wasn't much more than a sand spit that divided the Pacific Ocean from Mission Bay. Even before Papa moved there, he used to bring Rumor and Mary to the beach so they could tumble in the cold surf of the Pacific, then run across the strand and plunge into the warm water of the bay or ride the merry-go-round and eat candied apples.

Rumor rang the bell for the motorman to stop at the amusement center, where people in dresses and suits, sailor uniforms, and swimsuits all strolled along Ocean Walk. Red-and-white-striped tents and umbrellas crowded the sand. People from all around the city ventured to the beach to relax and forget their troubles. Relief workers, hobos, and bigwigs all stripped down and sunned on the same sand.

Surfers rode the frothy waves, and children chased the surf out, then ran from it as it came back in. At the amusement center, seagulls waited to tear apart unattended lunch sacks as the Giant Dipper roller coaster clanked and rattled on its track, rising and dipping like the ocean swells. Lifeguards with sun-bleached hair stood watch in their towers, with their trucks and dories parked beside them. Rumor loved the smells of caramel, hot popcorn, and the ebb and flow of people and laughter.

Papa Jack made a living performing magic tricks for children along the seawall. He didn't earn enough money for a decent place to live, but he was *gettin' by. Money was money, as long you came by it honestly,* he would say, proud that he never took any government relief. If only Mother believed that, she might take him back. After Papa lost his job at the cannery, Rumor remembered many nights of one-sided yelling as Mother told Papa Jack that he needed a decent job—that he needed to be a better provider and set a better example for their girls. Now Papa worked in the fresh air and sunshine of Mission Beach, dressed in a red-and-white-striped waistcoat, straight out of a barbershop quartet. He pulled pennies out from behind the ears of children and made seashells disappear, all for the coins that people tossed into his upturned cap on the walkway.

Rumor and Mary waited while two little girls, in matching Shirley Temple dresses and pink hair bows, stood before Papa. He wrapped a scallop shell into his handkerchief and made it vanish. Tucking the empty hankie into his shirt pocket, Papa Jack patted his knee and the youngest girl climbed on, her little bare legs dangling in the air. He whispered something into her ear and she giggled. Papa tapped his cheek with his finger, and she planted a kiss right where he indicated. A woman rushed up with two vanilla ice cream cones melting down her fingers. She looked angry but relieved to find her children. She called them over. The youngest slid off Papa's knee and ran to her mother. Papa smiled at the woman, but she didn't look pleased.

Once the woman stormed off with her girls, Rumor and Mary ran to Papa Jack, and he wrapped them up in one of his world-famous bear hugs, squeezing until they squealed.

"Look at how grown-up my girls are."

"We saw you just last week," Mary said.

"I know, I know, but you girls change from Sunday to Sunday."

Rosa, an old Mexican lady who always sat next to Papa by the seawall, wove crosses, fish, birds, roses, and dolls from palm fronds, laying them out for sale as they dried in the sun.

"Donde es Esmeralda?*"* Rumor asked her, using the little bit of Spanish she remembered from school.

"Alla." She pointed to the shore. Esmeralda, a ten-year-old with one long black braid hanging down her back, walked with her baby brother balanced on her hip. Rumor couldn't tell if Rosa was their mother or their grandmother, and Papa Jack wouldn't let her ask because it would be rude.

Papa pulled two nickels from his cap and offered them to Rumor and Mary, with an outstretched palm. "Run and get yourselves a concession," he said, bending to lift his crate and close up for the day.

"Get me a candied apple, will you, darling?" Mary asked, holding her nickel out to Rumor. "I want to say hi to Freddie." Mary leaned against the seawall, unbuckled her heels, and pranced across the sand to the lifeguard tower.

Three sailors in their navy-blue sailor suits and white caps waited in line behind Rumor, making wisecracks about girls who strolled by, poking each other in the ribs saying, "Hey, get a load of that hot number" or "Holy mackerel, I'd like to get a hook into that one." They carried on as if completely unaware of Rumor's presence in front of them. Not that she needed the attention, but Rumor thought it would be fun to practice flirting, especially since Mary wasn't next to her, distracting them. After all, she was practically sixteen. Brushing her hair back from her face, Rumor turned, smiled, raised her hand, and wiggled her fingers in a dainty wave.

The taller of the three sailors, a handsome Buck Rogers type, winked at her.

Rumor smiled again, waiting for him to say something.

He leaned forward. "I think it's your turn, girlie," he said.

Rumor turned and saw the boy behind the concession counter staring at her. "What'll it be?"

Too embarrassed to think straight, she forgot what she wanted to order. Rumor simply stood at the front of the line, gawking at the menu board.

"Mind stepping aside until you decide?" the clerk asked. He looked barely older than Rumor. Pimples dotted his face, and he wore a paper hat—but he still managed to make her feel like the fool.

The three sailors took Rumor's place at the counter and ordered.

"Hey there, good-looking." Papa Jack's voice came from behind her, and she wondered if he'd seen what had happened.

"You don't want to get mixed up with the likes of them. They're infected with squirrel fever."

Papa always knew the right thing to say.

Mary leaned against a long leg of the lifeguard tower, swinging her heels by their straps. Rumor wondered if Mary knew the effect she had on poor Freddie, an old classmate who'd fallen under her spell. He unnaturally puffed out his chest as Mary swished to and fro, brushing her dress back and forth across her legs. If he only knew she planned on marrying a film star or movie producer—rich or famous with a shiny Rolls-Royce and a mansion perched on the edge of a cliff. Not a boy in a lifeguard tower, who rode a bicycle to work.

Papa Jack plucked a handful of popcorn from Rumor's sack, motioning out to sea where a pelican soared above the water, just beyond the breakers. It crashed into the sea headfirst. Bobbing to the surface, it floated for a moment, stretched out its great wings, and lifted back up into the sky. The pelican circled back and again crashed into the sea. After the fourth time, it popped up with a fish wriggling from its beak.

"Things don't always come easy. Sometimes, you just gotta keep trying," Papa said.

Rumor didn't know if he was talking about himself, the pelican— or her.

"Sorry about that," Mary called, sand flicking out behind her as she skipped toward them. "I'm so fond of Freddy. I just couldn't stand not saying hello."

Papa rented and lived in Mrs. Bailey's garage, a wooden box on the side of a sandy lane just two blocks from the beach. The house itself was a white Craftsman bungalow with sailor-blue trim. Papa called the garage his castle. But in truth it was only a box of planks with one window and cockeyed double doors held shut by a rusty latch—a dinghy dead astern of Mrs. Bailey's house. A wire, looped between the house and garage, provided electricity to Papa. It gave Rumor comfort that the steps to Mrs. Bailey's kitchen stood only six feet from the garage. She'd never let Papa starve.

Inside the single room, Papa had a workbench, table, and an old canvas army cot left over from the Great War. Crates of junk metal, wood, wire, and scraps cluttered the floor and were stuffed in every crevice available. A frayed electrical wire snaked out from beneath his bed, and a can of oil sat in a ring of darkened wood on his table, next to an open tin of Campbell's soup with a spoon still in it, and a jar of Tootsie Rolls that Papa kept for the neighborhood kids. Papa's mess used to drive Mother right up the wall. She called him a pack rat. He'd tell her that inventors needed things; you never knew what odd scrap of wire or rubber or tin would be the one thing you required. Some fragment of glass or broken lamp could spark an idea. Of course, she'd tell him that he was not an inventor, because inventors made things that became products and brought money into the house. She'd tell him that she needed a man who could support a family, and dreamers don't put food on the table.

Papa swung one of the doors wide open, letting the sunlight wash into the dim room. Rumor noticed a shiny wooden radio with golden knobs on his workbench.

"You bought a radio?" Mary asked.

"Nope," Papa Jack answered with a mischievous smile.

"Someone gave it to you?" Rumor guessed.

"Nope. It's not mine."

"Whose is it?" Rumor asked.

"It's yours," Papa said.

"Ours? How's it ours?" Mary ran her hand over the smooth wood. There were only a few small nicks in it.

"Well, I just happened to procure it from a gentleman. It was broken, so we made a trade. I took a peek under the hood, made a few adjustments, and voilà—it works."

"Thank you, Papa." Mary hugged him.

"What about Mother?" Rumor asked, knowing they couldn't take it home. There'd be no way to explain it.

"Got it all figured out," Papa said. "I'll smuggle it over in the middle of the night with a big red ribbon tied around it. I can picture it now—your Mother opens the door to get the morning milk, and there's a nice big gift from her secret admirer."

"That should do it," Rumor said, knowing Mother's weakness for male attention. She prayed it would work, though. There'd be hell to pay if Mother found out they'd been sneaking over to Papa's.

Tucked under the workbench was an overturned surfboard with a propeller and motor bolted to the bottom. Blue wires reached out like the tentacles of a sea anemone. "A new invention?" Rumor asked.

"Working on a motorized surfboard to ride in the bay, but it's working me more than I'm working it."

"I hear the world's fair will have all the wonders of the future," Rumor said.

"Will it?" Papa unbuttoned his vest and hung it on a nail sticking out of the bare wooden frame.

"I heard it will have a robot, a talking kitchen, and a radio wave that can pop corn without the use of heat."

"Well, I'll be."

"You should go there and talk to the inventors. Maybe you can make something they'll put on display."

"My stuff wouldn't hold a candle to a robot or a talking kitchen."

If only Papa could sell some of his ideas and make a decent living, maybe Mother would let him come home. "You don't know till you try," Rumor said.

They spent the rest of the afternoon strolling in their bare feet on the beach. Mary searched for unbroken sand dollars while Papa and Rumor stood in the surf, letting it wash over their toes. Two little girls ran beneath a kite flown by their father as their mother rested on a blanket nearby.

"Mother's not happy," Rumor said.

He didn't answer but nodded as if it didn't surprise him.

"She's drinking and going out dancing with Ruth." Rumor waited for him to respond, to react. But he did nothing. "Do you think she'll ever let you come home?"

The man's kite hovered above them, snapping in the breeze. Gulls screamed and the waves curled their foamy lips before collapsing into nothing but a frothy wash.

After a long time, he finally answered. "No."

As the sun dipped halfway between heaven and horizon, they wandered back to the streetcar station. They had to be home by dinner. Settled onto the wooden benches, they pulled away. Papa Jack stood alone at the amusement center with his arm in the air. Every Sunday, Rumor hated her mother.

As Rumor and Mary crested the hill, their courtyard came into view. Seven identical two-bedroom bungalows. All coral-colored plaster with Spanish tile roofs. The front doors all faced each other around a square filled with thick-branched potted plants, palms, twisted juniper, gardenia, hibiscus, and oleander.

A girl in a pure white dress and a wide-brimmed sun hat stood on their porch. She seemed about to knock but stopped herself.

"Who's that?" Rumor asked Mary.

"I haven't a clue, darling."

As they got closer, Rumor could tell she was a woman and not a girl. A small lady with curly blond hair. She looked fit and bronzed, as if she'd just returned from the Caribbean. Maybe she was a woman who had made it to sea.

"Hello," Rumor said. "We're home. Can we help you?"

Rumor had never startled anyone before. The woman took one look at her and almost fell backward off the step. Regaining her balance, she sidestepped off the porch and disappeared around the far side of their bungalow.

Rumor didn't know why, but she hightailed it after her, cutting between their bungalow and the Harringtons'. Rumor made it to the back street, right behind the woman.

"What do you want?" Rumor called out.

The woman stopped and turned toward Rumor. She looked familiar, but not.

"Mary?"

"No."

The woman's brows pinched together. She seemed to be studying Rumor's face. "Is your mother named Wavey?"

"Yes," Rumor said. "Who are you?"

The woman put her hand to her mouth. "Good God," she said before turning and running off.

"Who are you?"

The woman glanced back at Rumor but kept going.

On May 29, 1935, the California Pacific International Exposition would open at eleven o'clock in the morning—without them. Rumor had sulked around for three days, hoping to wear Mother down so she would take them on opening day. It didn't work. Mother gave no explanation, so Rumor didn't know if she refused because of the nudists, because of the money, because Rumor had school, or because Mother just plain didn't care. On opening day, Rumor faked being sick and slept in with Mary. Ever since Mary had graduated the year before, she'd done everything she could to rub it in—when Rumor's alarm clock went off, Mary would stretch in an overly cinematic style and lounge around in bed while Rumor dressed for school.

Mother banged around in the kitchen. The smell of coffee and fried eggs oozed in under their closed door. Rumor dozed off and on to the clinking of plates, running water, the flushing toilet, and the low hum of their new radio. Papa's trick had worked, and Mother had propped it up on the end table like a trophy. She left the ribbon around it, probably to remind everyone that she had an admirer. It felt like summer already as Rumor's alarm clock quietly ticked next to her bed instead of ringing her awake.

The floor creaked and their bedroom door swung open. Mother stood in the doorway in her waitress uniform—a high-buttoned pink dress, head scarf, and apron, all trimmed with thick black ribbon. It was the exact uniform every waitress at Pinkie's Cafeteria wore. "You sure you're sick?" she asked.

"I threw up."

She went to the side of the bed and put her hand to Rumor's head. "You're not running a fever. Mighty suspicious on opening day."

"Maybe it's something I ate."

"Maybe, but it's quite a coincidence." Mother put her hand on her hip. "Well, Mary'll take care of you, and I'll ask Mrs. Reed to keep an eye out."

Ten minutes after the front door shut behind Mother, Rumor threw the covers off.

"I knew it," Mary said from her pillow.

"You can leave my Academy Award on my nightstand," Rumor said on her way to the bathroom.

After her shower, Rumor found Mary sitting at Mother's vanity in her new corset and silk stockings, trying on different shades of Mother's lipstick and making kissy faces in the mirror. Mary's new work outfit hung on a hook on their bedroom wall, as if it were a work of art. It looked like a drum major's uniform, but Rumor did have to admit that it outshone Mother's. Mary's red dress had gold-ribbon trimming and huge brass buttons down both sides of the bodice. When Mary showed off her pillbox hat to her, Rumor teased that she'd once seen an organ grinder's monkey wearing one just like it.

"You coming?" Rumor asked.

Mary set the lipstick down on Mother's mirrored tray. The bright red on her pale face made her look like one of those Japanese geishas in *National Geographic* magazine. "Coming where?"

"Opening day!" Rumor said.

"Mother asked me to watch you."

"Fine, watch me at the Exposition."

"We don't have any money."

"We're not going in. We'll just watch the parade march in the gates."

"What about Mrs. Reed?"

Rumor just gave her a look. Mary knew how often Ruth's mother napped during the day. "If need be, we can easily slip out the bedroom window instead of through the courtyard. Mother'll never know."

Mary posed once more in the mirror, patted her hair down, then said, "Fantastic. We'll make it a wonderful, crazy adventure."

During the entire walk to Balboa Park, Mary jabbered on and on about starting her new job and all the people she'd meet. Her scheme was to reel in a film star. They'd marry, move to Beverly Hills, and go to all the Hollywood premieres. Rumor could just picture Mary in the cinema in her red monkey suit, batting her eyes at all the men.

A drum cadence rumbled in the distance.

"Oh no, we're going to miss it!" Rumor took off at a run with Mary tip-tapping behind in her heels. "Get the lead out," Rumor called back.

Rumor squeezed into the line of people just in time to see the Marine Corps Band and Color Guard rounding the corner, all perfectly buttoned up in crisp uniforms and marching in perfect rank and file to a drum cadence. Each soldier stared straight ahead with solemn eyes. Rumor wondered how they could look so serious when they were headed into the world's fair. The drum major raised his staff, signaling the entire block of men to lift their brass trombones, saxophones, and trumpets to their mouths. The sun flashed off the instruments, and the air erupted with music and cheers from the crowd.

In the wake of the band, a long string of motorcars followed, some with their tops down and people perched on the seat backs. Others reached out windows, waving to the poor saps left behind on the side of the road. As far as parades went, this one didn't compare to one filled with clowns and Boy Scouts, floats covered in bunting, and more than one marching band. But this parade wasn't meant to entertain the crowd. She imagined it as more of a royal procession, meant to impress the riffraff. *Look at us, we are privileged and going into the fair. Wish us a merry time.* Rumor felt like running to one of the cars and begging to get in.

On the heels of the motorcade filled with bigwigs, a disordered horde of civilians trailed, waving and blowing kisses. The women wore hats and gloves, and the men were dressed in suits and ties. Small children rode on their fathers' shoulders as the older children skipped and danced in their Sunday best, all bursting with excitement. An onshore breeze ruffled the tops of the palms and pressed the ladies' dresses tight against their backs, making the hems wave forward toward the entrance of the fair.

Rumor wished she could be one of them, lost in the tide of people, pulled forward to see the wonders of the world. They'd grown up going to Balboa Park anytime they pleased, crossing the Cabrillo Bridge, which looped across the ravine and into the park, but now a mass of people marched in as they stood outside, unable to enter.

Rumor wanted in. She wanted to run and catch up with all the lucky people to see how the workers had transformed the park into a magical wonderland.

Rumor and Mary waited until the tail end of the parade wiggled through the entrance. Then they, and all the other unlucky people, wandered off in different directions. Back to boring homes and chores and jobs.

"At least we got to see the band," Mary said. "They led the people in just like the Pied Piper of Hamelin."

"Then I wish I were a rat," Rumor said, glancing back at the entrance.

Everyone had something exciting to look forward to, except for her. Mary had started work and talked of nothing but the crowds of cinema-goers, and how she peddled her candy and cigarettes to them, calling out *Tootsie Rolls, Jujubes, Raisinets, Baby Ruth, Lucky Strikes, and Chesterfields.*

It seemed as if all the other students at Rumor's school had already gone to the Exposition, even with the nudist colony there. Rumor had to listen to them brag about seeing the Ford Building that looked like a gigantic washing machine, where you could see an entire car built on an assembly line, the Hollywood Hall of Fame with studio sets, Mary Pickford's stage curls, and Charlie Chaplin's shoes. Rumor had to hear about the Crime Never Pays exhibit with John Dillinger's bulletproof car, and, of course, Zoro Gardens Nudist Colony, where you could save yourself twenty-five cents by peeking through the knotholes in the fence.

One day, on her way to science class, Rumor spied a group of boys huddled together in the school courtyard. An occasional head popped up like a periscope. Knowing they were up to no good, Rumor snuck up behind them. Squeezing into the group, she caught them red-handed, gawking at postcards of naked women. In their shock at her sneak attack, they froze, giving her the upper hand. Rumor grabbed the cards and dashed out of the cluster. "What're you gonna do? Tell on me?" she said, waving the cards over her head.

"Come on, Rumor, give 'em back."

"I think Mr. Bradford would love to see these." The top card showed a completely nude woman standing in front of a hibiscus bush, with a bunch of long-stemmed gladioli cradled in her arms. She looked familiar. The pack of boys regained their senses and started toward her, but Rumor wanted a better look at that picture. Clutching the card to her chest, Rumor tossed the rest of them into the air. Images of a dozen naked ladies flipped and fluttered like giant confetti. As the boys scattered, plucking up the cards, Rumor escaped, tucking the one she'd kept between the pages of her *Introduction to Science* textbook.

When Rumor got home from school, she found Mary lounging on the couch, her feet up, paging through the *Ladies' Home Journal.* Mother had already left for work, leaving dirty dishes in the sink and the radio on. It irked Rumor that her mother received so much pleasure from the device. After kicking Papa Jack out and divorcing him, she shouldn't get the benefit of anything he gave them. And Mother acted so smug about having a secret admirer.

"How was school, darling? You have no idea how delightful it is to not have to sit in a hard wooden chair and be lectured at all day," Mary said, licking her finger to turn the page.

On her way to their bedroom, Rumor knocked Mary's feet off the armrest. "I can imagine how trying school must've been for you, not knowing how to do anything but apply lipstick and swing your behind for all the boys."

Rumor tossed her schoolbooks on the bed. They bounced once and fanned out, causing the naked woman to peek out from the pages of the text.

The soft melody of "Stormy Weather" drifted in from the living room as Rumor examined the postcard. On the bottom, written in white letters, was *Zoro Gardens, California Pacific International Exposition, San Diego, 1935.* The woman gazed off to the side, smiling as if lost in a daydream, completely nude. The more Rumor looked at it, the naughtier she felt, but she couldn't put it down. The small pixie nose and rounded cheeks of the woman in the picture looked very familiar.

"Mother won't be—"

Rumor jumped at Mary's voice behind her.

"Don't sneak up on me." Rumor tucked the postcard back into the pages.

"I wasn't sneaking, darling. What were you doing?"

"Nothing," she said, stacking her textbooks and taking them from the bed. "Just going over my science notes."

"Figures. Mother won't be home for dinner, so I guess it's soup and crackers again."

"Tip your head to the side a bit," Rumor said to Mary.

"Why?"

"I think you look like somebody."

"Really? Who? Jean Harlow or Rita Hayworth? Most people say I look like them." She tipped her head to the left and the right.

Mary looked just like the woman on the postcard.

"Who?" Mary asked, still posing.

"Oh, I got it," Rumor said. "You look like Harpo Marx."

Straightening her shoulders and turning on her heels, Mary said, "Go chase yourself."

For two weeks, Rumor kept the card hidden in the closet, tucked into the pocket of her heavy coat. She'd never seen a naked woman before. Besides herself. Mary and she only stripped down to their slips or bloomers and brassieres in front of each other. This woman stood out-doors, cool as a cucumber and completely unashamed. The petals of the gladioli in her arms curled back and brushed against her bare breast. She was not just an image in a photograph. The woman was a real person who had the same nose and cheekbones as Mary.

After school on Friday, Rumor came home and found the same woman on their front porch again. She was frozen in a pose as if play-ing statue, her fist half-raised and about to knock, but she didn't. Afraid the woman would run off again if she saw her, Rumor crept behind a hibiscus bush in front of the Harringtons' house. This time the woman wore a flowered dress with a waistband and a wide-brimmed sunbonnet with a yellow bow on it. She finally brought her knuckles to the door and knocked lightly. After only a fraction of a second, without waiting for an answer, she turned to leave.

"Wait," Rumor called, stepping out from behind the bush. "Who are you?"

The woman's eyes swept the courtyard and came back to Rumor. "What's your name?"

"Rumor."

Dropping to her knees, the woman buried her face in her hands and cried.

Rumor expected the door to their bungalow to swing open and for Mary to appear, but it remained shut. Glancing around the courtyard to see if anyone was watching, she stepped to the woman's side and touched her back. From above, the woman looked even more like Mary, both were so small and wispy. If Mrs. Reed or Mrs. Keegan had peeked through their drapes at them, they would probably assume that she and Mary were just having another little tiff.

Rumor bent down next to her, not wanting to talk to the top of her bonnet. "Who are you?"

The woman turned her head and looked at her. At a distance, her eyes had also resembled Mary's, but up close, Rumor could spot the difference. Mary's were breezy and happy-go-lucky, but this woman's eyes seemed full of heartache.

"How old are you?" she asked.

"I'll be sixteen this summer."

"Oh, dear God." The woman sprang up so fast, Rumor had to catch herself from tipping backward. She ran off again, but this time Rumor didn't follow. Instead, she went inside and dug the postcard out of her old coat pocket. Without a doubt, it was her. Mother must know her. Rumor knew better than to ask her mother anything personal, so she propped the postcard on the counter, leaning it against Mother's ashtray.

About half an hour later, footsteps sounded on the walkway in the courtyard. Mother pushed the door open with one hand, a bag of groceries in the other. Behind her, Mary stood with another bag. Both of them were laughing.

Rumor waited on the couch, watching Mother walk toward the kitchen. She stopped at the postcard. The grocery bag fell out of her arm and thumped to the floor with a dull crack, then the smell of pickle juice. "Addie," she gasped.

"Who?" Rumor asked.

Flipping the card over, she asked, "Where'd you get this?"

"She came to the door," Rumor answered.

"And she gave this to you?"

"No. I took that from some boys at school, but it's her. Mary and I saw her before, but she ran off."

"You didn't tell me someone came by?" Mother asked.

"Who is she?" Rumor asked.

Mother took another look at the postcard. Tears ran down her face as she tore it in half, lined up the pieces, tore through them again, lined them up, and tore again and again. Rumor had never seen her mother cry before—ever. Dropping the segments into the ashtray, Mother set a match to them, then another and another. The smell of sulfur swirled up in the threads of smoke from each dying match.

"Who is she?" Rumor asked again.

"Nobody," Mother said on the way to her room, slamming the door behind her.

The postcard didn't burn. Even with all that effort, Mother only charred the jagged and torn edges.

"Now you did it," Mary said. "We'll never go to the fair."

"There's something about her. She's familiar." One by one, Rumor picked the charred picture-puzzle pieces of hair, breast, flowers, shrub, and face out of the ashtray.

"Who is she?" Mary asked.

"I don't know," Rumor answered. "But now we know her name is Addie."

CHAPTER THREE

ADDIE

Addie stripped off her clothes and hung them on a peg in the dressing room. She dreaded the day, knowing it would be filled with boy-sailors, whooping and hollering at them after months at sea, but on the bright side, she'd found her sister. And nieces. Two of them, not just Mary.

At first she'd gone straight to the Eucalyptus Street house, taking a taxi through downtown, where she recognized the Marston Company department store, Jessop and Sons, Owl Drug Company, the U.S. Grant Hotel, and Spreckels Theatre. She remembered her first ride through the city on the trolley all those years ago. She'd imagined herself shopping with Wavey in all the stores and going to the theater to see a moving picture, but that had never materialized, not with a new baby in the house and the influenza epidemic. Things hadn't lived up to her expectations then. Hopefully, it would be different this time.

The house was smaller than she'd remembered and painted a dull yellow rather than white. It showed its age. The walkway had cracked and the oleanders had exploded, creating an impassable barricade around the backyard. Addie remembered when Ty had planted the scrawny little shrubs. A curious neighbor, seeing her standing in front of the house, informed her that Wavey no longer lived there. The neighbor must have picked up on Addie's distress and told her that Wavey had moved somewhere on Bankers Hill. The neighbor, an old woman who Addie didn't recognize, went into her house and came back minutes later with Wavey's name and address scribbled on the back of an envelope. "It was right in the phone book," she said, handing the address to Addie. And that was how she found out that Wavey had remarried and her last name was now Donnelly.

Addie had never imagined a second niece. Rumor was the spitting image of Wavey. Almost as if Wavey had been frozen in time, but without the blue eyes. Addie didn't know what she'd expected. Time never stood still. It kept right on going, with or without you.

The dressing room was a cold square of cinder blocks with nothing but wooden benches, a flush toilet, and a single shower, as bare as a jail cell. All the ornamentation was on the outside for the visitors. From the garden side, an artificial facade of stone and plaster covered the cement blocks, creating a miniature Mayan temple with mysterious geometrical shapes that transported the visitors into an ancient world where aboriginals roamed in the nude—young, beautiful, well-proportioned aboriginals of European descent, of course.

Heinrich's favorite sign hung by the exit for the nudists to see every time they passed into the garden. He had it painted on tin, like an advertisement, but instead of plugging Smoke Mac Cigars, Drink Coca Cola, or Motorists Relax With Lacquerwax, it promoted his motto: "To Know What You Prefer, Instead of Humbly Saying Amen to What the World Tells You You Ought to Prefer, Is to Have Kept Your Soul Alive—Robert Louis Stevenson." Addie always wondered if she kept her soul alive or if she simply said amen to what Heinrich preferred. She went where he wanted her to go, ate what he wanted her to eat, and followed the schedule he wanted her to follow. Did she prefer that life or had she only preferred the simplicity of the life that Heinrich offered as she hid from her past?

Addie stepped out onto the terrace with as much composure as she could muster, trying to ignore the fact that she was in the middle of the world's fair wrapped in nothing but the cool morning air that pinched at her nipples. A wooden stockade fence kept their garden secluded from the rest of the fair, like an elaborate and lush animal enclosure. Addie didn't mind. It kept her from having to see the horrified faces of children, prim women, and old fuddy-duddies shocked at their nudity. Unlike the colony, expositions were for the voyeurs; anyone was welcome to gawk as long as they coughed up a quarter. When at the fairs, she usually tried playing make-believe, like she had done when she first arrived at the orphan asylum, pretending to be invisible. She tried convincing herself that if she didn't look at the customers, they couldn't see her—or, at least, they couldn't see into her.

Below in the garden, Giselle, Yvette, Clara, Dottie, Lucille, Daisy, Lilly, and Eva hunched around the campfire, their bare backs arched, rounding off at their rumps. The women clasped their arms around their knees in the final moments before the gates opened—when hunching, yawning, and scratching were still allowed. They looked like a group of cavewomen crouching in the dirt. Heinrich and Frieda, king and queen of Zoro Gardens, were probably in the other make-believe temple, orchestrating the preparation of breakfast to make sure none of the caterers slipped in a crumb of bacon or sausage. Who knew where Joe was off to, and Sal probably already sat in the ticket booth, waiting for the crowds.

Ida, a redhead from Texas whose white skin constantly burned and peeled from the sun, stepped out of the dressing room behind Addie. "Holy Toledo, it's cold," she said, cupping her bare breasts in her hands. "Better than Chicago, though. It was so clammy and sweaty there, I felt like a greased pig all summer."

"Isn't that the truth," Addie said.

Ida appeared to have gotten over her disappointment that Mae West had visited the fair but hadn't bothered to come to the colony.

They descended the flagstone steps, rough and cold on Addie's bare feet, into the garden for another day filled with hours and hours of their fair routine: exercise, sunbathing, and the sun-worship pageant. Thick tropical plants, eucalyptus, and fig trees provided them with shade, but not protection from the crowds of watchers. Spotted black-and-white cowhide rugs stretched across the bare stones, like an entire herd flattened in supplication to Zoroaster, the ancient mystic the garden was named after. The cowhides seemed odd, being that Heinrich preached vegetarianism and wouldn't allow even a smidgen of meat at the colony. Addie wondered where Heinrich thought the insides of all those cows had gone.

Addie squatted next to Giselle, a former French ballerina with a slim figure and a long neck. Always upright and graceful, Giselle even huddled by the fire with poise. She and her younger sister, Yvette, had come to America with a ballet company, and due to some sort of scandal that they kept tight-lipped about, they were given the boot.

Addie held her hands out to warm them at the campfire.

"Bonjour," Giselle said. Something caught her eye and she looked up toward the dressing room. *"Oh mon dieu!"*

Addie followed her gaze to see Joe strutting down the steps with his Bible in the crook of his arm. His cheetah-print loincloth shielded all his sensitive areas, front and back, as stipulated—only for the men—by the fair's board of directors. Joe's bushy hair, beard, and scrawny legs reminded Addie of an aborigine she'd once seen in the back of a *National Geographic*, except the man in the magazine wasn't covered in body hair like Joe.

"Looks like we're in for it," Ida said. "If Joe don't watch himself, Heinrich's gonna toss him out by the scruff of his neck."

Joe's sermons amused Addie, but she worried for Joe; they weren't exactly what you'd call respectable. Although you wouldn't know it to look at him, Joe came from a wealthy family. He'd been thrown out of the Divinity School at the University of Chicago, and out of his father's home shortly after that. Joe joined the colony last year at Chicago's Century of Progress. Who knew what compelled Heinrich to roll out the red carpet for Joe, unless he hoped Joe had some trust-fund money tucked away somewhere.

Many times Addie had considered asking Joe for clarification about the Ten Commandments—about how many of them you could break and still get into heaven. Or if there was any way around them. But every time she'd worked up the nerve to ask, he'd do something stupid, which made her question his understanding of the workings of God. One time, he'd dropped a piece of firewood on his foot and cursed up and down, using the Lord's name in vain in ways Addie had never heard before. Another time, she caught him and Lilly behind a hedge of manzanitas, their sweaty bodies intertwined and getting to know each other in the biblical sense. After that, Addie decided that even though Joe knew the Bible chapter and verse, he did not have the proper judgment to advise her.

Joe stepped before Addie and the other women gathered around the campfire, his goosefleshed congregation. He attempted to appear pious but only looked ridiculous, with his knobby knees and loincloth. With a clearing of his throat, Joe began, "Dear ladies, I have finally discovered my true calling. The Lord has led me to this colony. I have been confounded as to the reason until now."

"Get on with it," Daisy said. "We don't need a long explanation."

"*Rapide,*" Yvette said. "The gates will be opening soon."

Joe straightened up, pulled a folded paper from his Bible, and began, "This is the beginning of my new book. Not so much a book. I'm writing my own bible."

"Good God," Daisy said. "Take a few steps back, so when you're struck by lightning, we don't get hit."

Joe took two steps back, cleared his throat again, and read, "In the beginning, God created light, earth, water, grass, fruit trees, day and night, the moon and the stars, and all the living creatures of the sea, the air, and the earth. Over all this, he gave man dominion. And man was naked. Nudity did not create sin. Nudity is chaste, it is only the sinful mind that is indecent and corrupt."

A chorus of giggles came from the gathering; they all recognized Heinrich's exact words about nudity and sin. Addie couldn't believe Joe had the nerve to mock Heinrich in front of everyone. Talk about insolence.

Joe paused a moment, a well-trained actor timing his next line: "And so, Heinrich sought to spread the word. If the masses could only witness the medicinal benefits of heliotherapy, they too would strip off the clothing that asphyxiated their pores, and let their flesh breathe in light and air. His dream was not for himself but for the improvement of the human race. But, alas, the dream lacked financial support, so Heinrich, like a prophet of old, went from town to town with his message. With him, he brought his disciples, the very examples of robust humanity, to frolic naked for the masses."

Addie glanced around the garden, keeping watch for Heinrich or Frieda. She didn't know why she cared whether Joe got tossed out or not, he'd brought more trouble than good, but he did amuse her.

Joe kept going, his voice rising like a pastor about to hit the climax of his sermon, "And so it was. In a tropical garden at the world's fair, Heinrich spread out his literature . . . and his disciples."

More giggles.

"But the powers that be spoke and bridled Heinrich's dream. They enclosed the garden with a seven-foot fence and decreed that a loincloth should cover the men. The prophet and his disciples obeyed and sought communion with nature in the lush tropical garden within the fence. And the garden was good. A forest primeval with giant palms and creeping vines. A tropical dream of a bygone civilization, with two

Mayan temples, carved deep with picture writing, and tucked behind towering eucalyptus and fig. Heinrich saw that it was good, and for a mere two bits per person, the multitudes could witness the freedom of outdoor living and the life-giving properties of age-old sun worship."

After a long, dramatic pause, "But all was not good, for one man in the garden had tasted the freedom of nudity and refused to be suffocated in a loincloth." Joe grabbed the edge of his loincloth and yanked it off.

The women gasped.

"Heavens to Betsy, you're gonna get us all thrown out," Ida said. "The officers will be here any moment."

Daisy stood up and advanced on Joe just as Heinrich stepped out of the smaller Mayan temple that served as their kitchen. Joe scooped up his loincloth and ducked behind a bush, continuing, but now ad-libbing his sermon, "And then the Lord spoke. 'How did you know that you were naked?' And the man answered, 'I have been given knowledge from the serpents of the fair's board of directors.'"

Just then, the gates swung open, then shut again as the two officers on duty that day stepped through wearing their usual tweed suits, always black or brown, and fedoras. They each carried a lunch box, a thermos, and the daily newspaper. Heinrich looked about to blow a fuse. His face turned red and the veins on his neck pulsed as his eyes darted back and forth between the officers descending the walkway and Joe crouched behind the bush. The fair's board of directors required officers from the San Diego Police Department to be stationed in the garden to make sure the nudists behaved in a "moral capacity." Just as Heinrich took his first step toward Joe, Giselle and Yvette popped up and began pirouetting around the grounds. Two nude dancing ballerinas would surely warrant more attention than one Joe in a bush.

Before Addie could plead with Joe to put his loincloth back on, he stepped out, fully covered again by the cheetah-print cloth. He nodded at Heinrich, tucked his Bible under his arm, and sauntered to the opposite side of the garden. The officers were none the wiser.

"What happened?" Heinrich asked the group of women still around the fire.

Addie always thought Heinrich looked like an exact replica of Johnny Weismuller. She wasn't the only one, either; people frequently asked him for his autograph. And sometimes, he gave it to them.

"Not a darned thing," Ida said. "Joe was just talking to us when his loincloth just up and fell off."

Heinrich narrowed his eyes and looked at Dottie. "Is that the truth?"

Dottie nodded. "That loincloth's been giving him trouble. I think he needs some suspenders on it."

Addie could barely keep a straight face, praying Heinrich would leave before she burst into laughter. Luckily, Giselle and Yvette returned to the fire. Heinrich thanked them for their quick thinking, then turned back to the kitchen.

Tinny music from an old German waltz drifted in from the fairground speakers, not yet drowned out by the laughter and excited voices of the wash of people who would traipse in at any moment.

"Smart thinking," Addie said to Giselle and Yvette.

"Merci, madame," Giselle said.

"Her name is Addie," Ida said, with a trace of her Texas accent breaking through. "*Madame* is not a compliment in America. *Madames* run brothels."

"Excusez-moi," Giselle said. "I apologize for my ignorance."

"I accept your apology," Ida said.

Giselle harrumphed. "I said it with sarcasm, but of course, you would not comprehend."

"Let's not start the bickering already. We have the whole day ahead of us," Lucille said, always trying to maintain the peace.

Like clockwork, the squabbling always began right at three weeks on the road. Every single trip. After the newness wore off, the women began to miss their comfortable beds at the colony, and the long, empty hours in the garden tested their nerves.

The tide of people rushing in from the front entrance must have startled two pigeons, because they suddenly swooped out from under the eaves of the Palace of Better Housing next to the garden, fluttering their wings aimlessly, then righting themselves and disappearing into the fair. On cue, the women spread out around the garden.

Clara and Addie sat on their usual cowhides, as far away from the viewing ramps as possible; neither of them liked the attention. Above the tapping of shoes, laughter, and the excited voices of hundreds of people, they heard the barker call out, "Beautiful women in the nude. Step into the garden and see a modern Eden. Beautiful women in the nude."

Heinrich always waited for a line to form outside before opening the gates to Zoro Gardens. He called it herd mentality; people were followers, and when they saw a line, they wanted to be a part of it. The voices rose outside the gate, eventually engulfing the calls of the barkers. Addie's heart raced, worrying as she did every day that when the throngs flooded in, the single wooden rail separating the nudists from the audience wouldn't hold the crowd back. When the gates swung open, a mass of sailors in dark blue uniforms and other men in black, brown, and beige suits poured down the ramp. A few women broke up the crowd, either not willing to wait outside or coming in to keep an eye on their men. Heinrich waited for the audience to file in, filling the ramps and getting their initial eyeful before he clapped his hands twice, rallying the nudists in his German accent, "Time for gymnastic."

They all jumped up and jogged to their usual positions, arranged by height with the shortest in front, conforming to Heinrich's aesthetics. Unfortunately, being the shortest always put Addie in row one, column A, right in the front. They formed a four-by-three square of jumping, arching, and sweating flesh. The crowd churned and hooted as they realized the women would be exercising in the nude, right in front of them. The excited mass of men whistled and jostled each other, vying for spots closest to the railing. One sailor straddled the bar, swinging his white cap above his head like an imaginary lasso. Another jumped for a low branch of a fig tree, grabbing hold and swinging back and forth, as if trying to get enough momentum to launch himself into the garden.

A voice came from the upper ramp. "Hey, doll, look over here."

Another man yelled, "How 'bout you and me makin' some whoopee?"

Addie reached to the left, then right, then twisted and swayed through the choreographed moves as Clara beat on the tom-toms. An older man, maybe in his fifties, in black slacks and suspenders, stood silent with his jacket draped over an arm, taking long drags from his cigarette and slowly exhaling a long plume of smoke—silent and staring directly at Addie. Addie wondered if the man had a daughter her own age. Did he consider his daughter virtuous and Addie some sort of a floozy? His square chin reminded Addie of her own father, and she tried to remember if her father had smoked or not. She tried to ignore him, wishing herself invisible.

Clara transitioned into a faster rhythm, signaling for them to flow into a single line for a few laps around the garden. Addie led with Giselle right behind her, then the rest, still arranged by height. Over by the fence, a tree branch unnaturally dipped and swayed. Two boys had climbed out on the limb and dangerously clung to it, like curious bear cubs, unaware that it could snap at any moment. Addie knew better than to look up, but the movement had startled her. And there, through the leaves, she caught the eye of one of them. A boy in a brown cap. He couldn't have been more than ten or eleven. The look of utter shock and amazement on his face made Addie realize that the sight of her and the other ladies would be something he'd never forget. It was possibly his first glimpse of naked women. Their images would probably forever pervade his memory as his first taste of lewd and unholy thoughts. The first chink in the innocence of his childhood. Circling, Addie passed the end of the line. Daisy's, Ida's, and Dottie's ample breasts undulated with their strides, slapping together, heaving to and fro. Oh, what would the boys think of that?

After the morning gymnastics, Addie settled by the brook to cool her feet in the water as Heinrich, Frieda, and Clara brought out trays filled with oranges, grapefruit, melons, and breads with jams and jellies. Luckily, the officers had shooed the boys out of the tree and back into the fair, so Addie didn't have to think about them watching her.

The crowd, disappointed by their lack of movement as they ate breakfast, began to taunt them.

"Come on, doll, let's see those titties jiggle."

"Aww, come on now, the fun was just getting started."

For an extra ten cents, visitors received a souvenir booklet that described the philosophy of naturism, their vegetarian diet and exercise regimen, and the names and brief descriptions of each of the nudists—complete with photographs of them sunning, exercising, or participating in their favorite hobbies. Two of the customers, both young men in tweed pants and caps, wadded up pieces of the literature and hurled them into the garden, only to be immediately escorted out by the police officers.

Frieda, a blond Jane to Heinrich's Tarzan, with a perfect hourglass figure and firm breasts, waved Addie over. Frieda sat sideways on a stool with an easel propped before her, perfectly angled so as not to block the view of her body. Heinrich knew better than to anger the visitors by allowing the women to hide behind props like a cheap sideshow.

"Guten Morgen," Frieda said when Addie approached. She swished her brush through a shiny blob of yellow paint, smeared it in a dry spot on her palette, and then dipped the brush into the blue. "You will sit for my painting today?"

Addie ran her fingers through her hair, combing out the last of her morning tangles. Frieda posed her on a medicine ball with her legs crossed and her hands on one knee, as if arranged upon a chair in someone's living room.

Frieda didn't have her usual relaxed smile. Addie figured it was because of the criticism from some of the local nudist colonies, calling them frauds and commercial exhibitionists. The newspapers ran with the stories, of course, degrading them with headlines that referred to them as "nudies" and saying they were given a "verbal spanking" from the other colonies. In turn, Heinrich had tried to discredit the other groups, calling them "Sunday nudists" and not true nature lovers like his colony. He told the papers the other groups went around dressed up during the week in their underwear, collars, and stockings, only shedding their clothes on Sundays. According to Heinrich, they were hypocrites, just like swindlers who rob people blind during the week and then show up at church on Sunday, pretending to be pious.

Heinrich was truly dedicated to naturism—but by trying to get his ideas across to the general public, he only set himself up for ridicule. To non-nudists, Heinrich and his group were laughingstocks, people to poke fun at. Ida had told Frieda not to "let it get in her craw," which was a funny thought for a nudist.

Addie shifted her weight, making the medicine ball roll beneath her. Men hooted and called, but Addie tried to listen past them. She tried to ignore the knotholes in the fence that went black, then glowed for only a moment before another Peeping Tom put his eye to it, turning it black again. The knotholes blinked on and off all day, like a signal lamp on a distant ship communicating across the sea. The only part of the fair visible from the sunken garden was the second floor of the Palace of Better Housing, heavily ornamented with plaster motifs of masks, knobs, and naked women with their breasts hanging down like ripe figs—their arms were crossed over their heads, and it looked as if they bore the entire weight of the roof on their shoulders. Instead of dwelling on the voyeurs lining the ramps and the bluestockings seeking to throw them out, Addie sought out the sounds of children screaming as they rode on the Loop-O-Plane or slid down the giant waxed slide. She imagined the families mesmerized by the exhibits, musicians, and shows. Addie wondered if her sister, Wavey, had visited the fair, if she had walked right past Zoro Gardens with her two daughters, sipping Coca-Colas and never knowing Addie was there.

The encampment, where many of the fair workers "hung their hats and housed their brats," as Daisy liked to say, was a huddled mass of tents all crammed into the canyon behind Gold Gulch, the forty-niners' mining-town exhibit. In the camp, the sounds of dance hall music and BBs pinging off metal targets rung above the laughing and whooping of barefoot children running roughshod through the maze of canvas tents, seemingly unaware that they did not have a home nor grieving when their playmates moved on. They'd never known anything else. Smells of pork and beans cooking over sagebrush fires hung in the smoky air, all prepared by the women who followed their men, scrubbed their clothes, and bore them their children. Worried that each night of love could bring another mouth they could not feed and another body they could not clothe. Clotheslines stretched between tents waved tattered banners of cotton dresses, trousers, and shirts. Stovepipes were stuck through canvas sidewalls or poked out the doorways. Open flaps exposed lumpy mattresses and storage crates upturned and used for furniture. Like most workers' camps, it lay hidden; the ugly scab of humanity separated from the dreamworld of the fair.

Addie and Daisy, now dressed in their training suits—blue pants with elastic waists and zippered jackets—made their way past the women in threadbare dresses, toiling over their camp stoves or little fires. The women either flashed sideways glances or ignored Addie and

Daisy altogether, probably lumping them in the same stewpot with the prostitutes at the back of the camp—women who ignored their biblical roles.

One woman, slumped in a wooden folding chair, nursed an infant, her pale breast looking too thin to offer any nourishment. Her toddler, tied to her waist with a rope, pulled his tether taut, reaching for a mangy cat that sat flicking its tail right beyond the boy's reach. At a huge tent, patchworked like an old quilt, with canvas, gunnysacks, and oilcloth, a gray-haired woman moved about a smoking stove, shifting the lids. The entire thing, rusted like an abandoned motorcar at the bottom of a ravine, had probably been packed around with them for years, traveling from job to job and staining their hands red every time they touched it. Inside the tent, four mattresses lay on the ground, thin and lumpy and probably packed with horsehair.

"Good evening," Daisy called to the woman, but was acknowledged with only a reproachful scowl.

"Oh, Mrs. Hoity-Toity dressed in rags thinks she's too good to greet the likes of us," Daisy said to Addie, loud enough for everyone in the proximity to hear.

Addie wished Daisy wouldn't taunt the women. Live and let live. But Daisy still had that attitude of a ward of the state—strike first and strike often.

The next three tents were circled together like covered wagons, and in their middle were three very young women in gingham dresses, probably new brides and none of them over nineteen years old. They giggled together with their hair newly done up and dresses smoothed over their knees. They waited around a table made of planks and overturned crates. The table was set for six, with tin plates and cups and freshly picked gold and purple wildflowers springing up from an old tin can. They looked like little girls playing house, waiting for the boys to join them for tea, as if it were all fun and games. But it wasn't. In a few years, they'd be as worn out as the rest of the women in the camp.

Camp life mimicked city life. Segregated, everyone congregating with their own kind. These families on the west side of the camp looked straight out of some Hooverville, breaking their necks just to feed and clothe themselves. The traveling road shows, like the colony, each had their own quarters grouped together on the east side. Toward the back, on the south side, was where the single men as well as the Mexican and black families took up residence. And finally, the prostitutes lingered along the southern edge, up all night in the red lights of their lanterns.

Heinrich had their pure white tents erected on wooden platforms, keeping the canvas up and out of the dirt and looking like a sterile bandage on the dirty skin of the humanity around them. The six tents, precisely spaced and uniform, created a U surrounding an unused courtyard, raked smooth every day in long precise pinstripes, without a fire pit, piles of wood, a stove, table, or crates. Naked, clean, and impersonal.

Addie and Daisy climbed up the two steps of their platform and clomped across the wooden deck and into their tent. In the dim light, Daisy groped for the opening to Hobbs's cage as Addie rolled and tied back the flap to let in the last little bit of sunshine and to air out the musty smell of mothballs and kerosene. Two army cots, puffed up with feather beds and quilts, lined the walls, with Daisy's wardrobe trunk between them.

Hobbs clutched onto Daisy's wrist with his scaly gray talons. His cage, the gigantic metal Taj Mahal, took up an entire corner of their tent. "You see your sister yet?" Daisy asked.

"Went to her house twice."

"Good. How'd it go?" Hobbs sidestepped up Daisy's forearm, ruffled his feathers, and bit at himself like a flea-ridden dog.

"She has two girls. I didn't know about the second one." Addie wondered who Rumor's father was, glad that Wavey had found love and a stable family.

"Good for you. Butter her up real good so you can slide on in when Heinrich sends you packin'." Daisy stuck her arm back into Hobbs's cage, nudging him onto his perch. "And don't you go doing your usual ostrich routine, sticking your head in the sand at the first sign of trouble. You've got to get some backbone and learn to stand up for what you want."

Daisy opened the top drawer of her trunk and pulled out a pair of stockings and garter belt. Digging deeper, Daisy extracted the hummingbird flask and her silver cigarette case. "I'm going out tonight. If I'm not back in the morning, feed Hobbs for me."

It had started. Daisy's nights out, and Addie all alone in the tent with nothing but an obnoxious parrot and hours and hours of nothing to do, which, since they'd arrived in San Diego, were filled with memories that landed on her like mosquitoes, silent and stinging. "He doesn't let me feed him."

"You'll be fine. Just keep your fingers out of his mouth this time." Daisy took a swig from the flask and wiggled into a blue chiffon dress, stockings, and heels.

"You're getting all dolled up."

"Got a date. You should try it sometime." Daisy held out some setting lotion and a handful of wave clips. "How about some finger waves?"

Addie began combing, smoothing, and clipping Daisy's hair into a series of waves.

"What do you have against men anyway?" Daisy asked. "It isn't natural."

Addie combed some setting lotion onto the next section of Daisy's hair. "I don't have anything against men. I'm just not suited for marriage." She pinched up a long brown lock of hair between her fingers and clipped it in place.

"Have you ever had a man?"

"Yes. Practically engaged." Which wasn't a lie. Wallace had asked her to marry him. Addie had dated a few men who had come through the colony, but the moment they touched her, it brought back the memories. The fear and the guilt always put an end to it.

"A broken heart, how predictable. You've gotta get back up in that saddle. If nothing else, the ride is a lot of fun."

Addie wished Daisy would find a steady man, not the type she dallied with: the drunks, gamblers, showmen, two-bit hustlers, or discontented married men with no intention of leaving their wives. She needed someone with a stable job who was willing to marry a woman with a grown son. Addie hoped it for Daisy's sake, but even more for Sal's. Daisy was counting on Sal taking care of her as soon as he was grown, but that was a heavy burden for a boy, especially considering Daisy's temperament.

"Who's the lucky man?" Addie asked, clipping another sleek brown wave and moving to the other side of Daisy's head.

Daisy sifted through her makeup kit, eyeing Addie and smearing on some Chinese-red lipstick. "Fred from Ripley's. You remember him from Chicago?"

"The fire-eater?"

Daisy reached for her silver cigarette case, put a cigarette between her greasy red lips, and flicked her lighter. "Fireproof."

Fireproof, maybe, but definitely not Daisy-proof.

CHAPTER FOUR
RUMOR

Rumor had only one thing on her mind, but Mother wasn't talking. Since she'd attempted the little bonfire in the ashtray, Rumor had seen little of her. She had barricaded herself in her room that entire night, leaving the bag of groceries right where she'd dropped it, with pickle juice darkening the bottom of the bag and seeping onto the floor tiles. Even after Mary and Rumor plucked the pickles from the shards of glass, rinsed the Campbell's soup cans and the deviled-ham and tuna cans, their entire bungalow still smelled like pickles.

Rumor and Mary buttoned their sweaters and crossed their arms against the cold as they stepped off the streetcar. The deserted amusement center surprised Rumor. Usually on weekends, lines of people strung out from the concessions, fun house, carousel, and the Giant Dipper. But today, the carousel turned around and around, the lonely horses rising and falling to the music of the pipe organ, without a single child aboard.

Thick fog muffled the rattle of the empty roller coaster and dulled the cries of the gulls, while the smell of salt, fish, popcorn, and caramel hung in the moist air. It felt eerie, walking through the amusement center as carnival music played and rides turned around for nobody.

Papa Jack slouched on his lemon crate in his red-and-white-striped vest, his back against the seawall and his bony knees poking out to the sides. Rosa squatted next to him, her palm-frond crosses, fish, birds, roses, and dolls scattered around her on the vacant walkway.

Papa's cap sat upon his head instead of lying upside down on the empty pavement, waiting for donations. He stood as Rumor and Mary approached. "Here comes my sunshine," he said with his arms outstretched.

Rosa's hands blindly twisted together strips of palm fronds—the beak and head of a bird emerging from the tendrils. Esmeralda waved her fingers at them from beneath a wool blanket wrapped around her and Juan, who lay asleep in her lap.

When Papa bent over to scoop up his crate, the knots of his spine popped up under his vest. *"Buena suerte a usted el día de hoy,"* Papa said to Rosa.

"Gracias, Jack, *"* Rosa said, her hands not pausing.

With no tourists on Mission Beach, shopkeepers lounged in chairs outside their stores, and concessionaires leaned out over counters, gazing up and down the walkway. As they passed Robinson's Bait and Tackle, Mr. Robinson, in his shirtsleeves and butcher's apron, called out from his doorway, "Afternoon, Jack. Got some extra ghost shrimp and mussels if you want to take your girls fishin'."

"Thanks, Gil. Don't think they're dressed for fishing today. Maybe next week."

Papa hardly ever took them fishing anymore. When they were younger, they'd go a couple of times a month. Once, Papa took them surf fishing. He had waded in the water, hurling his bait into the waves in giant swinging arcs. Rumor had followed him out, clinging to his pant leg as the breakers washed across her chest. Mary waited on the beach, making a mermaid castle—towers of dripping wet sand that looked like an underwater coral palace. Papa got a bite, and just as the tip of his rod bent to the surf, a huge roller tore Rumor from his leg. All she remembered was tumbling underwater, her face scraping against the bottom, and gulping in salt water for what seemed like forever and not knowing which way was up. Papa's strong hand snatched Rumor from the surf and he carried her to shore, where she threw up all the water, the salt burning her throat and nose. Papa had lost his rod and reel. Rumor always pictured a fish out there, still towing it around behind him. The scare had turned Papa's face all white. After that, they always fished in the bay with their bobbers floating on calm water. But now that Papa lived right by the beach and bay, they hardly ever went. Rumor didn't know if it was because she and Mary were older, or because of the divorce, but she missed it.

Mr. Moody leaned out the tiny walk-up window of his ice cream parlor. "Thanks for fixing my freezer, Jack."

"Anytime," Papa called back.

"How about an ice cream for your girls? On the house."

While Mr. Moody scooped the ice cream onto cones, he and Papa discussed the lack of tourists, both coming to the conclusion that the Exposition had lured them away.

Licking their ice creams, Rumor, Mary, and Papa strolled along Ocean Walk, on their way to Papa's castle by the sea. A group of pelicans soared over in formation, and two gulls rummaged in a tangled wrack of kelp and surf grass. They passed coral-and-white-plastered beach houses with Spanish tile roofs and wooden bungalows with whitewashed fences. Rumor lagged behind, watching the surf roll in, a gray froth trailing across the sand when it receded. Mary slid her hand into the crook of Papa's arm. He bent and kissed the top of her head, leaving his face in her hair for a long moment; Rumor wondered if he recognized the scent of Mother's setting lotion.

Papa fumbled with the padlock and latch that held his cockeyed doors shut. When they swung open, Rumor noticed two more radios on the workbench.

"You have more radios?" Mary asked.

"Just fixing 'em. They're not mine."

Rumor twisted the dials, as if trying to tune in to a station, but of course, the radio sat unplugged and silent.

"She's a beauty, isn't she?" Papa asked.

"Papa Jack?" Rumor asked, unable to let it go another minute. "Who's Addie?"

Papa ran his finger around a dusty oil stain on his workbench. In his silence, Rumor realized he knew who Addie was.

"Why are you asking?"

"She came to our house."

"What did your mother tell you?"

"Nothing," Rumor said. "Mother wasn't home."

Papa stood silent. He had that look on his face. The same look he'd had when he'd told them that their dog, Smokey, had been hit by a car. And the same look he'd had when he'd told them he was moving out.

"Do you know?" Rumor asked.

"I need to go for a walk," he finally said, turning toward the open door.

Rumor started to follow, but he put his hand up. "Wait here. I need to sort a few things out." Papa buried his hands in his pockets, like he always did when contemplating, and left.

"Lovely, darling. Now look what you did," Mary said. "Can't you let things be?"

Rumor took a Tootsie Roll from Papa's jar, unwrapped it, and popped it into her mouth before lowering herself onto the edge of his unmade bed. Sand infested everything, making her itch as if the grains were millions of tiny fleas. A layer of grit covered the cement floor and accumulated in the ripples of Papa's bedsheets. His wool blanket looked as if it had sand woven into the fibers. Poor Papa didn't have anyone to take care of him.

"Help me shake this out," she said to Mary, tossing her an edge.

They stepped outside with Papa's blanket and stretched it tight between them. Rumor looked both ways down Kennebeck Court, but Papa wasn't in sight. "Think he'll tell us?" Rumor asked Mary, lifting and flicking her side.

"Uhh." Mary squeezed her eyes shut. "You got sand in my eyes." She rubbed them, blinking, with the slack blanket in her hands.

"Aren't you curious?" Rumor asked.

"Of course I am. But if she's anyone important, she'll come back and we'll find out." They both pulled the wool fabric taut and snapped it in violent waves with their eyes shut tight. "That should be good enough."

They folded the blanket and got busy cleaning the rest of Papa's garage. Rumor lifted a corner of the sheet and shook the sand to the floor while Mary found a paper sack and dropped in empty cans of Franco-American spaghetti, deviled ham, and corned beef. Fat, lazy flies rose from the cans when she lifted them, buzzing and spiraling in slow motion.

"Girls," Papa said, appearing in the doorway. "Secrets are easy to keep when you're not asked directly. But once you are, they turn into lies, and I won't lie to you."

Rumor smoothed the wrinkles from the blanket and looked up.

Lowering himself onto the single chair in his garage, Papa patted his knees like he did when they were little.

Without thinking, they both obeyed. The tin cans clattered inside the sack as Mary dropped it. Rumor plopped down on his left knee and Mary on his right. Rumor wished she could reverse time, stop the clocks and rewind them to when they were younger. They used to climb onto Papa's lap and he'd read to them from the book of nursery rhymes with bright-colored pictures of "Jack Be Nimble," "Little Bo Peep," and

"Mary, Mary, Quite Contrary," Mary's favorite, of course. But now that they were grown, there wasn't as much space, and Mary's knobby knees poked into Rumor's. Small black dots of beard shaded Papa's jawbone, making Rumor wonder if he was running out of razor blades.

Papa stroked Rumor's hair, his fingers working through it and tickling her back. He used to tuck them into bed, rubbing their backs until they fell asleep. Another thing Mother had stolen from them.

"Addie's your mother's sister," Papa said, twisting a strand of Rumor's hair around his finger then sliding it out. Rumor imagined the tiny ringlet it left uncoiling down her back.

"Mother has a sister? And we've never known? What happened?" she asked.

"You know how tight-lipped your mother can be, so I don't know much." Papa's voice sounded throaty, as if he wished he could swallow his words. "I've never met Addie, but I do know that she's your mother's sister."

One of the many things Rumor loved about Papa was that he was always on the up-and-up, *honest injun,* he used to say with his hand raised in the air. But here was something he'd hidden from them. Papa stopped talking, and they sat in silence except for the sound of a fly buzzing and bumping into the glass window.

"Don't tell your mother I told you."

"Why would we?" Rumor asked. "We're not supposed to be here in the first place."

"Oh, right," he said. "Almost forgot."

Mother must have ordered him to keep the secret. "Did you love Mother?" Rumor asked.

"Rumor," Mary said, with her newly acquired tone of reprimand that made Rumor want to pop her in the mouth.

Ignoring Mary, she asked again. "Did you?" If Papa didn't want to answer her, then he wouldn't.

"I loved her then. And I still love her now," Papa said. "Not sure she ever loved me, though, but that's alright, I guess. I had a nice family. Mary was my little sunshine and you were my little love bug. You girls made everything right. We had some good times, didn't we?"

Almost every weekend, Papa had taken them on one exploit or another: touring the La Jolla Caves, ruins of old missions, the gold mines in Julian, or the Scripps aquarium. Rumor would never forget the very last adventure they went on. Three years earlier, when she was twelve and Mary fifteen, he took them down to Tijuana, where they browsed through the curio shops, through rows of painted pottery and woolen blankets, coconut masks and tiny guitars, dresses in every color of the rainbow and dolls with ceramic heads and limbs. Papa bought them sugarcane and Mexican jumping beans. Rumor remembered that it had gotten too late to go home, so Papa rented them a hotel room that smelled funny and had yellow stains creeping up the walls. They hadn't brought their pajamas, so Papa bought them silky kimonos to sleep in. Rumor's was red and Mary's had little bluebirds all over it. Papa wore a gigantic black sombrero, pretending to be a matador by waving his jacket next to his baggy pant leg as Rumor and Mary charged at him like two bulls. Even though they were too big to jump on the bed, Papa let them. Rumor never knew what happened to their kimonos; they had probably forgotten them in Mexico.

The next afternoon, when they'd returned home from Tijuana, Mother had smoke coming out of her ears. All Rumor heard before Mother ordered them outside was "You better not have harmed a hair . . ." They sat on the front step as Papa's and Mother's muffled voices rose and fell until dinnertime. After a silent meal, Mother ordered them to their bedroom, where they buried themselves beneath the covers and tried to sleep. When they woke up the next morning, they found Papa waiting on the couch next to his packed suitcase. Mother sat at the table, smoking a cigarette and stirring her coffee, the spoon clinking as it swirled around and around. Papa said he'd waited for them to get up, because he couldn't go without a hug. And Mother forbade them to ever see him again. Their own father.

Luckily, they'd figured out a way to sneak over to see him every Sunday. Rumor didn't know what she'd do without Papa. Mother might hate him, but that didn't mean they should lose him.

Outside the garage, a woman's voice called out, "Ruby Anne, time to come in."

Papa Jack offered them some of the Tootsie Rolls, but they both shook their heads. "Did I ever tell you girls that I ate a tree once?"

He had told them, hundreds of times, but it was their little joke.

Again the woman called, "Ruby Anne."

"How'd you eat a tree?" they asked in unison.

"From the bottom up," Papa said with a big grin.

They laughed, as usual.

A woman's head appeared in the open doorway. She had an apron tied over the top of her flowered dress. "Sorry to bother you, Jack. Have you seen Ruby?"

"Not since yesterday," Papa said. "Do you need help looking for her?"

"No, I'm sure she's not far. If you do see her, though, will you tell her it's time to come home?"

Papa agreed and she left, calling out to her little girl.

"It's getting late. You two should get going."

Papa Jack walked them to the station, where only a smattering of people rode the Giant Dipper and played in the surf, even though the sun had finally come out. As the streetcar pulled away, Papa stood with one arm raised good-bye, alone for another week on his Isle of Despair.

A young man across from them stared at Mary and winked when she glanced up at him.

"I figured it out," Rumor said to her.

"Figured what out, darling?"

"Addie."

Mary rolled her eyes.

"I think she's your real mother."

Mary's eyes grew wide.

"Why else would Mother burn the postcard? And why did Papa act so strange when we asked?"

"For crying out loud," Mary said a bit too sharply. She glanced up at the man, checking to see if he'd noticed their little scene, then lowered her voice and whispered, "You should have your head examined."

The bungalow smelled of boiling ham hock, with the slight tinge of pickle juice still lingering in the air. The house looked spotless and "Minnie the Moocher" drifted from the radio. Mother danced around the kitchen, swaying her hips to the music and chopping carrots for the bean soup bubbling on the stove. Her white apron covered the front of a pink smock that Rumor had never seen before, and a scarf covered her curly hair. She almost looked like the picture of a real mother. Her ashtray rested on the counter with several old cigarette butts squished into it. A new cigarette leaned against the edge, burning itself out, and a mason jar filled with fresh white gardenias sat on the kitchen table. Ruth, Mother's friend from across the courtyard, sat in one of the kitchen chairs, unrolling strips of homemade noodles and placing them in rows on a dish towel to dry.

"Why's there a bowl of unpickled pickles in the refrigerator?" Mother asked. No "Hi, sweeties" or "Welcome home." She moved over to the counter and took a drag from her cigarette, staring at them with her biting blue eyes.

"The jar broke when you dropped the groceries," Rumor said, studying the woman in her mother's apron and wondering who she really was. Rumor watched as the ashes from her mother's cigarette fell onto the counter. It crossed Rumor's mind that maybe Mother had lied about Addie to protect Mary and her, but that thought evaporated with the sudden recollection of Mother hurling a vase across the room at Papa Jack. Maybe she just liked to run people off.

Ruth picked up a slice of noodle dough in her thick, mannish fingers and unraveled it. "Where have you girls been?"

Rumor and Mary glanced at each other. Who did Ruth think she was? Mother had stopped asking them where they went on Sundays a long time ago, probably tired of hearing them go on and on about the sermon or picnics they'd been invited to with real families. As long as they arrived home in time for dinner, Mother didn't ask. Ruth should mind her own business, but Rumor knew better than to show disrespect to an adult. If she did, Mother would beat her up one side and down the other.

Rumor stared directly into Ruth's eyes. "After church, we went lawn bowling with a girl from my school and her family. Her father is a member of the lawn bowling club. And he's a member of the yacht club too." Rumor could feel her mother's irritation. Mother had no desire to hear about the lives of people who would look down their noses at her, but Rumor kept going. "Her mother brought a picnic lunch with fried chicken and potato salad."

Mary left halfway through the lie, closing their bedroom door behind her, probably also to avoid Ruth's typical round of questions about whether or not Mary had a beau. Ruth frequently lectured Mary about getting married while she was still young enough to *get her claws into a man.* Ruth had never been married, and by the looks of it, she hadn't been a hot commodity to begin with. She never gave that advice to Rumor, though, probably deeming her unmarriageable in the first place.

"Two girls your ages shouldn't be taking advantage of other people. I swear, it's like you're little beggars using the church to prey on people right after they've been brainwashed about Christian charity." Ruth extracted a pack of cigarettes from her bra and shook one out.

Rumor opened her mouth, about to tell Ruth to put her two cents' worth of useless advice where the sun doesn't shine, but before she had a chance to say a word, Mother said, "Go ask Mary if she's seen my red nail polish."

Mary sat cross-legged in the middle of their bed, surrounded by magazines and a Sears Roebuck catalog, leafing through them and jotting notes in her old school notebook. It was the same notebook from which, on her last day of school, she'd torn out every single page with anything educational written on it. Then she'd rolled the pages up and stuffed them into an empty milk bottle. Before corking the bottle, Mary added a little note to it that said, "I hereby bestow my formal education to the bottom of the deep blue sea. May it forever rest in peace." Mary and Rumor walked down the hill to the end of Municipal Pier, where Mary gave it a *bon voyage* and tossed it into the bay.

"What're you writing?"

"I'm making a list of what I'll buy with my wages." She was rubbing it in that she'd soon have money, and Rumor wouldn't, but Rumor wasn't about to bite.

"Mother wants to know if you've seen her red nail polish."

"How would I, darling?" She wriggled her unpainted fingernails in the air. "You think Mother would let me put a speck of color on my nails?"

When Rumor went back to the kitchen, Ruth had gone, leaving half the noodles unrolled. Mother stirred the steaming pot of beans, with a lipstick-stained cigarette pinched between her two fingers.

"Wednesday is my last day of school," Rumor said to the back of her mother's head.

"Is it? Bet you're glad."

"Is that lady your sister?" Rumor asked, far enough away so Mother couldn't whack her head.

"That's none of your business." Mother brushed some escaped tendrils of hair from her eyes and reached into the cupboard. Holding three bowls out to Rumor, she said, "Make yourself useful."

"The lady on the postcard looks like Mary," Rumor said.

"Drop it."

Rumor knew to shut up, so she set the bowls on the table, one in front of each of their chairs. From the living room, "Let's Dance" blared from the radio. Every day since Papa had dropped off the radio, Mother had turned it on the moment she got in. The other day, when Rumor came home from school, she found her mother on the couch puffing on a cigarette. Her nasty feet, with the toes unnaturally squished together and pointed like the tip of a high-heeled shoe, were propped on a pillow while Duke Ellington sang "Cocktails for Two." It took everything she had not to scream at her mother. She had no right to get a moment's pleasure from Papa Jack's gift.

Mother grabbed hold of Rumor's wrist, startling her. Rumor tried to pull her arm away, but Mother squeezed tight, pulling her toward the living room and swinging her hips. Her mother spun around, face-to-face with Rumor. "Come on, let's cut a rug."

Ever since Mary and Rumor began to walk, their mother danced with them. Recently, she'd taught them how to swing dance, and that's what they did. She spun Rumor around the living room, twirled her beneath her arm, and rolled her out and back to Benny Goodman and his orchestra. Rumor's head collided with her mother's armpit, and they laughed. When the song ended, they both were breathing hard, glistening with sweat.

Mother lifted Rumor's chin and studied her with those intense and fractured blue eyes, so close that Rumor could smell the perfume she dabbed behind her ears. "Some things need to stay in the past," Mother said before turning and going back to her cooking. "Unroll the rest of those noodles, will you?"

***

The last week of school was murderous. With the Exposition within spitting distance from the high school, the music and the screams of people swooping, plunging, and looping on the amusement rides swept over on the breeze. Every now and then, Rumor could have sworn she smelled fresh-baked pastries, roasted chicken, waffles, or chocolate. All the tantalizing delights that she might never experience.

Three days before the end of the school year, half the students played hooky to go to the waterfront and welcome the fleet to San Diego. The entire city would be there to welcome ninety-two battleships, cruisers, destroyers, aircraft carriers, submarines, oilers, and minesweepers into the harbor. Rumor regretted not going, sitting in half-empty classrooms with all the Goody Two-shoes and reading her textbook under the glaring eyes of substitute teachers—even the teachers had contracted the same one-day illness that very day. But by noon, the students began straggling back, disappointed because the fog had prevented the fleet from entering the harbor. Just after the school bell rang at the end of the day, the fleet must have broken through, because sirens and horns blared. As Rumor made her way down the hill toward home, the sounds of a brass band, then the roar of a squadron of planes flying so low over the city it looked as if they had sprung up from the depths of the sea, reverberated between the buildings. Squadron after squadron passed overhead, their silver wings sparkling against the sky. Rumor had to cover her ears as the hundreds of planes swept over the harbor and up toward the Exposition, thundering and vibrating her very bones.

At the harbor, people packed the waterfront and piers. Bands played, appearing to pantomime their songs as the concussion of the planes drowned them out. People waved flags. Banners tied to buildings and all along the streets read "Welcome, Fleet." There was even a civilian ship cruising around the giant battleships and aircraft carriers, all decked out in streamers and with its own band blaring into the deafening fanfare. Rumor had read in the newspaper that the fleet would bring in sixty thousand men to San Diego, who would take turns at shore leave to swarm through the city and Exposition for Fleet Week. It seemed as if everyone in the whole world would see the Exposition. Except for her and Mary.

On the fifteenth day of June, Rumor's summer vacation officially began, but she still woke up at the crack of dawn. She tried to doze off, tossing and turning until Mary whined, "Darling, you're driving me mad."

Too many thoughts floated around in Rumor's head. The world's fair tortured her. All the wonders of the future, a midget village, Ripley's Believe It or Not Odditorium, the midway, Gay's Lion Farm, performing horses all the way from Arabia, nudists—and especially her new aunt, Addie—were so close, but still out of reach. It was worse than Christmas, because then, she could at least peek under the wrappings.

Rumor quietly dressed and stepped outside to get the milk bottle from the porch. Dew made tiny glistening beads on the grass in the courtyard, and Little Benny screamed a tantrum from the Parkers' bungalow. Rumor had babysat him a few times, but it wasn't worth the money. He was a biter. She still had teeth marks on her arm from the last time. Mother called Mrs. Parker a *wallflower* who couldn't raise her voice even if she stood on a chair, and that was why Little Benny ran the show.

With the morning so clear, Rumor wondered if she could see all the way past Point Loma and out to sea. After putting the milk bottle into the refrigerator, she went to the corner. Without the fog, the lines of all the rooftops, telephone poles, and streets stood crisp and sharp. The ships filled the harbor with military precision, wedged in side by side, so close it looked as if you could skip deck to deck all the way to Coronado

Island. Papa called the sailors bluejackets, Mother said they were boys, and Mary thought them charming. Rumor imagined them sailing the seven seas, standing at the railings as they approached distant lands or sinking down into the depths in their submarines while zoophytes and schools of fish drifted past their portholes.

When Rumor returned to the bungalow, Mother sat at the kitchen table reading a *McCall's* magazine, with a cigarette burning in the ashtray and the percolator on the stove with the burner turned high. Her dark curls sprung out below a white terry-cloth turban.

"Is Mary up yet?" Rumor asked.

"No." Two one-dollar bills sat on the table next to Mother. She slid them toward Rumor. "This is for you and Mary to go to the Exposition." Mother tried to hide her smile behind the magazine.

"Really?" Rumor wrapped her arms around her mother. "Thank you! Thank you! Thank you!"

"That's enough of that. Take your money and wake your sister up."

"You're not coming with us?" Rumor smelled a rat. Why would Mother let them go alone, knowing that her sister, Addie, was there?

"No, I have to work. Maybe you girls can find the best things, then show me around another time."

"We get to go more than once?"

"Maybe. That's all the money I can give you, so make it last."

The fair. The world's fair. All those weeks of waiting finally behind her. Today was the day. And they could go wherever they wanted without Mother. The first thing on the agenda would be to find Aunt Addie. Rumor had no idea what she'd say to her aunt once she found her, but something would come.

Rumor rushed into the bedroom. "Come on, Mary, we're going to the world's fair."

She mumbled something and rolled over.

"We need the whole day. We're missing it." Rumor took hold of Mary's arm, trying to pull her limp body into a sitting position, but she grumbled and flopped back down. Rumor wished she could zap Mary with an electrical charge.

By the time Rumor had changed into her dark blue Sunday dress with the yellow roses, Mary sat on the edge of the bed, stretching. She still had on her nightgown and wave cap and was no closer to being ready. Rumor pulled Mary's Sunday dress from the closet and billowed it out on the bed, right next to her. Choosing Mary's old rubber-soled shoes, she placed them at Mary's feet.

Mary wrinkled her brow. "I don't want those. They're little-girl shoes."

"We'll be walking all day. You need something comfortable. I don't want you slowing me down and whining about blisters."

Mary scooted closer to the edge until her feet touched the floor. "Go on out so I can change."

Rumor plucked two giant squares of shredded wheat from the box, dropped them into a bowl, and scooped two spoonfuls of Cocomalt into a glass. Then she filled both with milk. Steam rose from the percolator on the stove, and coffee erupted into the glass knob. Positioning herself between her mother and the coffeepot, she poured a bit into her Cocomalt. She needed every drop of energy she could get.

Mother looked up from her magazine. "You must promise me to stay away from that nudist colony. It's no place for two young girls."

Maybe there wasn't a rat. Maybe Mother trusted them. Crossing her fingers behind her back, Rumor promised.

Mary finally emerged from the room in her peacock-blue dress and rubber-soled shoes but disappeared straight into the bathroom. The minutes ticked by. Rumor had time to wash her breakfast dishes and make Mary some toast with jam. She stood outside the bathroom door with both dollars in her purse and Mary's toast wrapped up in wax paper. "Come on, Mary, we're burning daylight."

"Don't rush me, darling. Perfection takes time."

Mary finally finished and they were under way. Little Benny still bawled next door. Old Mrs. Keegan rested in a chair on her porch, where every warm day she could be found in her housedress and slippers, with a flowered scarf over her head, always smelling like mothballs and rose water.

"Morning, Mrs. Keegan," Rumor called out to her.

"Where are you girls going?" she asked.

"To the world's fair. We'll tell you all about it when we get back."

Mrs. Keegan called them over with a crooked finger. With shaky hands, she reached into her pocket, pulled out her change purse, twisted the clasp, and extracted two nickels for them. "You go ahead and have some fun, now."

Mother would throttle them if she found out they took Mrs. Keegan's money, but it made Mrs. Keegan feel good, and they sure didn't mind. Mary and Rumor interlaced their fingers and skipped away, finally on their way to the fair.

They'd crossed the Cabrillo Bridge many times before, its arches looping over the ravine below. But this time, the world's fair and their aunt Addie waited on the other side. The Tower of the Science of Man rose up like a Spanish cathedral, higher than the eucalyptus and palm trees. Next to it, a gold-blue-and-green-tile dome glistened in the sunshine. People bunched up at the ticket booth and turnstiles, speaking languages Rumor had never heard before. Mary clenched Rumor's hand, either out of excitement or fear of getting separated, but probably both. The line moved slowly. All the weeks of waiting, and now more time wasted. Children fidgeted and tried to pull away from their parents to look over the edge of the bridge. Rumor didn't go too close to the railing. It gave her the willies.

Kids at school called it Suicide Bridge because so many people had jumped to their deaths from it. One time, Rumor dragged Mary on an adventure to the bottom of the canyon, and they'd found a group of boys fishing in the lagoon. The boys told them stories about ghosts that lingered beneath the bridge and how they'd seen watery faces looking up at them from the bottom. Rumor figured the boys were just trying to scare them away. It worked.

A ways up the bridge, Rumor spotted a man in a long white smock with a real turban on his head. Behind them, a man smoked a sweet-smelling cigar, and a woman, probably his wife, fanned herself with an elaborate Asian folding fan painted with birds and cherry blossoms. It was as if the whole world had come to their doorstep.

Finally, they got to the ticket booth. "Two children," Rumor said.

"But I'm . . ." Mary started to say until Rumor kicked her in the shin.

Rumor pushed fifty cents through the little slot in the window. When they moved away, she whispered to Mary, "It's twice as expensive for adults. You don't look like one anyway."

Rumor handed their tickets to the gatekeeper, a lanky man in a red velvet sombrero with gold trim. She felt as if she'd jump out of her skin in excitement. Rumor wanted to push through the crowds and run in to see how the park had transformed. But as she stepped through the turnstile, it came to a sudden halt. Mary hadn't waited for Rumor to exit before she started through. The gatekeeper pulled Mary back, letting the bars rotate again.

Finally they were in. They'd made it.

The park exploded with life. Colorful flags and banners snapped in the breeze, and flower beds overflowed with blossoms. A mariachi band played in a courtyard, and women in bright-colored dresses twirled around the men. People brushed past them, smelling like Aqua Velva, lavender, cigarettes, and exotic scents. Despite the many times Rumor had been to Balboa Park, she felt disoriented.

"Watch out," a man said, grabbing Rumor's arm and pulling them toward him.

A rolling chair with two passengers darted by. The driver, an athletic-looking college boy in a blue-and-gold uniform, glanced back, tipping his hat in apology.

The man let go of Rumor's arm. He smelled spicy and foreign. "Can't stop in the middle of the thoroughfare," he said with a peculiar accent. His gray whiskers hung long over his mouth, which wetted the bottom edges.

"We'd better keep moving or find some place to stop," Rumor said to Mary.

Mary let go of Rumor's hand to dig something out of her purse. Rumor kept walking, moving with the crowd. She wanted to get into the heart of it, to let the whole Exposition surround her. To let it swallow her.

She didn't know where to begin. To the right of the first plaza, a band played "Stars and Stripes Forever" to a sea of people in the Spreckels Organ Pavilion. Clutching the map she'd gotten at the ticket booth, Rumor made her way to a bench. When she turned to show Mary, Rumor realized she'd disappeared. She'd already lost Mary. She should have known better. Mary always daydreamed. One time, when they were little, Mother took them to the zoological gardens, and Mary wandered off somewhere between the apes and the penguins. Mother had searched the canyons, pulling Rumor behind her, past the polar bears, lions, tigers, seals, and ostriches. They circled back through a different canyon, past the swans and all the way to the reptile house. A zoo worker finally found Mary crouched and trembling in the bushes next to the camels. Mary had been hysterical, gasping and breathing in gulps. She wanted to go home, spoiling the entire trip. They didn't even get to see the elephants.

Mary wasn't going to ruin this trip. They'd finally made it to the Exposition, and Rumor didn't want to waste her day looking for Mary. Stepping up onto the bench for a better vantage point, her heart sank. Rumor had never seen so many people in one place. Thousands of men, women, and children swarmed about like a gigantic school of minnows. She looked for a blond head moving in hesitation or against the flow of people, but couldn't spot Mary. Cupping her hands around her mouth, Rumor yelled, "Mary, Mary, Mary," but the chatter and music coming from every direction drowned her out. Single and double rolling chairs, all pushed by boys in uniforms, swam through the crowds. An occasional cowboy hat or sombrero floated by.

"Can I help you?"

Rumor glanced down. A shiny policeman's badge flashed up at her. His hat rode so low on his head that Rumor could barely see his eyes. She'd never spoken to a policeman before, and in truth, they intimidated her. They always seemed so stiff-necked and serious.

"Are you lost?" he asked when Rumor didn't answer him.

"No, my sister is." Rumor couldn't tell if he was angry with her or trying to help. "She was right behind me."

The officer held his hand up to Rumor. The dark blue sleeve of his uniform had three gold bands sewn around it. Rumor wondered what they meant. She'd seen enough uniforms in her life to know that every pin, stripe, or patch stood for something. "Come on down. We can't have girls falling off benches."

"But I need to find my sister."

"Come down and I will help you."

Rumor didn't want his help. His help would probably take up her whole day. First, Rumor needed to find Mary, then she needed to strangle her. Rumor climbed down without taking his hand.

The officer, much taller than he had seemed from the bench, pulled a small leather notebook and pen from his pocket. He looked like a young James Cagney. "What is your name?"

"Rumor Donnelly."

"How old are you, Rumor?"

This was going to take forever. Rumor pictured the rest of her day, answering questions and being babysat by the police until they either found Mary or called her mother to come get her. Mary ruined everything.

"Eighteen," Rumor said with conviction, staring straight into his eyes. She'd found that people didn't trust or believe you if you didn't make eye contact.

He tipped his head down, as if looking over some nonexistent glasses. "You don't look eighteen."

"That's what everyone tells me."

"And your sister? How old is she?"

"Nineteen."

"I see."

"Thank you for your help, Officer, but I'm sure she's close by." Rumor tried to sound grown-up.

"Well," he said, taking a step back, "if you change your mind . . ."

"I appreciate your offer." Rumor waited until he turned and walked away.

Afraid to attract any more attention, Rumor didn't climb back on the bench. After about twenty minutes of watching the crowd for Mary's blond head and peacock dress, Rumor spotted her at the top of the steps of the Palace of Fine Arts. Mary stood with her hands clasped together, scanning the crowd. When Rumor made it through to her, Mary raced over and clung on to her arm.

"There's a tremendous number of people here, darling," Mary said. "I believe we ought to hang on to each other."

Below the steps, down in the plaza, a sea of white sailor hats, black and brown derbies, fedoras, and an endless rainbow of women's hats all rolled and flowed in pools and currents, around fountains and down the avenues. Rumor wanted to dive down into it and be one of the people adrift and cut loose. They made their way down the steps to a reflecting pool.

"If we get separated again," Rumor said, "we'll meet right here at this pool. The one on this side of the archway."

Mary agreed and they sat down, unfolding the tiny park map, about the size of a pack of cigarettes. Hunching over it to see the itty-bitty writing, they each pointed to different areas. Mary wanted to see the Hollywood Hall of Fame. Rumor wanted to see the Ford Building, and they both wanted to see the Midget Village, Crime Never Pays, and the Days of Saladin with performing Arabian horses. They decided to head toward the midway, which just so happened to pass right by Zoro Gardens and their aunt Addie.

"I don't think we'll have time to see it all in one day," Rumor said.

They made a start down the Avenue of Palaces. Close to the end of the street, they came to the Commerce and Industries Building, which, according to the map, was now called the Palace of Better Housing. It was a tan-and-coral building carved with masks, shells, snakes, cupids, and cornucopias overflowing with fruit. A balcony with a black wrought-iron railing and huge doors of glass bulged over the main entrance. Along the top, seven kneeling women, all carved into the stone and completely topless, crossed their arms over their heads, hunching beneath the roof. The bare breasts of the women hung down for everyone to see.

Rumor had always been fascinated with the kneeling women across the top of the building, sneaking glances up at them when Papa or Mother wasn't looking, and wondering why they were there. Now it seemed obvious. They'd been waiting for this world's fair. Right next to them, in a sunken garden, lay Zoro Gardens Nudist Colony, completely surrounded by a wooden stockade fence.

A barker, dressed in shirtsleeves and woolen cap, shouted, "Beautiful women in the nude. Step into the garden and see a modern Eden. Beautiful women in the nude."

Every knothole in the fence was manned. Men bent down or crouched along the fence, with their hats tipped back on their heads and one eye peeping in. Groups of high school boys milled around, trying to get the courage to look too.

"Where are you going?" Mary asked.

"We're going to visit our aunt Addie," Rumor answered.

"Surely not. That's a nudist colony."

Digging in her wallet for a quarter, Rumor set a course dead ahead toward a cinder-block ticket booth dwarfed beneath a giant marquee that read "Zoro Gardens" in huge black letters.

Mary stayed put, in a halfhearted attempt at defiance. "What about Mother?" she asked, "Don't be obstinate, darling."

But Rumor ignored Mary, knowing she'd eventually give up and join her.

A scrappy but good-looking fellow, who looked only a couple of years older than Rumor, sat in the ticket booth.

"You girls lost or wanting to join up?" He winked a teasing green eye.

"Neither," Rumor said, holding out her quarter. Mary gazed off, pretending she wasn't standing in front of a nudist colony.

"It's a quarter each. You do know this is a nudist colony?"

"Of course we know."

"Don't get many young girls wanting to come in. Matter of fact, you have the honor of being the first two. What are you, twelve years old?"

He knew full well that they were older than twelve. "Is it your job to take our money or to pester the customers?" Rumor asked.

"You're a live wire. I'll be glad to take your money, but no refunds. Once you pass me, you've gotten your money's worth."

Rumor held out their quarters. Instead of taking them, he reached through the opening and clasped her wrist. "What do you want in there, toots?"

"We're here to see our aunt. She's one of the nudists."

"Is that right?" He leaned back with his hands behind his head and elbows poking to the sides. "And what would her name be?"

"Addie."

"Addie what?"

Rumor realized that she had no idea. "Do you have more than one Addie?" she asked.

"Addie Bates," Mary whispered in her ear.

"How'd you know that?"

She shrugged her shoulders. "That's Mother's maiden name, isn't it?"

"Addie Bates," Rumor said.

"We have an Addie Bates, but I'll tell you what. Even if I let you in there, you can't talk to her now. Why don't you keep your quarters and come back when all the fairground lights come on? She's off by then, and I'll have had time to talk to her to see if she wants to see you."

The clip-clop of horse's hooves made Rumor turn around. A mounted police officer stared at her from the other side of the walkway. She didn't want to put her faith in this ticket seller, but she didn't know what other option she had at the moment.

"Okay, we'll come back."

As they turned to leave, he whistled. "Nice chassis you got there."

Rumor glared at him, but he just sat in the ticket booth with an impish smile on his face. Oh, how Rumor wished she could slap him. Just then, a man backed away from one of the knotholes. Without thinking much about it, Rumor hurried to the spot, fired a look at the imp, and placed her cheek against the coarse wood. Mary gasped.

Rumor held her eye to that peephole for the longest thirty seconds of her life, trying to ignore the voices behind her.

"What does that girl think she's doing?"

"What has this world come to?"

"For shame!"

Beneath thick, twisted fig trees, naked women sunbathed and gig-gled, unashamed of their nakedness. Their breasts and smooth golden flesh blended in with the lush garden of milkweed, passion vine, and lilac. Rumor didn't know there could be so many different shapes of breasts and hips. One blond woman, who looked as if she could be in a glamour magazine, sat behind an easel and fluttered a paintbrush across a canvas. Another woman with long hanging breasts sat cross-legged on a cowhide as a redheaded woman brushed her hair into a cascade of silky amber waves. They could have been fairies in an enchanted garden—until Rumor noticed the lines of people ogling at them. Then it felt dirty and she backed away.

Casting another glance at the ticket seller, who gaped back at her with raised eyebrows, Rumor turned and strutted off with Mary right behind her.

"Why'd you do that?" Mary asked.

Rumor didn't answer.

They strolled down the street as if nothing had happened, but the images from the garden had burned themselves into Rumor's brain.

"It's a sin. Why'd you do that?"

"Don't get yourself all in a tizzy," Rumor finally said. "I didn't see anything. Only plants. Just a beautiful garden." But Rumor reviewed the trapped image, trying to pinpoint their aunt Addie.

CHAPTER FIVE

ADDIE

As soon as Addie set foot into the dressing room, her skin turned to gooseflesh. It felt a good ten degrees cooler than in the garden. The damp chamber of cement blocks reminded her of the old root cellar where she and Wavey used to play as children. She longed for the earthy scent of dirt and potatoes instead of the antiseptic smell of Clorox—Heinrich's favorite disinfectant.

Sal entered from the opposite doorway, tugging at his collar. Rings of sweat darkened his shirt beneath his arms. "How do people bear these godforsaken things?"

He looked different in clothes, not so wholesome and robust. The cheap trousers and wool cap pigeonholed Sal, making him appear no different than one of the thousands of desperate young men willing to work long hours for little pay. Back at the colony, Sal's youth, bronze skin, and strapping muscles gave him the appearance of a Greek hero—like Jason ready to hop aboard the *Argo*. Funny how clothing could make a person appear worthless and shabby when they were not.

Addie sat down on one of the wooden benches, beneath the rows of warm-up suits and dresses. She crossed her arms over her breasts, not because of the chilly room but because there's a difference between nude and naked, and it all boils down to a single person in clothing. Even if it was Sal.

"Clara said you wanted to see me," Addie said.

"Two girls came to the ticket booth, claiming to be your nieces."

Oh God. How'd they know to come to Zoro Gardens? They knew she was a nudist? This was not how Addie had imagined it. Not at the fair. She had pictured meeting them, all proper in her dress, gloves, and stockings, sitting on Wavey's couch and sipping iced tea. "Was their mother with them?"

Sal unbuttoned his shirt and flapped it to cool himself. Sweat darkened a giant *V* down the front of his undershirt. "I only saw two girls."

"What did they look like?"

"The girl I talked to had long brown hair and was full of sass. The other one just stood there like the cat got her tongue."

"What did the quiet one look like? Brown hair? Blond? Was she tall or short? Was she beautiful?"

"You don't know?"

"It's been a long time."

"A tiny thing with blond hair, just like you."

Sweet Mary. Addie remembered Mary's blond hair, all light and fine like dandelion fluff, but that was true for most babies, wasn't it? Addie had always thought it would eventually turn dark, what with both Wavey and Ty's Black Irish looks.

"Are you sure their mother wasn't with them? She looks like the dark-haired one."

"I didn't see anyone but the girls, and they walked off alone."

Of course they did. She was a fool to think Wavey would ever want to see her. There are some things that cannot be forgiven. She left

Wavey without a husband, no way to support herself, and a tiny baby to take care of.

"Do you want me to bring them or not?" Sal asked.

"I don't know." Addie knew she shouldn't see them without their mother. But what if Wavey didn't know that she had come by? What if Rumor hadn't told her? What if Wavey had sent them with a message? Maybe an invitation to dinner. Then again, she couldn't imagine Wavey sending her daughters to a nudist colony. How she longed to see Mary. To see if she really did look like her. She'd love to meet Rumor and to hear how well Wavey's life had turned out after all. If she let this chance go by, she might never have another. But when it really came down to it, did she even deserve to see them? How had this already become so discombobulated?

"Well, you think about it. I gotta get going." Sal pulled his cap back onto his damp head. "I'll bring them to your tent just after dark. If you want to see them, that's where they'll be."

Addie watched as he buttoned up his shirt and tucked it back in.

"You okay?" Sal bent and kissed her cheek.

"Yes. You run along now, I don't want to be to blame if Heinrich sacks you."

Sal gave her a wink. "I'm more worried about coins accidentally slipping into the pockets of that new fellow we just hired."

Addie made her way back into the garden. Joe and Lilly stood poised with taut bows, ready to launch their arrows into a target on one of the trees. Daisy rolled a ball across the ground, and Hobbs, his feathers all dusty as if he'd bathed in the dirt, waddled behind it playing fetch. Clara, Dottie, and Eva lounged on cowhides, their heads tipped back, letting the sun drench their bodies. His body all greased with perspiration, Heinrich paused over his barbell, heavy with two giant balls of iron on either side. The nudists and the crowd moved slowly, everyone lazy and languid in the heat. Even the officers had stripped off their suit coats, one fanning himself with a newspaper and the other leaning back against the stone wall with his tie loosened and the top button of his shirt undone.

Addie stretched out on one of the cowhides next to Clara.

"What's wrong?" Clara asked.

Addie shook her head. "Nothing."

"Don't seem like nothing to me."

"My nieces. They're here to see me."

"You don't look too happy about it."

"I am," she said, forcing a smile.

Addie felt caught between the devil and the deep blue sea. She was damned if she didn't see them, and even more damned if she did.

CHAPTER SIX

RUMOR

The image of the garden floated in Rumor's head—a full-color exposure of flesh-and-blood women lounging around in the open air, naked as jaybirds. The nudists knew people gawked at them, but they seemed unashamed, as if they were merely sunning on the beach in their bathing suits. And what about the crowds of people who paid to see them? They weren't only curious young men or perverted bums. They looked like ordinary people, the type she passed by in the street every day, and some of them were even women. Adults always preached about right and wrong, sin and piousness, but there they stood, ogling at naked women. Mr. Robinson from the Bait and Tackle could have been there, or the man with the perfectly trimmed mustache from the newspaper stand, or Mr. and Mrs. Reynolds from Reynolds' Market. The crowd looked like everyday people who ran businesses and went to church on Sundays but then went to gawk at nude women at the fair. Rumor wondered if any pastors or priests lurked among the watchers.

She was starting to get the picture. Everything was a sham. Adults spanked their children for swiping a penny candy or for a bad word slipping out of their mouths, while those same parents went to nudist colonies, came home drunk, or hit their daughters in the head with a hairbrush if they cried when it ripped out chunks of tangled hair.

"Penny for your thoughts," Mary said, looping her arm through Rumor's.

"If you had a penny."

"A band!" Mary pulled her toward the Spanish Village.

In the plaza, a mariachi band, with half a dozen mustached men, played the "Mexican Hat Dance." Rows of silver buttons flashed down the legs of their tight pants. Giant sombreros, similar to the one Papa had bought in Mexico, hid their faces in shadows. Pairs of dancers, the women in bright red dresses and the men in suits of black outlined in glittering silver, swirled around each other. The men stomped a beat on the tiles with their boots.

One time, when Rumor was in the second grade, her teacher had paired the students up to teach them the "Mexican Hat Dance." She'd been coupled up with Roger, the nose picker, and was glad when the teacher told the boys they had to hold their arms behind their backs. The teacher plunked out something similar to the song on the piano, while Rumor and the other girls spun in circles trying to get their dresses to flare out and the boys began competing to see who could stomp the loudest. The mayhem that ensued caused the teacher to round the children up and march them back to the classroom for more lessons in spelling.

The Spanish Village looked more like a dream version of Mexico than what Rumor remembered of the real place. Here, white adobe buildings with looping arches and red tile roofs surrounded the courtyard and were filled with curios, art, flower shops, and restaurants. Everything was spick-and-span, and every single clay pot overflowed with red and pink geraniums, pansies, bougainvillea, or young olive trees. Instead of barefoot children begging for money, well-dressed children whined for ice cream, candy, and trinkets from the shops. Just like in Tijuana, though, a photographer took pictures of people wearing straw sombreros and sitting in a brightly colored cart attached to a zebra, which was really a white donkey painted with black stripes— except this donkey's ribs weren't showing and he didn't have flies buzzing around his eyes.

"Aren't these beautiful?" Mary held out a bouquet of turquoise, yellow, and tangerine crepe-paper flowers from the front of one of the curio shops. "I think I might buy one, darling."

"We're not going to use up all our money on novelties."

"Oh, that's sweet! You were just about to blow fifty cents, dragging me into a nudist colony."

"To see our aunt."

"I have absolutely no desire to meet a nudist, whether she's our aunt or not. Can you imagine, darling? Where would you look?"

"I'm sure she'll be clothed."

"But we know she's a nudist. I won't be able to think of anything else."

"You're naked when you take a bath, but I don't imagine your bare butt afterward."

Mary held out her hand. "Half the money's mine, so give it to me."

Rumor clasped the top of her purse. Mary would fritter it all away if given the chance. "Don't you want to come back another time?"

"They're only a nickel, so cough it up, darling."

Rumor handed her one nickel.

"Marvelous. What color should I get?"

Knowing how long it took Mary to make decisions, Rumor wandered around the shop, browsing through the rag dolls in bright-colored dresses, maracas, papier-mâché figures, clay piggy banks, and lifeless marionettes decked out in ponchos and sombreros. A fat rosy-cheeked man lifted one of the marionettes that dangled from a hook on the wall. The puppet was a tiny pistolero with guns in both hands, a sombrero, and a thick black mustache. With a grip on the wooden cross that controlled the strings, the man brought the puppet to life, making him bow at Rumor. When she laughed, the pistolero sprang into a frantic dance, hopping around with the slightest movements of the man's wrist. Brandishing both pistols, the puppet would've shot up the entire shop if they'd been real. Several children joined Rumor and sat cross-legged on the floor, mesmerized by the pistolero's drunken dance.

Rumor slipped away toward the back of the shop, happy to leave the man with his new audience. Striped wool blankets lay stacked beneath a wall full of coconut-shell masks that smiled blankly across the shop. The blankets looked exactly like the one that lay on the bed in their Tijuana motel room, except without the musty cigarette smell.

An entire village of skeleton figurines lurked in the back of the shop. *Día de los Muertos.* You couldn't grow up in San Diego without knowing about the Mexican Day of the Dead, but she'd never given much thought to it. Rumor had never lost anyone she needed to honor or pray for, except her dog, Smokey. But now that Aunt Addie had materialized, she realized that, whether you knew it or not, everyone had skeletons somewhere. She wondered how many other relatives she had, dead or alive.

"What do you think?" Mary asked, biting the stem of a yellow crepe-paper flower. "Do I look like a senorita?"

"Senorita Rosita who rode a big fat cheetah."

"Which was"—Mary paused, thinking—"the color of Velveeta."

"Drinking a margarita," Rumor added. "Maybe we should get a flower for our aunt Addie."

"You need to stop this madness," Mary said, the smile fading from her face. "Mother forbade us to see her."

"Senorita Rosita doesn't want to meet ya, so she rode her cheetah all the way to Costa Rica."

"Costa Rica doesn't rhyme."

"Close enough," Rumor said. "Come on, we're burning daylight."

Rumor grabbed Mary's arm and steered her toward the midway.

Barkers shouted, trying to pull the crowds this way and that. In front of the Crime Never Pays exhibit, a man in shirtsleeves and suspenders called out, "See John Dillinger's bulletproof automobile."

Men hollered from all directions, "Twenty-foot monsters," "Bathing beauties in jets of water," and "Come see Rossika, the tightrope-walking Arabian mare."

At Ripley's Believe It or Not Odditorium, a man called, "Feast your eyes on living, breathing freaks and monstrosities."

Rumor moved toward Ripley's Odditorium.

"Oh no," Mary said. "I couldn't tolerate looking at those frightful people. It's deplorable and makes me sad."

"Just because you don't look at them, it doesn't make them stop existing."

"They won't exist for me," Mary said.

And that about summed Mary up. If she didn't think about it, it didn't exist. It drove Rumor nuts. In Mary's world, not a single starving child or homeless family lived within the United States. Algebra, chemistry, and Latin had never been invented—but King Kong really did climb to the top of the Empire State Building, invisible men wrapped themselves in bandages, and young disadvantaged girls could marry rich Prince Charmings.

In front of a city of miniature adobe buildings, a giant barker, who made the buildings appear even smaller, shouted, "Over one hundred midgets right here. Come feel like a giant in their teeny, tiny town."

"What about midgets? You okay with midgets?"

"Of course, darling. I love midgets."

Mary stuck the wire stem of her crepe-paper flower in the front of her dress, pushing it down until the huge blossom flowered at her collarbone.

At a distance, the midgets looked like primary-school children playing dress-up, but as they got closer, Rumor could tell that they truly were adults. She'd never seen an actual midget before. Where did they all come from? An entire village of little people hurried about, going in and out of the butcher's, the post office, and the barbershop. One midget, who wore a sexy dress and looked like a diminutive Mae West, posed for pictures with the giant guests and their children, her hand on one hip and the other behind her head, just like her busty look-alike.

"They're adorable," Mary said. "I feel like I'm on a motion picture set."

"In a way, we are. They're all just putting on a show."

Rumor had to duck down to see inside the window of the barbershop. A tiny barber, dressed in a striped vest, similar to Papa's but half the size, clipped the hair of another midget covered in a cape. When the barber finished, he removed the cape and dusted off the man's neck. The customer, dressed in a three-piece suit and shiny black leather shoes, paid with a tiny dollar bill. As he strutted out the door past Rumor and Mary, he winked at them. His head came up only to Rumor's chest.

"Hello there, dolls," he said. "You ever need yourselves a sugar daddy, just give me a call."

They didn't reply, but once he rounded the corner of the telegraph office, Mary giggled. "I think I've had my fill of midgets, darling."

"He's just teasing us."

"Then why didn't you say anything back?"

"I'm not used to being flirted with, especially by a little person," Rumor said.

"I've seen Little Benny flirt with you," Mary said, smiling.

"Yeah, but he bites."

"Darling," Mary said as if she were the world expert on men, "I'm sure they all bite."

The rest of the day they visited as many exhibits as they could, including the Hollywood Hall of Fame building with its motion picture soundstage decked out for a Western, complete with saloon doors and a hitching post. They saw cartoonists create Silly Symphony cartoons in Technicolor and then went into a screening room to watch the film of dancing trees and flowers in full color. In a separate viewing room, they watched scenes from various motion pictures. The screen flickered with the images of Clark Gable, Bette Davis, Greta Garbo, Errol Flynn, the Marx Brothers, and Shirley Temple. The moving pictures bewitched Mary. Rumor had to pull her out or she would've spent the rest of the day hypnotized by the montage of scenes.

They watched workers assemble real cars in the canister-shaped Ford Building. It had a fountain on the front patio surrounded by rubber and pepper trees. The workers inside the building wore white suits and white shoes, looking more like hospital employees than factory workers. Guides pulled the crowds through corridors, moving them along the assembly line while loudspeakers explained the marvels before their eyes. At the end, finished cars rolled outside and were put up for sale. Behind the building, the Roads of the Pacific exhibit dropped down into the canyon, where guests could ride in real Ford cars to the bottom and back.

Before they knew it, the sun set, and the lights of the Exposition blinked on. Prisms of color lit up the bushes, trees, and buildings. Searchlights crisscrossed the midway, and the entire park transformed into an enchanted wonderland. A rainbow of color, mimicking the aurora borealis, shimmered over the Organ Pavilion. At the Firestone Singing Fountain, colored lights shone on sprays of water, synchronized in time with the music. Children listed against their parents or slept in their arms, while young men seemed to be electrified by the darkness.

"It's time to meet Aunt Addie," Rumor said.

"For crying out loud, Rumor. Can't you let it be?"

"She's our aunt."

"Mother doesn't want us to see her, and we should respect that, darling. She must've done something terrible." Mary pulled the flower out from her dress and wagged it at Rumor like their school librarian did when boys got into mischief. "And she's a nudist. Don't you think that's a sin?"

"Mother doesn't want us to see Papa Jack, and we don't respect that."

"That's different."

"Why? It's only different because we know him and we know Mother's wrong. She could be wrong about Aunt Addie too." Rumor swatted at the flower. "Get that out of my face unless you want to lose it."

"Mother asked us not to go there."

"No, Mother asked me not to go there. You're off the hook."

Mary didn't agree, but when Rumor turned toward Zoro Gardens, she followed behind.

CHAPTER SEVEN
ADDIE

As nightfall washed over the workers' camp, lanterns and fires glowed, illuminating the faces of men, women, and children, and giving them an eerie glow. Like a city of animated shadow boxes, the camp began its nightly display. Silhouettes moved inside tents, tending to children, bobbing in conversation, embracing, or hastening about.

Addie climbed up the steps of her platform and sat on the edge with her legs dangling above the dirt. Music from the fair drifted down into the canyon and intermingled with the camp's conversations, the clink of dinner plates, and the chirp of crickets in the scrub.

A man in front of a tent across the lane pulled his hat low over his eyes to play peek-a-boo with the little girl on his lap. She lifted the cap from his head, giggled at his funny face, then pulled it down again. Two boys poked at a fire, mesmerized by the flames and sparks that whirled up, like flaming moths, and dissolved into the night air.

The aroma of pork and beans cooking on a sagebrush campfire flavored the darkness, making Addie salivate. Like some people craved alcohol or tobacco or candy or sex, Addie craved meat. Not to the point she'd steal or commit a crime to get it but enough to create an urge that usually went unfulfilled. Addie remembered that Wavey had a cookbook with the most sumptuous meat recipes: beef balls, breaded lamb chops, corned beef au gratin, chicken à la king, pork croquettes, creamed beef, and pan-broiled steak. The cookbook was a combination of a newlywed woman's journal, housekeeping suggestions, and recipes. What was the author's name? Oh, yes, Bettina. Addie could never forget the title: *A Thousand Ways to Please a Husband.* Which seemed ironic. Wavey had done everything she could to please Ty, but in the end, it did her no good.

A little boy, leading his sister by the hand, passed through a circle of light, probably on the way to the toilets. The girl's knotty braid had unraveled, and tendrils of hair stuck to her dirty face.

Addie hoped she hadn't missed Sal and the girls. She didn't want to disappoint them. Oh, how she would love to see Mary. And her blond hair. Who would have imagined? If Mary had kept her blond hair, could Daniel have kept his too? Ty was so dark she had always imagined Daniel with a mop of mahogany hair so rich it could be mistaken for black.

A baby cried from one of the tents and a woman's soft pacifying coos quieted it to a whimper. Then, far off, a faint feminine voice called out, "Maddy, Maddy," a moment's pause, then "Maddy." Even though it had been over eighteen years, the woman's calls brought back every detail of the day Mary was born in that little house on Eucalyptus Street.

341 Eucalyptus Street
San Diego, California
May 9, 1917

Addie awoke to someone crying her name. Still not used to being away from the orphan asylum, it took her a moment to remember that she lived with Wavey. The clock in the living room ticked, then chimed twice. She lay with her eyes wide in the darkness, wondering if she'd imagined it.

"Addie." Wavey's voice sounded small and tired. Addie waited. Why would Wavey call for her? Where was Ty? It came again. "Addie."

Pulling on her robe, she stepped barefoot into the hall and put her ear to Wavey's door.

"Addie," Wavey cried out.

Addie turned the knob and pushed. The bedside lamp cast a weak light across the bed, but it was empty. "Wavey?"

"In here." It came from the bathroom. Wavey sat on the toilet with her nightgown bunched up around her hips. Her hair hung down, curly and wild just like it had when they were children. "The baby's coming. I can feel it coming."

"Where's Ty?"

"He went out."

"Out? In the middle of the night?" Ty knew it was almost time for the baby. How could he leave them alone?

Wavey moaned, "The pains are coming fast."

"You can't have it now. You have to wait for Ty."

Wavey clutched her thighs, digging her fingers into them as she bent forward, panting. When the spasm passed, she held up a hand, but the white imprints of her fingers were still clamped around her leg. "Help me lay down."

"I'll go find Ty," Addie said.

"There's no time." Wavey kept her hand outstretched to Addie. "I need your help."

Ty had assured them that he knew how to deliver a baby. He said women had been giving birth ever since Eve bore Cain, and even though Wavey acted as if she were the first to ever procreate, millions of women gave birth every day, and she was nothing special. Wavey had wanted to deliver her baby at a maternity hospital, where trained doctors and nurses knew what to do, but Ty refused. Damn him. Their very own mother died in childbirth. Where was he? Addie put one arm around Wavey's back and took hold of her arm with the other. Just as Wavey stood, she slid from Addie's grasp and onto the cold white tiles.

"See, I can't do it," Addie said. "I'm not strong enough." She wished she could run away, like little Delilah used to do at the orphan home, hiding until the trouble passed.

Wavey pulled her nightgown up. Red marks ran up and over her belly, as if she'd been scratching at the tight skin. It looked about to burst. Addie didn't know what to do, so she rolled up a towel and put it under Wavey's head, then ran for the front door. She stood at the edge of the porch steps, looking up and down the street, hoping to spot Ty, or anyone. Wavey needed help.

When Addie got back, she stood outside the bathroom door. Wavey screamed. She remembered her mother screaming the day before she died. Their father had said she went to live with God because the baby didn't want to come out, but somehow he did, because he was out when they buried them. He was out, black-and-blue and swollen. That can't happen to Wavey. She can't leave Addie all alone to go back to the asylum.

Addie stepped back into the bathroom. The tiles were colder on her feet than the wood floor. She wished she could lift Wavey and get her to the bed. She wet a washcloth, wiped her sister's face, and smoothed her hair back. Wavey's body shuddered as another surge of pain rushed through her.

Addie waited for it to subside, stroking Wavey's hair. She didn't know how to help her. Addie's voice quavered as she began to sing a song she remembered their mother comforting them with. "Golden cherub, close your eyes, dreams await you in the skies. Sleep, little baby, rest your head, off to dreamland where angels tread."

Wavey screamed and then, as the pain ebbed away, she said, "I think it's coming out. Look and see."

"Oh . . . I can't," Addie cried.

"You have to. I need your help."

Addie peered across her sister's swollen belly to her bare knees, thin, white, and sweaty.

"Please, Addie," Wavey breathed.

Addie stepped across the tiles until she stood between her sister's knees. She looked down just as Wavey bellowed again. Something pushed out, but it didn't look like a baby. There was no tiny little baby head with soft baby hair. It looked like a bloody sausage casing. Wavey stopped crying out, and it went back in.

"Something's coming, but I don't know," Addie said.

Another wave of pain pushed through Wavey's body, and it poked out again. Addie knelt and watched it come out, then go back in. Wavey raised up on her elbows and let out a long howl. It came out again, but this time something popped and a rush of water poured out. Instinctively, Addie put her hands at the opening, and the baby slipped out and into them. It was limp as a freshly skinned rabbit, wet and bloody and still connected to Wavey by a pulsing blue and bloody cord.

"Is it out?" Wavey asked.

Addie couldn't take her eyes from the lifeless baby.

"What's wrong?"

Addie watched, wondering if it would turn black-and-blue, like their baby brother. Its legs twitched, it gulped in a breath, let out a raspy cry, and turned pink. The hands clenched into tiny fists. "It's a girl."

She laid the baby on Wavey's chest, but the baby was still not free. The fleshy cord ran from the baby's stomach, down Wavey's belly, and back between her legs.

Wavey cried. "A beautiful baby girl. My Mary."

The cord slowly stopped pulsing. Addie didn't want to touch it and had no idea how to separate them. She decided to worry about it later and squatted next to her sister. The tears that she hadn't cried in a long time slid down her cheeks. "Oh, Wavey."

The baby stopped crying. She blinked into the light, quiet and alert.

"Look at her tiny fingers," Wavey said as she opened the small fist.

"What the hell?" A deep voice shattered the moment.

Addie jumped up, pulling her robe tight around herself.

"Oh, Ty," Wavey answered. "It's a girl."

"What're you doing on the floor? Why isn't the cord cut?"

"I didn't know," Addie started to answer, but he'd already left the room.

Ty returned a moment later with a kitchen knife and a piece of string. He stepped around them, mumbling, "Good Lord. I can't leave the house without things falling apart." He washed the knife off in the sink, knelt down, and cinched the string around the cord. He cut it and freed the baby from Wavey. "You have to push out the afterbirth."

"What?" Wavey asked.

"The afterbirth. It's still inside." Ty lifted the baby, holding her out to Addie.

Addie could smell the alcohol on his breath as she took little Mary from him. Ty put his hand under Wavey's head and lifted her up onto her elbows again. "Push just like you did when the baby came."

She pushed several times, and something bloody and lumpy slid out of her and onto the tiles. It looked like a giant cow's heart.

Addie gasped.

"She's fine." Ty stood up and extended his arms to Addie. She placed the baby into his huge hands. "Run some warm water and wash Wavey up. Get her a new nightgown and something for the bleeding. Then put her in bed." Ty left the bathroom with the baby cradled against his scratchy suit coat.

"He wanted a boy," Addie said. "You don't think he would . . . ?"

"Of course he wouldn't," Wavey answered.

"I already love her," Addie said, twisting the handle of the hot-water spigot. "I was so scared. But I thank God she was born into my hands."

Addie helped Wavey to the bed, propping the pillows against the headboard just as Ty came in with Mary wrapped in the yellow blanket with tiny white lambs and bells embroidered around the silk border. She and Wavey had taken their one and only trip downtown to buy it and to ride in the elevator at Carpenter's. Mary's wispy hair had begun to dry and spring up like dandelion fluff. Ty handed the baby to Wavey as Addie climbed onto the bed beside her sister.

"Go clean the bathroom," Ty snapped at her. "Wrap the afterbirth in towels and throw them outside in the incinerator."

Addie looked at him for a moment without moving.

"Now."

As she bent down to wrap the towels around the bloody afterbirth, the door to Wavey's and Ty's bedroom closed shut. Addie cleaned up as best she could, but the blood had stained a section of the grout, outlining the tiny white tiles in dark red. Ty would be angry about that.

CHAPTER EIGHT
RUMOR

The smart aleck sat trapped behind the glass of his ticket booth, right where they'd left him. "Well, if it isn't the live wire and her mute sister."

Rumor bit her tongue. She needed his help, but once he'd served his purpose, he'd better stay clear. "Have you told our aunt Addie that we wanted to see her?"

"I may have. What's it worth to you?" He leaned forward, nearly touching the glass, a funny look on his face. He reminded Rumor of the pig's head floating in formaldehyde in her school science lab.

"Never mind. I just thought she'd like to see her nieces. Thanks for your help anyway." Rumor turned from the ticket booth with Mary hot on her heels.

"Oh, thank the good Lord in heaven," Mary said. "We need to get home, Mother'll have our hides for being so late."

"We're not going anywhere except to see our aunt Addie."

"But . . ." Mary glanced back at the ticket booth.

"I'm just calling his bluff."

"Oh, come on, toots. You can do better than that," he called out through the little slot in the window.

"See?" Rumor said to Mary, turning back toward the garden.

Mary let out a loud sigh. "Mother's gonna kill us."

Standing in front of the booth again, Rumor crossed her arms and waited for the smart aleck to talk.

"Now, don't you go thinking that I did it for you," he said. "I did it for Addie. She needs some family."

He propped a "Closed" sign in the window and stepped out a side door. He seemed taller without his ticket booth. Rumor thought about making a wisecrack about how she preferred talking to him in his specimen jar but figured she shouldn't push her luck.

"Follow me," the smart aleck said.

Rumor and Mary fell in step behind him. He stood about six foot tall, and his scraggly brown hair sported a home-cut look—not quite even in the back and an unshaved neck. He looked like something out of the laundry bin, his trousers and shirt worn but clean. An unbuttoned waistcoat and rolled-up shirtsleeves rounded out his rumpled ensemble.

He stopped and spun around. Rumor almost ran smack into his chest. "Holy crap."

"Name's Sal," he said, holding out his hand.

Rumor looked at it but didn't shake it.

"Rumor and Mary," she said, first pointing to herself, then Mary. That came out a bit dim-witted. She may as well have said *me Jane, you Tarzan*. He'd caught her off guard, that's all.

"Rumor . . ." he said, as if thinking aloud. "First time I heard that one."

Rumor waited for the wisecrack, but it didn't come. He just nodded his head once and turned back around.

"That boy makes you go weak in the knees, little sister," Mary whispered into Rumor's ear. "How charming."

"Shut your trap," Rumor said. "There are lots of ways to lose a sister at a fair."

They followed Sal down a deep and twisting gulch lined with eucalyptus and pepper trees, past the Palace of Better Housing and boring exhibits about construction, architecture, and home building. They came to a model town with over fifty doll-sized homes of different styles, all with tiny picture windows and porches and glowing with lights. Rumor imagined that's what a city would look like from an airplane—perfect little homes with nobody inside.

"Look how marvelous that one is." Mary pointed to a white two-story with a wraparound porch and red front door. "Could you imagine having an upstairs and a downstairs?"

"That would be my bedroom." Rumor indicated an upstairs window right next to a giant tree. "I could climb the tree to get in and out of the house anytime I wanted. And Papa would build us a tree house where we could sleep on warm summer nights."

Mary picked out a room for herself, and they both decided that Papa still lived with them, because if they lived in a perfect house, you'd have to be a complete family. They chose a bedroom on the first floor around the back for Mother and Papa. The entire second floor would be theirs. Without telling Mary, Rumor imagined Aunt Addie living next door in the storybook cottage with the high-peaked roof and shutters on the windows.

"I'm not your tour guide," Sal called from down the path.

When they caught up to him, he looked irritated.

"Next time you decide to stop and dawdle, I'm gonna keep on walking, and you can find someone else to help you," he said.

Hanging from the rustic wooden entrance of Gold Gulch, a banner read, "On the Stage, the Drunkard." Rumor should swipe that sign and hang it above Mother's bedroom door. It wouldn't be a lie. Gold miners in baggy trousers, suspenders, floppy hats, and neckerchiefs wandered through the crowds and unpainted shacks. Some of them looked more like bums than forty-niners, and they gave her the willies. Shooting galleries pinged as people aimed BB guns at the metal targets shaped like ducks, squirrels, bunnies, and eagles. Tiny lights floated under trees, blinking on and off like fireflies. A man in a bowler hat shot a weather vane, causing it to spin round and round. Piano music reeled out from a dance hall, and a dummy, lit from below by a blue light, dangled from a hang-town tree, tick-tocking in the breeze as people walked by licking their ice cream cones and sipping cold drinks. They passed a Chinese laundry, a blacksmith's shop, and a brown shack with a sign that read, "Gold Gulch Planter—Tin Coffins Made to Order." At the mill, a flume of water rotated a wooden wheel pressing out cider. And for ten cents, you could ride a burro. She giggled at the thought of Mary riding a donkey. Rumor would pay double for that.

An old forty-niner with a grizzly beard and floppy felt hat popped out from between two of the buildings. Mary let out a screech as the man put his arm around her waist.

"Evening, missy," he said. The lighting cast eerie shadows, distorting his face. "You're a nice little nugget. I'd like to stake a claim on you."

Mary stiffened but didn't slap or push him away.

The man bent down to Mary's neckline and put his nose into her crepe-paper flower, reaching to touch it.

"Hey." Rumor started to grab the man's arm, but before she could, Sal pushed between them.

"That's enough. You're scaring the poor creature."

"Didn't mean no harm."

Mary backed away from him and took hold of Rumor's hand.

"You got two of 'em. Don't be stingy, now." The man smiled, showing a gaping black hole where two front teeth should've been. "You can share with a fella, can't you?"

"You better get moving now"—Sal pulled his shoulders back and squared his feet—"if you know what's good for you."

"You don't need to be like that," the man said, limping away, mumbling, "Didn't mean no harm."

"I want to go home," Mary said.

"He should be fired for that," Rumor said.

Sal laughed. "He don't work here. He's just a bum who sneaks in. I've run him out of our camp several times for bothering the ladies."

"Have you reported him to the police?"

"Now, why would I do that? No one wants the police poking around our camp," Sal said. "Come on, we don't want to keep Addie waiting."

At the back of Gold Gulch, Sal pushed aside two loose boards in the fence, stepped through, and held them up for Rumor and Mary. As Rumor lifted her leg to step over the crossbar, Mary tugged her back. "What are you doing?"

"You know what I'm doing."

"We don't know him."

Rumor yanked her arm from Mary's grasp. "Fine. Stay here. I'm sure that bum would be more than happy to escort you home."

Rumor stepped from the fairgrounds, lush with plants and trees, to a dirt path and the shadows of chaparral lit by only the moon. Mary appeared right behind her, as she knew she would. Sal let the boards fall behind them. In the dim silver light, Rumor saw Mary pull her flower out of her dress and drop it to the ground. Up ahead, the only things visible between the canyon walls were the silhouettes of scrub brush and a few trees.

She looked back at the fence. Maybe it was a mistake. What if Sal planned to take them into the brushwood and rape or murder them? Or worse yet, sell them to white slavers down in Mexico? She'd heard stories of girls getting knocked out with chloroform-soaked rags and being taken down to Mexico. Just as Rumor was deciding whether or not to make a getaway, the silhouettes of a woman and little girl came around a bend in the canyon.

"You coming or not?" Sal asked, already partially down the path.

"Not," Mary whispered in Rumor's ear. "This is giving me the heebie-jeebies."

The woman and little girl came closer. Neither of them looked raped or drugged by chloroform. The little girl giggled and skipped ahead of her mother. If she had nothing to fear, neither did Rumor.

"Coming," she said, picking up her pace. As they moved farther from the noise of the fair, other sounds became more distinct. Voices mingled with the soft moan of a harmonica and a baby's cry. Around the bend from where the woman and little girl had appeared, they came upon an entire village of tents lit by lanterns and firelight. Some people cooked on open fires with cast-iron pots; some sat on wooden or canvas stools, peeling potatoes or washing dishes in tubs of water. Children ran through the tents in games of tag or kick the can.

"Sal!" A pack of barefooted children stampeded toward them. Rumor felt Mary's grip loosen. "Will you juggle for us? Please?" Smiles of anticipation appeared on their dirt-smeared faces.

"Only one time," Sal said. "I have some important business."

Sal pulled three soft leather balls from the inside pocket of his vest. The children watched, mesmerized, as he tossed them into the air, rotating all three with one hand.

When he stopped, they thanked him and ran off in a cloud of dust.

"You should be a clown," Rumor said.

"I could if I wanted. My mother used to date a clown."

Rumor had meant it as an insult.

"Astonishing," Mary said, her voice filled with sarcasm. "An entire sideshow wrapped up in one boy. You sure know how to pick 'em."

"Shut up," Rumor said, kicking a spray of dirt at Mary, dusting her white socks. "I don't like him."

"Hey!" Mary said, brushing the dirt from her legs.

They passed by two rows of tents and took a right at a group of white ones standing on wooden platforms. Glowing lanterns hung from posts on the corner of each porch. The tents, so different from the hodgepodge of green and khaki canvas around them, stood out as stark as a fleet of sailboats on the bay. Rumor recognized her aunt Addie sitting on the edge of one platform. She sat there, holding on to the lamppost, with her legs dangling over the edge as if she were on a life raft, floating all alone in the middle of the sea.

Finally face-to-face with Aunt Addie, Rumor had a thousand thoughts but couldn't utter a single word. Rumor had never met a relative, so she wasn't even sure of the proper etiquette. Should she hug her? Kiss her on the cheek? Shake her hand? But there her aunt Addie sat, in flesh and blood, not making a move to give Rumor a clue as how to behave. Their aunt. Their mother's sister, of all things. She wondered if her mother and aunt used to sleep together like she and Mary did. Did her mother brush her sister's hair? Did they make tents out of bedsheets or play hide-and-seek? How could her mother not even want to see her own sister? Rumor couldn't think of a single thing Mary could do that would make Rumor cut her out of her life for good.

Seeing Mary so close to Aunt Addie, the resemblance was unmistakable. Did Mary see it too? Anyone with a lick of sense would jump right to the conclusion that Addie and Mary were mother and daughter.

Aunt Addie seemed to be as tongue-tied as Rumor. She sat anchored to her porch, clinging to the lamppost, with her eyes stuck on Mary.

"Well, this is a first," Sal said. "Three silent women."

Aunt Addie looked as if she wanted to say something, but the words were caught in her throat.

Giggles came from the tent across the courtyard, followed by a deep and throaty laugh. Four shadows, three of them dancing, moved across the canvas.

"Why don't you all go inside where you'll have some privacy?" Sal said, putting his hand on Rumor's back.

His touch made Rumor flinch, as if a zap of electricity had discharged from his hand. Instantly, she remembered one of the lessons from Mr. Dixon's science class: If a plus-charged body and a minus-charged body are connected, it produces an electrical current. A positive and a negative. It finally made sense. And she knew which one she was.

Rumor and Mary waited on the porch while Sal ducked inside to light the lantern. Aunt Addie didn't budge except to cover her eyes with her hand. Rumor got the feeling that she didn't want them there.

A gigantic birdcage loomed right inside the doorway of the tent. Rumor instinctively reached out to touch it. With two giant hops, the red-and-green macaw clung to the bars with its talons. Rumor pulled her hand back just in time to see its beak open and snap the air, right where her pinky finger had been.

"Whoa there," Sal said. "You don't want to do that. Hobbs is a nasty bird."

"Why does she keep him?"

"He's my mother's bird, and God only knows why."

"Your mother?"

"Addie's roommate." Sal laughed. "Don't worry. We aren't related."

That's when Rumor noticed the two cots pushed against each wall of the tent. Thick feather beds with hand-quilted covers made them look like real ones, except for the crossed wooden legs poking out beneath them. Two open trunks, one with white and pink flowers on the drawers and the other marbled green, served as closets and dressers. Rumor had always wanted a trunk. A trunk and a ticket to sail across the sea.

"Have a seat." Sal motioned to the cot on the left side, then slipped out the tent flap.

"Let's get out of here," Mary said. "I've got a bad feeling."

"I'm sure she's just nervous."

"Didn't you see her? I think she's got a screw loose."

"Aren't you curious? Don't you want to know what happened?"

"Curiosity killed the cat, darling sister."

Sal's arm appeared in the doorway, lifting the flap. With his other hand, he guided Aunt Addie in. She wore gymnasium clothes, a zippered jacket and pants with elastic bands around her ankles. Mary looked off in the opposite direction of Aunt Addie, as if the wall of the tent were the most interesting thing in the world, and Rumor knew she was trying not to picture Aunt Addie naked.

"I'll leave you ladies to your visit," Sal said. "Addie, I'll be back in a bit to usher them home. I think these two would probably get lost in their own house." He winked at Rumor.

Oh, how she vowed to slap him one day.

Aunt Addie smiled sadly as Sal kissed her on the cheek and left.

"You kept your blond hair," Aunt Addie said to Mary. "I never thought, especially with both of your parents so dark."

"You know Papa Jack?"

Aunt Addie looked confused.

"Our father, Jack Donnelly," Rumor asked.

Aunt Addie's eyes rose, searching the air above their heads. "Uh, yes. Jack."

Silence.

"I never thought I'd see you again, Mary," Aunt Addie said. Tears slid down her face and she didn't wipe them away. "And Rumor, you are so much like your mother."

"I'm not like my mother. At all."

Aunt Addie's eyebrows pinched together. She went to the trunk in the corner, the one with the pink flowers, and took a box from the bottom drawer. Sitting down cross-legged on the wooden planks in front of Rumor and Mary, Aunt Addie slowly lifted the lid of a cigar box. On the lid, a little robin redbreast perched on a woman's finger. Inside, Rumor saw a pocket watch, envelopes, and postcards. Aunt Addie lifted out a lock of silky blond hair tied with a powder-pink ribbon.

"This is your baby hair, Mary." Aunt Addie caressed the fine strands between her thumb and forefinger.

Mary stiffened. Seeing the woman who was supposedly their aunt, but also a complete stranger, caressing Mary's baby hair as if it was one of her most valued possessions gave Rumor the creeps.

"You were so beautiful. Such a little angel," Aunt Addie said, gazing at Mary.

Seeing the terror on Mary's face, Rumor popped up, grabbed Mary's hand, and dashed through the tent flap. Behind them, their aunt called out, "Wait. I'm sorry. Come back. I didn't mean to . . ."

They hightailed it past packs of dirty children and families gathered around fires. Rumor felt their eyes on them as they ran through the camp. They plowed through scrub brush, not even looking for the path, heading only toward the glow and safety of the Exposition. The bushes scratched at Rumor's legs, but she kept running, Mary right behind her. When they reached the fence, Rumor noticed Mary's crepe-paper flower lying on the ground. She lifted the boards and Mary stepped on the flower, smashing it into the dirt as she climbed through.

They emerged back in Gold Gulch, doubled over and breathing heavy. When Rumor looked up, she saw a woman dressed—no, completely undressed—as Lady Godiva, riding upon a white horse through a throng of wolf-whistling men. The woman's creamy white legs draped down the belly of her horse, sidesaddle. Her wavy blond hair cascaded over her naked body, all the way down until it fanned out and blended in with the horse's hide. Four burly men with pipes in their hands flanked her, looking ready to knock in the heads of the throbbing crowd.

Bullets from the shooting gallery pinged off metal targets, and drunken men from the saloon called out to Rumor and Mary above the vigorous rhythm of a tinny piano.

"Hey, toots, what's your hurry?"

"Come over here, girlie. I've got somethin' for ya!"

"What have you gotten us into?" Mary asked.

"Let's get the hell out of here," Rumor said.

They ran, hand in hand, through the crowds of couples and packs of sailors. "Hey, watch it," one man yelled as they pushed between him and his date.

They made it back to the Avenue of Palaces and plopped down next to a pool as rectangular and flat as a mirror. The lights and image of the Botanical Building were reflected in the surface of the water, like one of those Impressionist paintings Rumor had seen in the Fine Arts Gallery, except this pool came alive with the shadows of giant koi fish gliding below the surface.

"You satisfied?" Mary asked, unbuckling her shoe. "That woman belongs in the loony bin."

"Papa said he'd never met her." Rumor set her shoes on the grass and pulled off her socks.

"And?"

"But Aunt Addie knew what color Papa's hair is, and she remembers you as a baby."

"Exactly. She's got a screw loose."

Mary placed her shoes next to Rumor's and the two of them sat in silence picking all the foxtails from their socks.

Two days later, Rumor heard someone whistling in the courtyard. Mother wasn't home yet from her shift at Pinkie's, and Mary had just left for the Cabrillo Theater. She peeked out the front curtain and noticed a man sitting in a chair right in front of their bungalow, whistling something familiar. What was that? After a few more notes, she recognized it: "Who's Afraid of the Big Bad Wolf." She realized that the man in the unbuttoned waistcoat and with scraggly, home-cut hair sticking out beneath his cap was no man. Sal!

Rumor yanked open the door and stepped onto the little square of cement porch in front of their bungalow.

"Hey there, toots," he said.

"How'd you get here?"

"Walked here on my own two feet." He'd moved Mrs. Keegan's green metal chair to the patch of grass directly in front of their step, leaning back in it as if he owned it. With the rear legs sinking into the thick blades of grass, he began tossing three leather balls into the air, rotating them around and around with one hand.

His carnival tricks might make the girls at the fair swoon, but they had no effect on Rumor. "My mother may be home any minute. You need to leave."

"She's not crazy, you know," Sal said, the balls still rotating in the air. "You should give her another chance."

Rumor considered going back inside and slamming the door on him, but he didn't seem the sort to leave without having his say.

The door to Mrs. Keegan's bungalow opened. When Sal turned to look, two of the balls fell into the grass. Mrs. Keegan was a stickler about her chair. Rumor had never seen anyone else sit in it. Rumor lowered herself onto the edge of her step and hugged her knees. Mrs. Keegan would take care of him, and hopefully before her mother got home. Sal must not have grasped the old woman's intentions, because he casually scooped up the balls that fell, then tipped back in her chair again.

"Pretty nice setup you've got here," Sal said. "Lived here long?"

"As long as I can remember," Rumor said.

Mrs. Keegan, in a pink housedress and with a broom clutched in her knobby hand, put a crooked finger to her lips, signaling Rumor to keep quiet as she slid her slippered feet toward Sal.

Rumor smiled down at the ground and noticed a pill bug creeping across the sidewalk. "Where do you live when you're not at the fair?" Rumor poked the bug with a stick until it rolled into a silver ball.

Sal must've heard Mrs. Keegan, because he turned around again. Mrs. Keegan stopped in her tracks and swept at the sidewalk, smiling like a harmless old lady.

"Just north of San Francisco," Sal said, looking back toward Rumor. "Addie's got her head on straight, you know. She's as true blue as they come and terribly upset that she scared you away."

"I wasn't scared. It was Mary."

Mrs. Keegan inched forward again, closing in on Sal with her old-lady shuffle.

Rumor did want to see her aunt. She had a lot of questions that nobody else would answer. "I don't have money to get into the Exposition again."

"You don't need money. I can get you in," he said just as Mrs. Keegan cocked her broom like a baseball bat. With her thin spider-veined ankles spread into a batter's stance, she took a slow but even swing at Sal's shoulder. At contact, his arms flew into the air. He lost his balance, fell over sideways, and tumbled onto the grass.

"What'd you do that for?" His voice cracked, making him sound like a little boy, as he scrambled up onto his knees.

Her cotton-candy head shook in anger. "For stealing an old woman's chair. Don't you have any respect for other people's property?"

"I was going to return it."

She raised the broom again, pouches of papery skin dangling beneath her upraised arms. "If you didn't break it first."

Sal raised his arms to protect his head and dodged toward Rumor. "Thanks for the warning," he said.

"Don't mention it." Rumor gave him a satisfied smile and then flicked the pill bug with the stick, sending it rolling across the cement and under the hibiscus bush.

"Meet me at the high school tomorrow night. After dark," Sal said. "I'll take you to see your aunt."

Rumor didn't have time to accept his offer or to tell him to get lost before he circled back around Mrs. Keegan, scooped up her chair, and put it back in front of her bungalow. He bowed as if it were his finale and then sidestepped stage left like a vaudeville song-and-dance man. Just like Mary had said, he was an entire sideshow wrapped up in one boy.

CHAPTER NINE

ADDIE

Addie knew there'd be hell to pay the moment she spotted Daisy stomping up the dirt lane in the moonlight, bowlegged like a cowboy and looking ready to ride roughshod over anyone in her way. Coping with Daisy's temper was the last thing she needed right then. Daisy was quite a spectacle, in high heels, a fancy dress, and clutching her handbag like a six-shooter. More than anything, Addie wanted to slip away, but Daisy spotted her.

"Goddamn, goddamn, goddamn." Daisy hurled her handbag at the tent. It hit the opening in the flap and slipped inside. Not a bad shot.

It had been an entire day of bombardment. All morning, wave after wave of military planes flew low over the Exposition, dropping dummy bombs on a mock enemy-supply camp. There must've been eighty different planes. And then another contingent came back in the early evening to finish it off and demonstrate the mighty power of the US Army. Along with that, Addie's regret over the visit with Mary and Rumor tormented her all day. She had scared them off and ruined her one chance.

And now Daisy. She looked ready to give Addie both barrels, which was the last thing Addie needed. Her head throbbed from the constant drone of airplanes. Addie never knew whether to talk or remain silent when Daisy was in a mood. She could just as soon let her have it for butting into her business as for not caring enough to ask. Addie found it best to test the waters with Daisy. If she clammed up, Addie let her be. If she spilled her guts, Addie listened. Daisy clomped up the steps, across the porch, and into their tent. Addie followed.

"That goddamn lug. I have half a mind to find out just how fire-proof he really is." Daisy sat on the edge of her cot and tugged off one of her heels and then the other.

Of course she wanted to unload on her this time. Just how much more grueling could Addie's day get? Daisy cocked her arm back, with both heels dangling behind her, and Addie ducked as the heels went flying over her head, hitting Hobbs's cage and sending him squawking and flapping against the bars. "That double-crossing lug."

Addie gathered up her perfume bottle and face cream, sliding them into the top drawer of her trunk. If Daisy damaged and broke her own stuff, that was her problem, but Addie was damned if she wouldn't protect her own.

"I caught him red-handed. With his dirty red hands all over some bimbo from that Sensations show." Daisy turned her back to Addie, pointing at the row of buttons sinking down her back, which Addie had just buttoned an hour earlier.

One by one, using Daisy's silver buttonhook, Addie worked her way down Daisy's spine, releasing the artificial mother-of-pearl buttons from the tight loops. If Addie only had a nickel for each time Daisy had man trouble, she'd be a rich woman.

"He's fooling around with a bimbo who makes a living by being shot out of a pool on a jet of water. She's only posing on a platform. Where's the skill in that?" Daisy's shoulders shook with anger. Behind them, Hobbs hammered his beak against the bars as if trying to break his way through them. "A fireproof man messing around with a water floozy. Now, if that don't take the cake."

Addie wanted to console her, but what could she say? There would be others? She deserved a steady man? She still had Sal, and this wasn't the end of the world? Addie had heard Ida and Lucille gossiping the day before, saying that they'd heard Heinrich would let Daisy stay in one of the guest cabins if Sal worked off the cost of her room and board. Should she tell her?

"I thought we had something. Fred and me. We had some history from last summer in Chicago." Her shoulders relaxed a bit, making it easier for Addie to slip the buttons out. "I thought we'd set up house together. Maybe get married."

Addie made it down to Daisy's waist, and the dress slipped from her shoulders. She slid out of it, unclipped her garters, and rolled her stockings down her legs, one at a time. Bent over like that, each nub of her spine poked up through her silk slip.

"You still might," Addie said. "This girl may only be temporary. Maybe he's just on a lark."

Daisy stood up, dropping her stockings on the bed like two shed snakeskins coiled up on her coverlet. "Cut the crap, Addie. If I need you to placate me, I'll let you know."

Daisy lifted her slip over her head and dropped it next to her dress, which was puddled up on the rough floorboards of their tent. "Will you get my brassiere?"

Addie unclasped Daisy's brassiere and it dropped to the ground.

"I thought he'd be my ticket."

Addie reached out and put her hand on Daisy's back. For a brief moment, Daisy melted. Her muscles relaxed and she let out a sob before shrugging Addie's hand away. "I don't need your sympathy. Who are you to give me anything?"

"Heinrich said you can stay in one of the guest cabins when we get back. Sal can work off your rent." Addie hadn't meant to say a word to

Daisy about Heinrich. She'd always avoided being the bearer of news, good or bad, especially bad, but it slipped out.

Daisy's head cocked to the side, as if she were trying to hear a faint sound, before she slowly turned to face Addie.

Uh-oh, Addie knew that look.

"How generous of Heinrich. A nice neat way to keep Sal over a barrel. How long have you known?"

"It's just gossip."

"So you're talking about me behind my back?"

"No." Addie took a step back. "I just heard it."

"From who?"

"I can't remember. I just heard it and thought you'd like to know."

"You need to worry about your own goddamn problems and butt the hell out of mine. Did you make amends with your sister yet?"

"I'm working on it," Addie said, not mentioning how she'd made a mess of the one chance she'd had. She shouldn't have met her nieces behind her sister's back. And she shouldn't have acted like a crackpot, pining over that lock of Mary's baby hair.

"Well, good for you," Daisy said, the color rising up her neck.

Addie took several steps back, recognizing the signs.

"You're just gonna have a swell life with your family while Heinrich keeps Sal working his tail off just to keep me trapped in a tiny cottage." Her voice began to rise. "Well, la-di-da, Little Miss Addie, living the good life." Daisy stepped toward her, her breasts and fists shaking with anger.

Addie backed toward the tent flap, feeling for it with her fingers. She'd be damned if she'd turn her back on Daisy. One time, Daisy had grabbed a handful of Addie's hair. She'd realized what she'd done and let go before it ripped out of Addie's head, but it had hurt like hell. Addie finally felt loose canvas and ducked out.

***

Addie felt like an escapee from a sanatorium, slinking through the encampment and into the Exposition, still dressed in her training suit, but she needed to get away from Daisy and give her time to cool down. Back at the colony, she could just disappear into the woods or wait things out on the dock, with her feet dangling in the lake. Here, it was either wander around the workers' camp or through the Exposition.

With colored lights and a full moon illuminating the buildings and trees, the whole thing felt like a dream. Addie wished she could wake up and find herself back in her bed at Sleepy Valley, where she only had to follow Heinrich's schedule and she didn't have to think, where she didn't have to remember how she had betrayed her sister and how much she had lost because of it. Addie followed the flow of people toward the midway, where searchlights sliced through the night sky. Barkers called to the crowds, and machines pinged and whizzed and cranked out tinny carnival tunes. People screamed on the Swooper, the parachute jump, and the Loop-O-Plane.

A man walking next to her reached into his breast pocket and took out a fistful of bills, causing the three children with him to prance around like hungry puppies. The man licked his finger and flipped through the bills, extracting one at a time and holding it out to each of the children. Once they'd snatched up their cash, they skipped off toward the Race Through the Clouds roller coaster, all jazzed up in American flags and tiny white lights.

Addie wondered which rides Mary and Rumor had ridden. Did they visit Gay's Lion Farm or the Snake Farm? Or did they like exhibits like Ripley's and the Two-Headed Baby? Did they see the trained chimpanzee named the Duke of Wellington? Did they visit the Indian Village?

The young couple in front of her, a sailor and his girl, veered off toward the House of Mirrors. Addie wouldn't go in there for a million bucks. The thought of being lost in a house of mirrors, with her own image reflected all around her and the images of others slipping in and out, gave her a feeling of panic. She hated being watched. And it seemed she always was.

People stumbled out the exit, laughing and clinging to one another. Those people must not have a past that haunted them—nothing to stare back at them from the corridors of angled mirrors.

At the orphan asylum, they would dare each other to walk up the dark staircase backward, holding a candle and looking into Anna's hand mirror. If you did it right, you'd see the face of your future husband. The first time Addie tried it, she saw nothing but her own ghostly image. The second time, the image of a distorted, almost skeletal, face stared back at her. She'd dropped the mirror, creating a web of cracks, and run to her bed to hide beneath the sheets. Harriet had told her that seeing the skeleton meant that she'd die before getting married, and since she'd broken the mirror, she'd have seven years' bad luck on top of it. And she did.

341 Eucalyptus Street
San Diego, California
July 17, 1918

Out back, Ty looked like a gravedigger with his lantern and spade. He paused and tipped a silver flask that shone in the moonlight to his mouth, then came the flare of a match and the orange glow of a cigarette.

"What're you looking at?" Wavey asked from behind Addie. Mary's towel-dried hair curled in damp little circles all over her head.

"Ty," Addie said. "What's he burying?"

Wavey put Mary down and looked out at her husband. "Maybe one of Miss Mabel's cats?" She gave Addie a wink. "He's planting some oleander bushes to give us some privacy from Miss Mabel. He doesn't like her meddling."

Addie didn't have a kind word to say about Miss Mabel. The day after she'd arrived, an officer from the police department showed up, stating that he'd received a call from the neighbor that a delinquent girl from an orphan asylum had moved in and needed to be monitored. So twice every week, just around noontime, he came by to check on her. Wavey usually stepped out onto the porch and spoke with him in private, only occasionally forcing Addie to show her face to him. The officer, Officer Darby, seemed kind enough—young and with a twinkle in his eyes. His presence always reminded Addie that because she was an orphan, people judged her a reprobate, a kleptomaniac, a liar, or just a generally wicked girl, without knowing her or giving her a fair shake, but Wavey seemed to look forward to his visits, checking her hair and pinching some color into her cheeks before answering the door.

That night, Addie fell asleep to the scraping of Ty's spade against the soil and the occasional metal ping when he hit rock. By the time the back door slammed and the sound of Ty's boots stomped across the kitchen, the grandfather clock had chimed twelve times. Who dug holes in the middle of the night? Ty hardly ever slept, always lurking around the house with his bottle of Scotch.

The next morning, a line of eleven open holes, each about two feet in diameter, divided their yard from Miss Mable's.

The nighttime digging went on for two more evenings, until holes surrounded the entire backyard. The following morning, as Addie dressed Mary in a little white dress with tiny little cows jumping over moons embroidered along the hem, she heard the rumble of an engine in the drive. Two Mexican men backed up a delivery truck full of shrubs, aiming the tailgate toward the backyard. The oleanders were all splotched with red flowers, and their root balls were wrapped in burlap and twine. It would be years before the tiny bushes grew into a true barrier.

Addie balanced Mary on her hip as she made her way to the chicken coop to collect the morning eggs. A salty breeze blew in off the ocean. Addie had imagined visiting the beach with Wavey, letting the tide wash over their bare feet, but they had not gone once. Ty couldn't tolerate the sand. He did not like the feel of it on his feet, and he said that it got into everything and you couldn't get rid of the grit.

The men unloaded the truck, taking trips back and forth, dropping oleander bushes next to each hole. She didn't look in their direction, but she felt their eyes on her.

"Bring Mary over." Miss Mabel stepped between two of the holes, right into their backyard. "I'll hold her while you collect the eggs."

"No need," Addie said. "Mary likes the chickens."

"Nonsense, child. It'll take you twice as long. Bring her to me."

When Addie handed Mary over to Miss Mabel, the baby reached back for her and whimpered, "Ah-ee." Addie never knew if she was saying *Addie* or *auntie*.

"You keep Mary away from these bushes, do you hear?" Miss Mabel said.

Addie looked down at one of the spindly bushes. "What could she do to them?"

Mary wriggled, trying to free herself from Miss Mabel's grasp. "They're poisonous. Deadly poisonous. My father, God rest his soul, was a doctor. He'd never consider planting poisonous plants around *his* children."

"We should tell Ty."

"I've already told him. That man doesn't listen to anybody. I told him to go look it up in the library, if he didn't believe me, but do you think he has any intention of that?" Miss Mabel shifted Mary to her other hip. "Go on now, get your eggs. And hurry, she's getting heavy."

The moment Addie turned to leave, Mary screamed and reached out to her. "Ah-ee, Ah-ee."

"Oh, hush, hush," Miss Mabel sang, trying to soothe her distress.

The more she sang, the louder Mary cried.

Inside the henhouse, Addie reached her hand into the soft pine shavings of the nesting boxes. Only three eggs again. Aunt Bessie wasn't laying. If Ty found out, he'd behead, pluck, and plop poor Aunt Bessie into the soup pot for dinner. Ty had named all the barnyard chickens after his father's sisters: Aunt Bessie, Aunt Gertie, Aunt Biddy, and Auntie Pearl. He didn't like any of his aunts and couldn't wait to lop off the heads of their namesakes. Addie liked Aunt Bessie the best because of her fluffy feather legs. Mean Aunt Biddy pecked at the other three, so Ty had debeaked her, which made her look funny with her mouth in a permanent pucker—just like Miss Mabel.

"Everything okay?" Addie heard Wavey calling out from the house.

"Fine, dear," Miss Mabel said. "I'll get her quieted."

Addie heard the screen door bang shut. "Thank you for your kindness," she heard Wavey say, "but it's past her nap time and she's fussy."

Addie latched the door to the henhouse just as Wavey climbed up the back steps with Mary. Addie pulled two skinny carrots and an onion from the vegetable patch as the chickens bobbed and scratched in their run, their jerky movements reminding her of the flickers at the movie palace.

As one of the Mexican men passed by Addie, he whispered under his breath, something in Spanish. She didn't know what he said, but the way he said it made her flesh crawl.

"Addie," Miss Mabel called from her yard. "Come over here, dear."

Miss Mabel held a handful of blossoms she'd plucked from Ty's new plants. "You put these up out of Mary's reach, then give them to Ty when he gets back. Tell him they're poisonous."

She held them out to Addie, but she didn't touch them. Ty would be furious that Miss Mabel had plucked the flowers off his new plants.

"Take them, child, and make sure you keep them away from Mary."

When Addie stepped into the kitchen, Wavey pressed her fingers to her lips. "She's asleep."

"Did you know the new oleanders are poisonous?"

"Where'd you hear that?" Wavey asked.

"Miss Mabel." Addie held out the handful of red blossoms, already turning limp and bruised in her fist. "She asked me to give these to Ty."

Wavey took them from Addie's outstretched palm and tossed them into the wastebin. "No need to get him upset. It took him a long time to dig all those holes."

"But what about Mary?"

"I'll talk to him about it. There's a way to approach matters, and there's a way to make them worse."

***

The front door slammed and Ty's voice boomed into the kitchen. "Wavey?"

He'd come home early, which was unusual with the labor shortage. With so many men gone to war, the ones left behind had to fill in.

"Wavey?" he yelled again. Addie never understood why men had to be so loud.

Mary awoke and cried from her crib. Turning off the gas flame from under the pot of lamb stew, Addie hurried past him to get the baby.

"Where's Wavey?" Ty had two bunches of flowers clasped in his fist. Roses and lilies.

"She went to the market."

"How long has she been out?" Ty followed Addie through the kitchen and into her and Mary's bedroom.

"Not long," Addie lied, realizing that Wavey should've returned long ago. She lifted Mary from her crib and laid her on the bed to change her. She unfastened the safety pins and pulled off the soggy diaper.

"Let me help." Ty's voice came from directly behind her. Before she had a chance to step away, his belt buckle poked into the small of her back. He stunk of sweat and stale cigars. He grabbed both of Addie's hips, his fingers pressing hard into her bones. Ty pushed himself against her, the fingers of one hand working at her dress, inching it up. "How long should she be?"

Addie couldn't speak.

"I asked you a question."

"Any minute" was all that Addie could get out.

Mary twisted on the bed, rolled to her stomach, and scooted toward the edge. "The baby," Addie said.

Ty backed away, let out a harsh laugh, and left the room. Addie lifted Mary and, slumping to the floor, hugged her to her chest. How had Wavey married such a man? How could she look into his meaty face and feel any sense of love? How could she crawl into bed with him at night? The thought of Ty's hands on her sister, and Wavey allowing it, made Addie sick. How had things come to this? Addie was a fool to think there was any safety here. This wasn't the end of it; she could just feel it in her bones. Mary wriggled out of Addie's grasp and toddled away, bare bottomed, toward the door.

"Addie." Ty stood in the doorway and lifted the naked baby in his arms. "You better keep a better eye on her. We can always ship you back to that orphan home. And don't you think for a second that I won't."

He patted Mary's behind and sat her down on the floorboards. Mary pushed herself up and tottered over to Addie on her bare feet, grabbing Addie's sleeves as she climbed up onto her lap. Ty wasn't in the doorway any longer, but Addie imagined him lingering somewhere close by. She closed the door and leaned against it.

After what seemed an eternity, Wavey came home.

"Where have you been?" Ty's voice hammered through the house.

"We ran out of flour," Wavey said.

"I didn't see you at the market on my way home from work."

"I went straight there and back."

Addie held her cheek to the cool back of the door. She didn't know how long to wait. She couldn't imagine why Wavey had been gone for so long. Officer Darby had come by to check on Addie as usual, and as soon as he left, Wavey had asked her to watch the stew so she could go to the market. Addie had a bad feeling the two were connected but prayed they weren't. Ty would kill Wavey for something like that.

"Addie," Wavey called. "Why's the stew off the burner?"

Addie stepped out of the bedroom with Mary on her hip and followed Wavey's voice into the kitchen. "I had to take care of Mary."

Ty lowered himself into his chair at the head of the table and picked up the newspaper Wavey had placed at his spot—unopened; they weren't allowed to read the paper until he'd finished with it.

"Did something happen?" Wavey asked.

Addie shifted Mary to her other hip. Ty didn't respond.

"No," Addie said.

Wavey looked from Addie to Ty, but he ignored them, only turning the page of his paper. Addie noticed a headline as he readjusted it, "Body of Missing Wife Found Buried In Backyard," and the image of Ty digging in the moonlight came to mind, and she believed that he could do it.

"You two gonna keep standing there?" Ty growled without looking up. "I worked all day and I'm hungry."

"Sorry." Wavey looked back over at Addie. "Why don't you take Mary out back and play with her?"

Addie lowered Mary onto the grass next to her rubber ball, then sat down on the back steps. Mary tried to push herself up on the ball, but she tumbled over, rolling onto her side. Scrambling back onto her hands and knees, she crawled toward Addie.

"It's hard to relax with you staring at me like that." Ty's voice filtered out through the screen door. "Get me a drink, will you?"

"Did something happen with Addie while I was gone?"

"She wasn't watching Mary properly and I had to say something." His newspaper rustled. "Could be that."

Addie felt like screaming through the dusty mesh of the screen door, telling her sister that Ty had touched her. That he scared her. That he'd caused it all. Mary grabbed at Addie's skirt, trying to pull herself up.

Ty's deep voice resonated in the kitchen. "I've caught your darling little sister lying to me several times."

Addie wanted to burst through the door and scream at him, but that would only prove his point. She hated him.

"That doesn't sound like the Addie I know," Wavey said.

"Maybe she isn't the Addie you remember. I've heard about those orphan asylums. How could it not have corrupted her?"

Addie scooped Mary up onto her lap. She put her nose into Mary's hair, breathing in her soft and innocent baby scent.

CHAPTER TEN

RUMOR

Rumor didn't need Mother's permission. She'd never liked the game of Mother May I—having to ask for the go-ahead every time she wanted to take a baby step here or a scissor step there. And since the answer would most likely be "No, you may not," with no logic or fairness applied whatsoever, she stopped asking. So without a lick of permission, Rumor decided to give Aunt Addie another shot. She didn't agree with Mary that she belonged in the loony bin, and curiosity got the best of her. Curiosity may have killed the cat, but what was the alternative? Living with your head in a daydream, like Mary? No, thanks. And to top it all off, the timing was perfect. Both Mother and Mary had to work the night Sal had asked her to meet him at the high school. Rumor offered to escort Mary to her job, which thrilled Mary since she hated going anywhere alone. Besides, the walk to the Cabrillo Theater was only a few blocks out of her way.

Mary, sporting her drum major uniform and monkey hat, click-clacked down the street, acting all grown-up and glamorous but, in reality, wobbling in her heels like a tightrope walker.

"Oh, darling, did I tell you about a certain gentleman who winked at me last Friday night at the cinema?"

"Yes, you did." Rumor rolled her eyes. "Three times."

"I'm dreadfully sorry if I bore you, sister. It's just so exciting. I tell you, with this job, I'm going to marry a star."

"Only a star?" Rumor asked. "Would you settle for a director?"

"I suppose I would. If I had to. Do you think directors get invited to all the glamorous parties? Or is it only the cinema stars?"

Hundreds and hundreds of lights outlined the front of the cinema, spelling out "Cabrillo," illuminating the archway, and forming starbursts that looked like Fourth of July fireworks. Two ushers in red coats and black trousers attached red velvet ropes to golden posts, creating a route directly to the ticket booth. Mary wobbled under the marquee that listed in bold black letters: "Claudette Colbert," "Richard Arlen," "Ronald Coleman," and "Elissa Landi." As Mary passed by the ushers, they tipped their hats, but she ignored them. On either side of the entrance, under the words "Now Playing," two movie posters in glass cases advertised: *Three-Cornered Moon* and *The Masquerader*. An old man sat inside the ticket booth, like a figure in a snow globe. It looked claustrophobic with nothing but three walls and a window. What did he do between customers? Play solitaire? One of the ushers opened the heavy wooden door for Mary, and she disappeared through it as if making her grand entrance into the lobby.

At night, the city seemed muffled, a dull symphony of rumbling cars, the distant crooning of someone's radio, and the muted laughs of tipsy sailors over on Broadway. Rumor hadn't wandered the streets at night since Papa had moved out. He used to take them to the top of Cortez Hill, where they would lie back on the high school lawn and stargaze. Rumor could easily pick out Orion's belt and the Big and Little Dipper, but Papa showed them where to find both of Orion's hunting dogs, Canis Major and Canis Minor. And also, Hercules, Centaurus, Scorpius, and Virgo.

Once she was at the top of Cortez Hill, Rumor tried to pick out the porch light of her bungalow but couldn't figure out which tiny speck it could be—a tiny pinprick just like all the other points of light in the city. Looking down on the houses made her feel small, as if her troubles were nothing. The pool of downtown lights abruptly ended at the harbor, usually a dark abyss but now so crowded with ships that the glittering deck lights created their own constellations across the bay.

Rumor had never been to the school at night alone. It gave her the creeps. Everyone called it The Gray Castle because of its stone walls and turrets. At night, the ivy creeping up the walls, like the plague, looked black. Rumor cut through the triangle of lawn in front of the main school building without seeing any sign of Sal. Maybe she'd missed him, or maybe he was full of hot air and never had meant to come in the first place.

A faint whistle echoed from the shadow of the main entrance. Rumor's heart rose to her throat, nearly choking her, until she recognized the tune—"Who's Afraid of the Big Bad Wolf"—again. Damn him to hell and back.

"You're late," Sal said. "I thought you chickened out." He leaned against the front door of the school, with one hand in his pocket as if he owned the place. "You go here?"

"Yes."

"Pretty ritzy."

"Do you go to school in San Francisco?"

"I haven't been in a classroom since I was ten years old."

"Isn't that illegal?"

"We don't get many truancy officers at the colony." Sal smirked. "And the ones we do get don't give a hoot whether I attend school regularly or not."

"You don't get any education?"

"I didn't say that. Just not in a schoolroom."

"Are you a nudist?"

Sal tipped his head back and laughed. "Can't sneak anything past you."

Rumor couldn't imagine seeing her own mother naked. Or Ruth. Or heaven forbid, Mrs. Keegan. What kind of a mother would raise her son in a nudist colony?

"Should we get going?" Rumor asked.

"Well, since you were late, we have to wait. Addie has the nightly pageant tonight. We'll head over soon."

"Nightly pageant?"

"The ancient sun-worship ceremony."

"Are they naked?" Rumor asked.

"Of course. Who'd want to watch it if they weren't?"

Rumor wondered how many naked women Sal had seen in his lifetime. And men. "What about your father? Is he a nudist also?"

"I have no father." Resentment flickered in his eyes for a second, but then it vanished. He pushed himself up from the step. "Okay, toots, let's go."

They headed up Twelfth Street, then into a canyon on the opposite end of the camp, picking their way down a path toward a dim glow of orange firelight and lanterns.

"What's it like working in a ticket booth?" Rumor asked.

"Isn't it obvious? I take money and give out tickets. That's it."

"That's not what I mean. How do you pass the time between customers? It seems as if it would get rather monotonous."

"Monotonous? That's a big word. They teach you words like that at your fancy school? If you mean ho-hum, yes, it gets rather ho-hum."

The sounds of laughter, a flute, a banjo, and a baby's cry drifted toward them. On the outskirts of the camp, a deep, scratchy voice rumbled out from the base of an oak. "Who's there?"

It reminded Rumor of the troll in *Three Billy Goats Gruff*.

"Hey, Vern. It's Sal."

When Rumor was in the second grade, her class performed the play. She was the middle billy goat gruff.

"Got yourself a little snuggle pup there, do ya?"

"Watch your mouth, Vern."

"Aw, when did you get all high-and-mighty? She's one hot number. What do you say, girlie? You wanna earn a buck?"

"She's not that kind of girl," Sal said.

Vern raised himself to his feet, his dark form towering over Sal by at least twelve inches. He really was a troll and reeked of sour cheese and alcohol. With one arm across his protruding belly, he bowed. "Pardon me, your highness. Didn't mean no disrespect." His bald head shone like oil in the moonlight as he peeked up at Rumor, revealing several dark gaps where teeth should have been.

"Lay off it," Sal said to Vern, taking hold of Rumor's wrist and pulling her behind him.

"Just havin' some fun," Vern said. "Don't go off all half-cocked now. I'm just lonely out here with nothing but the rabbits and weeds."

Once out of earshot, Rumor asked, "Why's he out here?"

"Not sure. He has an old lady. Guess she kicked him out."

They continued on a bit farther until the outlines of tents and the orange glow of campfires materialized. A row of six dingy tents lit with red lanterns crouched against the outer rim of the camp. As they crept closer, Rumor noticed some ladies sprawled outside, dressed in worn-out evening gowns. The dark shapes of three boys hid behind a group of trees, spying on the women. A man ducked out through a canvas flap, pulled his cap onto his head, and tucked the back of his shirt into his pants. A woman appeared behind him, running her fingers through her tousled hair. Without a backward glance, the man stepped across the lane and disappeared.

"Is that . . . ? Are those . . . ?" Rumor didn't quite know how to put it.

"Prostitutes?" Sal asked.

"Yeah."

"You really are as sharp as a tack." Sal laughed.

Rumor clenched her fists and bit her tongue as she followed Sal into the maze of tents. Six men played cards at a slapdash table made from crates and fence slats. A lantern sat off center, casting light on the cards and a small pile of pennies. A baby wailed, followed by a shushing, sweet hum. The occasional orange dot of a cigarette glowed bright, illuminating a scruffy beard and nose.

They finally came to the square of familiar white tents with the glowing lanterns on their platforms. They were vacant, with all the flaps tied shut. Sal thumped up onto Aunt Addie's porch. He lowered himself on the edge of the wooden slats and patted the spot next to him. "Take a load off."

Rumor joined him but sat on the opposite side of the space he had indicated. "How long do you think she'll be?"

He pulled a silver chain, and a pocket watch emerged from his trousers. "About fifteen to twenty minutes."

"How long have you known my aunt?"

"For as long as I can remember," Sal said. "I think she came to the colony when I was two or three years old."

"You've always been a nudist?"

"Yep. Been running around bare-butt naked ever since they took a diaper off me."

"Oh."

"It's not what most people think. After a while, a breast is no different than an elbow or an earlobe. Everyone is unique, but the same. It's how God made us."

"How God made us?" Rumor said, shifting her weight on the wooden slats, wondering what any of the pastors would say about that. She imagined words like *blasphemous* and *sacrilegious* and *heathen*. "I don't think God intended for us all to be running around naked."

"And why not? Everyone comes into the world naked as a jaybird. Clothing is man-made, not God made, and people judge others by the quality of the clothes they wear."

Shabby clothing hung from the tent lines and ropes strung all around the workers' camp. The tired banners of tired people. And she saw what Sal meant. Looking at the clothes, she could almost imagine the people who would step into them.

"Clothing suffocates the body," Sal said. "Our cells need sunlight to renew."

Rumor tried to imagine a naked society but couldn't get past the image of bare butts sitting on the slick wood of a trolley seat or at a school desk. It was unsanitary and impractical, no matter what Sal said. If everyone went around naked, she'd carry around her own personal handkerchief to sit upon.

"You alright?" Sal asked.

"Huh?"

"You're mighty thoughtful there."

"But all advanced societies wear clothes."

"And all advanced societies are commercial. Money is power. And who says advanced societies are happier?"

"The naked aboriginals in the *National Geographic* don't look happy."

With that, Sal let out such a belly laugh that a pack of dirty little children, dressed in ragged clothing and hand-me-down shoes, came running over to them, begging for Sal to do some tricks.

Aunt Addie stepped into the light of the lantern in the same white chiffon gown she'd worn the first time Rumor had seen her on their porch, looking more like an apparition rather than a full flesh-and-blood person.

"You came back," Aunt Addie said, glancing around.

"Mary's not here." Rumor wondered if that disappointed her aunt.

"Oh no." Aunt Addie smiled. Her two front teeth crossed slightly, just like Mary's. "I was just wondering if you brought your mother with you." Addie stepped up onto the platform, and Rumor got to her feet and followed her aunt into the tent.

"I'll wait around in the vicinity this time. How's that for a big word, hotshot?" Sal said.

How could he be so aggravating?

Aunt Addie settled cross-legged on one of the cots with her dress bunched up, exposing her calves, smooth and athletic. She patted a spot next to her for Rumor. The birdcage in the corner had a brown blanket draped over it, but she could hear the parrot rustling around inside, a dry and crackling noise, like snapping twigs.

"I'm sorry I scared you last time. I had no intention . . ." Aunt Addie's curly hair bobbed as she spoke.

"I understand."

"Does Mary?"

"She had to work tonight. That's all."

"What about your mother? Does she know you're here?"

Rumor didn't know how to answer that. If she told the truth, Aunt Addie might ask her to leave. If she lied, Aunt Addie might go to visit her mother thinking all was well, and then all hell would break loose. "No, she doesn't know."

"I want to see you more than anything, but I'm afraid your mother will never forgive me for seeing you behind her back."

"She doesn't have to know."

"I want to have a chance to talk with her, and I'm afraid this will ruin that."

"Maybe we can work together to get her to come around. She won't know I'm here. Scout's honor."

"You're a Girl Scout?" Aunt Addie asked.

"No." Rumor smiled. "But you can trust my word as much."

"You remind me of—" But then she stopped. "You have your grandmother's hair."

Her grandmother? Until that instant, it never struck Rumor as odd that she had never seen a single photograph of her grandparents. Photographs were rare in the olden days, but you'd think her mom would at least have one. Why hadn't Mother told her that she had her grandmother's hair? It would have been nice to know. Mother used to slap Rumor's hand every time she tried to touch the antique perfume bottle or mirrored tray on her mother's vanity. As Rumor got older, her mother explained that they were fragile antiques that had belonged to her grandmother, but that was all she'd ever said about her. Rumor tucked her hair behind her ears and twisted a finger through it, leaving a long ringlet spiraling down her shoulder. "The color of my hair or the wildness?"

"Both," Aunt Addie said. "You didn't know that?"

"Mother doesn't like to talk about the past."

Aunt Addie laughed. "I think that may run in the family."

"I know she died when Mother was young, but I don't know how."

Aunt Addie looked pained, then she reached over and patted Rumor's knee. "Your grandmother died in childbirth. It was a boy, but he died too."

"Oh, I'm sorry."

"That's okay. It was a long time ago."

"Your grandfather took her death awfully hard. One night he went for a walk in the woods and a terrible snowstorm snuck up on him. They didn't find him until the spring when the snow thawed."

"And you and my mother?"

"Our Uncle Henry and Aunt May took your mother in. She hasn't told you this?"

Rumor shook her head.

"I got sent to an orphan asylum."

"An orphanage?"

"More or less."

"Why?" Rumor couldn't imagine losing her parents and then her sister. Why would anyone do that to two girls?

"Aunt May and Uncle Henry couldn't afford to take both of us, and your mother was old enough to help around the farm. I would've only been a burden."

"How old were you?"

"Eight."

"And my mother?"

"Thirteen." Aunt Addie patted Rumor's knee again. "Don't you fret for us. It was a long time ago."

Rumor didn't know how to bring up the question about Papa Jack. She looked over at the other bed, Sal's mother's cot. It had a feather bed with a quilt tossed crookedly over it. Rumor's neighbor, Mrs. Reed, made quilts out of old clothing. She wondered what they used to make quilts at a nudist colony. Maybe people had to surrender their clothing when they joined up, and the quilts were made from that.

"It's my turn now," Aunt Addie said.

"Turn?"

"For a question. We can trade questions."

"Fair enough."

Aunt Addie seemed to be turning something over in her mind. Was she afraid to ask it?

Rumor smiled at her. "I can handle more than you think."

"Who is your father?"

"What do you mean?" The hairs on Rumor's neck pricked up.

"What's his name?"

"Jack. Jack Donnelly. But you said you knew him. That you were there when Mary was born."

A funny expression washed across Aunt Addie's face.

"I asked Papa," Rumor said. "He told me that he never met you."

Aunt Addie's hands trembled before she tucked them under her legs. Rumor waited for her response. As the moments passed, Rumor began to wonder if her aunt did have a few bats in her belfry or if she was hiding something. The sound of footsteps outside the tent interrupted the silence. Rumor cursed Sal. He had the worst timing. But it wasn't him.

A lady with bobbed dark and wavy hair walked in. She had thick eyebrows, manly and scowling.

"Oh, Daisy, isn't she lovely?" Aunt Addie sprung up and put her hand on Rumor's shoulder. "This is my niece, Rumor."

Daisy gave Rumor the once-over and harrumphed.

"Daisy is Sal's mother," Aunt Addie said.

"She knows Sal?"

Aunt Addie hesitated and didn't answer.

"Yes, I know him," Rumor said.

"She's kidding, Daisy. She hardly knows him at all. He only took a message from her."

Daisy turned away and rummaged through a drawer in the trunk between the two cots. She apparently didn't find what she was looking for because she turned back empty-handed. "Why is Hobbs still covered up?" She took hold of the brown blanket and yanked it off, sending the parrot into a dry, brittle flutter.

"I just got in and—"

"How'd you like to be under a blanket all day?" Daisy dropped the covering to the floor and left without another word, stomping heavy-footed across the porch and down the stairs.

"It's getting late," Aunt Addie said. "You should be heading home."

"But . . ."

Rumor followed Aunt Addie onto the porch. Down at the end of the lane, she noticed a moonlit shadow that resembled Sal. He was bent down talking to a group of camp children. Aunt Addie hugged her, and she felt fragile to Rumor, like a hummingbird, and she smelled of honey and lilac. "You probably shouldn't come again until I talk with your mother," she said.

"But—"

"I'll do it soon."

Rumor nodded, but didn't promise. Aunt Addie remained on the porch as Rumor stepped down, heading toward the silhouette that looked like Sal. Rumor glanced back one more time, and Aunt Addie waved to her just before stepping back into the yellow glow of her tent. As Rumor got closer, she saw Sal was bent down on one knee, with a little girl sitting on it and two boys clambering up his back.

A strong hand grabbed Rumor's arm. Her first thought was Vern. Someone's fingers dug into her bones, sending a shooting pain all the way up her neck, and pulled her into the gap between two tents. But it was a woman, her face so close that Rumor couldn't focus. Her teeth looked like little squares of Chiclets clenched together. Rumor gasped and tried to scream, but the woman covered her mouth. Rumor kicked and scratched, pulling away long enough to recognize Daisy.

"You stay away from my Salvation." Her breath smelled of black licorice. "Do you hear me?"

Rumor tried to wrench her arm free, but Daisy tightened her grip.

"You stay away from him, you dirty hussy."

Rumor's heartbeat pounded in her ears and she couldn't breathe or scream or answer. She had never felt so helpless.

"Answer me, you dumb bitch."

Rumor nodded and managed to mutter, "Okay," before Daisy pushed her away, shoving her back into the dusty lane, where she landed on her butt. Rumor grabbed two handfuls of dirt and chucked them at the empty spot between the tents where Daisy had ambushed her. The barrage of dirt and pebbles sprayed against them on either side, feebly pattering against the canvas.

Rumor brushed herself off and walked over to Sal. He looked up at her, and his eyebrows pinched together. "You okay?" As he stood, a little boy lifted off the ground, clinging to Sal's neck with his filthy, scrawny arms.

"Of course I am."

"You're awfully red."

Rumor didn't answer him.

"Oh, I understand." Sal unclasped the boy and lowered him to the ground. "You're just swooning over me."

The girl giggled.

"Take me home," Rumor said.

"See what I mean? She's all over me, wanting to take me home with her." He winked at the group of children.

"Get over yourself." Rumor crossed her arms. "You gonna take me home, or should I head out on my own?"

"I'll take you. You don't need to get all in a lather."

"No, don't go." The little girl with long blond wisps of hair hanging in her face hugged Sal's leg.

"I'll be back," he said.

"But we have to go to bed soon."

"Then I'll see you tomorrow." He pried her from his leg and set her down next to the others.

"Are we leaving or not?" Rumor asked.

The little girl stuck her tongue out at Rumor before they all ran off in different directions.

Rumor trudged behind Sal, not saying a word. They passed the men playing poker, now slurring their words and slapping their cards down hard on the planks. Rumor kicked at the sagebrush as they passed by the prostitutes' tents.

Sal stopped in the middle of the scrub. "What's eating you?"

"Nothing."

"Quite the moody thing, aren't you?"

"Could you just shut up and take me home?"

"Ooooh, and testy too."

"What's your name?" Rumor asked. "Your real name."

"You know my name."

"Is Sal short for something?"

"Yeah, it's short for Salvation. What's it to you?"

"It's nothing to me. Absolutely nothing. "

"Then what are you all pissy about?"

"Your mother threatened me. She told me to stay away from her Salvation."

"Shit." He kicked at the ground, blasting dirt against Rumor's legs and down into her socks.

"Hey!"

"Sorry. Sorry about my mother." He turned and continued on. "And the dirt."

Rumor had to scamper to keep up with him. After they emerged from the canyon and made it to the high school, Rumor said, "I can make it from here. You can go back now."

"It's late. I'm walking you all the way," he said without slowing down.

When they approached the bungalow, Rumor noticed her bedroom light on and hoped it was only Mary and not Mother waiting for her.

Sal left her on the front porch with nothing but a final "Sorry."

"Where have you been?" Mary asked as she entered their bedroom. Mary must have just gotten home. She unbuttoned her skirt and slid it down her hips into a ring of fabric around her feet. She looked so grown-up in her corset and garters with silk stockings. Rumor felt like a child as she unbuckled her shoes and pulled off her socks filled with dirt and foxtails.

"Is Mother home?" Rumor asked.

"No. Where have you been?"

"I went to see Aunt Addie."

"You know Mother doesn't want you to, and Aunt Addie isn't quite right in the head."

"I don't care what Mother wants. All she does is chase people away. I swear, we would be better off living with Papa Jack. At least we'd be with someone who loves us."

"Don't be so obstinate," Mary said, pulling her nightgown over her corset. "She's our mother. Of course she loves us. She just works dreadfully hard to keep a roof over our heads and food on our plates. You need to show some respect." Mary wiggled out of her corset. It dropped out the bottom of her nightgown.

"Show respect for what? For going out drinking and dancing and bossing us around?"

Rumor changed into her nightgown and slid into bed, but she couldn't sleep. Her heart pounded in her chest, blocking out all other noise, and she couldn't stop picturing Daisy's teeth and feeling her fingers digging into her arm.

CHAPTER ELEVEN
ADDIE

The fair stretched and yawned itself awake with the rolling of carts and the clinking and knocking of concessionaires setting up for the day. The smell of popcorn and scones drifted down into the garden, where Addie and the other nudists huddled by the campfire, warming their flesh and waiting for the sun to move over the garden. Addie held her hands out to the dancing flames as she squatted, compact, with her knees to her chest. She was glad for this time before the crowds arrived. Breakfast would come after the guests and after the morning exercise. Stimulate the blood, then feed the body. Lucille and Dottie looked as if they'd been through the wringer, with their swollen eyes and tousled hair. A late night and an early morning are not the best recipe for a chipper attitude.

The officers slipped in the gate and made their way down the ramps in the same tweed suits and fedoras, carting their familiar lunch boxes and newspapers. Even when they were reading the dailies, Addie felt as if their eyes were still on her. Addie hated being under their microscope, pressed down between two glass slides and expected to act normal.

The fair's board of directors claimed they'd stationed the officers to protect them, to make sure the crowd didn't get out of control, but they all knew it was also to make sure they stayed in line. The nudists were expected to behave with decorum; Heinrich had made that clear to the colony from day one.

"Did you girls hear the news?" Ida called out, hurrying toward Addie and the group of nudists by the campfire. As she ran, an open newspaper pressed to her naked body like rubbish against a fence picket.

"Where have you been?" Frieda asked. "Heinrich has been asking for you all morning."

"Heinrich's not my daddy." Ida held the newspaper tight against her breasts. Addie wondered if she'd have black newsprint tattooed across them when she removed it.

"What's the news?" Yvette asked, standing in the creek and ladling handfuls of water over her shoulders. It dribbled down her breasts, forming little droplets that dripped off the ends of her cold nipples. She only did it to show off while the others sought nothing but warmth. Daisy had remarked that she could do it because even an ice cube was several degrees warmer than Yvette's soul.

"You'll never guess," Ida said, squealing like a child. "It's about Gold Gulch Gertie."

"You mean the girl who rides around like Lady Godiva?"

"The very one."

"She got bucked off her mule?" Dottie guessed.

"Nope." Ida wiggled behind the newspaper, barely able to contain herself. Maybe she could create a new sensation, dancing nude behind a newspaper, sort of like Sally Rand but without the fans.

"Her ass died?" Lilly said with a roll of her eyes.

"Lilly! How can you say that?" Ida said. "Besides, it's a mule, not an ass. An ass is a wild donkey."

"Of course you'd know that. You're nothing but a backwater Texas bumpkin," Lilly said. Usually, Ida would have jumped all over her for that comment, but she clearly didn't want to ruin her guessing game.

"Good God," Daisy said. "Tell us already."

"She was arrested," Ida said. "Thrown in the hoosegow."

"*Ach je!*" Frieda said. "What did she do?"

"Indecent exposure."

Everyone fell silent and Ida turned the headline toward them. In bold black letters: "Lady Godiva Disrobes, Police Enter, Burro Balks, Show Ends."

"Bluestockings!" Frieda said. "I'll wager they are the cause of it."

"But what about us?" Dottie asked. "We're indecent."

"Next thing you know, they'll try to pin something on us and send us to jail too."

"Heinrich needs to do something," Lucille said.

"*Ja,*" Frieda said, looking deep in thought.

One sharp whistle, quite different from the wolf whistles of the customers, trilled from across the garden. Heinrich's call to attention. Everyone froze like children in a game of Statue, watching to see what or who Heinrich wanted. He stood in his he-man pose on the exercise grounds, looming over the heavy barbell and pointing at Ida. She did have black smears of ink across her breasts, but not the perfect mirror image of the headlines, like Addie had imagined.

"I'll be back in two shakes," Ida said, turning and sauntering toward Heinrich.

Frieda nodded, smiling to herself. "Have any of you heard of a woman named Aimee Semple McPherson?"

"Is she a nudist?" Lucille asked.

"*Nein,* not a nudist." Frieda smiled. "She's a female—what do you call it? An evangelist? And she's coming here to the Exposition."

"A female preacher? Do they allow such a thing?" Dottie asked.

"*Ja*. And it is said that she is drawing bigger crowds than P.T. Barnum and his circus ever got. Many believe that she is a messenger of God. She is one of those, what is the American term? A holy roller?"

"I've heard of her," Lilly said. "She does miracles—makes the blind see and the cripples walk. That sort of sham."

"You can fool some of the people some of the time, but you can't fool five thousand people three times a day," Joe said, putting his two cents' worth in. "They call her Sister Aimee. She's got her own temple in Los Angeles that seats five thousand, and she fills it three times a day. She's got to have something. And boy oh boy, wouldn't I like to find out what it is."

"Maybe you can run off with her," Lilly said. "I hear she's in need of another husband."

Frieda didn't seem to be following the conversation. "I think it could work," Frieda said.

"What?"

"I will invite this Sister Aimee to tea. Here in the garden."

"Aren't the preachers the ones trying to shut us down?" Dottie asked.

"*Ja.*" Frieda nodded, smiling. "That is the beauty of it."

"Why would she have tea with you?"

"The publicity," Frieda said. "She is a woman with a cause, just like me."

"I see where you're going with this," Joe said. "If we can get some respect from Sister Aimee, maybe the other churches will ease up on us."

"What about her past? The scandals?" Lilly asked.

"That is the magnificence of it. Because of her past, she won't be so quick to pass her judgment," Frieda said.

Addie couldn't imagine what sort of a past a preacher, especially a woman preacher, could have. "What did she do?"

Addie had never known Lilly to be so animated. She usually kept to herself, downcast and only speaking in monotone when she had to.

This Sister Aimee must've made an impression. "She's been widowed once, divorced twice, and she went up on felony charges for staging her own kidnapping so she could run off with a married lover," Lilly said.

The way Addie figured it, Sister Aimee had broken at least four of the Ten Commandments, maybe even five. If Sister Aimee could break God's commandments and still be a preacher and a messenger of God, what did that mean for Addie? "Did she go to jail?"

"Nein," Frieda said.

Lilly started back up, her dark eyes sparkling, "And that's the best part of the whole sham. The evidence mysteriously disappeared and eyewitnesses refused to testify. The charges were dropped."

"How do you know all of this?" Addie asked.

"It was in all the papers."

God's forgiveness? The people's forgiveness? No prison time?

Frieda leaned in close, whispering like a child with a secret, "Aimee Semple McPherson is my hero. I have been to the Angelus Temple. It was unbelievable, like a Hollywood show, with all the lights and choirs and glamour. Sister Aimee is a charismatic and sexy woman."

Addie couldn't imagine a sexy preacher. All the ones she'd ever seen were old and stern.

"Do you think she'll come?" Addie wanted to talk to this Sister Aimee. Maybe she could help her find the peace she needed.

"Ja, I don't see why not," Frieda said. "I am not asking her to take her clothes off. I am simply asking her to tea."

Daisy paced the rough boards of their tent, walking the same line back and forth, just like Hobbs on his perch. She stewed, mumbling about the betrayal of her fireproof man and plotting her revenge against him. Maybe she'd lie in wait outside the Odditorium for her chance to pee in his shoes or to hide the oily carcasses of anchovies in his bedding. One time at the colony, Addie had witnessed Daisy spitting in the orange juice of a male guest the morning his wife joined him. He'd been sowing his wild oats with Daisy for three days before his wife had arrived, and even though he'd disclosed his marital status from the beginning, Daisy didn't take well to witnessing it in the flesh.

Daisy shook out the brown blanket and draped it over Hobbs's cage, tucking him in for the night.

"Why didn't you ever get married?" Daisy asked as she turned the knob on the kerosene lantern until it went out, making everything disappear into the darkness. "You're the sort of woman a man would lose his mind over."

There was a biting tone in Daisy's voice that put Addie on alert. Addie wasn't about to share any more information about her past. She could imagine Daisy's outrage if she told her there was a man who had lost his mind, but that he'd been her sister's husband. And that she had given birth to his son, who would have been two years younger than Sal—if he had lived. That was something she should've divulged long ago, and Daisy wasn't in the right frame of mind to forgive her. And she probably never would be.

"I'm barren," Addie said. "A man wants children to carry on his name."

"You can still get married. Then when children don't come, act surprised."

Aunt May had given her that exact same advice after Daniel's birth, when the doctor told her that she'd never be able to have another child. Probably because Aunt May wanted her to get married so she would be rid of her.

"How are things going with your sister?"

"They're fine."

"You haven't seen her yet, have you?"

Addie didn't answer.

"I figured. Sure hope those girls haven't been sneaking behind their mother's back. That could ruin everything for you." When Addie didn't answer, Daisy said, "She's kind of a ratty thing, isn't she?"

"Who?" But before Daisy could answer, Addie knew she meant Rumor. "She's not after Sal."

"She better not be. No cut-rate floozy's gonna take him away from me."

Rumor was a beautiful and wholesome girl. And Daisy knew it. If not, she wouldn't be so worried.

Addie awoke in the middle of the night, clutching her hands to her chest. She heard feet shuffling in the dirt outside their tent, the strike of a match, then the sound of footsteps moving around. Daisy breathed rhythmic and throaty, oblivious of the noise outside. With wide eyes staring into the dark, Addie tried to make out shapes in the tent. The silhouetted dome of Hobbs's cage materialized against the light canvas on one side of the door. She couldn't remember the dream she'd had just before waking, but it was disquieting. Hobbs must've woken too. He shuffled around in his blanketed cage and began knocking his beak against the bars, like an inmate tapping a signal with a tin cup. That was it. In her dream, she was crammed in a cell with all the other ladies of the colony—Frieda, Daisy, Giselle, Clara, Ida, Dottie, Lucille, Yvette, Lilly, and Eva. They all waited at the open door of the cell while the jailer released them one at a time. Addie stood at the end of the line and couldn't see him. As each woman passed, he let them by. But when Addie approached the door, a huge arm swung across her chest, knocking her to the ground. She looked up, right into the eyes of Ty. With a sinister laugh, he said, "And where do you think you're going?" just before he slammed the cell door, leaving her inside. Alone.

After an interminable minute of Daisy's breathing and Hobbs's tapping, it hit her. If Gertie went to jail, they all could go to jail. If she was arrested, she'd have to provide her name. Was she listed in the San Diego Police Department's files? She had no idea what Wavey had gone through that last afternoon. She'd tried writing Wavey, but all her letters were returned unopened. All she ever received from her sister was one envelope with a death notice cut from the newspaper that read, "Briggs, Tyrone Fulton, d. December 19, 1918, 32, Influenza. Benbough Funeral Parlors." No note, no details, no explanation, no forgiveness. Addie had left Wavey holding the bag and had no idea how she had worked things out.

341 Eucalyptus Street
San Diego, California
October 23, 1918

The smell of Ty's cigar smoke slithered under the door and into Addie's bedroom. His lurking felt even more dangerous to her than the Spanish flu that crept through the city. A mockingbird trilled outside the window. It seemed impossible that something so tiny and vulnerable as a bird could continue to sing with so much heartache and fear all around it. The board of health had closed the schools, theaters, churches, libraries, and beaches. The streets were deserted except for a few people coming and going in gauze masks. Two weeks earlier, Ty had come home with a sack filled with flu preventatives and remedies, including masks, Aunty Flu medicine, and camphor balls they wore in pouches around their necks, which Mary kept trying to pull off, choking herself.

With the covers pulled up to her neck, Addie watched the gap of light along the bottom of the door. Occasionally, the floorboards creaked and two dark shafts interrupted the beam of light, pausing before moving on. The stink of camphor and cigar smoke choked her. Mary shifted in her crib on the other side of the room, sighed, then gave a tiny giggle in her sleep. The grandfather clock chimed. One, two, three, four, five, six, seven, eight, nine, ten, eleven times. The light on the other side went out and the gap disappeared. Addie listened for his footsteps and the sound of him opening and closing his own bedroom door, but all she could hear was a dog barking down the street and the rattle and clopping of horse hooves moving past the house.

Addie dozed off but awoke when the clock chimed again. One, two, three, four, five, six, seven, eight, nine, ten, eleven, twelve. Mary cooed and the house lay silent. Ty must've gone to bed. Outside, the mockingbird called out for a mate, trilling incessantly. One night a few weeks ago, after hours of the bird chirping without end, she heard Ty curse and stomp out the back door. She'd gone to the window and saw him stark naked, with his pistol pointing up into the branches of the sycamore tree. The moon illuminated his thick back, butt, and thighs. The bearlike heft of him startled Addie. She'd never seen a man fully naked. Only Wallace and his boy parts flopping out of his unbuttoned trousers. Ty fired the gun. One loud crack echoed through the houses and set all the neighborhood dogs off. When he turned, his man part stuck straight out, rigid and shiny in the moonlight. Addie ducked below the window ledge and hunkered in the darkness of her bedroom, feeling dirty and ashamed that she'd seen him. After a while, the dogs quieted and the night fell silent. The next morning Addie looked for the carcass of the bird, but never found it.

But now she couldn't get rid of the feeling that Ty waited on the other side of her door. She listened, heard nothing, and dozed back off and dreamt of Ty digging his holes in the backyard, tipping his flask in the moonlight, a lantern illuminating the bottom half of his face. The point of his spade striking the ground over and over. She didn't know if she was dreaming or awake when she heard the groan of her bedroom door. Where the door had been solid and shut, it now seemed an open, dark hole with a black form in it. When the floorboard creaked and the latch clicked shut, she knew it wasn't a dream. She could smell his sweat and aftershave. She lay still, pretending to be asleep. Maybe he'd go away. She waited. The floorboards creaked again.

She heard the strike of a match, and Ty's face flared into view. He held the flame to a candle on her bedside table and shook out the match. Addie remained motionless, only her eyes following Ty. He held the candle over Mary's crib, peering down at his sleeping baby. Addie prayed that was all he'd come for, but she knew it wasn't. Addie closed her eyes for only a second, but when she opened them, Ty loomed over her in his bathrobe. He set the candle on her nightstand and pulled the tie that held his robe shut. It fell open and Addie got one brief glimpse of his privates and black hair before his hand clamped down on her mouth and her nose, crushing her lips against her teeth. She tasted blood.

"Don't you make a sound," he whispered, smelling of Scotch and rancid cigar.

Addie tried to bite down on his calloused hand, but he pushed harder and she couldn't close her jaw. His hand tasted bitter. She couldn't breathe. Grabbing his wrist, she tried to pull it off but couldn't budge it.

"If you don't lie still, I'll suffocate you." His breath dampened her neck. "Do you understand?"

Addie tried to nod, but it felt as if her jaw would crack.

He lowered his hand, freeing her nose. She sucked in, hungry for the putrid air, feeling her nostrils flare open and shut. With one hand still over her mouth, he yanked the covers from Addie's body and pulled her nightgown up to her waist. She kicked and fought beneath him.

"Hold still or I'll kill you."

She went limp. Addie remembered his man part in the moonlight, and her whole body began to shake. "No, please," she tried to say, but his hand smothered her words, leaving them in her throat. He pushed her nightgown up over her breasts and stood over her, looking. The mattress sank under his weight as he straddled her, all black hair and sweat, half man, half bear. *Please, God, let Mary wake up. Let her howl and bring Wavey into the room.*

Faint and unable to get enough air through her nose, she tried to suck some in from between his fingers. Ty pushed a knee down between her clamped legs. *No, no, no,* Addie screamed in her head, but he jammed his knee down, forcing her thighs open. It felt as if he'd ripped Addie in two, thrusting and grunting. His sweat stung her eyes, and she couldn't help but cry against his hand.

He finally collapsed on top of her, his heavy weight burying her into the mattress.

"You say a word," he said, panting, "and I'll send you right back to the orphan asylum. You'll never see your sister or Mary again." He released the pressure on her mouth, waited, then slid his sweaty body off of her.

Even after he left, Addie still felt his weight on her. She slid off the bed and onto the cold floor. Mary stirred, whining in her sleep. Addie crawled across the floor and pulled herself up by the bars of Mary's crib. It felt as if she'd been split open like the dressed deer Mr. Hayes had hung from the walnut tree to bleed out. A warm flow dribbled down her thighs. Mary twitched and whimpered as if she were having a bad dream. Addie placed her hand on Mary's back until she quieted. The candle still burned, and in the dim light, Addie saw a gash of blood across her bedsheet. She pulled it off and dragged it behind her toward the bathroom.

Addie pushed the rubber plug into the bathtub drain and opened the hot-water spigot. Cold water gushed out. Someone tapped on the door, but she didn't answer. Wavey's voice came through the crack. "Addie, are you okay?"

Addie didn't respond.

"Addie," Wavey said, "are you feeling sick?"

"I'm fine. It's just my time." Addie tried to keep the tears from her voice. "I had an accident." She held her hand under the rushing water until it turned hot.

"You need any help?"

"No."

Addie could feel Wavey lingering at the door, listening. Once the tub filled, Addie dropped the sheet into it. It billowed out like a giant pillow. She stepped in and it collapsed around her body. Her nightgown inflated, then sank, clinging to her body as it absorbed the hot water burning her skin and stinging her privates. She felt as if she'd faint when she scrubbed herself with the bar of Lifebuoy, filling her insides with soap. She scrubbed until the pain peaked and couldn't get any worse. She found the bloodstain on the sheet beneath her and pulled it above the surface, rolling the bar of soap over and over, scouring until only a dark shadow of blood remained. Addie stayed in the tub until the water cooled and goose pimples covered her body. She peeled off her wet nightgown and dropped it into the water, then pulled the rubber plug.

Addie wrapped a towel around herself and pressed her ear to the bathroom door. No breathing, creaking floorboards, or cigar smoke. She creaked open the door and stepped into the hall. The bedroom still flickered with dying candlelight and Mary still slept. Addie changed into a clean and dry nightgown, blew out the flame, and fell asleep on top of her bare mattress.

Addie awoke the next morning to the chugging hum and pop of the washing machine in the backyard and a raw pain between her legs. Mary stood at the bars of her crib in a wet nightgown and soggy diaper. She noticed a faint stain on the mattress, where her blood had seeped through the bedsheet. After changing Mary and draping the pouches of camphor around their necks, she stood with an ear to the door and the baby balanced on one hip, listening for Ty's voice or his heavy footsteps. When she heard neither, she stepped out. Ty had left for work.

Addie had no appetite. She poked the tines of her fork into her egg and watched the yolk run out the holes. Wavey spooned porridge into Mary's mouth; between bites, the baby made pulp of a wedge of toast.

The chickens clucked out in the coop, sounding agitated and nervous. Addie wondered if one of Miss Mabel's cats was taking pleasure in taunting them again.

At the orphan asylum, Addie had learned to keep it to herself when a farmer or one of his sons touched her. The farmers were upstanding members of the community, and she was nothing but an orphan in an asylum and, like all reprobates, prone to telling tales just to get out of work. Was this any different? And even if Wavey did believe her, how could she protect her? They had no money and no place to go. But by not telling, was she a traitor to her sister? Addie remembered her lessons on the train ride from Kansas and how a lady must govern her tongue—for words are like sparks on dry timber, and carelessly spoken words can burn down the whole neighborhood.

"I think it's Bessie who's not laying," Wavey said.

"Don't tell Ty," Addie said, regretting how quick and urgent her words came out when she noticed the quizzical look on Wavey's face.

"You're awfully upset about a chicken."

"He'll kill her if she's not laying."

Wavey reached over and put her hand on her sister's arm. "I washed your bedsheet and nightgown. You left them in the bathtub. They're in the wash basket, wrung out and waiting to be hung on the line."

Addie nodded. She imagined Ty dragging her to the train station with nothing but her valise and a ticket straight back to the orphan asylum, or Wavey whisking her away to keep her safe from Ty. Either way, she'd be shipped off, forever separated from Wavey and Mary. She kissed Wavey on the cheek and stepped outside to hang her sheets.

CHAPTER TWELVE

RUMOR

Mother had left a path of clothing from the front door to her bedroom, kind of like a witch leaving a trail of bread crumbs for some unsuspecting man. One red heel lay tipped sideways on the rug just inside the entryway. The other stood upright with the toe pointed at the bathroom, as if it were waiting to get in. Her silver beaded handbag gaped open on the kitchen table, her lipstick, compact, cigarettes, and tissues spilling out of it. On the floor, a red hat and one glove lay tangled in a silver shawl with wispy fringe, the tail end of it trapped in the door. Rumor dumped the rest of the contents of Mother's handbag onto the table, looking for her change purse.

"What in the world are you doing?" Mary asked.

"Getting the church offering." Rumor twisted the clasp on the change purse. "What do you think I'm doing?"

"That's stealing, darling."

"She gives it to us every Sunday." Rumor pinched two nickels from the belly of the purse. "I'm letting her sleep in."

"How kind of you."

Rumor slipped the coins into her own handbag and tossed the coin purse onto the heap of Mother's belongings on the table. "She'll never know. Is it my imagination, or has Mother's drinking gotten worse ever since the fair opened?"

Rumor poured two glasses of milk, scooping in the last of the Cocomalt. She stirred until the powder dissolved and a light froth covered the top.

"It's probably because of her sister," Mary said, gathering Mother's clutter from the floor.

"What are you doing?" Rumor placed Mary's chocolate milk on the counter. "Let her pick up her own mess. And you can't blame Aunt Addie, she's not opening Mother's mouth and pouring in the booze."

"She might as well be."

"Oh, is that so?" Rumor picked up Mary's glass of Cocomalt and dumped it into the sink. "Then I guess it's your fault that your breakfast just went down the drain."

"That is so childish, darling."

"And so is Mother's drinking."

"Personally, I've never witnessed a child drinking alcohol." Mary stuck her chin in the air and slowly turned her back on Rumor. "Have you, darling?"

"I didn't mean literally, I meant figuratively. I would explain those words to you if I thought it would do any good."

Earlier, they had decided on Saint Joseph's Catholic Church that day, so Rumor pulled the lace doilies from both arms of the couch, wadding one up and hurling it at the back of Mary's head.

"Now, that is childish," Mary said, plucking the doily up from the floor and stepping out into the courtyard.

Outside on the street, Rumor gazed out over the harbor. A blanket of gray hung along the shore. She imagined Papa making his way to the amusement center in his red-and-white-striped vest, carting his crate to his spot for another foggy day on his Isle of Despair. Bright blue skies and sun shone on their bungalow and the rest of Bankers Hill, and in a few hours, Mother would wake up hungover and then lounge around the house all day, listening to her favorite music on Papa's radio.

The good things about the Catholic churches were the standing, sitting, and kneeling. It kept you awake. They also smelled mysterious and sacred. The bad thing was the Latin. Rumor couldn't understand most of the mass, only the occasional words that sounded like English—*et in unum dominum Jesum Christum*, which probably meant "we are one in the dominion of Jesus Christ." But both of them knew to cover their hair with one of the couch doilies, to dip their fingers into the holy water and cross themselves when entering the sanctuary, to kneel at the end of a pew before sitting down, and that they should not get in line for the bread and wine because they hadn't taken the classes to do that. Men ran most of the services, only letting women play the organ or sing in the choir, but the Catholic churches were men only. Altar boys in robes marched in with a giant wooden cross and candles while the priests swung a shiny silver ball with burning incense and magically turned water into wine—things too sacred for women. They did have nuns, but they only sat in the pews, like everyone else.

With her mother's doily draped over the top of her head, Rumor knelt when the rest of the congregation dropped to the prayer benches. Mary wore hers farther back, more for fashion than as a sign of respect. When it came time for the people to line up for the communion, Mary and Rumor sat back, letting people slip past them. One by one, they'd stick out their tongues for the wafer, then sip from a golden goblet that the priest wiped off between each person.

As the line progressed, Rumor pressed her hands together and prayed, "God, please bless Mary, even though I'm still mad at her, and Papa Jack and Aunt Addie. And Mother. Bless her and make her a better person. Forgive me for taking Mother's money with no intention of putting it in the offering, but it is so I can see my papa, and I don't think that is too big of a sin. Please forgive me for lying about seeing Papa and

Aunt Addie. And please strike Sal's mother with a tiny bolt of lightning. Not enough to kill her, but just enough to teach her a lesson. Amen."

The people at the amusement center wrapped themselves in jackets, sweaters, or beach blankets, huddling in the sand, flying kites, which sagged and struggled in the foggy air, or combing the beach for shells. Rosa sat alone by the seawall, her skirt fanned out and covering her crossed legs while she twisted her palm fronds into a fish. Rumor asked Rosa where her papa was, but Rosa just put her hands in the air and said, *"Yo no se."*

"I hope it's not something frightful," Mary said. "You don't think he's sick, do you?"

"I guess we'll find out."

"I hope not, darling. You know I don't do well with illness. I was never meant to be a wet nurse."

"Nursemaid."

"That, either." Mary's heels tapped on the pavement as they made their way down Ocean Walk.

Two sailors in their blue uniforms and white caps approached from the opposite direction. As soon as Mary spotted them, she stuck out her chest and made sure her dress swished back and forth like a dinner bell. When they passed by, one let out a low, long whistle. "I think I just saw a dream walking by."

Why Mary put on such a show for some sailor boys not worth her time was beyond Rumor.

They found Papa and two other men sitting on upturned crates outside his garage. The three of them puffed on hand-rolled cigarettes and talked politics. The men looked as if they'd just rolled out of a breadline. Rumor hoped they weren't trying to get handouts from Papa. He didn't have much to spare.

"Things are turning around," one man with a hooked nose and bowler hat said.

"At least here in San Diego. The Exposition's bringing in jobs and money," the other said, flicking the butt of his cigarette across the alley. It landed at the base of a dented garbage can. "People are squawking about FDR and his New Deal, saying it's all riding on the backs of the middle class, but I'll tell you something, at least FDR is trying to give a hand up to the working man."

Papa smiled as soon as he spotted Mary and Rumor waiting by Mrs. Bailey's fence. "Come on over, girls. Sam, Harry, these are my beautiful daughters, Mary and Rumor."

The men stood and pulled their hats from their greasy heads. "Pleasure to meet you," Harry said, smiling tight, probably trying to hide his black front teeth. "We'll leave you be. Give you time with your girls."

Papa waited until Harry and Sam disappeared around the corner, then looked to see if the coast was clear before whispering, "Wait till you see what I've been up to." He glanced around again, then cracked open the door of his garage, just wide enough for them to slip in.

A little girl sat on the cement floor with the parts of an electrical fan scattered about. She held a screwdriver to a motor, loosening the wires and dropping the screws into a pile in front of her.

"You have a new daughter?" Rumor asked.

"Oh, heavens no." Papa laughed. "This is my helper, Ruby Anne."

She looked to be no older than eight, maybe only six, so Rumor wasn't sure how much help she could be.

Papa pulled two crates out from along the wall and set a glass jar half-filled with screws in front of Ruby. "Put the metal in this one, all the wire in this one, and the screws go in the jar," he told her. "Then that's enough for one day. You've earned your Tootsie Roll."

Ruby sat cross-legged in a blue-and-white bathing suit, the crotch of it gaping open on one side and exposing the bare mound of her privates. Rumor didn't want to embarrass Ruby, but she couldn't let her sit there all exposed like that. She whispered into Ruby's ear, "Your bathing suit needs some adjustment."

Ruby looked down and tugged the crotch back into place as if it were no big deal, then plucked several screws from the ground with her tiny fingers. The screws clinked into the jar as she dropped them in one by one. Once Ruby finished sorting the pieces into the jars, she placed the screwdriver on Papa's workbench and went straight for his candy jar.

"You sure are pretty," Ruby said, staring up at Mary and nipping off the end of her Tootsie Roll.

Mary put on her one of her imitation-starlet smiles. "Why, thank you."

"You should probably be heading home, Ruby," Papa said to her.

"Thanks, Mr. Donnelly," Ruby said before slipping out the open crack of the doors.

Rumor had been so surprised at seeing the little girl that she hadn't noticed all the radios crammed on Papa's workbench. Papa reached in his pocket and pulled out a wad of money. He flipped through the bills, fanning them in front of Rumor and Mary. They were mostly ones with a few fives mixed in. A lot of money for Papa.

"Where'd you get all the cash?" Rumor asked.

"Fixing and selling radios. I made a deal with a man who runs a pawnshop. He takes the radios in, working or not, and I fix them. He gives me a dollar or two and resells them. I even got myself an employee that I pay in Tootsie Rolls. Not a bad deal."

Papa seemed truly happy, as if he'd got some of his pride back.

Papa split his wad of money in half and held it out to Rumor. "Here, give this to your mother."

"She doesn't deserve it," Rumor said, her voice a bit harsher than she'd intended. "I mean, she doesn't need it."

Papa looked surprised.

"You keep your money, Papa Jack. Get yourself a nice place to live."

"I got me a place. This is good enough for the likes of me."

"No it isn't," Rumor said, ignoring Mary's scowls.

The money still hung in the air between them. If Mary dared reach for it, Rumor would slap her hand.

"You girls have the things you need?"

"Yes, Papa, we're doing fine. And Mary's getting herself a movie star, so she doesn't need it, either."

He folded both halves of the wad back together and slid them into his pocket. "Okay, but if you girls need anything, you let me know."

"We will, Papa," Rumor said. "Maybe you can save up and get yourself a car. Then you could come pick us up on Sundays."

"Wouldn't that be the ticket?" Papa said.

That afternoon, Papa treated them to cotton candy and a roller coaster ride on the Big Dipper. They had to practically force Mary into the car, and she screamed the entire ride. Afterward, Mary felt sick to her stomach, forcing them to spend the rest of the day on a bench, watching the ocean and the crowds. Mary must really have been feeling green, because she didn't even notice the sailors and lifeguards who strolled by right in front of them. An onshore breeze blew in, chasing out the fog and snapping the flags inland.

Rumor watched two little girls screaming in delight as the surf washed in across their knees. When she was little, she'd wrap kelp around her waist and swish it back and forth like a hula skirt. She liked how the slippery fronds brushed against her legs. She also liked to skip rope with the long golden stems of bull kelp or chase Mary down the beach, snapping it like a whip.

When the sun dipped low, she and Mary climbed aboard the street-car and pulled away from Papa for another week.

"I don't like that Papa has Ruby working for him," Rumor said once they'd cleared the station. "She's only a little girl."

"You sound jealous, darling." Mary still looked a bit green. "You afraid that he's replacing you?"

"No. It just doesn't seem right."

"You know how much Papa loves children," Mary said. "He's just being nice to her."

Rumor wondered if maybe she was a bit jealous, worried that Papa would one day get married and have another family.

Their electric fan did nothing more than swirl the hot air around the living room. Mary lounged on the couch with a wet rag draped over her forehead. Even with windows open on both sides of the bungalow, the curtains lay unfurled, not catching even a hint of breeze. Rumor swung the front door wide open. Mrs. Keegan sat in the shade of her porch, fanning herself with a red-and-black oriental fan. Even the radio sounded listless, with slow-crooning melodies drifting out.

"This must be what the doldrums are like," Rumor said.

Mary cocked her head to the side. "I don't hear anything."

"At sea. The doldrums are when . . . Never mind," Rumor said. "I wish we could go to the Plunge and spend the rest of the day floating in the pool."

"I wish you'd stop pacing, darling. Just watching you is wearing me out." Mary picked up Mother's *McCall's* magazine and fanned herself. "You got streetcar money?"

"If I did," Rumor said, "I wouldn't be here."

Rumor had been fidgety for days. A girl could go crazy sitting around the house. The only thing she'd done all week was go to the cinema with Mary to see *Three-Cornered Moon*, starring Claudette Colbert, a predictable and harebrained film about a rich girl whose mother lost the family fortune in the crash and had to find ways to earn money. Elizabeth, the character Claudette Colbert played, ended up marrying a doctor, like all the women in moving pictures did to solve their problems. Rumor wished they'd make movies where women solved their own problems without having to be rescued. Of course, Mary argued that would be ridiculous—why would a woman go through so much trouble when all she had to do was look pretty?

Rumor wondered what was going on at the Exposition. Was it Catholic Day, Canadian Day, or Women's Relief Corps Day? Mary had wanted to go to the fair on Danish Day, thinking that anyone who showed up with a pastry could get in at a discount, until Rumor explained it was for people from Denmark. In Europe.

"I'm gonna make some lemonade," Rumor said.

"To sell?"

"No, to drink. I'm sweltering."

There was a lemon tree on the corner of Fourth and Ivy, two on Juniper, and a whole grove of them on Albatross. With her hair twisted up off her neck, and a paper sack, Rumor headed out on a lemon quest. Heat waves rippled across the asphalt, and thick tropical leaves hung like wilted lettuce. A woman sat in the shade of the lemon tree on the corner of Fourth and Ivy. Rumor couldn't rightly pluck the woman's fruit with her sitting right under it, so she made her way to Juniper. There, a group of children took turns holding a hose over their heads and dousing themselves with water in one of the yards. Since Rumor didn't know which child belonged to which house and she couldn't risk any of them tattling on her, she headed over to the grove on Albatross.

Rumor picked the lemons from the trees along the perimeter, not daring to wander into the orchard. You never knew who might be in there. There could be a drifter, ex-con, or a kidnapper. People hid in orchards all the time and you never knew who you'd come across.

Stepping back into their courtyard, she noticed Mary had moved out to the lawn and was sprawled out like a rag doll on a blanket beneath the one tree. It wasn't much of a shade tree at all; a beautiful jacaranda with purple flowers, the branches were airy, allowing sunlight to filter through and creating only spotty shadows on the lawn. A straw hat covered Mary's face. Heaven forbid she ruin her perfect complexion. Mrs. Keegan still fanned herself, and now Mrs. Parker and Little Benny had wandered out. Mrs. Parker slumped on her front step with her dress pulled up over her knees and tucked between her legs. She gazed off toward the back wall of the storage closets while Benny dug holes in the dirt.

By the time Rumor made the lemonade and two butter-and-sugar sandwiches for her and Mary, she wondered if it was worth the effort. She'd wasted more energy making it than she'd get from consuming it. Those kids with the hose had the best solution. Mary sat up when Rumor came out with her lunch, and the two of them ate to the sound of Louis Armstrong singing "Lazy River."

Little Benny held up a wriggling earthworm, trying to get his mother's attention. When she didn't respond, he pulled it in half and flung one end at her. It hit the side of her head and then dropped to the cement. Except for the movement of her eyes to Benny, Mrs. Parker did nothing. If Rumor had done that to her mother, she would have been slapped up one side and down the other. Mrs. Parker seemed to have something big on her mind. She usually doted on Benny.

"Thanks for lunch," Mary said, lying back and pulling the hat over her face again. She left half her sandwich to dry in the sun.

Rumor took the plates into the house, placing them next to the sink for Mary to clean, since she'd made lunch. As Mother always said, "The cook doesn't do the dishes."

Outside, Mrs. Keegan raised a fuss. Rumor wondered if Benny was throwing worms at her now, but as soon as she got to the door, she saw the problem. Sal. He stepped up onto the porch of their bungalow while Mrs. Keegan screeched from her chair, "It's you again, is it? Come over here, young man. I want to have a word with you."

Mary peeked out from under her hat, shook her head, and covered her face again. Rumor reached out to take hold of Sal's sleeve but noticed the big rings of sweat under his arms and thought better of it. "Come in, quick. What're you doing here?"

"Well, it's obviously not for the hospitality of your neighbors." He stood in the middle of the living room, sizing up the place. "Nice radio."

"Thanks, it's my father's."

Rumor noticed his eyes stopping on an ashtray filled with cigarette butts. "Got any smokes?"

"Do you smoke?"

"Who doesn't? I smoke when I can get them." He gave Rumor one of his high-and-mighty smiles. "Don't tell me little Miss Sneaking-out-of-the-house doesn't smoke."

"Even if I had any, I wouldn't give them to you. Go bum one off someone else." Rumor realized what a sight she must be. She hadn't even brushed out her hair before twisting it up, and the sundress she wore was from last year and hugged her breasts a bit too tight. "So, why are you here? I'm sure you didn't come all this way to bum a cigarette."

"Addie's asked me a couple of times if I'd seen you around, so I thought I'd bring you to her."

"Did she specifically ask you to get me?"

"No, but I can tell she wants me to."

"Oh, so you're telepathic too? You *do* belong in a circus."

"You coming or not? I don't have all day."

"Yeah, I'm coming. Give me five minutes." Rumor started toward her room to change and brush out her hair. "Why don't you wait out in the courtyard?"

"You think I'm gonna rob you? Your front door's standing wide open."

After slipping into her newest school dress, Rumor ran a brush through her hair and neatly twisted it up. When Rumor came out, she found Sal on their sofa reading her mother's *Ladies' Home Journal.* He lowered the magazine with raised eyebrows. She thought he was about to compliment her or whistle, but instead he said, "Is this the sort of fiction they're feeding you ladies? 'Kisses are the language of love. Don't be a delicatessen,'" he scoffed. "Or even better, 'So Glamorous, So Brave.'"

"Did you come here to poke fun at my family or to do a good deed for Aunt Addie?"

He dropped the magazine and saluted her. "To do a good deed. Boy Scout's honor."

"They have Boy Scouts at the nudist colony?"

"Of course they do. I just got my badge in naked rowing."

Rumor shook her head. "Let's go."

Back in the courtyard, Mary still lay in the shade. Mrs. Keegan must've either gone in for her nap or to fetch her broom. Little Benny spooned mounds of dirt onto the sidewalk.

"Want to come with us?" Rumor asked Mary.

"Us?" Mary asked, peeking out from under her hat brim.

"Me and Sal. We're going to see Aunt Addie."

"Heavens no," she said. "When will you be back?"

"Before Mother, that's for sure."

She just shook her head. "You're gonna get caught."

At the camp, people wilted in whatever shade they could find. Even the children had stopped running around like wild dogs and instead lay panting under the trees. At the nudists' tents, three women—one blonde, one brunette, and a redhead—lounged in the shadow of the one directly across from Aunt Addie's. They all wore short-sleeve sundresses and had the golden skin of sunbathers. It was the same tent where the women's shadows had danced and giggled the first night she'd been to the camp.

"You looking for your mama?" the redhead asked in a slow Southern accent.

"No. We're looking for Addie," Sal said.

"Either way, they're both still holed up in the garden. We're taking a breather, but I'll be darned if it ain't cooler in there. I'm sweating like a whore in church."

"Mind your language, Ida," the brown-haired woman said. "Can't you see she's a child?"

"Who's your pretty little girlfriend?" the blond one asked.

"She's not my girlfriend."

"Figured not." She giggled with a sideways glance at the lady next to her. "Mommy wouldn't like that."

Sal gave her a hard stare. "This is Rumor. She's Addie's niece."

"Well, I'll be," Ida said. "I heard Addie had family coming around. Nice to meet you."

"Do you mind if she waits here with you for a while? I'll be right back," Sal said.

Rumor wasn't happy at being dumped off or babysat. She would've preferred just waiting at Aunt Addie's tent, alone. The women looked nice enough, and healthy, but, good Lord, they were nudists. She wondered if they wore anything under their dresses or if they just threw them on over their naked bodies, without brassieres, girdles, or any sort of undergarment.

The moment Sal disappeared down the lane, all three of them began chattering in unison.

"Are you crazy?"

"Have you met his mother? She'll eat you alive."

"I'd like to get my hands on him."

"Girls, girls. You're scaring her half to death," the one with auburn hair said. She had a round face and short bangs. Sweat dotted her upper lip like dew. "Sorry, we didn't mean to upset you. I'm Lucille."

"I'm Ida," the one with the curly red hair and Southern accent said, then pointed at the blonde. "And that is Dottie, but most people just call us the chickens, being that we're always together. I guess 'the chickens' is easier to say than Ida, Dottie, and Lucille. And to tell you the truth, I don't mind, as long as they don't dip me in batter and drop me in the deep fryer."

"Nice to meet you," Rumor said, not really sure yet if it was nice or not, but she knew that was the proper thing to say. "I've already met Daisy."

"And you're back? Hats off to you. This girl's got some gumption," Ida said. "I like her already. Did Daisy threaten to skin you alive?"

"More or less. She said to stay away from her Salvation. What kind of a name is that anyway?" Not that she had any room to talk, with her name and all, but *Salvation* seemed a bit much.

All three of them jumped off the platform, creating a semicircle around Rumor.

Ida glanced around before continuing, "From what I've heard, when Daisy was about fourteen years old, her father began taking liberties with her. If you know what I mean."

"Now, Ida, you know that's just talk."

Rumor wasn't used to adults talking so freely in front of her. When she realized what they'd just said, she thought she must've misunderstood.

Ida waved Dottie's words away with one hand. "Daisy became pregnant by her own father. As soon as he found out she was carrying his child, he sent her to a state home for troubled girls. Can you imagine?"

No, Rumor couldn't imagine. Wasn't that inbreeding? Didn't it cause birth defects? She imagined Sal with extra toes or half-female and half-male body parts. Their science lab at school had jars of animal embryos floating in formaldehyde: a tiny two-headed sheeplike thing, a duck with three webbed feet, and a piglet with no snout—all pickled and pasty.

"Daisy named her baby Salvation. They took him away from her as soon as he was born and sent him to a home." Lucille poked her head up like a periscope and looked around as if she were making sure the coast was clear before whispering, "I heard the doctors did an operation so she couldn't have any more babies."

"It's called sterilization," Ida said, correcting Lucille.

"I thought they only did that to insane, violent criminals," Rumor said.

"If a doctor determines you're unfit, feebleminded, immoral, or delinquent, they sure don't want you breeding and making inferior babies."

"Do people have any say in it?" Rumor asked.

"Not if you're in an institution."

"Daisy didn't have any say. The same day she had Sal, they fixed her like a stray dog. But as soon as Daisy growed up and got out, she made a beeline for her Salvation. Took a lot to get him back too."

"She's raising him to take care of her when she gets too old," Dottie said. "You see, that's why he's her Salvation. He's her old-age pension plan."

"Yessiree," Ida said. "And she's seeing to it that he gets the best education she can provide for him."

"He said he hasn't been to school since he was ten years old," Rumor said.

"And he was telling you the truth. Once he turned ten, Daisy figured he was reading, writing, and doing arithmetic good enough. He was ready for a real education." Both Ida and Dottie nodded in agreement with Lucille.

"You see"—Ida jumped back in—"Daisy provides Sal with nothing but the best training."

Dottie leaned in real close and whispered, "Pays for it on her own back, if you know what I mean."

Rumor wasn't a hundred percent sure she understood, but she nodded.

"She dates men in different trades and gets them to teach their skills to Sal," Lucille said. "He's a smart one too. Learns quicker than anyone I've ever known."

Good Lord. Sal trusted these women? Serves him right for leaving her behind like a child.

"Dottie, do you remember when she dated that plasterer? What was his name? Wasn't it Larry?" Ida asked but didn't slow down long enough for anyone to answer. "Sal learned so much in three weeks that Larry was sending him off on jobs by himself. Soon as Daisy found out he'd got everything he could, she dropped the plasterer like a hot potato and started going with that carpenter. What was his name? George? Good-looking too! Dark brown hair and strong arms. Do you girls remember his arms?"

"Uh-huh! Who could forget those arms?" Dottie said.

"And she's dated a mason, a plumber, and an electrician," Lucille said. "That plumber was a piece of work. When she broke up with him, he beat her black-and-blue. Do you girls remember how he wouldn't leave her alone? Heinrich had to get the sheriff after him, and he still didn't stop. Finally, Heinrich took matters into his own hands and hired a group of men to beat that plumber with clubs. They left him on the side of the road and we never saw him again. Dead or alive."

"The most confounding one of all, though," Ida said, "was the clown."

"I've never understood that one." Dottie giggled. "He was only five foot tall, bowlegged, and bald as a monk. A sloppy drunk too. He hung on Daisy like a lap dog."

"Sal liked him, though," Lucille said. "I think he felt sorry for him."

Well, that explained Sal's juggling-clown routine that awed the children in the camp.

"Do you girls remember his name? Was it Irwin or Ira?"

"Irvin," Ida said. "But his clown name was Rickets."

"Isn't he the one who gave her that parrot?" Lucille asked. "I felt sorry for him myself."

"Of course you did, Lucille. You feel sorry for everyone," Ida said. "I didn't. That man was so ugly, I bet his mama had to tie a pork chop around his neck to get the dog to play with him. How many chances do you think a man like him has to date a nudist? He knew it wouldn't last, but he sure enjoyed the ride while it lasted."

"That's a horrible thing to say." Lucille scowled at Ida.

"What's a horrible thing to say?" A deep voice came from behind.

Rumor looked up to see Sal standing right behind Lucille.

"Oh, howdy, Sal." Ida's voice changed into a long and slow drawl. "Nothing. Lucille was just being Lucille and telling us what bad chickens we are."

"Heinrich's wondering why you three aren't back yet. They're about finished with lunch."

"How mad is he?" Lucille asked.

"Pretty mad," Sal said. "You better run off quick."

They hurried off down the lane of tents and turned left, out of sight.

Sal stepped closer, standing in the spot where Ida had been. "So, what were you girls gossiping about?"

Rumor couldn't look at him, the son of his own grandfather. What kind of deformities did he have? Did he have extra nipples or maybe a forked tongue or something pathological? Could he be a murderer?

"Oh, I see," he said. "Damn them."

Rumor glanced up. Sal's jaw tightened, and the tendons in his neck popped out. She needed to get away from there. From him. She couldn't stay a single moment longer, not even to see Aunt Addie. Rumor circled around Sal and headed in the same direction the chickens had gone. She ran toward the music and metallic pinging of the Exposition, around the canyon wall, through the scrub brush, and back through the fence slat into Gold Gulch.

Rumor should've stayed home. She wished she were lying on the grass with Mary, completely ignorant, with a sun hat over her face. Her head spun with thoughts of two-headed sheep and doctors doing abhorrent operations. Of doctors sedating her with ether and then waking up to find they'd hacked out parts of her insides. Of not having control. No choice. No freedom. Could her mother drag her to a hospital and authorize that? This put a whole new angle as to whether or not she should defy her wishes.

Rumor kept going, past a crowd of people watching a stagecoach holdup, past a Chinese laundry, and past an Indian selling blankets and jewelry. She emerged from the canyon and onto the Avenue of Palaces, surfacing into the enchantment of well-dressed people. Not nudists and prostitutes and dirty children. Parents walked hand in hand with their children, who skipped beside them licking ice cream cones and pointing to things that amazed them. Thousands of happy voices rang out around her. Some spoke German, some French, and some spoke in languages Rumor didn't even recognize. Manicured green lawns and flowering bushes stretched down the avenue. The smell of fresh-baked pastries filled the air, and people snapped photographs with their Kodak cameras. In the Organ Pavilion, the US Marine Corps band played, their brass instruments sparkling in the sun like diamonds of light.

Why should she care about Sal anyway? He wasn't anything to her. Just a ticket to see Aunt Addie.

Rumor heard Little Benny long before he and his mother rounded the corner into the courtyard. He bounded up the steps, pulling his mother behind him—a hand-to-hand tug-of-war, which Mrs. Parker was losing. "Snails and nails and puppy-dog tails, that's what little boys are made of." But what were big boys made of? It had been several days since she'd seen Sal, but she couldn't get the conversation with the chickens out of her mind. Maybe Rumor would've been better off not knowing. But really, what difference did it make?

"Good morning, Mrs. Parker." Rumor gave her a brief wave.

Mrs. Parker didn't answer, just gave a small and tired smile. She didn't look well. Rumor bet she didn't weigh a hundred pounds sopping wet. When they got close to their front door, she stopped and stared at it, frozen for what seemed an eternity.

"Need help?" Rumor called out to her.

She didn't move. Little Benny squirmed, twisting his little hand back and forth in hers, trying to wriggle free, but Mrs. Parker held tight.

"Everything alright?" Rumor asked, making her way over to Mrs. Parker.

As she approached, Little Benny began crying, "Hurts, Mommy. Hurts."

Rumor bent down, took hold of Little Benny's waist, and lifted him off the ground. "I got him, Mrs. Parker. You can let go."

But she didn't.

When Rumor looked up, she noticed a padlock on the outside of their door. Little Benny cried louder, "Hurts, Mommy."

Rumor put her hand over Mrs. Parker's. "I got him, you can let go." She still didn't. Tears slid down Mrs. Parker's cheeks, but she didn't utter a sound. "I got him, Mrs. Parker. Let go."

Rumor wriggled her fingertips between Mrs. Parker's hand and Benny's to pry them apart. It was only then that Mrs. Parker looked up and acknowledged Rumor's presence. When she freed Little Benny's hand, Mrs. Parker sank to her knees at Rumor's feet. It was as if he'd been the one keeping her upright the entire time.

"What does it mean?" Rumor asked. "Why's there a padlock on your door?"

"The rent." She was so quiet it took Rumor a moment to realize what she'd said. "Ben's been trying to get work. There's nothing."

Mrs. Parker didn't seem to be talking to Rumor or even aware of her presence—just mumbling out loud to the empty air.

"My mother's clock is in there. My grandfather's pocket watch, the china teacups, Benny's clothes. His toys. Everything's in there. Everything."

Little Benny arched backward, wriggling and kicking his feet. "Down. Me want down."

Rumor held tight. "Keep still."

"Down," he screamed and grabbed hold of Rumor's hair. "Down."

"Ouch." She yanked on a lock of his hair. "No hair pulling."

Mrs. Parker began sobbing. "We have nothing. What will we do?"

Rumor looked around the courtyard for someone. Anyone. Mrs. Keegan's chair sat empty on her stoop. The door to Ruth and her mother's bungalow was shut. The Harringtons' and the Pitts' doors were also shut, and she'd heard Mr. Hargrove leave for work an hour earlier. Rumor tried to keep a hold on Little Benny, but he squirmed and kicked. "Want to go for a walk, Benny?"

"No. Me want down."

"You want a Coca-Cola? If you're a good boy, I'll get you a Coca-Cola." That quieted him. Rumor left Mrs. Parker deflated on the grass and took Benny with her. When she opened the door to her bungalow, she felt relieved to find Mother sitting at the dinette, wearing her white terry-cloth turban, with a cup of coffee in front of her and a cigarette pinched between her fingers.

"What's wrong?" Mother had makeup smeared all under her eyes. Between that and her white turban and robe, she looked like a hospital patient with a brain injury.

"There's a padlock on the Parkers' door. Mrs. Parker is in the court-yard, crying."

Mother leaned the cigarette on the inside edge of the ashtray and rose to her feet. Rumor followed her to the door, switching Little Benny to her other hip. He was heavier than he looked. Before she knew it, Mother had lifted Mrs. Parker by her armpits and was leading her toward their bungalow.

"Coca-Cola," Little Benny whined. "Coca-Cola."

"Not now," Rumor said. "Be good and we'll go to the store in a bit."

"Coca-Cola now."

"We'll go soon."

Little Benny reached under Rumor's arm and pinched her in the tender spot close to the armpit.

"Owww!" Rumor instinctively slapped at his hand. "That's bad." Then she pinched him back.

He screamed and Mother shot Rumor a warning glare.

"If you don't stop, I won't get you a Coca-Cola at all."

Rumor opened the door to her and Mary's bedroom. Mary lay under the covers with her eyes closed. With all the ruckus, she couldn't really be asleep. Rumor plopped Little Benny on the bed. Mary looked up with squinty eyes, pretending to have just woken. She'd have to practice her acting if she ever wanted to be in the pictures.

"You have to keep an eye on Little Benny. Mrs. Parker needs our help."

"You watch him, darling," she said, rolling onto her side with her back to Benny. "Can't you see I'm sleeping?"

"Mother said you have to watch Benny," Rumor said, leaving the room and shutting the door.

Mrs. Parker sat on their sofa, her shoulders all hunched like a scared little mouse.

"Stay here with Nola," Mother said, storming out the front door, not even shutting it behind her. Rumor thought she'd go get Ruth, but instead, she headed directly for the manager's bungalow. The manager, Mr. Kaiser Pitt, and Mother never saw eye to eye. Something had happened between Mother and Kaiser right after Papa had lost his job, and ever since, she'd never uttered a kind word about him. Mother had said that his brain and his heart were the same size and neither bigger than the pimento in a canned olive. Since then, Mother and Ruth had referred to him as Olive Pitt instead of Kaiser Pitt.

Mother pounded on Kaiser's door. An oleander bush partially blocked Rumor's view, so she couldn't see who opened the door. All she could see was the back of her mother standing in her slippers, pink robe, and white turban on their stoop. "Ethel, is Kaiser home?" Mother said loud enough for everyone in the courtyard to hear.

There was a moment of silence, then Mother continued, "Why did you lock Nola and Ben out of their home?"

"I had no choice. This is between Ben and me. Now, you go on home."

"If it's between you and Ben, why did you wait until he was out looking for work and lock his wife and child out?"

"This is none of your business."

"It sure as hell is my business with Ben out and Nola sitting in my living room with nowhere to go," Mother yelled. "That was chickenshit of you to do it in the morning, leaving Nola and Benny locked out."

"I did what I had to do. It's my job, and I ain't about to lose it by being sentimental."

"What about all their belongings? That's all they have."

"They'll be sold to make up for what they owe."

"You are heartless," Mother said in that tone of voice she had that sounded more like a voodoo hex than a simple insult.

By then, Mrs. Harrington, Ruth and her mother, and Mrs. Keegan had emerged from their bungalows, drawn out by all the commotion. Ruth joined Mother on Kaiser's stoop.

"At least let Nola get some of her personal belongings."

"Sorry, can't do it. Go on now and mind your own business before I call the police."

"How much do they owe? How much so they can get their property?" Mother asked.

"If you want to help, then take care of Mrs. Parker," Kaiser said. "Ben can come talk to me when he gets home."

"You just wait, Kaiser. You'll get yours. What comes around, goes around."

Rumor knew it would be best to make herself scarce. Mother would be in a ripe mood, especially after she looked in the mirror and realized she'd been traipsing around in public looking like a hospital patient. The first thing Mother did when she got back to the bungalow was to order Rumor and Mary to take Benny to the park.

"I promised him a Coca-Cola," Rumor told Mother.

Mother dumped all the coins from her change purse onto the table. "Take what you need." Then she opened her silver cigarette case, plucked one out with her crimson fingernails, and lit it, sucking in until the tip glowed orange. With the cigarette pinched between her fingers, she massaged her temples. The smoke looked as if it rose up out of her right ear, and Rumor thought how funny it would be if she had a cigarette in each hand, making both ears steam—just like in the cartoons.

Mother looked up at her. "What are you waiting for?"

Mary still slept, with the covers pulled up, burying her head. Little Benny had emptied everything out from the bottom two drawers of their dresser and sat scribbling on Mary's catalogues. Mary's shorts, shirts, and bathing suit lay scattered all around him.

"Mother said we have to take Benny to the park right now."

Mary groaned. "I'm sleeping. Doesn't anyone around here understand that a working girl needs her rest?"

"Mother's orders."

***

By the time they returned home, Mother had changed clothes and looked like a normal human being again. She, Ruth, and Mrs. Parker sat at the dinette, with Mother and Ruth both clutching hands of playing cards and teaching Mrs. Parker how to play pinochle.

"Fix Benny some lunch, girls. There's soup in the cabinet," Mother said without even looking up from her hand. "The goal of the game is to win tricks. I dealt, so Ruth leads to begin with. After that, whoever wins the trick will lead."

Rumor bit her tongue. Wasn't it Mrs. Parker's responsibility to take care of her own son? Mary took Benny into their bedroom while Rumor opened the only can of Campbell's soup they had left—the mock-turtle soup, untouched for over a year. And rightly so. It would be good to get rid of it. As Rumor stood over the pot, stirring and waiting for it to boil, someone knocked on the door. Mrs. Parker looked up in relief.

"Maybe it's Ben," Mother said, pushing back her chair to answer.

Mr. Parker stood on the stoop in his sloppy suit and tie, with his hat cocked sideways on his head and a glassy gaze in his eyes.

"Yes, your family is here," her mother said.

"We're locked out," Mr. Parker slurred.

"Your family has been here all afternoon while you were out." Mother paused. "Out getting soused."

He stumbled over to his wife and knelt at her feet. He put his head in her lap and cried, "I'm so sorry. I've tried every day. So sorry. Tell me you love me."

Rumor didn't know why she felt embarrassed—it was Mr. Parker making a fool of himself—but she did. She stirred the soup and pretended she couldn't see or hear anything. There really was truth in the saying "A watched pot never boils."

Mrs. Parker put her hand on her husband's head and smoothed his hair back, petting him like a dog as he muttered, "What'll we do?"

Mother did not condone such weakness in men. Rumor waited for her eruption.

"First of all, you're going to get sober, and then you're going to talk to Kaiser about getting your belongings," Mother said in that tone that made Rumor cringe. "After that, maybe your head will be clear enough to figure out what you're going to do next."

Rumor stood at the stove with her head down, pretending she wasn't listening, until Mother snapped at her, "Rumor, put some coffee on while you're in there. I'll be right back."

Mother stepped outside, banging the door shut behind her. Ruth helped Mr. Parker to the couch, where he sat limp and disheveled. Mrs. Parker scooted next to him and patted his hand. Just as Rumor got the coffee going, Mother returned.

"Mrs. Keegan said your family can stay in her guest room for a week or so until you can find a place to go, but you're not going over there in your condition."

Mother came into the kitchen and yanked the spoon from Rumor's hand. "Go over to Mrs. Keegan's and help her get her guest room straightened up. And help her change the linens on the bed."

Mother, who loved bossing everyone around, was in her glory. Rumor knew better than to draw attention to herself when Mother was in that state, so she blindly obeyed, thanking her lucky stars she wasn't the one stuck watching Little Benny. Served Mary right.

Mrs. Keegan's house smelled like old lady—like rose water and mothballs. Some old ladies had lots of cats, but since Kaiser wouldn't allow pets, it looked like Mrs. Keegan kept plants instead. Potted plants covered every flat surface, with vines drooping down the sides of tables, the piano, and windowsills. Plants of every size, with round leaves, long leaves, and frilly fronds, crowded the coffee table and end tables. Little statues and knickknacks filled the gaps. Little Benny would have a heyday at Mrs. Keegan's. Rumor took a deep breath, remembering that plants released oxygen during photosynthesis. With all these plants, Mrs. Keegan must have extra oxygen in her house, but Rumor couldn't tell a difference.

"Thank you for your help, dear," Mrs. Keegan said. "The fresh sheets are in the cupboard next to the bathroom."

Rumor had figured that was where they were. All the bungalows were exactly the same layout, and it was the only logical place for linens and towels.

Just as the sun set, the Parkers were finally settled at Mrs. Keegan's. Mary said Benny screamed the entire time Rumor was helping Mrs. Keegan, and he wouldn't eat his soup. Mother tried to smile and tell Mary he was just tired and had a tough day, but Mary said Mother was at the end of her rope too.

Once they'd left, Rumor and Mary plopped down on the couch. Mother joined them, leaning back and propping her feet up on the coffee table, which they were not allowed to do. She exhaled a weary puff of smoke at the ceiling.

"What do you think they'll do?" Mary asked.

Mother shrugged. "Don't know. Ben hasn't had work in a long time."

Someone knocked at the door. Again. Mother dragged herself up. "For Christ's sake, what now?"

Rumor couldn't see who it was, but she saw Mother stiffen. "This isn't a good time."

"Oh, please. Just ten minutes." It sounded like Aunt Addie.

Rumor jumped up from the couch to get a view, and indeed, it was Aunt Addie standing on their stoop. "Aunt Addie?" Rumor said.

"You shouldn't have come back." Mother began closing the door.

"Please, Wavey, only ten minutes."

Of all the days, Rumor thought, Aunt Addie couldn't have picked a worse one.

CHAPTER THIRTEEN
ADDIE

It was either twilight or dusk, Addie could never remember the difference. A fog hovered dark and murky over the sea, but directly above, the stars twinkled and crickets had begun their nightly ruckus. She walked down the palm-lined streets, the same path to her sister's home she had taken the other two times, playing the reunion over and over in her head. She pictured Wavey wrapping her arms around her, letting all the years slide away, and pulling her into the house to catch up, like two schoolgirls after a long summer break.

The bungalows, most with their lights on and curtains drawn for the night, huddled together on the side of the hill overlooking the bay crowded with steel warships. Wavey seemed to have done well. The bungalows were tiny but clean and in a good neighborhood. What Addie wouldn't give to have been a part of it. To have lived across the courtyard from her sister as her girls grew up, joining them for dinner or loaning them a cup of sugar or milk when they ran low. She envisioned the girls begging to stay the night at her house. She'd have let them stay up late drinking Coca-Cola and playing mahjong.

It was all her own fault that Wavey had disowned her, and she knew that, and what she wouldn't give to take it all back. But what would their lives have been like if Ty and Wavey had continued on? Certainly, Rumor would've never been born.

Standing on the stoop, she paused. What if Wavey wouldn't see her and forbade Rumor to ever come back to the fair? Her visit could ruin the one connection she did have. Maybe she should've sent a letter, but she had a whole pile of letters that Wavey had never opened, all of them sent back "Return to Sender."

Voices murmured from behind the door. She recognized Wavey's and Rumor's. Addie closed her eyes and listened to her sister. She couldn't make out the words, but the cadence and pitch were as familiar as her own breath. The only thing between her and Wavey was a single door. A door, seventeen years, and an unforgivable sin. Addie raised her fist to knock. A moth the color of ash fluttered around the porch light, in a dainty but dangerous dance. What if Wavey wouldn't see her? What if she slammed the door shut—again—and for good?

Addie knocked. Three small raps. The voices stopped, and footsteps sounded on the other side.

"For Christ's sake, what now?" The door swung open and there she stood. Wavey. Close enough to touch. It took everything Addie had not to drop to her sister's feet and beg her for forgiveness. Addie wouldn't have recognized the woman standing in the open doorway if it wasn't for her startling and fractured blue eyes. Wavey had always been thin, but now her chin and cheekbones jutted out and she'd chopped off her hair, blunt and severe. Her eyes iced over. "This isn't a good time."

"Oh, please. Just ten minutes."

"Aunt Addie?" Rumor's cheerful voice came from behind her mother.

Wavey closed her eyes and puckered her lips. "You shouldn't have come back."

"Please, Wavey, only ten minutes."

Wavey peered past Addie, glancing around the courtyard. She took
a deep breath and stepped aside.

Addie looked for something familiar in Wavey's home—the writing desk, the couch, the table, the Victor Victrola—but saw nothing,
only the grandfather clock with the pendulum swinging back and forth
behind the glass door. And the newly familiar faces of her nieces, with
looks of expectation and dread on them.

Wavey shut the door and led Addie to a bedroom. Wavey lowered
herself down on the bed, with her arms crossed tight over her chest.
Addie thought that she'd be angry or break down crying and forgive her,
but not this, not this bottled-up and unwavering look. What if she went
to Wavey and pried her arms apart? Would it let loose all the feelings
from the past seventeen years?

Addie noticed Wavey still had the same dressing table she'd had on
Eucalyptus Street. Their mother's mirrored tray, rimmed with gold-fili-
gree roses, sat on one side of the table. Perfumes, lipsticks, and compacts
floated on the surface, with their inverted images reflected below. Addie
traced her finger along the back of a silver hairbrush engraved with flowers and vines. She could almost feel Wavey brushing her hair, like she
used to do every morning, telling her that she had the hair of an angel.

"I'm holding you to ten minutes," Wavey said. Addie didn't turn
to look at her. Instead, she observed her sister's reflection in the triple
mirror of the dressing table. With the angled side panes, it held three
different reflections of Addie but only one of Wavey in the center frame.
When their mother had died, the neighbor had draped a blanket over
their mirror so their mother's soul wouldn't become trapped in it. Had
Wavey done the same when Ty died? Could Ty's soul still be stuck inside
it? Addie didn't feel any sense of him. Instead, it felt as if she and Wavey
had been the ones frozen inside the glass for all those years.

Wavey still sat on the edge of her bed, her arms clasped tight and
her foot tapping as if it counted down the seconds until Addie's ten
minutes were up.

Addie lifted a perfume bottle and breathed in the light scent of lilac. "I remember this perfume bottle. It was Mother's, wasn't it?"

"Yes, you can have it."

"That's not what I came for."

"What *did* you come for?" Wavey asked.

Addie inhaled more of the perfume. What would their lives have been like if their mother had never died? Would they have been farmwives living a buggy's ride away from one another, with everyone congregating at their parents' house for Sunday dinners and holidays?

"What do you want? You want me to tell you I forgive you?"

"Yes," Addie said, "I need you to forgive me."

"I forgave you the moment it happened. You were a child."

"You said you'd send for me and you never did."

"There's more to it than you know."

"What? Please tell me so I can understand. You have no idea how terrible it is to wait year after year without a word from you."

"I sent you Ty's death announcement. We covered it all up for you."

"We?"

Wavey didn't respond.

"Who?"

"It doesn't matter anymore."

"But after everything blew over, after people forgot, couldn't I have come back?"

"You murdered my husband."

Addie winced at the word *murder*. She would never escape it. "Then you haven't forgiven me."

"Oh, I forgave you." She raised her gaze, meeting the reflection of Addie's eyes in the mirror. "But I didn't trust you."

"Trust?" The sound of her own voice surprised her. It sounded as if her words were wrapped in cotton.

"You'd been at that orphan asylum for so long." Wavey paused and then said, "I was afraid you'd hurt Mary too."

Addie's head spun. "How could you think I'd . . . ?"

"And now, after all these years, you show up out of the blue. I thought you were dead." Wavey's voice shook, sounding half angry, half heartbroken. "After your baby died and you ran off from Uncle Henry's . . ."

"You knew about Daniel?"

"Yes. Aunt May contacted me when you ran away. They were beside themselves with worry. She hoped you'd come to me."

That surprised Addie. She'd figured it was a relief for Aunt May and Uncle Henry not to have her as a burden. "Could I have come to you?"

Wavey shook her head. "No."

"I didn't think so," Addie said. "Daniel was Ty's son."

"I know," Wavey said. "And Mary's brother. And my nephew. And my husband's illegitimate son. You should've let them know you were okay. Let one of us know. You even stopped sending me letters."

"But you never opened them. You sent them all back to me."

"After all Aunt May and Uncle Henry did to help you out, that's how you repaid them? I got a letter from them last Christmas, and they're still asking about you."

"But . . ." Addie had no words. Wavey was right. She'd just run off, not a word, not a letter, nothing.

"And look what you're doing to my girls now."

Addie couldn't speak. She shook her head. No. No. She hadn't hurt Rumor or Mary. She would never harm them. "I haven't—" But before she could finish, Wavey interrupted.

"A nudist colony, for Christ's sake?"

Addie grabbed hold of the dressing table. The entire room spun. What did she have to show for her life? Six years in an orphan asylum? A murder? Living in a nudist colony, and now lying around a garden for men to ogle at her? How had it all come to this? All those years ago, when Wavey had sent for her from the orphan asylum, she had thought that her dreams had come true—but dreams had a way of drifting off into the ether.

"What's done is done," Wavey said. "But you need to stay away from my family."

Addie took a deep breath, but she couldn't pull enough oxygen into her lungs. She needed to get out. To get some fresh air. She pulled the door open and tumbled over Rumor, who'd apparently been eavesdropping. What had she heard? Addie scrambled to her feet and made her way to the front door. A rush of fresh air hit her.

"Aunt Addie?" Rumor's voice followed her from the bungalow as she ran across the courtyard. "Aunt Addie!"

341 Eucalyptus Street
San Diego, California
October 24, 1918

Ty burst into the house with his face flushed and shirtsleeves rolled up above his elbows. He was the sort of man who filled the house the moment he walked in, leaving no room for anyone else to breathe.

"Where have you been?" Wavey asked, weaving the needle through her embroidery and setting it aside on the couch.

"There's my wife," Ty said, slamming the door behind him. "Fetch me a drink."

"You were at the tavern? What about the flu?"

"Nothing can live in a bottle of Scotch. Not even the flu bug."

Ty lifted the hat from his head and flung it toward the couch, but instead, it flew across the room, falling at Addie's feet.

"Are you deaf? I said to get me a drink."

As Wavey passed by him, he snatched her by the waist and pulled her to him like a rag doll. He smashed his lips onto hers, so hard Wavey's head bent back unnaturally, making it look as if he'd broken her neck. Addie waited for Wavey to slap him, but she only pushed at his solid barrel chest with no effect. If only he'd been hit by a truck or had fallen into a ditch on his way home. Was it a sin to wish someone dead? When he released her, Wavey wiped her mouth, leaving a smear of blood across the back of her hand.

As soon as Wavey disappeared into the kitchen, Ty's glassy eyes turned on Addie. They hardened, then slowly drifted down her body to his hat lying at her feet. He shifted his weight toward her, but before he could take a step, Addie bent down and lifted his hat from the floor. The smell of sweat-soaked wool swept by as she tossed it to the other side of the couch. It landed upside down next to Wavey's embroidery hoop.

An evil, tight-lipped smile stretched across his lips as he continued toward the couch. Addie pushed herself to the far end, praying for Wavey to come back in with his drink. She hoped her sister would bring the entire bottle. Maybe another glass or two would do him in. When Ty reached the couch, instead of grabbing for his hat, he picked up Wavey's embroidery hoop. She had a lace-edged handkerchief stretched tight across it.

Ty exhaled a laugh that sounded as if he'd been punched in the stomach. "What is this piece of shit?"

Growing up without a mother, neither Wavey nor Addie had been taught needlework.

"Roses," Addie said, hoping he'd leave it be before Wavey came back into the room.

"Looks like someone blew a bloody nose into it." He tossed it on the coffee table with so much force that it skimmed across the top and dropped to the floor.

Addie felt his gaze on her but wouldn't look up. Out of the corner of her eye, she watched his trouser legs, waiting for any movement toward her and planning what to do. They swayed unsteadily at the far end of the couch. Would she be able to duck around his reach and make it to the bedroom for her hidden scissors? Or into the kitchen for a butcher knife?

When Wavey returned, her eyes fell on her embroidery hoop, lying upside down on the floor, and a look of confusion, then sadness washed across her face. Addie wished that she had picked it up, but she'd been too afraid to move. Ty dropped down in the middle of the couch and patted the spot to his left for Wavey. She handed him the glass filled with Scotch, a squeeze of lemon, and a splash of water—the way he always took it—before sitting down. When she did, Addie could barely see her with Ty's massive, bear-sized body between them.

"Put 'Danny Boy' on the Victrola," Ty said, slurring the words together into something that would be unintelligible if Addie hadn't known it was his favorite.

"Mary's asleep," Wavey said. "It'll wake her."

Addie hoped Mary would wake up so she could go tend to her.

"It's my house and I'm tired of you telling me what I can and cannot do because of the baby. The baby doesn't pay the bills."

He swatted at Addie, cuffing her in the back of her head so hard that it dazed her. "Do what you're told."

Addie had never touched the Victrola. She'd been under the impression that it was off-limits to her. She had no idea how to operate it and had seen Wavey do it only one time. Mr. Hayes had one at the orphan asylum, but none of the kids were allowed near it. She opened both doors wide, hoping to wake Mary. Sliding the phonograph from its sleeve, she placed it on the spindle and cranked the handle. Nothing.

"The break, you imbecile," Ty said.

Addie's eyes darted over the machine at several knobs and levers, unsure which one to touch. Someone moved behind her. She tensed, ducking her head down and bracing for another blow. But instead of a hard hand striking her, a smooth and delicate one reached across the machine and moved a lever toward the front of the cabinet. The phonograph record began turning. Wavey moved the big arm to the side, unfolded it, and placed the needle on the outside edge of the phonograph. Addie would have never figured all that out. After a few scratchy seconds, the music erupted from the front of the cabinet. Wavey swung the doors in, lowering the volume.

As Ty downed the rest of his drink in one gulp and closed his eyes, Addie moved toward her bedroom. "Don't be unsociable, sister." Ty slurred the word *sister* with venom. "Come sit with us."

Wavey gave her an apologetic look but said nothing. And did nothing. She wasn't the same sister who used to step in front of her, protecting her and taking the punishments. What happened to the sister who'd lashed out at the men when they'd taken her away to the orphan asylum? What had Ty done to her? Addie had felt safer at the orphan home, where she had to worry only about girls stealing her belongings or Wallace dropping his pants to shock her. The only men she'd had to watch out for were the farmers, and then they only touched you. You also had a chance of getting a good one, and even if you didn't, it was only during planting and harvesting seasons. Not the nightly threat of rape here in her sister's home. If not for Wavey and Mary, Addie would beg to go back.

Addie waited through the whole rendition of "Danny Boy," hoping Ty would fall asleep. He sat with his head back and eyes closed, his hands limp at his sides. He hadn't moved through the entire song.

With the final line, she glanced over at him. Still not moving.

A fuzzy, scratching sound came from the Victrola. Addie hurried to lift the needle, afraid it would wake Ty.

"Put on 'Don't Bite the Hand That's Feeding You,'" he said in a groggy voice.

Just as Addie placed the needle on the edge of the phonograph, she heard him get up. This time, she knew it was him behind her. She turned around to watch him stagger the last two steps toward her, his face sweaty and slack. "How about a dance, sister?" Again, the word *sister* sounded as if it left a bad taste in his mouth. "This is your song."

He reached for her waist with his thick arm, encircled her, and hugged her tight to his body, squeezing the breath from her. The two of them staggered around the living room in a grotesque and spinning dance. The muffled words from the Victrola drifted around them in circles. With one ear pressed tight to Ty's chest and the other muffled by his thick paw, the only words Addie picked up were *dream* and *starving* and *tyrant*. The first time Wavey spun into her vision, their eyes caught for a brief second. Wavey, still on the couch, had a look of dread on her face. The next time, Wavey had pushed herself up and was standing between the couch and the coffee table. Addie didn't know what Wavey planned, but she looked so little and insignificant. If only she had a weapon. A poker from the fireplace or Ty's gun. Would Wavey dare to get his gun? Addie wished for the Wavey she used to know. She wanted her wild-haired sister who'd do anything to save her. But the next time Ty spun her around, Wavey still stood in the same place, timid and pleading. As her mouth moved, Addie picked out "only" and "child."

"I'm dancing with my sister." Ty's words vibrated, thick and resonant, through his chest and into her ear. "She likes dancing with me, don't you, sister?"

Addie took the opportunity to fight back. Maybe she and Wavey could stop him together. Addie stomped the heel of her shoe onto Ty's foot. He didn't wince at all, but he did stop dancing. Anger flashed into his eyes, and in a snap, alert and no longer seeming drunk, he shoved Addie backward. As she fell, she saw him turn on Wavey. Before Addie could get back to her feet, Ty grabbed hold of Wavey's neck and threw her into the side table, just as the song ended. The crack of Wavey's head hitting the edge split the silence, and the dull scratching and scratching and scratching of the phonograph needle oscillated through the living room. Just as Wavey's body slumped to the floor, their mother's porcelain bowl slid off the table and cracked into pieces next to her. Ty's laborious breaths seemed to consume all the oxygen in the air. Addie, lightheaded and gasping, ran into her room for the scissors under her pillow. When she got back, she found Ty bending over Wavey's body as if he were about to scoop her up in his arms.

"Leave her alone," Addie screamed, running at Ty with her fist raised and the scissor points aimed at his back.

Ty turned just in time to grab her wrist. He twisted. Pain shot through her arm, and the scissors dropped from her feeble grasp, clanking onto the bare floor. Ty looked down at the open blades and smiled. "Didn't they teach you anything at the asylum, little sister?"

He lifted the scissors to her face. "Scissors are not a weapon." He knocked her to the floor, and with a knee on her back, he took a handful of Addie's hair. "They're for cutting."

With one cheek pressed into the cold wooden floor, she looked at Wavey surrounded by broken pieces of porcelain and felt the scissors ripping through her hair, handful after handful. Mary cried from her crib, but Ty ignored her, cutting and cutting as the needle scratched around and around. Addie finally heard the scissors drop to the ground, and Ty's weight lifted from her back. Mary's cries had become hysterical.

"Mary" was all that Addie could get out.

"I'm not done with you yet," Ty said, pulling her up by her waist. Her feet never touched the floor before he flung her onto the coffee table, facedown, pulling her skirt up and bloomers down.

"No," Addie cried. "Please, no."

"Girls who misbehave get a whipping."

She heard him unbuckle his belt and the swish of it moving through the loops of his trousers. Within seconds, she felt the first stinging lash on her bare skin. He struck her five times, but she refused to scream or cry out. Addie kept her eyes on Wavey, hoping she'd move. Praying she wasn't dead. The embroidery hoop with the red stitching lay on the floor, halfway under the coffee table. Ty finally stopped whipping her but kept her pinned her down with one arm. When he finally lifted it, he grabbed both sides of her hips and thrust himself into her from behind. She yelled once from the surprise and the pain. He mated with her like an animal. He was nothing more than an animal. When he finally finished, he left her naked and bent over the table as he scooped Wavey up in his arms.

"Is she alive?" Addie asked.

Ty didn't answer, but Wavey let out a groan before he disappeared down the hall and into their bedroom with her.

CHAPTER FOURTEEN
RUMOR

Friction is the enemy of all motion. The rougher the surface, the slower you go, and Mother was about as smooth as the cheese grater. Mother loved making things forbidden. *You may only have one cookie. No eating before supper. You may not go outside after dark. You are forbidden from seeing your papa. You may not speak to your aunt Addie. Stay away from the fair.* If Mother knew about Sal, he'd be forbidden too.

Rumor never cared much for any of the *forbidden* words, such as *prohibited, off limits, do not touch, no trespassing, stay off, stay away,* or *don't open until Christmas.* Nobody liked to be told they couldn't do something, especially not Rumor.

When Sal had prevented her from going into Zoro Gardens, she'd peeked in anyway. It seemed like a challenge. There were certain dangers associated with some challenges, but she was smart enough to know the difference. She wouldn't be dumb enough to go on the rocks at high tide or to drink a bottle of poison. But in her mind, most dangers were either minimal or imagined. Some people just liked putting limitations on others. They liked having the power to say "No, you cannot do that." They liked to decide what was good for someone else and then take away that person's right to decide for themselves. But there was no adventure in life if you did only what was safe and allowed.

Eve still ate the forbidden fruit. And obviously people didn't stay away from the Forbidden City or we wouldn't know anything about it. And what about forbidden treasure? Who could resist treasure, let alone forbidden treasure? If there were two doors and one said "Come On In" and the other said "Do Not Enter," it was only common sense that whatever lay behind the *do not enter* door would be much more exciting. There would probably be a schoolteacher or a pastor waiting behind the *come on in* door.

So with Mother now forbidding her to step "one single foot" in the Exposition or to have any contact "whatsoever" with her Aunt Addie, what was a girl to do?

The day was an unusually hot one for San Diego, more like you'd imagine the desert. But that was suiting. Most forbidden trips were taken across the desert anyway, like in *The Arabian Nights*, or across the sea, like in *Treasure Island*. They always included some sort of danger, although Rumor had no fear of a jinn or pirate, just of Mother—who could be a little bit of both.

Most of the guests at the Exposition waved fans in front of their faces and sipped cold drinks, moving listlessly down the avenues like some slow-motion picture show. As usual, men lined the wooden fence of Zoro Gardens, peeping through the knotholes free of charge, while streaks of sweat darkened their shirts down their spines and under their armpits. Cicadas buzzed like electric wires, and long lines of people waited their turn for an ice cream or Coca-Cola.

Trapped behind the glass of the ticket booth, Sal looked like a turkey roasting in an oven, all plucked and buttered up. His hair hung in wet clumps across his forehead, and his shirt gaped open, exposing his golden skin. He looked ready to be carved.

Rumor stepped up to the ticket window, but she wasn't prepared for Sal's look of displeasure.

"Adults only. Move on."

"Come on, Sal, don't be sore. I need your help."

"Of course you do. Why else would you be talking to me?"

"I'm over all that. I don't care about your . . ." Rumor didn't know which word to use; *incest* seemed rather insulting. ". . . heritage."

"My heritage?" Sal said.

"You know what I mean. Don't be such a baby. It just surprised me is all."

"I appreciate your ability to stomach my *heritage*," Sal said. "And not that it's any of your business, but I know what the chickens told you, and it's not the truth. My mother was raped by a neighbor boy. Her father disowned her because of it, but he never touched her."

Behind Rumor, a man coughed. She cringed, afraid to turn around, fearing the face of a police officer frowning down in displeasure at her choice of attractions. But when she stepped aside, a regular man, dressed in shirtsleeves and suspenders, slid his quarter under the glass window and disappeared into the garden, holding his ticket in his hand.

"Can you tell my aunt Addie that I'm here?"

"No can do." Sal crossed his arms over his chest. He'd rolled up his shirtsleeves, and Rumor noticed that his forearms were much more muscular than they'd seemed just days before.

"I'm sorry I judged you. There, does that make you feel any better?"

A laugh burst out of Sal, almost like a giant hiccup. "It's not because of that."

"She's still here, isn't she?"

"She's still here, but she doesn't want to see you. I don't know what you did. I've never known Addie to turn her back on anyone, but I got strict orders."

"It wasn't me; it was my mother."

"Sounds like Little Miss Royal Lineage has some skeletons in her own closet."

The clomping of horse hooves on pavement caused Rumor to turn around. A mounted police officer, probably cooking beneath his coat and not in a pleasant mood, headed straight for her.

"At least tell her I came by."

"I can do that," Sal said.

"Thank you," Rumor said, noticing the amused smile on his face before she dashed off toward a crowd of people gathered around a mariachi band. The trumpet sounded about as languid as the wilting crowd. The flags and banners hung limp in the scorching air, and gardeners moved from potted plant to potted plant, trying to revive them with their watering cans. Rumor headed toward the exit, praying she'd beat her mother home.

When Rumor opened the front door, she found Mother sprawled on the couch in her silk bathrobe. A sweaty glass of lemonade, probably spiked with something, stood on the end table. Mother turned her head toward Rumor, with her usual drunken glare. A cigarette dangled from two fingers, and cigarette butts, all with bloodred lipstick stains, filled the ashtray. Her robe had come untied, and the inside curve of one of Mother's bare breasts peeked out. "Where you been?"

Rumor took two steps toward her bedroom.

"You stay right there." Mother pushed herself up off the couch and staggered toward Rumor. Without her heels, Mother stood five foot five, a good inch shorter than Rumor. Face-to-face with Rumor, she breathed out stale smoke and booze-breath. "Who do you think you are?"

Rumor took a step back, but her mother grabbed hold of her arm.

"You been sneaking around that nudist colony? You been going behind my back?"

"No."

"Don't you dare lie to me." She let go of Rumor's arm and took a limp swipe at her face.

"You're drunk."

"Don't you talk to me like that." She took another swipe, lost her balance, and fell to the floor. She curled onto her side, with the cigarette still pinched between her fingers, and passed out.

Rumor plucked the cigarette from her mother's grasp and snubbed it into the ashtray before lifting her mother up by the arms. "Come on, let's get you to bed."

Rumor flopped her onto the bed sideways, then swung her dangling feet up with her. Tendrils of dark hair hung across Mother's cheek. Her face sagged into the bedspread, smearing her lipstick up into a foolish smile. Rumor smoothed the hair away from her mother's face before folding the other half of the bedspread over her.

CHAPTER FIFTEEN
ADDIE

Addie had never seen anything like it. Never before had she witnessed such a cross-section of humanity, all come to hear one preacher. The crowd resembled that at the horse races or Ringling Bros. and Barnum & Bailey. She wondered if President Roosevelt himself could draw such a crowd. They squeezed past cripples, sailors, drunks, a man with a grapefruit-sized goiter on his neck, old people, and tiny children perched upon the shoulders of their fathers. There were even a few of the midgets from the Midget Village, and Addie wondered how they'd ever be able see anything but the backsides of the people in front of them.

Word had it that Sister Aimee had arrived at the gates with a two-mile-long motorcade. All the bigwigs from the fair had greeted her at the west entrance and led her procession into the Exposition. Now the horde had washed into the open arms of the amphitheater, a giant lake of dirty, shifting, and roiling masses stretching all the way from the Plaza del Pacifico to the edge of the stage.

At first, Heinrich had forbidden Frieda and Addie from going to the revival. He said that he'd lost enough nudists to gospel shouters, who denounced them as sinners and wanted to save their souls.

According to Heinrich, evangelists were nothing but soapbox preachers who frightened people with damnation. They claimed to save people from sin, only to hop the next train out of town with pockets fat on the offering money.

Frieda had to work her magic with Heinrich, sidling up to him and caressing his chest with her cheek. "I want Addie to see her. We won't bring any money, and we promise not to be saved." She'd looked over at Addie. "You promise, don't you, Addie?"

"Cross my fingers and hope to die," Addie had told Heinrich.

Heinrich had protested, "What about the colony? We owe it to the customers to have our queen in the garden."

"It will be dead today. There are so many Christians at the fair for Sister Aimee, even the sinners will be too ashamed to approach the ticket booth."

Heinrich had reluctantly given his permission. And now Addie followed Frieda, hand in hand so they didn't get separated, weaving in and around people from all walks of life. Joe was somewhere in the crowd; maybe he'd already connived his way backstage with Sister Aimee, pretending to be a real preacher rather than a dropout. Heinrich probably wouldn't mind losing Joe to the gospel shouters. Since he'd joined the colony, he'd proven himself more trouble than he was worth—unless he really did have a trust fund. Frieda led Addie all the way to the front end of a colonnade. Two young college boys sat atop the short wall along the east arm of the amphitheater.

Frieda, putting on the theatrics, fanned herself with a pamphlet. "Oh my, I think I may faint from the heat," she said loud enough for the boys to hear.

One of the boys poked the other in the ribs. "Say, they sure look like two of those nudies."

The other nodded and spoke up. "You ladies are welcome to our seats."

Before Addie knew what happened, the boys had hopped down, and two strong arms scooped her up, plopping her on the edge of the wall, with Frieda right next to her.

"*Danke,*" Frieda said.

"You ladies look mighty familiar. Do you happen to work here in the fair?

The crowd shifted like one giant, rolling wave, pushing the boys closer, practically with their chests against Addie and Frieda's knees.

"Yes, we are nudists. Have you come by the garden?"

The taller boy, who had sandy hair and was wearing a straw boater, looked as if he was about to blush. The shorter one, the boy who'd spoken before, swept his Panama hat from his head and held it before his heart. "Well. Uhh. We . . . We haven't had the opportunity to enter."

"And yet you recognized us?"

The colony did have a pictorial guide of all the nudists and their philosophy. They may have seen their pictures there, but Addie suspected that these boys were more the *peephole in the fence* type.

"Let me see." Frieda created a circle with her index finger and thumb and held them out toward the eye of the shorter boy. "*Ja,* that eye is familiar. You ought to pay a quarter sometime and get the whole experience."

He blushed. "Yes, we will now, ma'am."

He looked as if he was about to start some lengthy explanation, when the organ came to life, piping "Onward, Christian Soldiers." The audience fell silent, and the boys turned their attention to the lines of white-robed vocalists who began marching down both sides of the colonnade toward the stage. One by one, the choir members settled themselves onto the risers. Addie figured there were at least two hundred of them. The organist changed songs and they filled the air with:

Holy, holy, holy, Lord God Almighty
Early in the morning our song shall rise to Thee.
Holy, holy, holy, merciful and mighty
God in three persons, blessed Trinity.

When the song ended, an undercurrent of electricity buzzed through the crowd, a silent anticipation like Addie had never witnessed. A fluttering of wings broke the silence as a flock of white doves flapped out of the great archway. Everyone's eyes followed them into the sky. The moment the last dove disappeared, Sister Aimee stepped onto the stage in a shimmering white satin robe. She cradled a bouquet of at least three dozen red roses, and a crimson cross hung across her breasts.

"She's stunning," Addie said to Frieda.

"*Ja*, she is imagined as the Greta Garbo of the Lord."

A woman from the first row of the choir stepped down and held her arms out, and Sister Aimee laid the roses across them. Then she raised her own hands up to heaven. "Oh, my beloved, I bring you a message tonight. It is a message directly from the Lord, our God." Sister Aimee's voice trembled. "I raise up my hands and cry out to all who are backsliding. All who have lost sight of the Lord. I have come to bring you back to our Father, back to the Prince of Peace, back onto the road to glory."

The audience chanted back, "Hallelujah."

"Praise the Lord."

"Amen."

"Ain't she something?" a man to the left of Addie said. And he had that look in his eye. The look she was ever so familiar with at the garden or she'd seen at Sally Rand's fan-dancing show, but never for a preacher.

"There is no darkness in faith," Sister Aimee continued. "There is everlasting light where the Lord dwells."

Long ago, Uncle Henry had taken Addie to a revival in a dirty tent with a sweaty half-drunk preacher condemning everyone, but it seemed as if Sister Aimee spoke from her soul, as if God channeled compassion through her. As if she were an angel of the Lord, an imperfect angel who had been forgiven by God. Even though she had sinned, He still gave her the grace to carry His word. Addie wondered how she had done it. Could Sister Aimee help her get forgiveness? Or was all of it nothing but a sham?

"It is only a show," Frieda whispered in her ear. "Do not get swept away in it."

Sister Aimee held her arms out, as if encompassing the entire audience. "Brothers and sisters, we are here at the world's fair, with all the gadgets of the future, but we dare not travel into that future without the faith and religion of our forefathers."

The crowd nodded and shouted, "Amen." It was the same crowd who had, just an hour prior, marveled at the technology of moving pictures, electric kitchen appliances, and a robot that smoked cigarettes and fired a gun. Addie silently chanted Frieda's words, *It's only a show. It's only a show.* But what if it wasn't?

"Everyone is searching for a cure to the ills of the modern world. We do not need Mussolini's fascism, Hitler's New Order, or Stalin's revolution. All we need is to return to the arms of our Father. We must return to the King of Kings."

"Amen, sister," voices cried out in response.

"Hallelujah."

"Praise the Lord, Jesus Christ."

"On a recent trip to the Orient, I had the opportunity to meet with an Indian statesman. I asked him if India would stop the suffering of its people and grant every one of them equal freedom. And do you know how he answered me? He asked me when the United States would recognize the equality of all its citizens—rich and poor, black and white, Indian and European."

Sister Aimee continued for nearly an hour, sharing stories of growing up on a Canadian farm and her mission trip to China, where she had lost her husband, and how the Lord had led her to the pulpit. She called for the salvation of drunkards, gamblers, womanizers, and lost souls. She denounced the teaching of evolution in the schools and called for them to teach Creation. All the while in the background, the choir chanted in a low murmur, singing "Shall We Gather at the River," "A Mighty Fortress Is Our God," and "At the Cross."

She didn't share any stories about her divorce and remarriage, her alleged kidnapping, the court battles, or the two men who'd died while searching for her in the waters off Venice Beach.

"Sinners, are you going to put off repentance until it's too late?"

The crowd began to squirm.

"Will you be ready when the great day comes? Are you ready?"

Several old ladies began babbling in tongues, sounding like witch doctors of some ancient aboriginal tribe.

Then louder, "Are you ready? If you are ready, please stand and come forward. Tonight, there's salvation with the Lord Jesus Christ. Rise and be baptized by the Holy Ghost."

A lady dropped to the ground, prostrate and trembling, mumbling, "Praise the Lord. Praise the Lord."

A timid man with disheveled hair and a wrinkled suit made his way forward, then a woman, and another, until the great mass of people churned and shifted, congregating into a channel of flesh flowing toward the altar, where Sister Aimee blessed them, one by one, to the shaking of tambourines and the chanting choir. Men and women clawed at Sister Aimee, reaching to touch her sleeve or the hem of her robe.

Addie slid down and moved toward the stream of moving flesh. Maybe just a touch. What would it feel like to be saved? To be forgiven? She took another step forward into the crowd, but a hand grabbed hold of her arm.

"*Nein,*" Frieda said. "You promised. Get saved another day, if that is where your heart lies."

Frieda led her away, pushing against the current of sinners on their way to salvation. Against the wave pulsing toward everlasting grace. The crowd was pressed shoulder to shoulder, holding each other up. Frieda and Addie broke through the back of the crowd and onto the Avenue of Palaces. Only a smattering of people roamed down the avenue, where flags hung in the heat without a trace of breeze to liven them. Addie noticed a line of ambulances parked along the Plaza del Pacifico. Attendants, dressed all in white, opened the back doors of the vehicles, pulling people out on stretchers and rolling them toward the amphitheater.

"Where are they taking them?" Addie asked.

"To be healed," Frieda said. "*Ach je*, do you see? That woman can cast a spell. I do not believe she cures the sick and crippled like they say, but she sure can work her magic with a crowd. That is what I greatly admire."

"I would've liked to have a word with her," Addie said.

"You will have your chance," Frieda said, winking at Addie. "She is coming to the garden for a cup of tea and a bit of publicity."

"How'd you get her to agree to that?"

"How could she decline? We have naked souls in need of salvation."

"Do you think she'll talk to me?"

"*Ja*, and maybe she'll baptize you in the nude. Just like a newborn babe. Wouldn't that make the headlines?"

Addie and Frieda squeezed through the back gate and into the garden. Everyone lazed in the shade, and just as Frieda had predicted, not a single customer stood on the ramps. The more Addie thought about it, the more she could imagine Sister Aimee visiting the garden. After all, Adam and Eve were nudists.

Once they'd made their way to the dressing room, Frieda pulled her dress over her head and kicked her shoes under the bench. Just like Addie, she hadn't worn stockings or a single undergarment. "Ah, my skin can finally breathe," she said as she stepped back into the garden.

Addie lowered herself onto the bench, staring at the cinder-block wall. She slid off one shoe, then the other, noticing Heinrich's Robert Louis Stevenson sign: "To Know What You Prefer, Instead of Humbly Saying Amen to What the World Tells You You Ought to Prefer, Is to Have Kept Your Soul Alive." She'd seen it so many times over the years, she rarely contemplated its message anymore. Was Sister Aimee's entire sermon telling the crowd what they ought to prefer? Didn't all preachers do that? When had Addie ever done what she preferred? Had she ever? Yes, she had when she'd decided to protect herself and Wavey from Ty, but that hadn't worked out so well. And she had when she'd run off from Aunt May and Uncle Henry's. Were either of those times an actual decision or only a reaction? What did she prefer? She wanted forgiveness, and she wanted a permanent home—preferably with Wavey and Mary and Rumor, but that didn't seem possible.

Addie turned toward the soft sound of bare feet on concrete to see Heinrich standing in the doorway. "What did you think of Sister Aimee? She is quite the enchantress. Do you agree?"

Addie nodded and lifted her dress over her head.

Heinrich sat down next to her. "Sister Aimee is as human as the rest of us. She has committed the very sins she rebukes. She is only a gifted performer."

It was more than a performance. Sister Aimee had conviction and passion and something that Addie couldn't describe. Something holy. But it wasn't Addie's place to disagree with Heinrich or to sell him on the idea of Sister Aimee's religion.

Addie stood up and hung her dress on one of the hooks. When she looked back at Heinrich, the thought came to her that he and Sister Aimee had been cut from the same cloth, so to speak. Heinrich believed in the beauty of living in nature and of shedding the clothes that represent status and materialism. He believed in fit and healthy bodies and of forgoing the sins of tobacco and alcohol. That was his religion. And that galvanized him as much as evangelism impassioned Sister Aimee.

"I've been thinking of my future," Addie said. "How long will you guarantee me a place at Sleepy Valley?"

It took Heinrich a moment to answer. Did he think she didn't know?

"Customers do not come to the colony to be surrounded by age. Not even the old ones. They come to feel fit and vigorous. They want to be surrounded by youth."

"What about Elsa?" Addie knew that wasn't a fair question. Elsa was his sister and had come from Germany with him to establish Sleepy Valley. And she ran the colony when they traveled.

Heinrich looked to the ground, almost like a shamed little boy.

"You're sending her away?"

Heinrich nodded. "Back to family. Germany has recovered from the Great War and there is finally peace and prosperity for the people."

"Does she want to go?"

"*Nein*, but she will go. She understands the objective of the colony."

"And you?"

"It is different for me. I'm a man."

Addie closed her eyes, not wanting to look at him. The inside of the dressing room was cold, the cement floor never given enough time to dry out between the nightly scrubbings with Clorox. Addie turned away from him, toward the garden and the sunlight.

"Whether you like it or not, there is a difference," he said to her back as she walked away. "An old man surrounded by beautiful young women is a picture of vitality. It is not the same for an old woman."

That was something Sister Aimee had been wrong about. We do not need to go back to the faith of our fathers.

341 Eucalyptus Street
San Diego, California
October 25, 1918

Everything had unraveled into one great and messy tangle—the world war, the flu, and daily peril at the hands of Tyrone Fulton Briggs. The city had all but shut down: no school, no church, no theater, no shopping. People roamed the streets in gauze masks, afraid of their own neighbors. Alive one moment and dead the next. It seemed as if God had decided to pluck the earth clean, the good with the bad. Addie prayed, begging God to protect her sister. How many hours had passed since Ty disappeared into the bedroom with Wavey? Was she alive? Would one more life make a difference to God?

Sometime during the night, as Mary slept and Addie lay awake staring into the darkness, everything had gone silent. The mockingbird had ceased calling, and not a single dog barked outside. There was nothing but the tick, tick, tick of the grandfather clock—measuring out all their lives. How many ticks did any of them have left? And who would decide that? It felt as if the entire city held its breath, wondering who would be next. Nobody was in control, were they? She had no power over the war or the influenza, but could she do something to help her sister? Wavey had always protected her. Maybe the time had come for Addie to repay that debt.

With the first glint of morning, when the hazy light gave shape to the objects in her room, a solution coalesced in her mind. Usually at that time, Addie heard Wavey packing a lunch for Ty. That morning, the kitchen was like everything else; there was nothing but silence. Addie tiptoed into the kitchen, putting on a pot of water to boil and dropping in two eggs. She wondered which of their chickens had laid them, half hoping it was Aunt Biddy; wouldn't that serve Ty right for debeaking her?

Ty liked his deviled eggs spicy with lots of crushed red pepper. Addie opened Wavey's cookbook, *A Thousand Ways to Please a Husband*, and flipped through the index. She found the recipe on page 38 in the chapter called "Celebrating the Fourth." That's what Ty needed. Some eggs with a bang. Still in bare feet, Addie stepped outside, across the grass, damp with morning dew, and plucked off two red flowers from one of the oleanders. Back in the kitchen, she opened her hand. The bruised flowers looked like clots of blood in her palm, reminding Addie of the roses Wavey was embroidering on her handkerchief. She chopped the oleander blooms to the size of red-pepper flakes, then sprinkled them in the bottom of a bowl. She added vinegar, mustard, melted butter, dried parsley, salt, and lots of Tabasco, just like Ty liked them. Once the eggs were hard boiled, she peeled them, cut them in half, scooped the firm yolks into the mixture, and mashed them with a fork. Looking down into her concoction, she began to worry, uncertain how toxic the oleanders were. Would they kill him?

Addie crept over to Ty and Wavey's bedroom door, being careful to avoid the squeaky floorboard, and put her ear to the door. When she didn't hear any movement, she slid open the left drawer of the sideboard and lifted out the key to the garden shed.

The inside of the shed smelled of wood and oil and gas. Ty's spades, hammers, hand trowels, and screwdrivers hung from nails pounded into the frame boards. Glass jars, partially filled with various shapes and sizes of nuts and bolts, lined a shelf above a tiny workbench. Another shelf held Ty's fishing tackle, a flashlight, and an old set of boxing gloves stuffed with newspaper. The lawn mower, with sharp rotating blades, leaned against one wall, splotched with oil and bits of dead grass. Addie circled around the clothes-washing machine, which Ty always kept protected under an old wool blanket, and made her way to the shelves along the back wall. High up, she found what she was looking for. A canister of "Rough on Rats." The image of a dead rodent, with the words "Don't Die in the House" across its body, curled around the can—feet up. And right under it, "Poison," in bloodred letters. She rotated the container until she saw the word "Arsenic." Addie slipped the can in her pocket and returned to the kitchen.

Addie peered down into her deadly mixture. Her heart pounded. She could dump it all into the trash bin and go back to bed. She could pack a bag and leave. But where would she go? Even the YWCA would be quarantined. And even if she could find a place to stay, what would happen to Wavey and Mary? Addie stared at Ty and Wavey's bedroom door. Behind it lived a monster.

Addie remembered lying in bed at the orphan asylum. When the lights were out and Miss Engels's footsteps had faded away, Harriet would frighten them all with eerie nursery rhymes. She could still hear Harriet's creepy singsong voice chanting, *And when the door begins to crack, it's like a stick across your back. And when your heart begins to bleed, you're dead, and dead, and dead indeed.*

Addie popped the lid off the poison. A grayish-white powder filled half the can. She wondered how many rats, mice, or gophers Ty had killed with the other half. Spooning out a quarter teaspoon of power, she sprinkled it into the yellow mixture and stirred until it disappeared into the creamy batter. It looked so smooth and innocuous. Could it be that easy? A true home remedy? She scooped the batter into the empty egg whites, then put the halves together and wrapped them in tissue paper. They looked like two little torpedoes in the bottom of Ty's lunch pail. She wrapped a thick piece of ham in another square of tissue and covered the eggs.

With Ty's lunch pail packed and on the sideboard where Wavey always left it, and the key in exact same spot in the drawer, Addie tiptoed into her bedroom. Mary stirred in her sleep, letting out a tiny whimper. Addie wondered if babies had nightmares, and if they did, what kind of monsters filled them. She lifted Mary from her crib and crawled into bed with her niece cradled against her and finally fell asleep.

CHAPTER SIXTEEN
RUMOR

When Rumor opened the door to get the milk bottle, she noticed Mr. and Mrs. Parker coming out of their bungalow. Mrs. Parker hugged a table lamp and an armload of linens, and Mr. Parker cradled a stack of pots and dishes. They carried them straight into Mrs. Keegan's apartment. Kaiser Pitt must've had a change of heart and let them get their things.

"You need some help?" Rumor called when they emerged from Mrs. Keegan's.

"Yes, bless your heart," Mrs. Parker said.

And Mr. Parker added, "You're a saint, just like your mother."

Rumor didn't think that yelling at Kaiser Pitt was very saintlike, especially since her mother seemed to enjoy putting people in their place, but it must have helped.

"I can't believe she paid our back rent so we could at least get our belongings," Mr. Parker said.

Mrs. Parker stepped up behind him and whispered in his ear.

Mr. Parker shrugged and whispered a bit too loud, "Can't unsay it now."

How did Mother always seem to get her bony, manicured hands on money? Rumor followed the Parkers back into their old bungalow. Nothing was boxed or wrapped as you'd expect for a move, but since it was only to the next bungalow, that was understandable. Nails stuck out of the wall, with framed pictures on the floor beneath them.

"You okay?" Mrs. Parker asked Rumor.

What could Rumor say? She was glad the Parkers were able to get their belongings and couldn't begrudge them. But as she made her way back and forth, she couldn't imagine where her mother had gotten the money. She pictured Papa Jack—fixing radios, pulling coins from behind children's ears, and making seashells disappear with his sleight of hand—reduced to begging for money at the amusement center. He could've used Mother's money. What had the Parkers ever done for Mother? Papa had been her husband. The father of her children. But she had no trouble leaving him out in the cold.

A strong offshore breeze tousled the tops of the palm trees, but the bungalows sheltered the courtyard, and only a mild breeze drifted through. Rumor kept glancing toward her bungalow, wondering if Mother and Mary were awake and aware that she was helping but too lazy to come out themselves.

Rumor and the Parkers made a dozen trips back and forth, moving items like a line of worker ants until every crumb had been transferred to their new nest, stacked into piles in Mrs. Keegan's guest room.

When Rumor returned to her bungalow, finally able to make herself some breakfast, there sat Mother in her silk robe and fluffy slippers, smoking a cigarette and sipping her coffee like the Queen of Sheba herself. Rumor bit her tongue, knowing that even if she asked about the money, Mother would only tell her to mind her own business.

"Make me a couple of eggs, will you?" Mother said. "Over easy."

"By all means," Rumor said, pulling the butter from their refrigerator, fully stocked with butter and eggs, milk and leftover meat loaf, lettuce, carrots, onions, fresh parsley, apricots, plums, and two bundles wrapped in butcher paper—one with "Broiler 75¢" written across it and the other with "Loin Chops $1.12."

"You got something to say to me?" Mother asked, taking a long draw on her cigarette and eyeing Rumor.

"Nope. Not a word." Rumor sliced off a pat of butter and dropped it sizzling into the overly hot pan, where it burned, turning brown before she had a chance to crack Mother's eggs into it.

Mary sat on the edge of the couch, painting her toenails with a brand-new bottle of clear polish.

"Mother'll slaughter you for putting your feet on the table," Rumor said.

"*Slaughter* is a bit overreactionary, darling. Besides, she's not home."

Footsteps sounded outside on the stoop, causing Mary to drop her feet, but they were followed by the lifting of the mail slot and the mail sliding in and dropping to the floor.

"When's Mother supposed to be home?" Rumor asked.

"Who knows." Mary refocused on the tiny brush, gliding it over her big toenail.

Rumor gathered up the mail, noticing a bill from the electric company and the mysterious letter Mother received every single month. It always had her name and address typed on the front by a typewriter with an off-center *V* and no return address. Mother always whisked it away, never opening it in front of them. One time, Rumor had asked Mother who it was from, and the answer was her typical *None of your business.*

Rumor held it up to the window and saw only a dark rectangle of paper inside. Nancy Drew would steam it open. Rumor easily snuck the letter past Mary and slid it behind the bread box as she put a pot of water onto the stove.

"What time did you say Mother would be home?" Rumor asked.

"Don't be obstinate, darling. I already told you I didn't know."

Rumor went around the house, making sure that every window was open, hoping to hear the tapping of Mother's heels on the pavement or walkway. She wished she could rig up some sort of a trip wire attached to a bell, but then anyone in the courtyard would set it off. Too bad she couldn't attach a bell to Mother, just like people did to their cats in order to protect the innocent little birds.

"Something's steaming on the stove," Mary called from the living room.

Clouds of steam rolled up from the pot. Rumor positioned her body between the pot and Mary's prying eyes before she slid the letter out from behind the bread box. Mother would kill her, well, not quite kill, but severely maim her if she caught Rumor opening the mail. But curiosity got the better of her. If Mother wouldn't be so secretive, she wouldn't be forced to such methods of sleuthing. Rumor passed it over the steam, then slid a fingernail under the edge. She felt a slight tearing of paper fibers, so she returned it to the steam. It didn't seem like such a lengthy process when Nancy Drew did it. Rumor glanced back at Mary, intent on her second coat of polish, before testing the seal again. It felt gummy enough to lift the flap. Inside lay a cashier's check from the Bank of America made out to Wavey Donnelly for the sum of fifty dollars.

"What're you cooking?" Mary asked.

Rumor slid the check back into the envelope and tried to seal it, but it wouldn't stick, all water-warped and rumpled. She brought it into her bedroom and tacked it down with school glue. Afterward, she tossed it on the counter with the electric bill, covering both of them with the phone book and hoping it would dry flat before Mother returned home.

"Why are you boiling water?"

"I was going to cook some macaroni, but I changed my mind," Rumor said, dumping the steaming water down the sink.

Fifty dollars? Who would send Mother fifty dollars every month? That explained the Kelvinator, the food, and the bungalow, but it created many more questions than it answered.

Sometimes it's the lack of noise that jolts you awake in the middle of the night, like the sound of the front door closing without the tap, tap, tap of Mother's heels on the floorboards. Or their bedroom door remaining closed, not opening for Mother to stagger in and plant her greasy kisses on their foreheads.

"Wake up," Rumor whispered, shaking Mary's shoulder.

She opened her eyes in that befuddled, half-awake, half-asleep way she had. "What's wrong?"

"Someone came in, but I don't know if it's Mother."

"Who else would it be?"

"I didn't hear her footsteps."

Mary pulled the covers up to her chin.

"And she didn't come in to kiss us." Rumor slid her legs over the side of the bed, knelt down on the floor, and pulled the butcher knife from between the mattresses. "It's probably her, but I need to check."

"Holy cow!" Mary said. "Where'd that come from?"

"Well, I sure can't depend on you to protect us." Rumor tiptoed to the door, pausing on each of the floorboards that squeaked. She put her ear against the door. Nothing. The glass knob felt cold in her hand as she slowly turned it and pulled the door open. Someone was breathing on the couch, deep and rhythmic.

"Do you see anything?" Mary whispered from the bed.

Rumor turned toward her. "Shhh."

Rumor stepped past the threshold of their bedroom door, just enough to get a peek at the couch. Someone was there. When they were little, she and Mary used to hide in the closet when they were scared. She remembered hours of crouching behind the clothes, shifting the shoes out from beneath them. They used to fall asleep, huddled together, breathing in the dust and smell of leather and mothballs. Maybe that hadn't been such a bad idea.

Rumor took another step toward the figure. It had to be their mother. Who would break into a house to sleep on the couch? On second thought, a hobo might. Or a bum needing a warm spot. She reached over with her knife pointed at the figure and clicked on the lamp. Mother lay passed out on her back with one leg on the couch and the other still on the floor. One of her arms dangled off the edge, with the straps of her shoes barely hanging over her slack fingers. Mother wore her new lilac dress, already ruined with a dark stain between her breasts. Her hat had slipped down and covered one eye, and her lipstick extended beyond the lines of her lips, making them look swollen.

Mary peeked out of the room.

"It's Mother," Rumor said. "Drunk again."

"It's all your fault, darling," Mary said. "You need to stay away from that nudist colony."

"What?"

Mary stepped into the living room in her new turquoise kimono. Her paychecks had been transmogrifying her, more and more each week, into a harlot—just like Mother. "Mother's gone off the deep end ever since Aunt Addie showed up and you started sneaking over to that nudist colony."

"You're blaming me?"

Mary didn't answer, she just straightened her shoulders and gave Rumor one of her *holier than thou* looks.

"It's not me. It's her own guilt over what she did to Aunt Addie."

"She's our mother. 'Honor your father *AND* your mother.' You're so obstinate."

"Look at our life, Mary. Mother doesn't know what she's doing. She divorced Papa. She's hardly ever home, and when she is, she's either drunk or hungover. She can't even bear to step foot into a church. And don't you ever wonder where all our money comes from?" Rumor advanced on Mary, backing her against the wall. "She's probably a prostitute."

As soon as the word *prostitute* slipped out, Rumor knew it wasn't that. Prostitution was more of a cash, *pay as you go* type of transaction, not a *check in the mail* type. "Or a blackmailer."

Before Rumor could get another word out, Mary slapped her across the face. Mary had never before been violent with her. Rumor grabbed a handful of Mary's hair. "Don't you ever slap me again."

"Ouch! Let go," Mary said. "You're ruining our lives. Everything was fine until you brought home that lewd postcard. And you're the one who keeps encouraging Aunt Addie. She's just like a stray dog, and you keep feeding her."

Rumor pulled, making Mary's head tip to the left. "Mother is ruining our lives. She pushes everyone away."

Mary let out a cry, then said, "She must have a reason."

"Oh yeah? And what was her reason for throwing Papa Jack out?" Rumor let go of Mary's hair and grabbed hold of her floppy kimono sleeve, plunging the knife clear through the fake silk.

Mary gasped.

"If you think Mother's all that honorable, then you take care of her."

"You're a brute," Mary said, fingering the wound in her kimono.

Rumor walked into their bedroom, but before closing the door, she held up the butcher knife. "And stay out or I'll slash up the rest of your clothes."

***

The best pastors hollered and turned red in the face, just like this one from the Bayside Church of God. He did a lot of finger pointing and asking the congregation for hallelujahs. His voice boomed, resonating within the walls of the church. Rumor felt as if she were inside a drum. "Spiritual darkness is black with sin. It corrupts the mind and binds its victims in the chains of vice and sexual depravity."

Mary had struck a pose with her hands in her lap, looking as if she were so virtuous that she didn't have a single worry in her head; as if had she died at that moment, Jesus himself would personally escort her right up from the wooden pew and through the pearly gates. Especially now that she was a victim—a kimono martyr. Either that, or she was imagining herself on a movie set and focusing on her role as the faithful parishioner. *Interior—First Lutheran Church. Midmorning light from stained-glass window illuminating the heroine, who sits with angelic look and hands serenely in lap, gazing off, unaware of her surroundings, as if she were in direct communication with God himself.*

The pastor raised a rigid finger toward the ceiling. "If we truly perceive the light of Christ, we will discover our mission in this world to be nothing else than to share that light with those around us. We have here, in the heart of our city, a world's fair. The fair brings wondrous things from around the world, but it also brings vice. I call on you to rise up against it and to show the city and its visitors the glorious light of God. We are directed to bring them out of the darkness of lewd behavior and into the light and forgiveness of the Lord. We must drive out the wicked. Close down that nudist colony and the Ballyhoo and drive them from our city. Purge the filth."

The pastor spit out his words as if he were firing them from a machine gun, spraying the congregation and hoping some of them would lodge into the people and fester. Filth? Aunt Addie wasn't filth. Was she? Wouldn't it show on her face or in her words? Why hadn't

Rumor noticed? And what about Sal? Was there something she missed that everyone else could see?

Rumor pictured the church members all marching down to the fair and driving out the nudists, descending into the garden and shooing them out by swatting them with their Bibles. And what about the prostitutes? Did they even know there were prostitutes peddling their bodies in the back of the camp? Or did they only care about the nudist colony because it was visible and they thought they needed to stand against it? Were they the same? And who was to judge?

"Let's go," Rumor whispered to Mary.

Mary gave her a confused look.

"I'm not feeling well." Rumor slipped out of the pew and tiptoed toward the gigantic door that had seemed so wide and welcoming when they'd entered.

Sitting in that church, Rumor had felt like yelling out the rhymes she used to chant at playground bullies: *I am rubber and you are glue, whatever you say bounces off me and sticks to you* or *Sticks and stones may break my bones, but names will never hurt me.* She'd thought those times were well behind her, but adults seemed to be just as vicious when mocking and condemning others. Mother, Mary, the papers, the churches—they all did it. Was there something in Aunt Addie she didn't see? Or Sal? Her mother was fully clothed, but she was a drunk. Kaiser Pitt wore clothes, but kicked people out of their homes. The pastor cast his judgment on Aunt Addie, Sal, and the entire colony, even though he had never met them. The pastor's words, just like glue, stuck with her during the entire trip on the streetcar. Was she lost in spiritual darkness since she did not see Aunt Addie as filth? Visions of looking through the knothole at the naked women in Zoro Gardens played over and over in her mind along with Mary's words that she was to blame for Mother's drinking. Was she such a sinner that she couldn't recognize it in others? What had caused her to open her mother's mail and stab Mary's kimono? And what about the tingling feelings she had around Sal?

Without waiting for the streetcar to come to a complete stop at the amusement center, Rumor made her way toward the door, balancing and anticipating the movements. Papa had always told her that she had good sea legs. Mary, on the other hand, would have staggered forward like a drunk, eventually falling flat on her rear or in the lap of a stranger, so she stayed put until the streetcar had come to a complete stop.

Papa Jack's spot next to Rosa was vacant again. Nothing but cement and sand and a few cigarette butts. Now that Papa had his radio-fixing business, he seemed to have taken a break from his magic tricks. Rumor missed seeing him in his striped vest, squatting on a crate with his knees jutting out to the sides.

A strong sea breeze had washed away all the clouds, leaving a faded blue sky. Red-and-white beach tents flapped in the wind as children with buckets and shovels built castles and dug forts in the sand. People in suits, dresses, sailor uniforms, and bathing suits lingered near the seawall, either gazing out to sea or watching the other people stroll by on Ocean Walk. They all seemed happy and content, not a bit worried if they were sinners or trapped in spiritual darkness. They couldn't all be good people. They had to have secret sins. The rumble of the roller coaster and screams of the gulls echoed along the beach just as they had before the fair and Aunt Addie had come to town. They had been there before Papa Jack had been kicked out. Before Mary got a job and began acting so much better than her. The same rumbling and screaming that had been there since she was a child. A constant, just like the ocean and the night sky. Some of the few things that had ever stayed the same.

Papa Jack's garage doors stood wide open, giving everyone a full glimpse of how he lived—always tinkering at his workbench and sleeping in a wooden box on nothing but a cot. A brief look of confusion moved across his face when he saw them. "Is it that late already? Sorry I wasn't at the station."

"We managed," Rumor said.

"Mrs. Bailey has a treat for you," he said. "Go on and I'll be there in two shakes of a lamb's tail."

Rumor had never seen a lamb shake its tail, but she imagined it didn't take much longer than a dog. Mary knocked on the wooden frame of Mrs. Bailey's screen door.

"Come on in, girls," she called.

Rumor and Mary took turns using the whisk broom that hung on a hook by the back steps, brushing the sand off their shoes before going in. The screen door squeaked as the spring stretched out, then banged shut behind them.

Mrs. Bailey pushed herself up from a chair at her kitchen table. She wore a pink housedress, and a scarf covered her white hair. "I made a spice cake with maple frosting this morning," she said. "Have a seat."

Rumor and Mary sat down at the table as Mrs. Bailey shuffled around, getting plates and forks and cups.

"You want help?" Rumor asked.

"No, no. You sit."

"Where'd the other half of your cake go?" Rumor asked.

"Oh, you know poor little Ruby Anne, who's always clinging to your Papa? I sent it home with her. Her family's been struggling ever since the accident at the cannery," she said. "Poor thing has attached herself to Jack ever since her father's been bedridden."

Mrs. Bailey put two cups and a bottle of milk on the table, then shuffled back for the plates. "Some of the neighbors don't think it's right, though, being that your Papa lives alone, but I keep telling them that he's just got a soft spot for children."

He did. Ever since Rumor could remember, he liked entertaining children, and they had always been drawn to him, waving and smiling at his silly faces.

"Are you spoiling my girls?" Papa's voice sounded through the screen door.

"You have the loveliest girls, Jack," Mrs. Bailey said.

"Yes, I know, but don't go telling them that too much, or it'll go to their heads."

"Would you like a cup of coffee?"

"No, thanks. It's such a beautiful day, I think we'll go for a walk on the beach. Would you like to join us? The air will do you good."

"Oh no, you don't need an old woman slowing you down. You all go on now and enjoy yourselves."

When they reached Ocean Walk, the tide was out and the waves rolled in, slow and smooth. Rumor sat down on the beach-access steps and unbuckled her shoes. Papa and Mary did the same. Sand flies swarmed in the decaying wracks of kelp, and little stars of bird tracks crisscrossed the sand.

They made their way to the tide line, where it was easier to walk. Mary lagged behind, looking for seashells.

Papa took Rumor's hand. "You hear about that woman pilot who landed at Lindbergh Field, setting a world record?"

"No."

"She flew upside down all the way from Agua Caliente, Mexico, to San Diego. She's the first person to fly upside down over an international border."

Rumor looked up, wondering if there were any women in the sky at that moment, and thought since women could fly, they could surely go to sea.

"The paper said that when she landed, she was covered in engine oil, looking not very ladylike. A reporter asked her how she got so brave, and do you know what she said?" Papa let out a chuckle. "She said she didn't know, because she got dizzy on a stepladder. Can you imagine?"

Rumor tried to picture the woman splattered in oil and surrounded by the press. What did it take for a woman to not only fly but to break a world record? Did she have to fight against people telling her that it wasn't ladylike or against the church? That a woman's place was behind her husband and she was master of nothing but her own home? Did some consider her a sinner too?

"You seem awfully lost in thought today," Papa said.

Papa's hand always felt dry and calloused. A man's hand. She looked back at Mary, who was bending down to explore something on the shore. "Do you think I'll go to hell?" she asked.

"Where'd that come from?"

"The pastor at church this morning talked about spiritual darkness. I don't always tell the truth, and . . ." Rumor paused, not sure she wanted to explain.

Papa didn't say anything, waiting for her to go on. That was something Rumor loved about Papa Jack. He never pushed her and never jumped to any conclusions. Whatever she told him, he wouldn't be angry and he'd always love her. Rumor looked down at the damp sand, at the little air bubbles that erupted after the tide slid away. "When Mary and I went to the Exposition, I looked into a peephole and saw in the nudist colony. I saw naked ladies."

Papa looked perplexed for a minute, pinching his eyebrows together in thought before he answered. "Well, curiosity can get the best of most people."

"I wasn't curious. I wanted to show somebody up. There was this fella that worked there who gave Mary and me a bad time, telling us that we were little girls, so I walked over and looked in."

Papa smiled and shook his head. "Yep, that sounds like my Rumor. A bit strong-headed, but not a sinner." He put his arm around her. "Don't worry about it."

"And—" Rumor started to say.

"There's more? Seems like you've been doing quite a bit of contemplating."

"Mary says that I'm causing Mother to drink."

He stopped walking. "Is she drinking a lot?"

Rumor nodded her head. "It's gotten worse ever since her sister came to town."

Mary ran up to them. "Look, I found a full sand dollar," she said, breaking the edges and chipping it to pieces with her fingernail.

"You're ruining it," Rumor said.

"You have to break it to get the doves," Mary said as she picked out the tiny white pieces. "They're God's promise."

"Actually," Rumor said, "they're the sand dollar's teeth."

Mary opened her purse and tipped her hand, letting the doves slide into the dark abyss before she ran off down the beach in search of more.

When Papa still lived with them, they'd return home from their trips to the beach all windblown and sticky with salt and sand and with treasures from the sea in the bottom of their buckets. Rumor still had some of the shadow boxes Papa had made for them, where they'd created their own underwater scenes with sea grass, algae, and shells. Rumor used to dry out the kelp floats in the sun until they shrank, looking like pointy little fish with wavy fins.

Once Mary had flittered out of earshot, Rumor continued, "Why does Mother have so much money?"

"Don't know. She's always been good at saving."

"Do you send her money every month?"

"I wish I could."

"Someone does. She gets an envelope in the mail every month. Her name's typed with the *V* raised higher than the rest of the letters. And there's money inside."

He looked puzzled. "Beats me. She's gotten that envelope ever since the day I married her. I had no idea there was money in it. How do you know there's money?"

Rumor knew better than to tell him about her detective work. He would not condone that. "I saw her open it one time. It's a bank check for fifty dollars."

"Fifty dollars?" he asked. "After all those . . . fifty dollars?"

Papa seemed to no longer be talking to Rumor. He gazed out to the sea as if puzzling something out.

"You okay, Papa?"

"Huh?" He looked over at Rumor as if she'd just appeared at his side. "Oh, yes. I need to get back now." He whistled to Mary and waved her in before turning away from the ocean and back toward his garage.

"We're going in already?" Mary asked when she caught up to them.

"Yep. I need to get some work done," Papa said, walking off. "You girls go on and enjoy the beautiful day. I'll see you next week."

"What did you say to him?" Mary asked.

"Nothing."

"Then why's he so upset?"

Rumor shrugged and turned her back to Mary. She didn't need any more of her accusations.

That night, Rumor sat on the courtyard steps, gazing out at all the battleships and destroyers in the harbor, packed in as tight as a can of sardines. By the twinkle of their deck lights, it was hard to imagine they were war machines, capable of so much death and destruction. She wondered how many tons of explosives floated just downhill from their bungalow.

Orion was just rising above the horizon, with his club and shield raised. Perseus, with his sword and clutching the head of Medusa, rose in the north. Why was everything armed and poised for battle? Everything seemed on the verge of attack. Even the church members who wanted to chase out the nudists. Why couldn't people just let others live their own lives without judging them? It seemed as if everyone wanted to shape the entire world around their own values. Even the battleships out there had to be armed and ready to defend the country from others with different ideas.

The pastor's words came back to her again. What was sin anyway? Murder is sin, but men are sent to war. Being proud is a sin, but people still seek power and money. Lust is a sin, but men go to girly shows and the city doesn't close them down. Addictive behaviors are sins, but her mother got drunk. Judging others is a sin, but the church condemns people. Papa had said that she wasn't a sinner, that she was just curious, but she knew the pastor didn't see it that way. Were they all sinners? Heaven must be an empty place if even thinking a thought made you a sinner.

CHAPTER SEVENTEEN
ADDIE

The second Fleet Week began two days after Sister Aimee and her entourage had headed back to Los Angeles. Thirty thousand enlisted men and officers descended upon the Exposition—all heading straight toward Zoro Gardens, the midway with its bawdy exhibitions, carnival rides, and shooting galleries, or the Ballyhoo and its girlie shows. Heinrich strutted around the garden, confident that he'd double the profits he'd lost while Sister Aimee graced the Exposition.

Addie found Frieda in the garden getting ready for the gates to open. She made her way down a line of cowhide rugs draped over the railings, beating the dust out with a stick. "I'm sorry about Sister Aimee," Addie said.

Frieda shrugged and whacked a cowhide. "I'm sorry you didn't get your baptism."

The newspaper had referred to it as the evangelist-nudist controversy and the last headline read: "Queen of Zoro Gardens Shunned by Aimee Semple McPherson." On the morning of the meeting, reporters had lined the viewing ramps, ready with their pens and cameras to capture the evangelist and the nudist clasping hands. But as the afternoon wore on and they'd smoked all their cigarettes, they'd wandered off one by one.

"The funny thing," Frieda said, "is that the papers say I was shunned."

Addie followed her. The row of hides looked like an emaciated herd of cows heading up the ramp. She hit the next one, sending little particles of dust into the air.

"I wasn't shunned. Sister Aimee didn't want others to see how much she and I are alike. We are more like sisters than enemies. Casting judgment is easy, but seeing yourself in another is not. We have both shed our traditional roles as women. Neither of us is satisfied to be . . ." Frieda furrowed her eyebrows, searching for the term. "Domestic prisoners. That's it, domestic prisoners."

A few of the girls emerged from the dressing room, naked and goose pimpled from the morning chill. They huddled around the campfire, seeking warmth, while Addie shivered by Frieda's side.

"The bluestockings will never understand." A hollow thwack sounded with each of Frieda's blows. "But Sister Aimee does, and that scares her. She and I have both taken the sexual, how do you say it, exploi—?"

"Exploitation?"

"*Ja*, exploitation of women and used it to our advantage. Look at how the men idolize her—with unholy thoughts, I'm sure. And the women long to touch her robes."

They moved to the next hide.

"Sister Aimee Semple McPherson and I are both naked and sexual women. She just leaves more to the imagination than I do."

Heinrich strode across the exercise grounds. "Five minutes," he called. "The gates will open in five minutes."

"Lend me a hand," Frieda said to Addie, pulling down a hide and handing it to her. "Women shouldn't condemn and judge each other. Aren't we all just trying to find our way?"

Wrestling with the weight of the hide, Addie followed Frieda toward the other girls. Frieda's smooth leg muscles flexed and relaxed in rhythm with her steps. She was right. Women needed to stick together, but they rarely did. She and Wavey hadn't.

Within minutes of the gates opening, hordes of sailors in dark blue uniforms with white caps packed the ramps. The word was that the line extended clear down the Avenue of Palaces, keeping mounted policemen busy quelling the pushing and shoving, even breaking up a few fistfights.

Addie settled behind Lucille, combing and braiding her hair, trying to pretend all the shouts and calls from the sailors had nothing to do with her. All of a sudden, a high-pitched scream pierced the air. Giselle, Yvette, and Ida scattered across the garden. A thick spray of water hit Giselle in the back. Male laughter and cheers rose from the crowd of men as she scrambled behind a bush. A single sailor stood braced and aiming a hose into the garden, rousing the mass of uniformed men behind him. He shot at Frieda's canvas, soaking it and causing Frieda to duck behind the trunk of a tree. Yvette ran in circles, her boobs making the show the sailors wanted. She dropped to the ground and pulled a drenched cowhide over her. Plants and flowers waved frenziedly as the sailor cleared the patio of sunbathing nudists. Water dripped from branches and soaked the ground, creating an artificial rainstorm in the garden.

The sailor pivoted and aimed the hose toward Addie and Lucille. "Run" was all she could say as she grabbed Lucille's hand and hid behind a eucalyptus tree . . .

"Come on, be a sport," the sailor called. "Here, kitty, kitty, kitty." His cap and kerchief were cocked to the side, and he laughed like a mischievous boy.

The two officers tried to reach the sailor, but the wall of men shifted, blocking them.

"Come on, ladies, let's see a little hoochie coochie."

Across the garden, Joe and Lilly stood steady, with arrows drawn tight in their bows and aimed at the men. All that held the sailors out of the garden was the single rail along the viewing platforms. The stockade fence swayed from the force of the line of men outside, lifting themselves in chin-ups to see what had caused all the commotion. It looked as if it would collapse at any moment, letting in a flood of excited sailors.

Heinrich planted himself between the mob and the nudists, but one man in a leopard loincloth against a whole horde of sailors didn't seem like much protection.

"We could make a run for the dressing room," Addie said to Lucille as the hose swept around, dousing the garden.

Lucille nodded. "Let's go."

But before they could start, Frieda sauntered out from behind one of the palm trunks, stopping in the middle of the sunbathing patio and holding her arms out as if saying *go ahead and shoot*. The stream of water caught her full on. A huge roar went up both inside and outside the garden. Daisy emerged from behind a plant and joined her. The two of them linked arms, sharing the spray. The foliage came alive as nude women emerged like forest creatures coming out of hiding. They made their way to Frieda and Daisy, linking arms into a long fleshy chain. Yvette crawled out from beneath the soaked hide.

"Might as well," Addie said, trying to wiggle her hand from Lucille's grasp, but she squeezed tighter.

"I'm with you."

Like a nude chorus line, they all joined arms, facing the hooting, whistling, and screaming men.

"Come on now, hoochie coochie."

A sailor jumped the railing, and an arrow whizzed past Addie, embedding itself into a tree just inches from his head. He froze, but several more sailors climbed over the rails. The water hit Addie with a cold shock. The mass of men moved forward, surging into the garden. Addie braced herself, not knowing what would happen but holding tight to Clara and Lucille. Heinrich's bare back and flailing arms stood out against the sea of blue-and-white uniforms, swinging and trying to fight them back. Just before the men reached the women, the gates swung open, whistles screeched, and three gunshots rang out. A line of military police ran in, circling the men and containing them. The men ebbed back, pushed by the MPs. The sailor with the hose lay facedown with the knees of one of the MPs pressed into his back. They handcuffed him and cleared the garden. Heinrich locked the gate.

Once the latch sounded behind the mass of men, Clara and Lucille relaxed their grip. Addie looked down the line at all the beautiful water-soaked women. A high-pitched crescendo of nervous laughter escaped until *"Nein!"* Heinrich boomed, livid, with blood dripping from his nose. "Next time, you run!"

One of the MPs had stayed behind. "Is everyone okay?"

"We will close the garden if the sailors cannot be controlled," Heinrich said, the veins in his neck pulsing and tight.

"We'll take care of it."

"See that you do." Heinrich stormed off toward the dressing room, cursing someone or something in German.

Sal rushed in, gripping the handle of the first-aid kit. Addie looked around; most of them had nothing worse than the shivers and sopping-wet hair.

Joe seized the moment, especially with Heinrich out of sight, standing up before them in his leopard skin with his arms raised above the sodden group. "Repent and let every one of you be baptized in the name of Jesus Christ for the remission of sins, and you shall receive the gift of the Holy Spirit. Be saved from this perverse generation."

Giggles were the only response Joe received from his flock.

"A wedding ring is an outward sign that a person is married. A military uniform is an outward sign that a person is involved in that particular branch of service. Similarly, water baptism is a symbol designed by God to identify a person as a disciple of Jesus Christ. Let us shrug away our sins as easily as we slip out of our clothes."

A deep cough from above made Addie look up toward the upper terrace by the dressing rooms, but instead of God glaring down at their rebellious impostor of a pastor, it was Heinrich. Joe ran off in the opposite direction, finishing his blessing on the run. "And those who gladly receive his word are baptized."

Addie felt a cold hand on her shoulder and turned to see Frieda. "You got your baptism after all."

"Yes, I did," Addie said, smiling.

Maybe being hosed by a sailor and blessed by a divinity-school dropout was the best she deserved anyway.

Addie never got the chill from the hosing out of her bones. She'd lain all afternoon on one of the damp cowhides, trying to absorb any warmth from the sun, but it never appeared through the overcast sky. She'd felt like rolling herself up like a blintz in the cowhide, with only her head popping out the top. She smiled at the thought, imagining the customers calling for her to be unrolled and Heinrich using his bare foot to push her, unfurling her like a carpet runner, only to expose a skinny, naked, and waterlogged woman.

Now, dressed in her dry training suit, she waited for the warmth to radiate inside it, but she was so thoroughly chilled, there was no ember to get it going. She wished she could cuddle up to one of the workers' fires, sneaking in with one of the families and getting a warm bowl of soup. That was what she needed, a bowl of soup. Maybe she could change into a dress and head back into the fair. The Cafe of the World was bound to have some chicken noodle soup, minestrone, or clam chowder. An aurora of colored lights glowed from the fair, looking warm and inviting. She felt like a little moth, flittering through the darkness of the camp, drawn to all the fires and the glow of light.

Addie rounded the corner to their group of tents and was shocked to find Rumor sitting on the edge of her platform. She waited in the glow of Addie's porch lantern, looking like some lonely figure in a motion picture show. It took a moment before Rumor raised her head, and in that moment, Addie wondered if she could duck back behind her tent, but by the time the thought passed though, Rumor had jumped down from the platform.

"Aunt Addie," Rumor said, coming toward her.

The cheer in Rumor's voice sucked the wind right out of Addie. She so badly wanted to put on a smile and embrace her niece. She wanted to get to know her and hear about her school, her friends, and how she and Mary and Wavey had been all these years.

"Your mother doesn't want you to see me."

"I don't care what my mother wants. She's nothing but a selfish drunk who throws everyone out of our lives."

The anger in her voice surprised Addie. "I'm sure your mother has good reason."

"No, she doesn't."

"Maybe there's more to things than you understand."

"There's not."

"There is when it comes to me," Addie said.

"If there is, that was long ago. Sisters don't hold grudges for that long."

Addie began to speak, but Rumor interrupted.

"No matter what it was. I can't think of a single thing that Mary could do to me that I wouldn't forgive. Nothing."

That warmth that Addie had hoped for began in her chest and rose up into her face. Her hands began to quiver. "I don't want to see you."

Addie could have gone her entire life without seeing the look on Rumor's face at that moment. She'd never wanted to hurt her. She wished she'd never shown up on her sister's porch and laid eyes on her niece. Life was easier not knowing what she was missing out on.

"You don't mean that," Rumor said, the words sounding caught in her throat.

"Your mother is right about me." Addie felt as if she'd get sick right there at Rumor's feet. "You're causing all of us more grief. I don't want to see you."

Rumor stood, speechless, but her eyes conveyed her pain and disbelief. They begged Addie to take it back. But she couldn't. "And Sal too. You've managed to almost get him fired, and you're upsetting his mother."

Addie couldn't take any more. She turned away from Rumor's pained face and ran back up the path to the garden, wishing she could erase all of her steps. Every single one, from the moment she'd spooned the poison into Ty's deviled eggs to the moment she'd stepped foot back in San Diego.

"Aunt Addie," Rumor called after her. "Please."

Addie kept going until she reached the garden's back gate. She pulled the string, unlatching it, and stepped through into the garden, where just moments before, she'd helped Frieda hang the cowhides over the railings to dry. Once inside, she closed the gate, leaned against it, and dropped into a heap on the ground. Calliope music, the ping, ping, ping and barkers of the midway, and the overriding notes of an orchestra in the Organ Pavilion mixed in with the deep, green smell of tropical plants—and of something dead. An animal? The scent was faint but unmistakable. She pushed aside a giant leaf, trying to let some of the light from the fair shine on the ground to see what it was, when she heard the scuff of footsteps coming toward the gate.

"Aunt Addie," Rumor called through the opposite side.

A whimper escaped from Addie, and she felt as if she couldn't breathe. She could almost feel the warmth of Rumor coming through the gaps in the boards.

"Aunt Addie," Rumor said, her voice soft and muffled, pressing in through the wooden slats. "I know you're there. Please talk to me."

Addie couldn't bring herself to say another hurtful thing to Rumor. She hugged her knees and dropped her head, rolling herself into a ball.

She heard the metal latch unhinge. The gate pressed against her back.

"Please," Rumor said, "just let me come in."

Addie knew she shouldn't have come to San Diego. She'd only unearthed the old pain and turned her sister's life upside down. She'd murdered Wavey's husband, and now she had turned her own daughter against her. Wavey was the one person she loved most in the world, and look what she'd done to her—again.

"Please," Rumor breathed through the boards, the words coming in right behind Addie's head.

"I'm sorry" was all that Addie could get out before she heard the whimpers of Rumor crying on the other side of the fence. "Please go home. I can't take it."

Addie felt the pressure release on the other side of the gate and the sound of footsteps retreating. Addie didn't move, staying curled up against the gate. A man's voice sounded through one of the knotholes on the other side of the garden. "Hello, dollies, want to come out and play?"

And another voice, sounding young and mischievous: "Ally, ally, oxen free. Come out, come out, wherever you are."

The rancid smell of decay drifted back toward Addie. She scooted around to the other side of the plant, intent on finding out what caused it.

"Hello, nudies," the calls continued.

Addie pushed one of the giant leaves aside, and a shaft of weak light lit the ground, illuminating the carcass of a dead mouse. A swarm of black ants crept across it. Bits of flesh and fur were still attached to the bones. Was it killed by poison? "Rough on Rats"? Arsenic? She remembered the red image of a dead rat on the canister and the words "Don't Die in the House" printed across its plump body. The odor of death rose up, clenching her stomach. She had to lay down before she got sick.

"Nudies, nudies, bet you're all cuties."

Addie crawled away from the mouse corpse, squeezing herself between the back fence and a gardenia bush. It smelled thick and sweet. Overpowering. Bits of gravel and twigs pressed into her cheek, reminding her of Ty, all those years ago, digging with his spade, shoveling, scraping, and leaving empty holes all around the backyard. How large had the hole been that held his coffin? Had Wavey dropped chrysanthemums onto it, standing above her dead husband, all alone, and looking down on what Addie had done?

341 Eucalyptus Street
San Diego, California
October 25, 1918

The pounding on the door came late in the afternoon. Addie scooped Mary up and hid behind their bedroom door, picturing angry policemen with batons and handcuffs—Officer Darby ready to drag her away. She wondered if the jail had a special place for girls. The pounding continued. Wavey hadn't been out of bed all day, lying in her darkened room, sick with a headache. Addie had nursed her, bringing in brown-paper-and-vinegar compresses. All morning, as she cleaned up the living room, throwing the shards of porcelain and clumps of her cut hair into the wastebin, she kept an eye on the clock, wondering when it would happen. She pictured Ty biting into an egg—he always bit them in half—then popping the severed part into his mouth and chewing both halves together. She had had time to stop it. She could've run to his work site and warned him. But now, with the pounding, she knew that it was too late. What had she done? Mary grabbed ahold of Addie's nose, playing their game of Got Your Nose, pretending to put it in her mouth and chew.

Through the crack in the door, she finally saw Wavey shuffling down the hallway. "Addie? Where are you?"

Maybe it was only a messenger come to break the bad news. When Wavey opened the door, a skinny man in baggy clothes stood with Ty's arm draped over his shoulder. He wasn't dead. He'd come home.

"Oh my Lord," Wavey said, backing up and letting them in.

"Afternoon, ma'am," the man said. "Your husband's awfully sick."

"The flu?" Wavey asked.

"Can't say, but that'd be my guess."

"We have a baby. Shouldn't we get him to the hospital?"

"That's what I thought, but he refused. Where do you want him?"

"That way," Wavey said, pointing toward her and Ty's bedroom.

Ty was an eerie yellow-blue color. Addie had never imagined she'd have to see him. What had she been thinking? That he'd simply disappear? *Don't Die in the House. Don't Die in the House.* Wasn't that what the can had promised? Mary pulled at Addie's nose again.

"'ose," Mary said, holding her fist up to Addie.

"Shhh," Addie whispered. "We need to be quiet little . . ." She couldn't bring herself to say *mice.* Addie had forgotten how much Ty hated hospitals. Or maybe he knew he wasn't sick and he'd tell Wavey that he'd been poisoned.

Ty's head lolled to the side, his face slack and rubbery. She'd never seen him so helpless and human. What had she done? As they assisted him past Addie and Mary's hiding place, she smelled vomit and diarrhea.

"Yucky," Mary said, wrinkling up her nose.

"Shhh, quiet." Addie's throat tightened, as if she too would get sick. "Auntie needs you to play in your crib like a good little girl," she whispered, lifting Mary over the rails before hurrying into the bathroom. Addie leaned over the toilet, resting her chin on the cold porcelain and wishing she couldn't hear them in the other room. Why had Ty come home? Had God sent him so that she could see what she had done?

"You got a big bowl or bucket?" the man asked.

She heard Wavey rummage through a cupboard in the kitchen and two thuds on the bedroom floor that sounded like Ty's empty work boots hitting the boards. The man spoke to Ty, but he only groaned back.

"This hits you like a hammer," he said. "God save the rest of us."

As Addie heaved into the toilet bowl, the door to the bathroom flew open. Wavey stood in the doorway with wild eyes. "Dear Lord, not you too."

"Not the flu," Addie said.

"What happened to your hair?"

Addie had tried to even it out with the shears that morning, but there wasn't much hope for it. A horrific retching sound came from the bedroom.

"You got that bowl?" the man called out.

Wavey rushed from the bathroom but returned a moment later when the man asked her for a wet towel. She put the back of her hand to Addie's forehead. "Where's Mary?" Wavey asked, sounding panicked.

"In her crib."

"We need to get her out."

"It's not the flu," Addie said. "We'll be fine."

"You don't know that. Did you see him? He's dying. He's brought us all the flu."

Wavey ran her fingers through Addie's short hair. "What happened?"

"Ty cut it," Addie said. "Last night."

Wavey closed her eyes and took a deep breath. When she opened them, she wrung out the towel, twisting and twisting, even when no more water came from it. She finally set down the towel and put one arm around Addie, pulling her into a hug. Wavey whispered, "I don't think he's gonna make it."

Once she left, Addie turned and retched into the bowl again, then lowered herself onto the cold tiles. Just a year and a half earlier, Wavey had lain in this exact spot and delivered Mary. Wavey's blood had stained the tile grout in tiny squares of red. Curled up on the floor, Addie listened to the man and Wavey as they tended to Ty.

"Ma'am, could you pull his pants off? We should wipe him down."

"Wavey," she said.

"Pardon me?"

"Wavey. You can call me Wavey."

"Yes, ma'am. And you can call me Jack."

"What happened?" Wavey asked.

"I don't rightly know," Jack said. "Just after lunch, he lost his color and doubled over."

His lunch pail! Addie hadn't seen it when they came in. Would the police find it? Had he eaten all the eggs?

Mary cried from the other room, "Mama."

Addie pushed herself up to tend to Mary. In their bedroom, Mary stood at the crib railing, trying to pull herself over. It wouldn't be long before she'd learn to climb out. When she spotted Addie, she put her arms in the air and, wiggling her fingers, cried, "Up, Ah-ee."

"Are you hungry?" Addie asked, lifting her over the rails.

With Mary balanced on one hip, Addie opened the cupboard and took down a jar of apricot preserves. As she moved toward the bread box, she heard a gasp behind her.

"What in heaven's name?" Wavey screamed. "You'll get her sick."

"I'm not sick."

"You don't know that." Wavey advanced on her and pulled Mary from her arms.

"Yes, I do."

Wavey's eyes focused on something behind Addie. She cocked her head, as if trying to make sense of what she saw. Addie turned to see what had caught her attention and noticed the canister of "Rough on Rats." She'd forgotten to put it back into the shed. When she turned back, Wavey's eyes had frozen in wide-eyed shock.

"You didn't," she said. "Oh, dear Lord, tell me you didn't."

Addie nodded her head once, causing Wavey to gasp again and cover her mouth.

"Everything okay out there?" Jack called from the bedroom.

"Yes," Wavey said, slipping the canister of poison into her pocket.

"We need help. He needs a doctor." She turned to Addie. "Take Mary into the bedroom. Quick. And don't let him see your hair."

"Miss Mabel, the neighbor, has a telephone," Wavey said to Jack. "Do you think you could go and ask her to use it?"

As soon as the door shut behind him, Wavey called Addie into the kitchen. With a shaking hand, she held the canister up to Addie. "He's dying. You've killed him."

"I had to protect us."

"By murdering him? Who are you to decide that? You know better than the Lord?" Wavey stood on her tiptoes and hid the canister on top of the kitchen hutch. "You need to get out of here."

"No, I'll tell them I did it. I don't care what happens to me."

"I do. You need to leave."

Addie followed Wavey into the bedroom where Ty lay on the bed, quiet. Wavey shook his shoulder, but he didn't respond.

"Da," Mary said. "Da, Da."

Wavey put her hand to his nose. "Oh my dear God, I think he's dead. You've got to leave right now. Before the ambulance gets here."

"Forgive me," Addie said. "Tell me you forgive me."

Wavey didn't answer. Instead, she turned to the closet, pressed herself into the back corner, and pulled out a dusty overcoat. She tugged a thick pouch from the pocket and opened it. Inside, Addie saw a wad of money. Wavey held out several bills. "This should get you to Uncle Henry and Aunt May. Galloway. Their surname is Galloway. They're in Dayton, Ohio."

"They didn't want me before. Please don't send me away."

"You're older now and can help around the house."

"No, please. What about you and Mary?"

"You should've thought about that before." Wavey nudged her out of the room. "Go pack, quick, before Jack returns."

"I don't understand," Addie said. "Why do I need to leave?"

"Miss Mabel and Officer Darby know you're from the orphan asylum. They've been watching you like hawks since you arrived. And when they see your hair . . ." Wavey pushed her out of the room. "Hurry, you don't have much time."

"What if they think it's the flu?"

"They won't, once they see your hair," Wavey said. "I'll send for you when it all blows over. Go!"

Addie stuffed her valise with as much as she could fit into it, surprised at how much Wavey and Ty had provided for her. Addie emptied out her top drawer, the one with all her underclothes and keepsakes. She placed their father's pocket watch, which Wavey had given to her, along with their mother's brooch and a lock of Mary's hair, into her valise. After that, all she could fit in was one dress and a pair of shoes. She'd come with less. Much less. She remembered the train ride from the school and her thoughts of oranges, sunshine, and white beaches. They hadn't been to the beach once. Ty couldn't tolerate the sand. Addie took one last look around the room. Whatever she left, she'd have again when Wavey sent for her.

Wavey was waiting by the back door with Mary on one hip and her new hat with the ostrich and peacock feathers in the other.

"This will cover your hair. I don't know how you will explain it to Uncle Henry, but you have an entire train ride to figure that out."

"Can't I just stay here?"

"No, you'll be the first suspect, especially with your hair all chopped off." She placed the hat on Addie's head. When Ty had brought it home for her a few months back, Addie had told Wavey that peacock feathers were bad luck, but Wavey had said that there is no such thing as good luck or bad luck, that God was the master of the universe and everything that happened in it. Addie couldn't help but feel that now Wavey believed her and wanted the hat out of the house. Then she felt guilty for thinking that her beloved sister would wish that upon her.

"You'll need to wear this." Wavey pulled a flu mask from her dress pocket. "The quarantine. They won't let you on the train without it."

Addie kissed Wavey and Mary before tying the mask over her mouth and nose. It caught her tears, absorbing them into the white gauze. She slipped out the back door in an unlucky hat and a mask, feeling like the criminal she had become.

CHAPTER EIGHTEEN
RUMOR

The smell of toast and butter-fried eggs wafted in from the kitchen. Like in the cartoons, the scent seemed to slither under her bedroom door and form itself into a vaporous hand, beckoning and enticing her to get out of bed. But Mother was out there and Rumor had absolutely no desire whatsoever to be in her presence. Rumor listened, waiting for Mother to run a bath or leave for an errand so that she could get some food. She was wondering how long she could wait it out when she heard something else. It wasn't the normal sounds of the radio or the birds chirping or the rumble of the occasional motorcar passing by in the street. She heard something out of the ordinary. An almost inaudible "No, no, you can't do this."

Rumor slipped out of bed. Mary and Mother sat at the kitchen table, Mother smoking a cigarette and foraging through the *Sears Roebuck* catalog and Mary poking her fork into a single fried egg with lacy brown edges. Both were completely unaware that something was happening in the courtyard until Rumor slid the living room window open.

Mrs. Keegan's shaky old lady voice drifted in. "You can't. I'm an old woman."

Kaiser stood on Mrs. Keegan's front step with a police officer behind him on the walkway. It seemed ridiculous that Kaiser needed police backup against an eighty-year-old woman. Mrs. Keegan spoke through the thin, open crack of her door. It couldn't be about the Parkers. They'd already left, headed for family in Kansas or Nebraska or Indiana—somewhere like that. She couldn't remember, but it was some big farming state.

The radio went dead, then Mother's voice came from behind her. "What's happening?"

"Kaiser's doing something to rile up Mrs. Keegan," Rumor said. "And he has the police."

"For crying out loud."

They listened. Kaiser mumbled something Rumor couldn't make out, then Mrs. Keegan cried, "Please, Kaiser. Where will I go?"

Mother stormed out the door, stomping across the courtyard before Rumor had a chance to take another breath. She'd seen Mother go toe-to-toe with Kaiser but never a police officer. Rumor followed her out.

"Go away. I'm an old woman," Mrs. Keegan said, trying to close her door, but Kaiser had blocked it with his foot.

"Kaiser," Mother yelled. "What're you doing?"

He turned his hard, determined face toward Mother. "Get lost. This is none of your business."

"None of my business?" When Mother used that tone, watch out. Kaiser had no idea what was coming, copper or no copper. "First, you throw the Parkers out. And now Mrs. Keegan?"

"I'm only doing my job," Kaiser said, his foot still wedged in Mrs. Keegan's door. "I've been warning her for two months now. This isn't a charity. Do you think I enjoy this?"

"Sure looks that way to me. Leave her alone. You're going to put her in the hospital."

The officer whispered something to Kaiser. He moved his foot, then *slam*, Mrs. Keegan's door shut. The lock clicked.

The officer approached Mother, taking his baton from a belt loop and holding it against his leg. "Please go back to your bungalow. Mr. Pitt has handled this legally and has an eviction notice."

"Please, Officer," Mother pleaded. "I give my word that I will have her out today. If you continue, she'll end up very ill. Let me handle it. I'll have her out by five o'clock."

If Rumor hadn't been so angry with Mother, she might've been proud of her, but she knew that Mother only liked the drama of it all. She liked being in the center of the action.

"Is that okay with you, Mr. Pitt?"

"She's had two months."

The officer took Kaiser aside. Rumor couldn't hear what they said, but Kaiser shook his head as the officer kept talking and gesturing toward Mrs. Keegan's closed door, then back at Mother. Across the courtyard, Ruth's door opened and she poked her head out. Then, without hesitation, Ruth stepped outside in her yellow robe and curlers covered with an orange scarf. She looked like one of those comedy acts where a man dresses up as a woman, and Rumor would have felt sorry for her if she wasn't always poking her nose into their business.

The officer left Kaiser standing alone, red faced and fuming, and approached Mother. "You have until five. I'll be off duty by then, but I'll have another officer come around to check. I'm gonna hold you to your word, now."

"Thank you, Officer. I'll take care of it directly."

He nodded toward Kaiser, then headed down the walkway and onto the street.

Ruth and Mother whispered together for a while, then Mother called out to Kaiser, "We're waiting for you to leave. She's not about to open her door with you lurking out here like a vulture. Go home, Kaiser, and we'll take care of it."

As soon as Kaiser passed by Rumor and Mary, they all went to Mrs. Keegan's door. Mother knocked but there was no answer. "Mrs. Keegan, it's me, Wavey," she yelled at the closed door. "Kaiser and the officer are gone. It's just me, Ruth, and my girls."

"How do I know they didn't put you up to it?"

"You know me better than that. Kaiser can go suck eggs."

The door lock clicked, and Mrs. Keegan pulled it open just enough to peek out with one watery blue eye before she opened it all the way.

A green-and-yellow afghan covered her couch, and pots of violets, ivy, and silver-dollar plants cluttered the entire apartment.

"Why didn't you tell us that Kaiser's been on you about your rent?" Mother asked.

"I didn't want to trouble you," Mrs. Keegan said. She stood there, a tiny, shriveled-up old woman in a housedress and slippers. She twisted together her blue-veined hands. "I didn't think he'd put an old lady out."

"Of course he would. Kaiser would put his own mother out if she didn't pay up."

Tears rolled out of her faded blue eyes. "I don't have anyone," Mrs. Keegan said. "You know I've never had children, and my husband's pension is all gone. I'd get a job, but who would hire an old lady?"

"There's the Department of Public Welfare. They're giving money to people to help them through. I don't know if it'll be enough to keep you here in your bungalow, but it will keep you fed and clothed," Mother said.

"Oh, dear, I'd be ashamed to take government money."

"Why?" Ruth said. "They're not ashamed to take your money."

"It's only to get you by," Mother said. "You have no choice."

"How about if you move in with my mother and me?" Ruth said. "We're having hard times too. Just last night, we were trying to figure some way to cut corners. You could have my room. I'd be perfectly happy setting my bedroom up in the living room. We never have company anyway."

"Oh, I don't know. I don't want to impose." Mrs. Keegan wrung her hands together so hard that Rumor worried her papery skin would tear.

"You'd be helping us. If you get yourself some welfare money, we can all split the costs. We'd all be better off."

"You check with your mother and make sure it wouldn't put her out too much."

Mother scanned the room. "Is all this furniture yours?"

"Feels like mine, I've been taking care of it for nearly twenty years. But no, we rented our bungalow furnished. Except for the bedroom furniture. That's mine."

"Thank God," Ruth said. "We'd have no place to put it."

"Okay, that's settled. We don't have much time," Mother said. "Ruth, you go talk to your mother and clear some room for Mrs. Keegan. Girls, go find as many boxes and crates as you can. Don't know what we'll do with all the kitchen appliances and dishes. You may want to sell some of it and get yourself a little cash right away. You think on it. For now, let's get it packed up."

Mrs. Keegan just stood there nodding, or shaking, Rumor couldn't tell which. With everyone helping, they had her packed and out in three hours. Of course, Mary suggested that they clean up the bungalow to leave it nice, but Mother, Rumor, and Ruth all sniggered.

"Fat chance," Mother said. "Let Kaiser clean it."

By lunchtime, they had Mrs. Keegan settled in with Ruth and her mother. Mrs. Keegan and Mrs. Reed, both too old to pack and lift, had a meal ready by the time they had finished. Glasses of lemonade and a pile of egg-salad sandwiches were lined up in the center of Ruth's picnic table. Mother pulled her sandwich in half and took a single bite before lighting a cigarette and gazing off, deep in thought. The sun reflected off the fractured blue prisms of her eyes. Rumor wondered what Mother was plotting. Maybe revenge on Kaiser. Maybe how to get rid of Aunt Addie. Suddenly, as if an invisible hand had twisted the barrel of a kaleidoscope, her eyes shifted. Mother stood, her cigarette dropping from her fingers and onto the ground. Rumor watched it fall. A thin string of smoke rose from the grass. When Rumor looked up, she followed her mother's gaze to see what had caught it.

A police officer, not just a normal-looking officer, but a bigwig—like a sergeant or chief—climbed up the steps to the courtyard. He had a thick walrus mustache and stared straight at Mother as he stepped toward them. Except for her rouged cheeks and painted lips, Mother's face was completely drained of color.

"Afternoon, ladies," he said, glancing around at the group, his eyes pausing on Rumor and Mary longer than the others.

"Clyde." Mother's voice trembled. "You're back?"

Clyde? Not *Sir* or *Officer* or *Sergeant.* Not even a *Mister.* Mother knew this man and knew him well. And he flustered her.

"They sent you?"

He cocked his head, looking perplexed. "Sent me?"

"To make sure Mrs. Keegan got out of her apartment?"

"I'm not sure I know what you're talking about." His mustache covered his top lip, so it looked as if only his bottom lip moved when he spoke. "I need to talk to you. Sorry to interrupt your picnic."

He put his hand out and Mother took it, stepping over the bench seat. The two of them walked off the same way he'd come. Once they'd disappeared, Rumor looked to Ruth. If anyone knew who he was, it'd be her.

"Who was that?" Rumor asked.

Nobody answered. Ruth shrugged her shoulders, looking as confused as everyone else.

"Should we follow them?"

"Your mother obviously knows him," Ruth said.

Mother had never brought a man around before. Rumor knew she'd gone out with scads of men over the past three years, but none had ever shown his face before. And a police officer? Her mother together with a policeman made no sense whatsoever. A banker, maybe, a salesman for sure, but not a cop. Mother wasn't exactly a rule follower.

Ruth stood up. "Well, we have a lot of organizing to do inside." She took Rumor's plate, even though she still had two bites of sandwich still on it, and stacked it on top of Mary's. "I'm sure she'll be fine. Come get me if she doesn't come back soon."

Mrs. Reed and Mrs. Keegan gathered the glasses and all three of them left, shutting themselves inside their house.

"Should we call the police?" Mary asked.

"He *is* the police," Rumor said.

"Do you think it could have something to do with Aunt Addie?" Rumor asked Mary.

Rumor paced the apartment as Mary stood lookout at the living room window for what seemed like an eternity. According to the clock, an hour had passed when Rumor finally heard shoes tapping on the sidewalk outside.

"It's Mother," Mary said.

When the door opened, Mother actually had a smile on her face.

"You're okay. Who was that man?" Mary asked.

"That is none of your business," Mother said, making her way to the radio and turning the knob. A man's voice sang out to "Chasing Shadows." Mother swung her hips, sauntering over to Mary. She took her in her arms and danced around the living room to the orchestra. Mother hadn't seemed so happy in a long time. And she didn't deserve it.

Rumor couldn't wait to see Papa to ask him if he knew anything about some old walrus-looking policeman, but she couldn't get out of the pew. The man next to her looked older than dirt and he moved like it too. The service seemed to have lasted forever, and now this ancient man blocked their exit. Patience had never been one of Rumor's virtues.

When they finally made it to the street and broke free from the horde of parishioners loitering in front of the church, Rumor noticed a woman zip around a corner onto Broadway.

"Is that Mother?" Rumor asked, getting only a glance of the back of the woman.

"Don't be preposterous," Mary said. "Mother has work today."

Rumor would recognize those skinny, scissor-stepping legs in high heels anywhere. Rumor took hold of Mary's arm and pulled her toward the retreating woman.

"Even if it is Mother, we shouldn't follow her, darling. She doesn't like us snooping around in her business."

"Go to the streetcar stop then," Rumor said. "I'm seeing what's up."

Rumor rounded the corner just in time to catch a glimpse of her mother disappearing into the U.S. Grant Hotel. Rumor felt like a real sleuth, uncovering her mother's secret life. She'd catch her right in the act. Of what, she didn't know at the moment, but it had to be something big.

The hotel smelled like money, all marble and emerald green—not all that much different than the Catholic church but definitely less holy. In the lobby, Rumor ducked behind one of the marble pillars.

"Is it her?"

"Jesus!" Rumor said, her heart almost literally in her throat. "I thought you weren't coming."

"I couldn't miss watching you make a fool out of yourself, darling."

The pillar felt smooth, colder than she'd imagined it would. A potted palm added extra cover as they peeked out at Mother, who was dressed to the nines in her lilac dress and the fox stole that Rumor hated. That thing, all hard-headed and smelling of mothballs, made her queasy. And if that weren't bad enough, the emaciated thing stared at you with glass eyes. Why would any woman would want to wrap a dead dog over her shoulders? Mother made a beeline for a man sitting on a green sofa. All Rumor could see was the back of his head, but she'd bet a dollar that on the other side of it was a gigantic walrus mustache. And sure enough, when Mother put a hand on his shoulder and he turned, there it was.

"It's him," Rumor whispered to Mary. "I knew it."

"It's like a love story," Mary said. "We shouldn't be here. It's not our business who Mother's boyfriend is."

"Like hell it's not our problem. You want him living in our house?"

Mary looked shocked at her use of profanity, but Rumor didn't care. Some things required cursing.

"Look at how she gazes into his eyes. That's true love," Mary said.

"How would you know what love looks like?"

"It's obvious, I see it every day at work."

"In the motion pictures?"

"Of course."

"That's not real. It's playacting," Rumor said.

"That's absurd, darling. Acting imitates real life, so therefore, it is the same as real life."

"Sometimes I think you have more empty space in your head than marbles."

"May I help you young ladies?" a deep voice grumbled behind them. They turned to see a fellow in a bellman's uniform looming over them. He looked awfully old for a bellman, with a fat paunch of a belly and graying hair.

"Uh." Rumor tried to think of a reason they were hiding. She couldn't rightly say they were spying on their mother. He'd have dragged them by their ears right over to her. "We just wanted to see inside."

"Well, you've seen it. Now move on."

Rumor looked back one more time. Clyde's hand stroked Mother's shoulder, looking as if he'd wear a hole right through it. She wouldn't admit it for the life of her, but it seemed as if Mary was right. They loved each other.

In the packed streetcar, Rumor stood and gripped the handrail, letting Mary sit in the only open spot. They both knew that Rumor had the better balance.

"Do you think he could be her brother?" Rumor asked, figuring that since they'd never known anything about Aunt Addie, either, maybe all of Mother's relatives would start coming out of the woodwork.

"I sure hope not," Mary said. "There's laws about looking at your brother like that."

When Rumor and Mary stepped off the streetcar, Papa was nowhere to be seen.

"I hope he's not dismayed about us not showing up last week," Mary said. "Poor Papa."

When they arrived at his garage, the crooked double doors were padlocked. Mrs. Bailey said that she saw him leave early in the morning with his fishing rod. They found him by the bay, wearing shorts, with a line in the water, his cap pulled low over his eyes.

"Papa!" Rumor said. "We were worried."

He looked up at them, his eyes glassy and watery. Next to him, in the sand and rocks, lay a bottle wrapped tight in a brown-paper sack, along with a pile of fence slats and a tin of chipped beef, opened and swarming with yellow jackets. Rumor had never seen Papa drunk before.

"Oh, didn't know if you'd be coming," he slurred. "Waited last week, but you never came." He made a limp swipe at a wasp that hovered next to his ear. "Figured you had better things to do than see your old papa."

"Sorry, Papa," Rumor said. "Mrs. Keegan got kicked out of her bungalow, and we had to help her move."

"We nearly went mad with worry about you waiting for us," Mary said. "But we couldn't rightly tell Mother we wouldn't help."

"S'okay." He waved his hand in the air. "Glad you're here now."

"Catch anything?" Rumor asked.

"Got two spotted bay bass." He pointed to a stringer anchored in the ground. "They like the ghost shrimp."

Rumor pulled the stringer until two bass emerged, strung through the gills. One looked to be about eight inches and the other about ten. "This will make a nice dinner for you tonight."

"Yep. Thought I'd make myself a bonfire on the beach and cook 'em up, but now that you girls are here, we can have 'em for lunch. Just need one more fish and we're set."

"That sounds marvelous," Mary said, but Rumor could tell by her face she didn't mean it. Mary liked things sanitary, which meant cleaned, cooked, and eaten indoors.

Mary wandered off looking for washed-up treasures while Rumor plunked herself down next to Papa.

Papa pointed at two men in a boat. "They pulled in a bat ray about an hour ago."

As soon as Mary had moved out of earshot, Rumor asked Papa what was wrong.

"What makes you think something's wrong?" he asked.

"Papa . . ." Rumor gave him one of her *you can't pull the wool over my eyes* looks.

"Never could fool you, could I?" He took a long swig from the bottle in the brown sack.

Rumor knew he wouldn't be this upset just because of last Sunday. Something bigger was eating at him.

"The police are putting the screws on me, and I don't know why. They won't let me be." He glanced up and down the bay. "Wouldn't be surprised if they're watching me now."

"Why would they waste their time watching you?" Rumor asked.

"Don't know."

A few of the yellow jackets became curious about what was in the brown-paper sack and began hovering over the bottle neck. Rumor had heard about people swallowing yellow jackets that had become trapped inside their bottles. They got stung and their whole throats swelled up. She shooed them away.

Mother's friend Clyde was a policeman. A high-ranking one too. And now Papa was being watched. Could it be about her and Mary? Would the police tell Mother about them lying to her and sneaking to Mission Beach to see Papa? "Do you know anything about a police officer named Clyde?"

Papa's brow wrinkled. "As a last name?"

"No, a first name."

"A while back, but he's long gone. Gone. Gone." Papa waved his hand at another yellow jacket. "Adios, amigo, and good riddance."

Papa took another swig from his bottle.

"He was in love with your mother, but I won out." He gave Rumor a silly half-aware grin. "No idea how I did it, but she chose me."

"Two fish will have to be enough," Papa said, reeling in his line. "But he's a goner. Moved away somewhere up north in Los Angeles or Santa Barbara or thereabouts."

"What was his last name?"

Papa gave her a quizzical look. "Why are you asking?"

"I think he's back."

"Darby," Papa said as if he had a bad taste in his mouth. "Clyde Darby. It figures he'd come back. Surprised it took him so long. I'm done fishing."

Mary was squatting by the shoreline, moving something around with a stick.

"Mary," Papa yelled, louder than he needed to for her to hear. "Let's go have us a bonfire and cook us some fish."

They left the tin of chipped beef for the yellow jackets, but Papa scooped up his bottle of booze. "Help me with this wood." He put a few slats under his own arm, then pulled the string of fish from the water.

Rumor followed behind Papa. His clothes were too big, and the string of fish slapped against his bare leg as he walked. If she didn't know that he was her Papa, she would've thought he was a tramp. That thought made her angry. Look what Mother had caused. How could she throw her husband, the father of her children, out onto the beach to scrabble for a living?

Once they made it to the ocean side of Mission Beach, Rumor and Mary gathered some dry kelp wracks as Papa dug a hole in the sand with his bare hands. When they returned, he piled the brittle tangles of black weed into the hole and lit them with his lighter. The same silver lighter he'd had as long as Rumor could remember. It had the initials JJD engraved on the side.

"Papa," Rumor said. "What does JJD really stand for?" They'd played the game over the years every time he had his lighter out. Papa always made up silly middle names, saying the initials stood for Jack Jabberwocky Donnelly or Jack Jellyfish Donnelly or Jack Jughead Donnelly, but Papa must not have been in a joking mood.

"John Jacob Donnelly. That's my name. Just ask the coppers."

CHAPTER NINETEEN
ADDIE

It had taken two days for Addie to get up the nerve to ask Frieda out for a drink. And now they sat at a table in the courtyard of El Cafe Solana in the Spanish Village. It was in an adobe-style building with a red tile roof, ornate iron bars on the windows, and potted palms in large clay pots. Being close to the midway, the sounds of clanking rides, excited screams, a calliope, and the shouts of barkers created a strange undercurrent to the flamenco music of the band in the cafe. A beautiful young hostess, dressed in a traditional Spanish costume, had seated them at the edge of the dance floor. During the two years they'd spent at The Century of Progress Exposition in Chicago, Addie had learned that everything was a show—including the band and their music and costumes, the hostesses, the food, and even where they seated the customers. Frieda looked like a goddess with her pale blond hair falling in waves around her bronzed face, and they were two unaccompanied women. Therefore, the hostess seated them closest to the dance floor where they could attract the attention, and cash, of single, male customers. Everything came down to presentation and atmosphere.

"The sun-worship ceremony went well tonight," Addie said. She had played the part of high priestess, instead of maiden or one of the queen's sisters, like she usually did. Of course, Frieda, being the most beautiful nudist and the wife of Heinrich, always played the part of the queen, daughter of Zoro, the sun god.

"*Ja*, it seems to have been successful, but it is getting—how do you say it? Perplexing? For me to tell. I play the same part night after night, and after a while, they all get blended together. I have done it so many times, I could do it while sleeping if I had to. And sometimes it feels as if I am sleeping."

A waiter approached with two glasses and a bottle of wine. "The gentleman at the other side of the patio sends his regards to the beautiful ladies, with this bottle of honey wine."

Addie knew that, by accepting the wine, they'd eventually end up with a man at their table, but she also knew that Frieda would use that as an opportunity to invite him to Zoro Gardens, and depending upon the size of his wallet, he might get a private tour of the gardens with her and a few of the girls.

Frieda sent him a nod of thank-you and one of her queenly smiles, and in return, he raised his glass to her from across the patio.

Once the waiter had uncorked and served the wine, Addie said, "I thought Heinrich banned all alcohol."

"An occasional glass of wine is acceptable. Wine is the nectar of the gods, is it not?" And with that, she held the glass up to Addie for a toast.

The wine captured the flickering candlelight around them, appearing to float inside the golden liquid like little fairy lights. Addie clinked glasses with Frieda, wondering if that was the last time she ever would.

"This has been a difficult trip for you," Frieda said. "You are not the light and feathery Addie that I know."

Addie felt the tears rising. She nodded and took another sip of the wine. It was sweet and sunny and reminded her of Sleepy Valley, of all the years of sunshine and swimming in the emerald lake and lying on the sandy beach, the assortment of people with their clumsy and beautiful bodies. She wanted to be there. Somewhere safe and far away from San Diego, where she did not feel welcome. There was nothing worse than feeling unwanted, like a burden on the people around you. She had felt that way from the time her parents died until she'd arrived at Sleepy Valley. Despite all her fears, she had hoped that coming back to San Diego could be a new start. A way to face the past, receive forgiveness, and be welcomed back into her sister's family, but that had not become a reality. "Can I go back to Sleepy Valley?"

"Now? While we are here at the Exposition?"

"My sister is here, and I thought . . ." Addie paused, trying to keep the tears back. "She doesn't want to see me."

"I'm afraid of what Heinrich will do if you leave," Frieda said. "Can you not, what do you Americans say, stick it out?"

"I could," Addie said, "but it's not so simple. My niece Rumor wants my sister and me to reconcile. She's persistent and it's causing a terrible mess. Rumor doesn't know what happened between her mother and me. She doesn't understand and is blaming it on her mother."

"Could you explain it to her?"

"I've tried, but her opinion's set. She thinks I'm covering for her mother."

Frieda swirled her wine around in the glass, staring down into it as if she were a fortune-teller trying to peer into Addie's future. Out of the corner of her eye, Addie noticed the gentleman who'd sent them the wine starting to get antsy. Addie dabbed at her eyes with her napkin. No man with what he had on his mind wanted to deal with a crying woman.

Frieda set the glass down onto the tiled tabletop and looked up at Addie with a resigned and saddened look. "I can speak to Heinrich, but there are concerns. You know about Eleanor?"

Addie nodded. "She was getting too old?"

"*Ja,*" Frieda said. "It is a terrible thing that causes Heinrich much distress. We are all like a family, but we are not a family. We cannot continue to support those who do not help to bring in the money."

"And Daisy and I are next?"

"*Ja,* Daisy for sure, but you still look very young, so Heinrich wanted to wait and see how much profit we make by the end of the fair. But if you cannot stay here for the Exposition, I'm afraid he will have no choice."

"What about Sal? Doesn't he help enough to keep Daisy?"

"You are worried about Daisy? Sal will support his mother whether they are at the colony or no. Maybe he will use his salary to pay for a cabin for Daisy at Sleepy Valley. Maybe he will not. That will be up to them, but Heinrich cannot continue to support her."

"If I left, would he keep Daisy on for a little longer?"

"That could be, but an old woman in a garden full of young and beautiful girls seems to break the spell."

"Wouldn't a skinny preacher in a leopard skin do the same?"

Frieda let out a laugh. "*Nein,* Joe makes the ordinary man imagine himself in his place, surrounded by beautiful and naked young girls."

"If I can't go back to Sleepy Valley, I don't know what I'll do," Addie said.

"Would you consider joining the army?" Frieda smiled. "Sister Aimee's army?"

"What would I offer her? I need a home and money."

"Nothing to offer her?" Frieda had a look of bewilderment on her face. "You need to start thinking. Sister Aimee is a businesswoman, no different than Heinrich, just on the opposite side of the customer's conscience."

Addie pictured Sister Aimee and tried to image what she could offer her. Sister Aimee had a whole choir of women and an entourage to take care of her every need.

"Do you see it yet?" Frieda asked.

"No."

"You could offer Sister Aimee a testimonial. Preachers like her depend on testimonials to keep the dollars dropping into the offering plates." Frieda, who normally had a healthy and fluid posture, sat up rigid, mimicking a look of reverent superiority. "My dear followers of Christ, I bring you our dear sister, Addie, who was once trapped in sin, exposing her naked flesh for the price of a home and food in her belly. But, I say, after attending one of my sermons, yes, I say, after hearing the word of the Lord, she has cast away her wickedness and came to salvation."

"Good evening, ladies." A deep voice sounded, breaking into Frieda's monologue. "I see you enjoy dramatics. Are you performers here at the fair?" He had a cleft in his chin and a strong resemblance to Bela Lugosi. If not for the fact that this man didn't have a Hungarian accent, Addie might have thought it was him.

"Won't you join us?" Frieda relaxed, shedding Sister Aimee's posture as fast she'd have shed her clothes if she could. "I wouldn't say performers, because we only do what we always do, but yes, we are exhibitionists here at the fair."

The man laughed. "Do you mean that you have an exhibit?"

"I mean both." Frieda laughed.

Frieda, not being a native speaker of English, found the variations of certain English words amusing and used them when she could.

"We are part of an exhibit and we are exhibitionists." Frieda leaned in, as if she were sharing a secret with him, and whispered, "We are nudists at Zoro Gardens."

The man's face flushed. "Well, that was the luckiest bottle of wine I ever bought." He picked it up and turned the label toward himself. "I'll have to remember the vintner."

Addie, not about to leave Frieda with some strange man, sat there, smiling when it seemed appropriate and pretending to follow the conversation. Frieda, even at her young age, seemed to understand life and how to get what she wanted from it. Addie had wasted her time hiding out, trying to forget the past instead of making a future for herself. And now, here she was, thirty-two years old with no home, no family, and very little money.

CHAPTER TWENTY
RUMOR

Mary's back was turned to Rumor and she breathed deeply, a tiny whistle with each exhale. The chirping of crickets and the distant bleat of the foghorn floated in the open window with the onshore breeze. Rumor lay in bed, listening to Mother's nightly routine—the rush of water in the bathroom sink, the sound of her padding to her bedroom in bare feet. When Rumor was younger, she used to sit on the edge of the bathtub, watching Mother get ready to go out on the town. Mother would take one long drag of her cigarette before leaning it in the ashtray. She'd turn on the spigot, and while waiting for the water to warm, she'd spread cold cream all over her face until it looked like the meringue on a lemon pie. She'd take one more long drag before wiping the cream off with a tissue, then finishing the job with a warm washcloth. Rumor used to follow behind Mother, into her bedroom, where Mother would sit in front of her vanity table, sucking on her cigarette and applying makeup from all the colored bottles and jars. Mother always called it *putting her face on.*

But now Rumor knew the truth. It was a man-catching face. Made-up, artificial, fraudulent, a swindle of a disguise.

Mother had forbidden Rumor to see Aunt Addie or to go to the fair at all. What would she do for the rest of the summer? Mother ran around town, meeting strange men in hotels, but kept her daughters locked up in the house, caged in a tiny bungalow even smaller than most of the animal enclosures at the zoo. But Rumor wasn't an animal, and as long as she still breathed and thought and desired, she had the right to want more than the tiny life Mother offered them. Didn't all adventurous women push against their boundaries? You didn't see Amelia Earhart or Louise Thaden sitting in a room feeling sorry for themselves because most of the aviators were men. You didn't see Nancy Drew sitting around, too timid to chase the next clue. And even if it turned out to be a red herring, she still had the experience. Rumor couldn't let the memory of Aunt Addie running away from her and shutting herself in the garden be the last one she had of her. She needed a proper good-bye, with a promise to find each other when Rumor turned eighteen, when her mother could no longer run her life.

Once Mother left, Rumor would slip out the window. What could she do to her? Then finally—the click, click, click of her heels across the wood floor and the door shutting behind her, off to throw herself at some unwitting man.

Mother usually joined Ruth, then they'd make their way through the courtyard and onto the street, where they'd pass by her window, arm in arm. Two women on a mission. But this time, Rumor heard only one set of heels, then the rumble of a car coming up the street, slowing and idling on the corner. She imagined Officer Darby behind the wheel, his hat pulled low over his eyes and his walrus mustache turning up at the corners as he smiled at her mother. A car door opened and shut, then the engine accelerated and rumbled down the street, growing fainter and fainter until it evaporated into the night and Rumor once again heard only the crickets and the foghorn.

Rumor slipped one leg out of bed and listened, again, for Mary's rhythmic breathing. Mary lay silent, but she wasn't asleep. Rumor couldn't wait. She needed to see Aunt Addie at least one more time and she couldn't see her during the day. The odds were that she'd be in the garden and hard to catch, so she'd go to her tent at night. Rumor stepped, as silently as possible, to the closet, but the door squeaked as she opened it.

"Where are you going?" Mary asked.

"Nowhere. Go back to sleep."

"Mother will be furious if you leave, darling."

"Only if she finds out."

Rumor slipped into a pair of slacks before pulling her nightgown over her head.

"Then I'm coming with you. I'm your big sister, and it would be outrageous if I let you disappear into the night. It's not safe out there."

"What could you do? You'll slow me down."

Mary clicked on the bedside lamp and flung back the covers like some starlet in a moving picture scene. Rumor felt like calling *cut!* and asking her to try it again, but this time with less dramatic flair.

"Follow me if you want," Rumor said. "But I'm not slowing down for you."

Rumor shimmied the window all the way up and swung her leg over the sill. Mary still hadn't changed her clothes, and Rumor knew there was no way on God's green earth that Mary would be seen in her nightgown and wave cap.

"Don't go." Mary took hold of Rumor's arm. "What about the bums and murderers?"

Rumor pulled her arm from Mary's grasp. "Don't be so melodramatic." She slipped out, landing between the wall and the gardenia bush. "It's not a full moon. Crimes happen during full moons."

"It looks full to me," Mary said, poking her head out.

"It's not full, it's waning. Now go back to bed." Rumor put her fingers on the bottom of the window frame. "Or I'll guillotine your head."

Rumor pushed Mary's head in and shimmied the window closed. Mary looked like a useless china doll behind the glass pane. Rumor gave her a wave and looked up and down the street before heading toward the lights of downtown. In the distance, but lost in the darkness, lay the hills of Mexico with all the half-naked children living in shacks and sucking on sugarcane. Could they see the glow from San Diego at night? Did they want what was just out of reach? And what about the sailors in the harbor? She imagined them playing poker and sharing stories of what they'd done on their last shore leave, counting down the hours until they got another, forced to stay aboard their steel islands anchored in the bay.

Rumor stuck to the outskirts of town, crossing back and forth across the street to avoid drunks and darkened doorways that smelled like urine. Thanks to Mary, Rumor imagined every shadow to be that of a murderer skulking around with a pocketknife or pistol.

The moon shone off the leaves of ivy that climbed up the walls of the high school, making it look much more enchanting than it was in reality. Inside, the halls and classrooms were no different than any other school, just tile and paint and glass cabinets filled with sports trophies, student artwork, and handmade posters encouraging the football team to slaughter their next adversary. Rumor's heart just about dropped from her chest when she noticed a dark figure lying on the grass gazing up at the stars, with his bony knees poking into the air. He lay in the exact spot where Papa used to take her and Mary. Could it be him? Did Papa still come to the city and lie under the stars, even with nobody there to tell his stories to?

Rumor looked up and spotted Orion and his hunting dogs. Her favorite story that Papa used to tell was about how Artemis had banished Orion to the skies for chasing after the seven sisters. Artemis unleashed Scorpio on him, its tail raised and ready to strike. Papa said that because

Orion appeared on the horizon as Scorpio disappeared, and Scorpio rose as Orion sank, some people thought that Orion chased Scorpio through the sky, trying to finally destroy it, and others thought that Orion runs away from Scorpio and hides from its deadly sting. Rumor had asked Papa if he believed that Orion was chasing or running. Papa said that he believed that Orion, unable to get the seven sisters out of his mind with them glittering and twinkling just before him, chased after the girls; while Scorpio, still under orders from Artemis, chased Orion.

Rumor wanted to run up to the figure to see if it was Papa, but what if it wasn't? The figure shifted his weight and stretched his legs flat on the grass. Muffled laughter drifted over from the fair. The stray notes from a calliope and a mariachi trumpet mixed together with the sounds of a distant orchestra. Rumor glanced toward the fair and all the lights and the dim ravine that cradled the encampment—and her aunt Addie. She then looked back at the man lying on the grass. If it was Papa, how would she explain being out at night all by herself? He might prevent her from seeing Aunt Addie, or he might insist on going with her. She kept walking. She'd never turned her back on her papa before. But that might not be him anyway, and Papa wouldn't want her approaching strange men in the dark.

As Rumor dropped down into the ravine, she looked for the path that she and Sal had taken. In the faint glow of the moon, it looked like nothing but dirt and the silhouettes of scrub brush and trees. Maybe she didn't need the path. The land dipped down, funneling directly into the encampment, so she couldn't miss it.

Rumor's shoe hit a rock and she heard it tumble away into a dry bush. Something cracked behind her, and a dark shape ducked behind a tree. Vern? A murderer? Darn Mary for filling her head with shadows. She hurried forward, brushes scratching at her legs and foxtails burrowing into her socks and pricking at her ankles. Rumor didn't realize she'd been holding her breath until she came upon the red lanterns of the prostitutes' tents and she let it out. Two of them lounged outside, wrapped in silk dressing gowns, sucking on cigarettes, and chugging out puffs of smoke with their throaty laughs.

"Think we got ourselves some competition?" one of them said. "Hey, girlie, you horning in on our business?"

Rumor was afraid to look them in the eye or to answer their taunts; it might just egg them on.

"Nice frock you got on there; is it cotton?" Both women laughed out loud. "Come over here, sweet pea."

"Yeah, come on over. Maybe we can get you some business. Lots of men like their girls still in ankle socks."

The only light came from smoldering campfires, lanterns, and moonlight. Dark figures slipped around between tents, and in the distance someone played a harmonica, a sad and lonesome tune. A smattering of tents glowed, creating silhouettes of lumpy furnishings and people moving about like shadow puppets. Only one of the nudist colony tents had an inside lantern on, and it wasn't Aunt Addie's. Rumor climbed up on her platform.

"Aunt Addie," she called through the flap, all tied up and battened down. No answer. She called again, "Aunt Addie."

Rumor heard the tapping and scuffle of that parrot, Hobbs, but nothing else. If he wasn't such a mean bird, she'd feel sorry for him being all caged up. The light inside the chickens' tent illuminated their figures, creating a shadow play of what could be a backstage scene of actresses preparing for the stage. Rumor didn't want to disturb them, but she'd come too far to turn back home.

"Hello," she called before climbing the platform steps.

"Who in tarnation?" a voice with Ida's distinct long drawl said.

"Sounds like Rumor, but she wouldn't be here this late."

"Oh, for heaven's sake, girls, why don't you open the flap and find out?"

Lucille's round face appeared in the opening. "Yep, I was right. It's Rumor."

"Well, invite her in already."

It looked as though all three of their traveling trunks had exploded inside their tent. They seemed half-ready for a night out, still in their robes and Dottie with curlers in her hair.

"Sorry to bother you," Rumor said. "Have you seen my aunt Addie?"

"If she's not in her tent, beats me where she is," Ida said.

"Could you come back a bit later?" Lucille asked.

"I have nowhere to go. Could you look inside her tent to see if she's there but not answering me?"

"That's trespassing, darlin'. If Daisy caught me going into her tent, she'd slap me so hard that by the time I stopped rolling, Franklin Delano Roosevelt wouldn't even be president anymore."

"I know," Lucille said. "Would you like to see the garden?"

"I don't know," Rumor said. It seemed forbidden somehow. Like the Forbidden City or a forbidden treasure: don't touch, stay away, do not enter.

"Nobody's there. Ain't nobody willing to pay to see a bunch of nudists hiding in the dark," Lucille said. "And when we get back, your aunt Addie may have returned."

No trespassing. Stay off the rocks. Prohibited. "Okay, take me to it," Rumor said.

Her words seem to have electrified the chickens. They scurried around, searching for sandals. Dottie pulled the curlers from her hair and dropped her brush into her robe pocket.

"Well, let's skedaddle," Ida said.

"You're going out in your robes?" Rumor asked.

"It's a nudist garden, silly," Lucille said. "Nobody's there."

Rumor followed behind the three silhouettes in silk robes that shone like pearl pastels in the moonlight. They veered off to the right, skirting around the back of Gold Gulch, approaching the garden on the opposite side of the main entrance, the same gate that Aunt Addie had disappeared through on Rumor's last visit. Dottie pulled the string and the small gate swung open.

"Welcome to Eden," Lucille said, motioning for Rumor to follow Dottie.

Through the gate, Rumor saw nothing but thick tropical leaves. Dottie parted the plants, allowing Rumor to step through. It was even more enchanting than she'd remembered from her brief peek through the knothole. It smelled of gardenia and honeysuckle. A tiny, moonlit waterfall slipped over rocks, creating a small pool surrounded by ferns. Dim outlines of stone terraces and ramps dropped down from the fair, ending at a wooden railing draped with what appeared to be cowhides. Tree roots, like giant tentacles, stretched across the ground and over the edge of a rock wall.

"Beautiful, isn't it?" Dottie asked.

"It's like a fairy story." Rumor brushed her hand across the leaf of a banana tree.

Dottie took hold of Rumor's hand, leading her to a flat rock by the waterfall. "Can I fix your hair?" she asked. "We'll braid some wildflowers into it and make you into a fairy princess."

Rumor pulled off her shoes and socks so she could feel the soft ground with her bare feet as Dottie stroked the brush through her hair. Ida and Lucille slid out of their robes, leaving behind lustrous pools of silk. Their nakedness shimmered in the moonlight, washing over their rounded hips as they collected flowers that sprung up between the rocks. Rumor, almost hesitant, turned around to see Dottie. She stood, caressing Rumor's hair, naked as a jaybird.

"Would you like me to put my robe back on, honey?"

Rumor shook her head.

"I don't want to make you uncomfortable. It just seems almost sacrilegious to wear clothes in the garden. It's unnatural."

Dottie looked like one of those women in classical paintings, like the ones in the art gallery, all smooth and round. Rumor half expected to see fat cherubs sitting at her feet and gazing down from the trees.

"It's okay," Rumor said, and turned to watch Ida and Lucille search for wildflowers.

Dottie worked the tangles from her hair without once pulling or ripping through it like Mother always had. The bristles glided across her scalp and down her back, causing her skin to tingle. Dottie ran her fingers through Rumor's hair, separating it and twisting the sections together. Lucille and Ida returned with blue buttercups and tiny yellow daisies. They stood on either side of her, slipping the stems into her hair, with their breasts so close to the side of Rumor's face that she felt the warmth coming from them. Rumor sat still, afraid to move one way or the other. When it was done, they backed away.

"Beautiful," Lucille said. "You are the fairy princess."

"Would you like to see what it feels like to be a nudist?" Dottie asked.

"Oh, don't scare her," Lucille said.

"I'm not trying to. I just thought she'd like to see how natural and free it really is," Dottie said. "We're the only ones here, if you'd like to give it a try. You're safe with us."

"Don't feel like you need to," Lucille said. "We won't be insulted."

Rumor didn't know what came over her. Maybe it was the garden or the moon. Maybe it was the fight with her mother or just curiosity, but she slid her sweater from her shoulders and let it fall to her feet. Dottie unbuttoned her dress, and Rumor pulled it over her head. She stood in nothing but her chemise and panties, glancing around the garden at the rocks and the tropical plants, trying to ignore all the music and laughter coming from the other side of the fence. If anyone were to peep through the holes, would they be able to see into the dark garden? Ida, Dottie, and Lucille watched her, then turned their heads when she hesitated.

"Only if you feel like it," Lucille said. "There's no judgment here."

Rumor slipped the straps from her shoulders and let her chemise drop to the ground. The cool air swept across her skin, brushing across her breasts and giving her a shiver. Rumor instantly knew this was not Eden like the brochures claimed, because she did not stand there without shame. She did not stand there without the thoughts of all the pastors and their words about spiritual darkness, but she did feel free and adventurous, pushing against expectations.

"You get used to it, darlin'," Ida said. "At the colony, we got children of all ages running around buck naked, without a care in the world."

"People bring their children?" Rumor asked.

"Of course they do. Families come to relax, get some sunshine and healthy food, and to get away from the city."

"And Sal?"

"Darlin'," Ida said. "I don't know what sort of notions you have about our colony. There ain't nothing wrong with nudity. You get used to it, and after a while, it ain't no big deal."

"Come on," Lucille said. "Let's all see if we can find some ripe figs that didn't bust open when they fell."

"The giant trees are figs?" Rumor asked, but somewhere, back in her memory, she knew that they were. She'd come here to Balboa Park with Papa many times; and in Palm Canyon, Papa had named the trees.

Rumor didn't know if it was a movement that caught her attention or the sound of someone breathing, but she looked to the left. A man stood half-hidden in the foliage. She must have gasped, because Ida turned toward him, also. The man took a step forward.

"Sal? Well, butter my butt and call me a biscuit," Ida said. "What're you doing hiding in the bushes? Planning some sort of an ambush on us?"

Sal didn't say a word. He just stood there, completely dressed, staring at Rumor's nakedness. She crossed her arms over her breasts when she noticed his chest visibly rising and falling with each breath. Was he angry at her? The next thing Rumor knew, Dottie and Lucille stood next to her, Dottie cradling several figs against her breasts.

"Looks like Sal has finally noticed that Rumor's a woman, not a little girl," Dottie said with a giggle.

Sal stood there, still watching. Rumor didn't know what to do. She wanted to run and gather up her clothes. She wanted to go home and crawl into her own bed, pulling the sheets over her head. She wanted to feel his hand on her bare skin. His lips on hers. Rumor didn't know what came over her, probably the same thing that always came over her when challenged, but without thinking, she lowered her arms, fully exposing her breasts, and walked up to him. He didn't budge. Rumor stepped so close that she felt the fabric of his shirt against her nipples. She stood on her toes, raising her face to him. And he kissed her. His warm hand slid around her waist, dropping down to rest on her lower back. He pulled her naked body tight against him and kissed her again.

But then he released her. And nudged her away. Her body felt suddenly cold where it had been against him. Sal reached into his pocket, pulled out a fifty-cent piece, and held it out to her.

Rumor felt the blood rising, and just as she prepared to slap his face, he said, "You shouldn't be here. Here's some money. Take a taxi home where you belong."

"I don't need your money," Rumor said, surprised she could speak at all with her blood beginning to boil.

Sal looked at her one more time, his eyes running up and down her body, then without another word, he took up her hand and placed the money in it. "Take it. It's too late to walk."

Rumor let the coin drop to the ground. He looked down at it, turned, and walked away. The brief warmth of his body made the air in the garden now feel chilly, and she shivered.

"I think someone's smitten," Ida said.

"I . . . I don't know . . ." Rumor said.

"I'm not talking about you." She winked. "I've never seen Sal act like that."

"Oh, Daisy's gonna kill us," Lucille said.

Sal had left Rumor standing there, naked and ashamed. He had walked away. Was she too much of a little girl? Could he tell that she'd never kissed a boy before? Rumor picked up the coin, ran over to the brook, and pulled on her chemise and dress.

"What's your hurry?" Ida asked. "Don't you go chasing after him now, you hear? Men like a woman who's hard to get."

But Rumor had no desire to see Sal. She needed to get away. How could she look at him again, knowing that he'd seen her naked? Every inch of her body. His hands had touched her and he'd kissed her. And he didn't want her. She could still feel Sal's hand on her waist, sliding around and dropping down her little-girl hips—nothing like Ida's, Dottie's, or Lucille's. Nothing like a woman. Just a little girl pretending to be a woman. She was too childish for Sal. He lived at a nudist colony around beautiful women—sexy, adventurous women. Who was she kidding?

Rumor didn't know what caused her to do it, but instead of going home, she directed the taxi driver to Mission Beach. To Papa's. She couldn't bear the thought of going home and lying in bed with Mary and waiting for Mother to come home from Lord knows where, maybe straight from the arms of that police officer. She unbraided her hair, plucking the flowers from it and dropping them out the taxi window as they rolled through town. She had never visited Papa's at night and prayed he'd be home. Rumor didn't have a plan B if he wasn't. She wouldn't have enough money for a taxi back, and the streetcar didn't run that late. She imagined the surprise on Papa's face when she showed up and wanted to feel his arms around her and to hear his soothing voice telling her that everything would be fine. She ran her fingers through her hair again, finding another wilting buttercup. She needed Papa's protective hug, not Sal's. She was a fool to ever think otherwise. She wondered if he'd gone back to his tent and made fun of her budding little-girl breasts and how she thought she was a woman but didn't even know how to properly kiss a boy.

When the taxi pulled to a stop at the top of Papa's street, she noticed bars of light coming through the boards of his garage. He was home.

She tapped on his door.

"Hello?" Papa said.

He sounded hesitant, and Rumor remembered that the police had been bothering him. "It's me, Rumor."

She heard his footsteps scuffing across the floor. The taxi driver still idled at the top of Papa's street. Was he waiting for her? A bolt scraped, metal on metal, and the door swung open.

"What's wrong?" Papa's face looked worried. "Is Mary okay? Your mother?"

"Everyone's fine."

He looked confused but stepped back to let her in. Rumor waved at the taxi driver, and his car moved forward, rolling away, down Mission Boulevard.

Papa gave her one of his shirts to sleep in. It smelled like Papa—of motor oil, sweat, and Aqua Velva. Papa had turned his back while Rumor slipped out of her dress and chemise. She buttoned it over her body but still felt naked in nothing but her panties and someone else's shirt.

The only time Rumor had ever spent the night away from home was when Papa had taken her and Mary to Tijuana, but then they all shared one bed, so she hadn't felt alone. Once she had been invited to Mary Jane Gilmore's house for a sleepover when she was in the third grade, but in the middle of the night, she slipped out in her pajamas and walked home. At the time, the prospect of staying at Mary Jane's house, with its strange smells and sounds, seemed more frightening than roaming the streets in the middle of the night.

Papa's garage felt like a different place at night too. The cool air from the ocean slid right between the planks. She'd brushed all the sand from the blanket on the cot, and brushed her feet off before getting in, but every time she moved, she felt the grains rubbing between her and the canvas.

At home, the streetlight gave their bedroom enough light to see the shapes in the room, but Papa's garage was dark except for thin slivers of moonlight between the boards. She felt as if she were inside a giant shipping crate that smelled of motor oil and hints of rotting food coming from the open tin cans of tuna, pork and beans, and deviled ham.

She pulled the blanket tight around her to keep warm against the moist air. As she lay there, she felt a thick fog, *as thick as pea soup* as Papa always said, move in and wrap itself around his garage. The fuzzy air seeped into the cracks where the moonlight used to be. Rumor imagined the fog flowing in from the sea, flooding the houses and lifeguard towers until they appeared to be adrift on a sea of gray mist, and at the amusement park, the silent carousel horses, frozen in midstride, jumping, prancing, galloping, or bucking—tossing and arching their heads to keep them above the surface.

Papa lay on the bare cement floor, shifting, trying to get comfortable. Rumor felt guilty for taking his only bed. She'd offered him the blanket, but he said he'd hear nothing of it.

"Are you okay, Papa?"

"Don't you worry about me. I've slept in worse places than this."

Outside, Rumor heard a cat mewling in the night. It sounded so mournful she imagined it singing its song for Papa.

"You feel up to telling me why you won't go home?"

It wasn't just that she didn't want to face her mother, prolonging the time until she was grounded; she wanted to talk to Papa about the garden. She needed to know that he still loved her. But once she'd seen

Papa's face and felt his big bear hug tightening around her ribs, shame had kept the words bundled up in her chest. She thought about how easily she had slipped out of her clothes with Ida, Dottie, and Lucille. How their nakedness made her feel confined and stuffy. The women looked so beautiful. Dottie's curvy hips, Lucille's full breasts, and Ida's long and slender legs seemed so natural and free and unbound from all conventions that she'd wished to feel that way too. But once Sal had appeared, her feelings of freedom changed, and she wanted him to desire her. She wanted to feel his hands on her skin. And it had happened. He did touch her as she'd hoped he would. And he'd kissed her. But she wasn't good enough.

"I did something wrong, Papa."

He didn't answer. He waited for her to decide what to say or to decide to keep quiet. Would Papa be disappointed in her? Would he be heartsick that she was no longer his innocent little girl?

"I went to the nudist colony."

"They let you in?"

"It was closed. I went with three of the ladies."

"Your aunt took you there?"

Rumor could tell that Papa didn't approve but was trying to understand.

"No, Papa. She wouldn't have taken me. I went with three other ladies. They wanted to show it to me."

"So, it was only a garden then? Since nobody was there?"

"We were there, Papa. And we all took our clothes off." Rumor heard Papa shift in the darkness. "The women were so beautiful. They didn't worry about what anyone thought about them. It seemed so natural and free. I wanted to feel that way too."

"Did they do anything to you?" Papa's voice sounded closer. "Did they touch you?"

"No."

She could hear more movement, and when Papa spoke again, his voice came from right beside the cot. "What was it like?"

The fog slipped in through the planks, pushing into the gaps of her blanket. Rumor tucked it around her, sealing herself from the cold air. Papa breathed hard and Rumor felt sad that she'd made him angry.

"As long as there were no men," Papa said.

She couldn't tell him about Sal. If she did, he'd have to tell Mother, and then that would ruin everything. She'd be grounded for the rest of her natural life.

"Did any of the women do anything strange? To each other?" Out of the darkness, Papa put his hand on Rumor's hair and began smoothing it back off her forehead, just like he'd done when she was little.

"No, Papa. It wasn't like that."

Papa's fingers moved more slowly. He picked up a strand of her hair and twisted it around his finger. When it felt tight and fully wound, he let it loosen and slipped his finger out.

"Am I a sinner, Papa? Sometimes I can't stop myself when I'm tempted."

Papa's fingertips brushed across Rumor's cheek and down her neck. She didn't like it and turned her back to him.

"I'm tired, Papa. Good night." The rest of the words slipped around in Rumor's head. *Sleep tight, don't let the bedbugs bite, and if they do, I'll take my shoe and beat them till they're black-and-blue*, but she didn't say them out loud.

The cot shifted, as if Papa had used it to pull himself up. Maybe his legs had fallen asleep from kneeling on the cold ground. But then, the blanket lifted, and she felt a chill across her back.

"It's cold." Rumor reached back, trying to grasp the edge and pull it back around her.

"It's okay; I'll keep you warm."

The cot creaked and the canvas strained against Papa's weight as he slid in behind her. It felt as if the entire thing would stretch so tight that it would snap like a guitar string. "No, Papa" was all Rumor could say.

"It's okay, love bug."

He used to always call her *love bug* long ago, but as she'd grown, he called her by her nickname less and less. It didn't feel right, having Papa in the cot with her, but where else would he sleep? This was his only bed and she was in it.

"I'll sleep on the floor." Rumor tried to sit up, to crawl over Papa, but he wrapped his arm around her, pulling her down. Her head knocked against the wooden bar. "Ouch. There's not enough room, Papa."

"Sure there is. Just relax." He pulled her closer, his entire body pressed against her backside. Something hard poked her.

"See, there we go." He stroked her hair again. His breathing came quick and warm across the top of her head. "What was your favorite nursery rhyme? Oh, yes. 'Hey diddle diddle, the cat and the fiddle. The cow jumped over the moon. The little dog laughed to see such a sight, and the dish ran away with the spoon.'"

Why had she come to Papa's? She belonged at home with Mary and Mother. Papa's garage was cold and she shouldn't be there. Maybe if she just went to sleep, and as soon as the sun came up, she'd go to the amusement center and wait for the first streetcar. Rumor wondered if Mother had come home yet and found her missing. Mother would be worried. She shouldn't have come.

Papa's hand slid down Rumor's side, stopping on her hip.

"I need to sleep now, Papa."

"Go ahead. It's okay."

Papa's hand felt like dry wood, rough with splinters and snags as it ran down her bare leg and back up again, over her hip and across her belly. Rumor lay still and unsure. Papa wouldn't hurt her. He breathed hot across the top of her head, and his hand, dry and splintery, rose up and grated across her breasts.

"What are you doing?" Rumor grasped his forearm. "You're hurting me."

"Lay still," he breathed. "It'll be okay."

"Stop it!" Rumor wriggled against his tight grasp. She put her feet against one of the wall studs and pushed. Everything tipped. Her stomach lurched like it did when she went on the Big Dipper, but the coaster always swooped up, and there was the rising feeling, the exhilaration of knowing they'd come close but didn't crash. Not the abrupt stop of hard ground. They hit the cement with grunts. Her head struck something hard.

"Are you hurt?" Papa touched her shoulder.

"Leave me alone," Rumor cried, shrinking away from him. The sand rubbed against her skin, raw and grating. She felt it in her hair and in her mouth. She couldn't get away from it.

"Oh God, what have I done?" Papa sounded like he had the day they'd returned from Mexico. The day she and Mary sat outside on the step, listening to him beg Mother for forgiveness.

"I'm sorry," he said. "It'll never happen again."

He had said that same thing to Mother, and now he said it to her. An image of her red kimono, and Mary's, with the little bluebirds on it, came to her mind. She remembered the smelly hotel room in Tijuana with the yellow stains on the walls. And playing matador with Papa and jumping on the bed. And Mother's words, *You better not have harmed a hair.* But he hadn't. He hadn't laid a hand on them, had he? No, she would've remembered that. But she and Mary had run about the hotel room in those kimonos with nothing on beneath them while Papa sat in a chair, watching them jump on the bed. And he swatted them on their behinds as they ran past his waving coat, pretending to be the mighty matador.

Rumor heard Papa moving around, but the darkness inside the garage smothered everything—even his silhouette. He could be anywhere. She listened to his feet scuff across the cement and scooted away from the sound. Then there was light. Papa had plugged in his lightbulb but hadn't looped the wire to one of his hooks, causing the single beam to swing back and forth like a pendulum. Papa stood against the wall with his back to her and his fists clutching at clumps of his hair. He let out a groan that sounded like "Oh God" before he began hitting his head against one of the studs in the wall. The knock of his head against the wood kept perfect time with the sway of the bulb. Each time it swung toward him, he hit his head. Each time it swung away, he groaned, "Oh God." The arc got smaller and smaller until the light hung static from the ceiling. When it stopped, Papa sank down onto the floor.

Rumor lay still, afraid to move. Papa seemed like a stranger. And she was on his floor, wearing nothing but one of his shirts and her underwear over her naked body. His hands moved through his hair, over the wall, across his knees and over his shoulders, clasping and unclasping into fists, pulling at the fabric of his shirt. He looked as if he wanted to tear something to shreds. Rumor put her hand flat onto the cement and pushed herself upright, trying not to make a sound. She paused, waiting to see if he'd noticed, before getting her bare feet beneath her. She stood. Papa only groaned and his hands pulled at his clothes and his hair. She stepped toward the door, remembering that Papa had latched it. She'd never been locked inside before. The door had always remained wide open. And then she thought of Ruby. Had she been shut inside? Rumor stepped carefully around the overturned cot and over a crate, afraid she'd stumble or send something rolling. She reached out for the bolt on the door. The sliding metal rod had screeched, metal grating against metal, when Papa had latched it. She couldn't leave without him knowing. She could do it fast and make a run for it, but if he chased after her, she didn't have a chance. He could overtake her. But what other option did she have?

She clutched the lever and tried moving it. Stuck. She jiggled it, remembering how cockeyed the doors were and knowing that she needed to lift one side to allow the bolt to slide. Before she knew it, Papa's voice came from right behind her. She winced and hunkered down, away from him.

"I can't let you go out there all alone."

Rumor tried to hold it in, but her cries came out in gasps.

"I'll go," Papa said. "You can latch the door behind me."

Papa pulled on his work shoes and, without tying them, came back to the closed door. He pushed the toe of one shoe under the lowest door and lifted with his foot as he undid the bolt, swung the door open just enough to slip out, then closed it behind him. Rumor saw the tip of his shoe poke back beneath the low-hanging door, and it raised up.

"Okay, latch it now," Papa said from the other side.

Rumor slid the latch and listened, waiting for footsteps to fade away, but she remembered the streets were nothing but sand, and unless he stepped up onto the sidewalk planks, she'd never hear them. She put her eye to the gap between two boards. Maybe she could see his shadow fade away into the fog. But instead of the empty night air, Papa's voice burst through the crack.

"I'm sorry, love bug. I don't know what came over me."

Rumor felt her anger boil up and she clenched her fists.

"I promise I will never do it again."

Rumor remembered him saying those exact words to Mother. Many times. She slapped the door with an open hand, right about where his words had slid through. "Go away."

She didn't hear anything for a moment, then came the slight sounds of his boots on the sidewalk planks. She listened to them fade away, until all that was left was the distant call of a foghorn and the rumble of a truck up on Mission Boulevard.

CHAPTER TWENTY-ONE

ADDIE

Addie heard the heavy clunk of boots stepping up onto her platform. She had no idea who it could be. The men of the colony would never wear such heavy boots, with their feet so unaccustomed to footwear.

"Addie Bates?" a deep voice called from outside.

Addie froze, afraid to answer. The voice sounded official and stern. She could pretend she wasn't there. But why would a lantern be left burning in an empty tent? He'd know someone was inside. If only she'd stayed out with Frieda a bit longer, maybe she'd be dancing to the flamenco music or wandering around the fair.

Addie untied the one bow that held the flaps shut and peeked out into the face of a ghost. It was too solid to be a real ghost, but she wished it were.

"Officer Darby?" she asked, not needing an answer. He'd grown a mustache and wasn't wearing a policeman's uniform, but she had no doubt it was him.

"Sergeant now. May I come in?"

Addie stepped aside, holding the flap open wide enough for his large frame. He removed his hat and ducked his head as he stepped in. Did he know that she'd poisoned Ty? Had he been waiting all these years for her to come back so he could charge her with murder? She imagined a case file with her name on it floating around in his file cabinet all these years, and every time he leafed through his files, her name flashed by, a constant reminder of the delinquent girl he'd been assigned to keep an eye on. The girl who'd disappeared on the very day her brother-in-law had died with flu symptoms.

"You can have a seat on the cot. We don't have chairs." Addie held an arm out toward her own cot, knowing better than to offer Daisy's.

"I won't be long."

"How'd you know where to find me?"

"Wavey told me you'd come back, so I made it a point to find out where you were."

Wavey sent him? Had Wavey figured out a way to be rid of her?

"Are you here alone?" he asked, lifting the edge of her coverlet and shining his electric torch beneath the cot.

Addie couldn't image who he'd think would be hiding in her tent. Except for Rumor. "Are you looking for someone?"

"Rumor's missing. Have you seen her?"

"No. I just got back from the fair. I was out with a friend." The sweetness of the honey wine in her stomach made her feel queasy.

"Mary said that she had come here to see you."

"This is where she would've come, but like I said, I've just returned."

"Do you have any idea where else she'd be?"

Sal was the first person to pop in her mind, but she couldn't sic a police sergeant on him. Sal wasn't too fond of coppers; and besides, if Rumor was with Sal, she'd be safe. "I can ask around."

"I'd appreciate that. Wavey is worried sick."

Addie sat down on the edge of her cot to buckle her shoes back on. "If I find her, want me to bring her home?"

"No need. I'll be asking around with you." He smiled, a wide and mischievous smile, with the two front teeth slightly crossed below his great mustache.

"You're . . ." Addie cocked her head, imagining him without his mustache, trying to remember the young clean-shaven officer who used to come by to check up on her. That was it. They had the exact same smiles. As a girl, Addie had never put it together. Now, looking back with a woman's perspective, she knew that Wavey had the look and lightness of a woman in love whenever Officer Darby stopped by— always coming at lunch, when Ty was away at work. "You're Rumor's father."

He stood rigid, both hands clasping the brim of his hat, and gave a slight nod.

Rumor had told Addie that her father's name was Jack Donnelly, not Clyde Darby. "Rumor doesn't know. Does she?"

"No."

Addie had so many questions. How did Wavey end up with Jack, the man Rumor and Mary thought to be their father? Talking to the girls, Addie knew that Wavey had never told them about Ty or that he was Mary's real father, and now, Addie realized that Jack wasn't Rumor's father, either. Had Clyde abandoned Wavey? "And you didn't feel it your responsibility to stick around and take care of Rumor?"

The muscles in his jaw tightened and he closed his eyes. "That's something you would need to talk to Wavey about." He turned and took a step toward the exit. "Rumor's missing, and that's what we need to focus on."

Addie didn't like the thought of bringing a police sergeant around to her friends. "Wouldn't it be better if we spread out? You know, divide and conquer?"

"This is my only lead at the moment."

At least he wasn't in uniform. She could just imagine everyone's lips clamping shut if she showed up with a cop. "Okay, but it would be best not to let them know you're a police sergeant."

"Whatever it takes," he said. "And, by the way, it's good to see you again, Addie."

"Do you think you can loosen up a bit? It's gonna be hard to pass you off as a civilian."

"I'll give it a shot," he said. "But I have a lot of years of training to forget."

"Never mind. I'll tell them you're a captain in the navy," Addie said, following him out of her tent. "That'll explain it. Or would you rather be a commander?"

"Captain's fine."

Sal's tent was dark, and so were Heinrich and Frieda's, and Lilly and Eva's. But the chickens' tent glowed bright; their three shadows and one male shadow created an animated parlor show. Their gay and giggling voices betrayed their drunkenness, making it the last place Addie wanted to take Sergeant Darby. Who knew what state of dress, or undress, they'd find them in? Clara, Giselle, and Yvette's tent had a lantern on inside, looking quiet and much less likely to humiliate her. It was bad enough that she had showed up with the nudist colony; she didn't need the chickens giving the sergeant the impression that their morals were as loose as their clothing.

"Hello," Addie called from the edge of the platform, not climbing up onto it.

"Who is it?" a quiet voice answered, obviously Clara's, since the two ballerinas had French accents.

"It's Addie, and I have a friend with me."

Clara opened the tent flaps and stepped out, looking like some sort of a fortune-teller, in a flowing red-and-purple smock and a purple turban covering her white-blond hair. She tucked in some stray strands at the sight of Clyde. "Is everything okay?"

"Sorry to bother you, but we're looking for my niece, Rumor."

"Oh, dear, is she missing?" Clara asked. "What does she look like?"

"She's fifteen and has long, curly brown hair. Have you seen anyone like that around here this evening?"

"I wish I could help," Clara said, "but I just got back about an hour ago, and I've been inside reading ever since. I haven't seen any young girls around here."

Turning away from Clara's tent, Addie stared at the only other option. Now the chickens' tent glowed, illuminating some bawdy girly show inside, with two figures gyrating around the tent like belly dancers while two other figures sat watching.

"I doubt they've seen her," Addie said. "They seem rather preoccupied."

"We can always ask," Clyde said.

"I don't think . . ."

Clyde must have sensed her apprehension, because he put his hand up, stopping her. "I'm a police officer, Addie. There's not much that I haven't seen."

Addie followed behind him toward the chickens' tent. Clyde, though older, still had the same well-built frame and slightly bowlegged walk that Addie remembered. As she watched him, it was as though he had been conjured straight from her past.

Again Addie called, "Hello," up to the chickens, without climbing onto their platform.

"Addie?" Ida's voice answered. "Come on in, we're having us a grand ole time."

"Could you come out here?"

"Don't be silly," Ida said.

Their tent reeked of cigar smoke and perfume. Addie felt as if she'd walked straight into a bordello filled with half-dressed women in silk robes. Empty bottles of beer, shoes, stockings, garters, discarded dresses, and even a fox stole lay scattered around the tent. They had obviously interrupted something, because Joe lay propped up on one of the cots, wearing nothing but a look of exasperation and a pillow across his lap. Addie gave the girls a look, pantomiming that they should cinch up their robes, which they did just in time, before Clyde ducked through the opening.

The girls' heads perked right up at the sight of Clyde.

"Where'd you catch this one, Addie?" Dottie asked.

"This is Captain Darby," Addie said. She could almost see the hairs rising up on Ida's head as she eyed him.

"A navy captain," Addie said.

Joe gave him a salute from his position on the cot. "I'd rise to attention, Captain, but don't think I can quite manage it at the moment." His words were muffled by the cigar protruding from his mouth.

Dottie giggled.

"Mind your manners, Joe," Lucille said.

Ida stretched and rose from her position on the cot. Her robe clung to every curve of her body, including her nipples, which poked up under the silk. "Great thundering Jesus. Just looking at that mustache is making me homesick," Ida said in her slow drawl.

"You can call me Clyde," he said, looking a bit ruddy in the face.

"We're looking for Rumor," Addie said, wishing the girls would've been out. "Have you seen her this evening?"

"Sure we did," Dottie said. "You should've seen her—"

"Is she AWOL then?" Lucille cut in. "I didn't know they let little girls into the navy."

"Clyde's her—" Addie began, but Clyde interrupted.

"I'm a friend of her mother. You say she was here?"

"Rumor was looking for Addie," Lucille said. "We didn't know where Addie was so we gave Rumor some money for a taxi."

"Last time we saw her, she was making a beeline, straight for the exit," Ida said.

"Which exit?" Clyde asked.

"I'm not a hundred percent sure, because we didn't follow her, but I'd assume she took the nearest, the east gate."

"How long ago?"

"Oh, quite some time," Lucille said. "I'd say at least a couple of hours. Wouldn't you say so, girls?"

"That'd be my guess," Ida said.

"Did she seem upset?"

Dottie's mouth opened as if she had something to say, but Lucille put her hand on Dottie's leg, causing Dottie to shut her mouth. It was obvious they were hiding something. Addie wondered if Clyde had sensed it too.

"Just disappointed," Lucille said. "She wanted to see Addie."

"Any idea where she went?"

"No. We gave her money for a taxi and told her to go home."

"If you remember anything else or see her around, will you let Addie know? Rumor's mother is worried."

Ida sidled up to Clyde and whispered in a husky drawl, "Maybe you and your grand ole mustache can come by another day, once Rumor's all snug as a bug in her own bed, of course, and I can show you some of my roping and riding skills."

Once outside, back into the dim light of the encampment and the smoky sage smell of dying fires, Addie took a deep breath and looked up at Clyde. "Really, they're nice girls. They're just a bit"—Addie tried thinking of a nice way to describe the chickens, but couldn't, so she settled on "vivacious."

Addie figured if there had been any hope of Wavey letting the girls come to see her, which there didn't seem to be anyway, but if there had been, it'd evaporated the moment Clyde had stepped into the chickens' tent.

"There's something they're afraid to say," Clyde said. "In front of me, at least. Do you think they'd hold anything back that was important to finding Rumor?"

"No. They're brazen, but they care about people. Especially Lucille. She would've said something."

"Mary said something about a boy named Sal. Do you know where I can find him?"

"No, I don't. But I can tell you, if she's with him, she's safe. Sal's a good boy, and he'd act like more of a big brother to her than anything."

"Which tent is Sal's?"

Addie hated to do it, but she pointed at the darkened tent, lit by only the dim lantern on the porch.

"You think he may be sleeping?"

"No. Would you like me to check?"

"If you don't mind."

Addie called several times and received no answer.

Clyde put his hands on the edge of the platform and sprang up onto it. If Addie hadn't been so shocked at the dawning fact that he planned on trespassing, she would've been impressed at his youthful jump. "Hello," Clyde called into the tent. "Anyone in there?"

When Addie saw him reaching toward the flap, she said, "We can't go in without permission."

But Clyde ignored her. "This is Sergeant Darby with the San Diego Police," he said, drawing out a billy club with one hand and untying the tent flap with the other.

Oh, good Lord, if anyone saw her bringing a police officer to their camp and letting him snoop around, she'd be out on her butt in the morning. It would be the ultimate betrayal. Addie watched his electric torch flashing around inside Sal and Joe's tent. He looked more like a cat burglar than anything else. If Heinrich came around the corner and saw him, he'd ambush Clyde, pounding him with fists first and asking questions later. She'd seen him do it before.

All this trouble was because of her. If she had never tried to contact Wavey, if she had never spoken to Rumor or encouraged her, none of this would be happening. Why couldn't she have let them be? She did nothing but bring trouble to Wavey.

Clyde finally emerged and turned to tie the flaps. Addie's nerves sent electrical currents all across her skin as she willed him to hurry and get off Sal's porch. Clyde stepped down the two steps leading to the courtyard, sizing up the area, glancing between the tents and under the porches.

"You doing alright?" Clyde asked.

"We respect each other's privacy. If they knew I let you inside . . ."

"I don't remember you having a choice." Clyde winked at her. "Well, other than waiting for the boy to appear, I don't know what else I can do here. Would you keep an eye out for him?"

"Yes, of course."

"If you find Rumor, will you bring her home? And if you find out any more information"—Clyde reached into his coat pocket and pulled out his wallet—"there's an officer stationed near the east gate. Show him this card and tell him you have information for me. He'll call it in to the station."

Addie took the card. The seriousness of Clyde's words and actions created a stone of worry in the pit of her stomach. What if Rumor was not with Sal? Where could she be? For the first time since Clyde had arrived, she realized that Rumor could be in danger.

Clyde nodded his head toward the chickens' tent. "Why don't you go back in and tell them I've gone. See if they'll give you any more information."

"You don't think she's in danger?"

"God, I hope not."

And Addie saw in his face, not the concern of a police officer, but the fear of a father. He did love her; and whatever his reason for not raising her or claiming her as his daughter, the love was there.

"I'll do all I can here," Addie said. "I'll see if the girls know anything else, and I'll wait for Sal to get back."

"I'm going back to Wavey's. Maybe she's come home."

"Does her father . . . ?" Addie started to ask, but stopped at the look on Clyde's face. Addie knew immediately that she'd said something wrong but had no way to take it back. "I'm sorry, I mean, the man she thinks is her father. Have you talked to him?"

"Jack? Is he in town?"

Addie felt as if she were suddenly stepping across a tightly strung high wire, afraid to betray Rumor's confidence but worried she was in danger. "He lives in Mission Beach, and they visit him every Sunday."

Something flashed across Clyde's face but disappeared as quick as it had come. Addie could have sworn that it was either fear or anger. It was replaced so quickly with the trained stare of a policeman, she didn't have time to tell.

"Do you know where he lives in Mission Beach?"

"No."

"You said *they*. Do you mean Rumor and Mary?"

Addie nodded, and before she could get another word out, Clyde set off toward the fair, she assumed in the direction of the east gate. "Will you send word when you find her so I don't worry?" Addie yelled to his disappearing form, and he raised one arm as if in answer.

When she stepped back into the chickens' tent, Joe had had enough. There was nothing more amusing than a naked, erect, and infuriated preacher hurling his cigar to the ground. The stogie barely made a sound nor did any damage, other than scattering ashes across the wooden planks. There followed the delight of watching him try to stomp the cinders out with his bare feet, all the while cursing the God he loved so much and the audacity of women, and griping, "Why can't a man have one single evening to enjoy himself without everyone and their navy captain traipsing through?"

Even though she'd barged in on the chickens too, they seemed to get just as much pleasure in watching Joe and trying to stifle their giggles as his johnson went from bouncing mad to sad and hangdog.

Addie almost felt sorry for him as he yanked on his official Sleepy Valley training pants and stormed for the exit, tripping on a discarded red heel and catching himself by grabbing on to Ida's shoulder, which unleashed her pent-up amusement, making all three of them burst into laughter.

"Sorry for ruining your evening," Addie said.

"Are you kidding?" Dottie said. "I'm glad to be rid of him. That man don't know when enough is enough."

"His welcome was as worn out as a hobo's britches," Ida said.

"What happened to your sister's navy man?" Lucille asked.

"He's out looking for Rumor."

Lucille sat down on a cot and patted the spot next to her for Addie. "She's probably home by now, just took some time to sulk is all."

When Addie sat down, Lucille put her arm around her and gave her a squeeze. "She's fine."

"You should've seen her," Dottie said. "We took her to the garden and she stripped off all her clothes, like it was nothing."

"She has the cutest little figure."

Addie withheld the urge to scream at them, needing whatever information they had.

"She's a natural, just like her aunt Addie." Lucille patted Addie's knee.

"And you should've seen the look on Sal's face."

"I think he got lovesick right then and there."

Addie took a deep breath, then let it out. "Is she with Sal now?"

"No. It was the strangest thing. After they kissed, he gave her money for the taxi and told her to go home."

"I thought you girls gave her the money."

"Oh no, it was Sal, but we weren't about to rat him out and get him all tangled up with a missing girl."

Addie imagined how humiliating that must have been for Rumor. "Was she nude when he kissed her?"

"Naked as a jaybird and looking like a wood nymph, with flowers braided all through her hair."

"Was he?"

"No, which made it look a bit unnatural, wouldn't you say so, girls? Sal's the nudist, but was fully clothed, and Rumor isn't a nudist, but was naked. It's a bit ironic if you think about it."

"Think about it?" Addie couldn't contain her anger any longer. "Think about it? Why would you take her there?"

"What's wrong with it? I don't see anything wrong, do you, girls?" Dottie asked.

"Hell, no," Ida said. "We got naked kids that ain't knee high to a duck, running all over the colony."

Addie felt herself shaking. "But their parents are nudists. Rumor's mother is not a nudist. You had no right."

What were they thinking? Even more, what was she thinking? She should never have come to San Diego. If it wasn't for Addie, Rumor would never have been in the position for them to take her into the garden. Wavey was right. She was a nudist, for Christ's sake. It's not like she came as one of Sister Aimee's entourage or as a secretary for one of the dignitaries or even as a waitress. She came as a member of one of the cootch shows. A spectacle, really. People didn't come to see the benefits of naturism. They didn't come to learn about sun worship or how clothing suffocates the cells. They came to pay a quarter for a thrill, to see a bunch of naked women and try to get them to jump up and down, just like they'd taunt the monkeys in a zoo.

"Are you alright, honey?" Addie realized that she'd doubled over and was rocking back and forth.

"Lay her down, girls," Dottie said. "I think she's having a spell."

"No," Addie said, rising to her feet to get out and away from them. "I just need some fresh air."

Shaking and queasy, Addie wandered back to her tent. A woman wearing a work jacket over her tattered nightdress walked by, holding the hand of a little girl, who was the spitting image of her tired and worn-out mother. Addie had the vision of the little girl growing up, getting married at sixteen, and carrying on another generation of poverty. She thought about all the fair workers in the encampment and how they'd pack up and move on once the Exposition had run its course. But to what? Another fair? Their hometowns, where they couldn't find work in the first place? There were so many of them. Addie had been isolated from the Depression at Sleepy Valley, never waiting in a bread line or sleeping on the streets, but now, if she left, what else was there for her? Maybe Frieda was right, and she needed to start thinking business. She could try Sister Aimee's church. The Angelus Temple was in Los Angeles, just a short train ride from San Diego. This far south, even if she had to sleep on the streets, it was at least warmer than most parts of the country. And she did have a bit of savings.

Addie closed her eyes and took three deep breaths, ashamed she was wallowing in her own troubles while Rumor was missing. When she opened them, she noticed Sal and Joe's lantern glowing inside their tent. Probably just Joe, still fuming from her interruption of his evening fun, but maybe Sal had returned. As Addie was getting up the nerve to call into the tent, possibly throwing Joe back into a tantrum, Sal stepped into the courtyard. He looked tired and smelled like rotting meat.

"Hey," Sal said. "You're up late."

"Where's Rumor?"

He shrugged his shoulders. "At her house?"

"She hasn't been with you?"

"No. My pal at Gay's Lion Farm asked me to help feed the cats and clean their pens. They were shorthanded tonight."

"Rumor's missing. Nobody's seen her."

Sal's eyebrows pinched together and he ran his hand through his hair. "Well," he said, as if searching his conscience.

"I already know about what happened in the garden," Addie said.

Sal nodded. "I'm sorry."

"Do you know where she could've gone?"

"No. I didn't mean to . . . I didn't mean to disrespect you or Rumor."

"You gave her taxi money and told her to go home?"

"It was the wrong thing. I know it upset her. I should've left the moment I saw them in the garden, but I'm afraid my libido took over my head for a bit."

"She's just so young," Addie said.

"I know," Sal said. "It's been eating at me. I'll grab some clean clothes and go to her house to see what I can do to help."

"I think it would be best for you to lie low. Her family was here, and . . ." Addie didn't know how to put it without telling her sister's business. "They have the police involved, and your name came up."

Sal looked puzzled for a moment, then he nodded. "If you need me, come get me."

She watched him climb up the steps of his platform and disappear into his tent, all the while thinking how she would miss him the most.

CHAPTER TWENTY-TWO
RUMOR

Rumor tried to sleep, hoping to force morning to come quicker, but her mind tumbled in the dark. Everything mixed together, the garden and Orion, figs, the fog, carousel horses, and naked bodies. Sal's hands on her and her father's hands on her, and the falling, the tumbling, the gasping for air that would not come. Papa's hands were supposed to pull her from the surf and put Band-Aids on her scraped knees. Who would do that for her now? At some point, she must have dozed off, because she awoke to a voice calling her name. A man's voice. Outside, she could see an electric torch sweep across the planks, lighting little slivers of it at a time.

"Jack." Someone pounded at the door. "Jack Donnelly?"

Rumor didn't answer. She lay still and listened.

"Jack Donnelly?" He pounded again, but it didn't sound like a human hand. He knocked with something hard, maybe a club? "This is the San Diego Police Department. We need to talk to you."

Rumor didn't move.

"Your daughter is missing."

"Hello?" Rumor stepped over to the door, grasping the latch in one hand. "How do I know you're with the police?" she asked through the gap.

"Rumor?" the man's voice called, sounding filled with relief. "Rumor, are you okay? This is Sergeant Darby. Your mother's friend, Sergeant Darby. Do you remember me from the other day?"

"The bolt won't slide unless you lift the door," she said.

"Is your father, Jack, in there with you?" She saw the tip of a nightstick under the door, and it rose.

"No. I'm alone." She slid the bolt and opened the door to the face of the sergeant and his big walrus mustache. She noticed that he wasn't wearing his uniform and thought it odd that he carried a club off duty.

Rumor followed Sergeant Darby up the wooden sidewalk to a shiny black car parked on the main road. She looked behind her, afraid Papa would see her leaving with a strange man and try to stop them. Papa wouldn't stand a chance against the sergeant, especially when he was armed with a club. Rumor wondered if he had a gun strapped somewhere under his coat, just like in the moving pictures. He opened the front passenger door for her.

"Can I sit in the back?" Rumor asked.

With a single nod, he swung the door shut, then opened the rear door. "Didn't want you to feel under arrest or anything."

Funny how she'd started the night hearing the rumble of his engine, and now her night would end with it also. Rumor tossed her bundle of clothes into the backseat and slid in, still wearing Papa's shirt that smelled of motor oil and Aqua Velva. She hoped she wouldn't get sick in the sergeant's car. Rumor made a pillow of her bundle and lay down across the seat, listening to the sergeant's shoes on the pavement, circling around the car and stopping at the driver's door. But he didn't open it. She imagined him giving Papa's neighborhood the once-over, on the lookout for Papa. Or had something caught his eye? It felt like many frozen moments before he climbed in.

The car engine turned over right away and they rolled down the boulevard. Rumor tried to imagine where they were, by how many turns they'd taken and an occasional glance up at the window, first at the top of palm trees sliding by and then the upper stories of downtown buildings and light poles and the streetcar cables, so she'd know they were close to home. She waited for the sergeant to interrogate her. Wasn't that what they did? But all he did was say, "How you doing back there?" and "Let me know if you need anything."

Rumor imagined Papa returning to his garage and finding it empty. She should have left him a note so he wouldn't worry. The road sounded different and she figured they were on the bridge. Why had she gone to Papa's? She'd ruined everything. If only she'd stayed home in bed, with Mary. She remembered the image of Mary on the inside of their window as she'd shut it earlier that evening. It seemed so long ago.

With each turn, her stomach rolled and she felt as if she were drifting out at sea, rising and falling on the swells.

"My stomach feels sick," Rumor said to the back of the sergeant's seat.

The car moved to the right and came to a stop.

"Let's get you some air." He helped her out, guiding her to the front of the car, where she sat on the road in the beam of his headlights. It seemed as if nothing existed beyond this spot, lost in the fog and bright lights of the sergeant's car. She shivered in Papa's thin shirt, the fog soaking right through it, but couldn't bear the thought of getting back into the swaying car.

"Here you go," the sergeant said, draping his coat over Rumor's shoulders.

It felt warm and smelled earthy, like the incense at the Catholic church.

They'd stopped somewhere by the tidal marsh, but in the dark and fog, Rumor couldn't tell if the tide was high or low.

When her stomach felt settled, she stood and turned toward the car to find the sergeant leaning against the front fender in his shirtsleeves and suspenders. All that time, he'd been so quiet she'd thought he was waiting in the warm car.

As they pulled up to the courtyard, Rumor noticed every lamp in their bungalow on, lighting it up like a luminaria. As the sergeant knocked on the door, Rumor stood and waited on her own front step, the bundle of her clothes clutched to her chest. Mother opened it, still dressed in her evening clothes.

"Oh, thank God. Where have you been?"

Rumor didn't answer. She couldn't deal with her mother.

"She's not feeling well and needs to lie down," the sergeant said. "I found her at Jack's."

Mother gasped but stood aside. "What are you wearing?" Mother sounded panicked, her anger rising. "Did he . . . ? Are you . . . ? You are forbidden . . ."

Mary sat on the couch in her pajamas and wave cap, with her hands tucked in and squeezed between her knees. She stared at Rumor with wide, frightened eyes, and Rumor realized that she had ruined everything for Mary too. She had pulled Mary down with her, and now they were both in deep water with nothing left to cling to.

"Maybe you can talk with her tomorrow," the sergeant said to Mother. "She's not feeling well and needs some sleep."

Mother opened her mouth to object but then closed it. When she opened it again, all she said was "Get to bed. You too, Mary."

Mary followed Rumor into the bedroom, leaving Mother and Sergeant Darby in the living room and the bedroom door cracked open so they could eavesdrop.

"Did he do anything to her?" Mother asked.

"I don't know. She didn't say anything and Jack wasn't there."

"He needs to be questioned. The girls have been going behind my back."

"Sorry," Mary whispered, "I had no choice but to tell. When he didn't find you with Aunt Addie or with that boy, Sal . . ."

Oh God, he went to the camp. Poor Aunt Addie. She imagined Sal being interrogated, but it served him right.

"How did you end up at Papa's?" Mary asked. "When Sergeant Darby came back from the fair and said you had left in a taxi, but then you never came home, I was beside myself, darling. A taxi driver would be a perfect murderer. All he'd have to do is wait outside the Exposition and his next victim would climb right in—"

"Shhh," Rumor said. "I want to hear them."

"I thought Jack lived in Los Angeles," Mother said, her voice sounding close to tears. "He was supposed to leave town. That was the agreement."

"You didn't file a report?" It sounded strange, having a deep male voice resonate inside their bungalow, a man intruding on their family and asking personal questions.

"I thought I'd save the girls from knowing. I thought that if I could only keep them away from him, they'd be safe."

"What agreement?" Mary asked. "Do you know about any agreement?"

"No." Rumor shook her head.

"Why did you go to Papa's?"

"I don't want to talk about it." Rumor climbed into her bed. It seemed like so long ago that she'd lain there, listening and waiting for Mother to leave, but it was that very night. Outside, the darkness had begun to fade. Pretty soon, the sun would rise and she'd have to face her mother. Rumor pulled the covers up and got a whiff of motor oil and Aqua Velva. She swung her legs back over the edge and sat up.

Mary still sat, perched at the foot of their bed, with her brain probably working double-time, trying to sort things into some sort of a melodrama. Rumor pulled Papa's shirt over her head, balled it up, and threw it at the wall. She stood in the center of their room in nothing but her panties, watching it hit and drop to the ground. Mary gasped.

Before Rumor could blink, Mary had leapt from the bed and swung their bedroom door shut.

"What has gotten into you?" Mary asked. "Get some clothes on. That's indecent."

Rumor sunk back down on the bed, and like the switch of a light, the room started to sway. It felt as if she'd been dropped overboard, into an icy sea.

"Oh, darling, you've got goose pimples all over you," Mary said, slipping something over Rumor's head. "Slide your arms in."

A chill sunk in all the way to her bones. She curled into a ball and pulled the blanket over her head.

"Mother," Mary called out. "Come quick, Rumor's shivering all over."

Rumor felt a hand slip beneath the covers and cup her forehead. "She doesn't have a fever, but she's clammy."

"It's been a long night," the sergeant said, from right beside her bed.

Why was he in their bedroom?

"Do you have some extra blankets?" he asked.

"Mary, go get some blankets," Mother said, "and the heating pad. It's under my bed."

"Damn him," Mother said. "What did he do to you, sweetheart?"

Mother's voice sounded muffled and far away, as if she were drifting off. Rumor curled up tighter and didn't say a word.

"Answer me," Mother sounded angry. "What did he do?"

"It's been a long night," the sergeant said. "It can wait until morning."

"That may be too late. I want him arrested tonight."

The blankets smothered Rumor and muffled all the voices that were floating over, pushing her deeper and deeper below the surface, tumbling in the surf, like when she was a child and the wave had snatched her from Papa's side, unsure of which way was up and unable to find the surface. But Papa had saved her, brought her into the air, and hugged her to his body as he carried her to shore.

"Papa didn't do anything," Rumor said. "He wasn't home when I went there. I'm cold and I'm tired."

Silence. Rumor held her breath because silence was the space when adults paused, deciding whether they believed you or not.

"Please," Rumor said. "I want to sleep."

"She's home safe," the sergeant said. "It can wait until she's rested."

The edge of her pile of blankets lifted, and a hand slipped in a warm heating pad, sliding it over her shoulder and down her back. She felt the pressure of someone's arms around her, then the familiar squish of her mother's breasts against her shoulder. Mother kissed the top of her head through the layer of covers. The slow warmth began to penetrate and she drifted off.

CHAPTER TWENTY-THREE
ADDIE

Sometime in the middle of the night or early morning, Addie heard someone climbing onto her porch again. In her half-dream, half-awake haze, she thought it was Daisy coming in for the night. But a man's voice called out, and she remembered. Rumor. Rumor was missing.

"Hello. Addie? It's Clyde."

"Come in." Addie sat up on her cot. She couldn't see anything but his silhouette as he came in the open flap, then stood against the white canvas.

"Did you find her?"

"Yes."

"Oh, thank goodness. Is she alright?"

"She will be. I found her at her father's. Thanks for that tip," Clyde said. "I've got to get home. This fathering thing about wore me out."

"You took the time to come here to tell me?"

"You asked me to."

"Yeah, I did, but I didn't think you would. Wavey isn't too pleased that I'm here. She doesn't want me around her girls."

"I know," he said. "But she needs you more than she knows. Don't give up on her."

Wavey needed her? Addie couldn't imagine. She remembered Frieda's words from earlier that night about how she had more to offer than she realized.

"I better go before I pass out. That other cot's looking mighty inviting."

"You're welcome to it." But as soon as the words came out, Addie imagined Daisy coming home to a big man with a walrus mustache asleep in her cot. The thought made her smile. She could just picture Clyde waking up to a naked woman sliding under the covers with him.

Addie walked into her tent to find Daisy sitting on the edge of her cot, her arms crossed, and Hobbs stepping back and forth across her letters, his sharp talons puncturing her carefully formed script. Daisy snatched a paper from under Hobbs, sending him into a flutter of ineffective flapping. He couldn't take wing but managed to keep himself upright.

"What's this?" Daisy asked, then began reading in a high-pitched and mocking tone, "'Dear Sister Aimee, My name is Addie Bates. I had the pleasure of attending your revival at the California Pacific International Exposition.'"

"You snooped through my trunk?" Addie advanced on Daisy, grabbing for the paper, but Daisy put out one arm and pressed her hand between Addie's breasts, bringing her to a halt.

"'Your words touched my heart,' blah, blah, blah, blah." Daisy's eyes slipped down the page, "Oh, here it is, the good part. 'I'm a sinner and have been displaying my naked body at Zoro Garden's Nudist Colony, all for a place to live, food to eat, and a bit of money.'"

"Give that back to me. It's none of your business."

"None of my business? You're selling us out to some two-bit preacher with a radio show? She'll be all over the airwaves, capitalizing on your salvation faster than you can say amen."

"I already talked to Frieda about it."

"Bullshit. There's no way Frieda would tell you to drag the colony beneath that swindling evangelist's feet."

"She did. She said if I give Sister Aimee a testimonial, she'll take me in."

"An *imaginary* testimonial. I swear, I wonder if you have any common sense at all. Tell her you were a prostitute or something. If you bad-mouth the colony, and it's all over the radio, the bluestockings will use it to turn the entire city against us. They'll be at our gate with pitchforks."

Addie could've sworn that was what Frieda had told her to do. She knew she'd told her to tell Sister Aimee that she was once trapped in sin, exposing her naked flesh for the price of a home and food in her belly, but now that she thought about it, she hadn't said anything about mentioning the colony.

"Why would you want to be some lamb for Sister Aimee anyway? You know what really happens to lambs?" Without waiting for an answer, Daisy continued, "They are led to the slaughter."

"Sister Aimee does a lot of good for people."

"Sure she does. All while lining her own pockets."

Daisy snatched another page from the cot, causing Hobbs to flatten his crest and growl. "And what about this one?" Hobbs snapped his beak, barely missing Daisy's hand. She went back to the high-pitched tone. "'Dear Wavey, Please forgive me for all the pain I have caused you. Could you please give me another chance? I could try to get a real job and help you and your girls. I am not the best cook, but I could learn, and I could help with the cleaning and laundry.'"

"I'm not going to stand here and be mocked," Addie said, turning toward the tent flaps. Before she reached them, Daisy had jumped up and grabbed her wrist. "Ouch! Let go of me."

"The hell I will. You're staying right here and talking to me. You know what's wrong with you, Addie?" Before Addie had a chance to respond, Daisy said, "You don't stay and fight for what's yours. You run away. This letter is nothing but begging, kissing your sister's ass, a song and dance. You're not even putting yourself on the line for the outcome, or you wouldn't have written the other letter to that two-bit preacher woman."

Daisy plunked down onto the cot, pulling Addie beside her. Daisy's hand clenched Addie's wrist, shackling her. Daisy picked up the last of the papers with her other hand. "And what about this one?" This time she read in her own voice, "'Dear Daisy, I'm sorry to leave you, but I need to find a permanent home. We both know what happened to Eleanor and that we're next.'" Daisy's voice thickened, as if she were struggling to keep her emotions in check. "'I love you and Sal, and you will forever have a place in my heart.'"

"Daisy," Addie started to say, but couldn't think of any words. She turned toward Daisy, reaching to put an arm around her, but Daisy shrugged her off.

"A letter? After all these years, just a fucking letter?" Daisy's words gurgled, sounding half-drowned in her throat.

"I'm sorry," Addie said. "I couldn't bear to—"

"Couldn't bear to what?"

"I couldn't bear to see you upset."

"That's chickenshit, Addie. If you're going to hurt someone, at least have the respect to face it."

Daisy's entire body trembled. Addie couldn't tell if she was about to start crying or about to strangle her. Instead, Daisy let go of her wrist and examined all three papers.

"You're not running this time," Daisy said. She held up the letter Addie had written to her and crumpled it into a ball. "You don't need this because you're going to talk to me and you're going to deal with my pain and my anger, whether you like it or not." She hurled the ball of paper across the tent. It hit the side and dropped onto the floorboards. Hobbs fluttered to the ground after it, wobbling like a stiff-legged old man as he stepped across the planks.

Addie felt the panic rise in her chest. She eyed the exit and wanted nothing more than to dash out of it and keep going, never looking back. She should never have come to San Diego. Coming here was stepping into her past, and it had solved nothing. She'd caused only pain for Wavey and her girls.

"And this one," Daisy said, waving the letter to Sister Aimee in the air, "is horseshit. You're not selling us out to someone who will exploit you, parading you in front of her parish like a little lost lamb and humiliating you on the radio." She ripped the page into tiny shreds and sprinkled them at Addie's feet.

"And the one to your sister. How many ineffective letters have you written to her?"

Addie looked over toward her trunk and saw her cigar box on the ground, open. "You went through my personal papers?"

"I did. Now, let bygones be bygones, and don't change the subject," Daisy said. "Have any of your letters made one lick of difference with your sister?"

Addie felt the tears rising, and her face beginning to flush. "No."

"Then what in the hell makes you think this letter will be any different?"

"I've been to her house three times. We even talked for a bit, but she told me to stay away from her and her girls."

"And have you?"

Addie nodded, and the tears let loose. She tried to stop and gulp some air, get ahold of herself, but her whole body shook and gasped as she remembered Rumor on the other side of the fence, begging her. Daisy put her arm around Addie's shoulders, pulled her close, and stroked her hair. She was right. Wavey would ignore the letter, and she would have nowhere to go once the Exposition closed.

Daisy pushed her away. "Okay, that's enough blubbering. It's time to pull yourself together."

Addie, still breathing in gasps, nodded her head and wiped her face with the edge of her coverlet. "I just don't know what to do."

"You fight for what you want. That's what you do. Go to your sister's house and tell her that you're not running off this time. That, even after the Exposition, you'll be staying in San Diego. Tell her that you're sisters, and you're there to work things out."

"She doesn't want me around her girls. She thinks I'm a bad influence and I'll hurt them."

"Are you a bad influence?"

"I've caused problems with her youngest daughter. She keeps trying to see me, defying her mother and sneaking around."

"That doesn't make you a bad influence. She's sneaking around because she wants to know you. If her mother would let you in, she wouldn't have to sneak around."

"And I'm a nudist."

"Being a nudist does not make you a bad person. I've known you for, what, fourteen or fifteen years? I have to say, you're one of the biggest Goody Two-shoes I've ever met. How many men have you slept with since you've been a nudist?"

"None," Addie said. "Men have been nothing but bad news for me."

"Are you a drunk?"

Addie smiled. "No."

"Do you think you're better than others? Are you an angry or jealous person?"

Addie shook her head. "No."

"If anyone would be a good influence, it would be you. You need to stop beating yourself up and see the beautiful woman inside." Daisy tapped Addie's chest with a hard finger. "You have a lot to offer those girls, and the biggest thing is your love."

Hobbs waddled back over to them, nipping at the shreds of paper by their feet.

"My sister won't see me because of something unforgivable I did when I lived with her."

"How old were you then?"

"Fifteen."

"So, first of all, you were a child, and secondly, you're her sister. I don't give a damn what you did, it's time for her to forgive you."

Daisy bent over and put her hand in front of Hobbs. He stepped up onto it, his talons spread out, unable to get a firm grip. "I've got a date," Daisy said, standing up and taking Hobbs back to his cage. She opened the door and held him before his perch, but he didn't step up.

"With Fred?"

"No," Daisy said. "Goddamn you, you stubborn fleabag. Step up." Hobbs refused the perch.

"A new man?"

"No. I've got a date with a water tart. She doesn't know it yet, but I found out where that girl Fred's been dating is staying. She can go to hell if she thinks she can take what's mine without a fight."

Hobbs finally stepped onto his perch with one foot. Daisy yanked her hand out, leaving him in a mass of flapping feathers and groping for the bar with his other foot as Daisy shut the door of his cage.

Addie felt as if her life had stretched taut, like the skin of a balloon, reaching the point where it would burst, either on its own or by some-one else's actions. Something was going to happen, whether she took action or not. She wanted to scream. Daisy was wrong about only one thing. She didn't always run. Once, she'd fought for what she wanted and had become a murderess. A poisoner. A sinner.

CHAPTER TWENTY-FOUR

RUMOR

Rumor awoke and dozed off several times to a bright bedroom and muffled voices on the other side of her door. Mostly Mothers and Marys, but at times she also picked out Ruths and Mrs. Keegans. The smells of toast and coffee and, later, of soup drifted through her dreams. The sound of their front door opening and closing pulled her from sleep on occasion, but she forced herself to close her eyes again. Kids played in the street; at one point, it sounded as if a child hid between the oleander bush and her window as another called out, "Ready or not, here I come."

The night before, Mother had said something about Papa leaving town. She'd said, "That was the agreement." What agreement?

The door to her bedroom creaked open. Rumor peeked out between her eyelids, expecting to see Mary, but instead spotted the brown mop of Mother's hair.

"Rumor, are you awake?"

She didn't answer.

The side of the bed sagged under her mother's weight. "Rumor." Mother shook her shoulder. "It's time to wake up now."

This was it. The hurricane named Wavey Rose Donnelly was on course, and it would be a direct hit.

Rumor opened her eyes and was surprised to see Mary in the room, also. A conspiracy. Mary stood there like the little China doll she was, her eyes painted wide open.

"I know that you girls have been sneaking around and seeing your Papa for a long time."

Not exactly true, Rumor thought. At first, Papa had done the sneaking. But in the past year and a half, they had done it.

"Seems like a sin to pretend to go to church."

"We did go to church," Rumor said. Mother's face tightened and turned red, so Rumor added, "and then to Papa's."

"You lied to me."

"He's our papa and we love him. You took that away from us."

"I was protecting you."

Before last night, Rumor would have flown into a rage, telling Mother that she was the one they needed protection from. That Papa was kind and loving and generous, and she was the one who left them home alone, coming home drunk several nights a week. She would have said that she was the one who didn't love them, but Rumor still felt the ghost of Papa's hand sliding up her bare hip, across her belly, and the rough sandpaper of his hand rubbing against her breast.

"What happened last night?" Mother asked.

What would happen to Papa if she told? She imagined the sergeant and several other officers kicking in Papa's door and arresting him. Rumor couldn't bear the thought that he'd go to jail because of her. Maybe she'd misunderstood. Maybe Papa had been asleep and didn't realize what he was doing. But then she remembered him whispering into her hair, *It's okay, love bug* and *Just relax.* Could she stand to lose her papa? He promised he'd never do it again.

"I went to the fair to see Aunt Addie, but she wasn't there, so one of her friends gave me taxi money to get back home."

Rumor could tell by the stiffening of Mother's body that she was struggling to hold in her anger just long enough to get the facts she wanted. And those facts were about Papa. Mother's anger always floated on the surface like a cork. "But you didn't come home."

"No. I went to Papa's."

"Why did you go there instead of home?" Her jaw clenched.

Rumor knew that Mother couldn't contain it much longer, so why not make her explode right then and there? She'd go berserk, storm out of the room, and Rumor could have some peace and quiet. "Because I didn't feel like coming home to find you drunk and sprawled out on the floor."

The sting of Mother's slap didn't hurt as much as she'd remembered. Mary gasped, "No, Mother," but did nothing to stop her.

"Did your papa . . . Did Jack touch you?" Mother asked.

"No."

Mother put her hand under Rumor's chin and lifted her head. "Look me straight in the eyes and tell me again."

Rumor's cheek felt warm, as if Mother's hand still lay across it. Rumor looked into her mother's splintered blue eyes but didn't say a word.

"Why are you protecting him? Do you know who he is?"

"Yes, he's my papa and he loves me."

"He's not . . ." Mother stopped and stood up, shaking. "He has a problem, Rumor. And it's a perverted problem. I was trying to protect you. I know that you hate me, and I don't blame you. You just don't understand."

Mother left the room, and moments later the front door slammed.

"Mother talked to me last night while we were waiting for Sergeant Darby." Mary paused, letting her words float in the quiet room.

Rumor didn't respond.

"Papa's been arrested before," Mary said. "For touching little girls."

"And you believe what Mother tells you?"

"I don't know what to believe, but it made me remember things. Things that felt peculiar at the time."

Rumor closed her eyes. "Shut up."

"It started to make sense," Mary said. "All the touching and how he'd comb our hair."

"Shut up."

"Remember the little girls at the amusement park sitting on his knee while he whispered to them, asking for kisses?"

Rumor clenched her fists.

"And what about Tijuana?" Mary asked. "We were naked under our robes. Don't you remember how he watched us in the bathtub?"

"No, I don't remember that at all. Shut up!"

"That night I woke up feeling cold. The blankets were off me and my privates exposed," Mary said. "I don't think I understood at the time, and I had completely forgotten about it until now, but Papa had been standing over me, and I think he was touching himself."

Rumor flung the sheet from her and pounced at Mary. She'd rip the hair right from her head if she didn't shut up.

Mary ran into the living room. Rumor slammed the bedroom door closed, leaning against it, then sliding down into a heap. Mary and Mother could just stay out there. She didn't need either of them.

"He watched as we jumped up and down on the bed." Mary's voice slipped through the crack. "What about Ruby?"

Rumor didn't know if she could ever face Papa again, knowing what he'd done to her and thinking what he may have done to other girls, what he might be doing to Ruby now. But she also couldn't imagine never seeing him again. Never going to the amusement center and finding him in his red-and-white-striped vest, sitting next to Rosa and doing his magic tricks. Never fishing in the surf with him or lying under the stars and hearing his stories about Hercules, the Gemini twins, and of

Orion and his hunting dogs. Could it all be one big misunderstanding? These new thoughts about Papa had nothing to do with the papa she loved. It didn't make sense.

Rumor heard a knock on their front door, then Mother's heels clicking across the floor. There was a man's voice. Not deep like the sergeant's. A moment later, a knock on her bedroom door. She didn't answer.

Mother barged in. "Rumor, Dr. Hoffman is here to see you."

Doctor? "I'm feeling better. I don't need a doctor."

"He's made the trip here and he will see you. I'll give you a moment to go to the restroom and do something with your hair."

As Rumor passed by her mother, she felt a tug on her scalp. "What's this?" Her mother slid something from Rumor's hair, tearing out a few strands. "A wildflower? Where'd that come from?"

Rumor gave Mother a blank stare, stepping past her without saying a word. What did it matter anyway? What more could Mother do to her? What else could Mother take away? How hard could she beat her? She certainly wouldn't forbid her to go to school in September.

Rumor caught sight of Dr. Hoffman standing in the living room, his hat in one hand and his black doctor's bag in the other. He looked older and much grayer. He'd always been friendly enough. When he'd gagged them with the tongue depressor or stuck them with needles, he'd given them a lollipop at the end of his exam.

Rumor skimmed over the top layer of her hair with the brush, making it look presentable enough. She remembered all the times Papa had run his hand over her head, twisting his finger up in the strands and leaving long ringlets. Maybe it was time to cut it all off.

When she returned to her room, Dr. Hoffman still stood in the living room. He had a very serious look on his face, not his usual big-toothed grin, which made his eyes squint almost completely shut.

Mother must have told him the sordid details of what she imagined had happened the night before.

As soon as Rumor sat back down on her bed, Mother said, "Since you won't talk to me, you've left me no other choice."

"No choice about what?"

"It's my duty to protect you, but you lie to me, sneak behind my back, and refuse to talk."

Mother's words felt ominous. That, combined with Dr. Hoffman's stoic face when she had passed him, started a churning panic in her stomach.

"You've left me no other choice," Mother said again, sounding more apologetic than angry, and that worried Rumor.

Mother opened the door and Dr. Hoffman stepped in. "Hello, Rumor," he said, sounding stiff and formal. None of the teasing—*So, I hear you've swallowed a sea urchin*—like he used to do whenever she had tonsillitis.

Mother left the room, closing Rumor in with the doctor.

He placed his hat on the dresser, covering Mary's porcelain figurine of a little Swedish milkmaid, and dropped his doctor's bag on the bed. Its handle had been worn smooth, and the leather looked recently shined, except for the edges where it was gray with dust. "Sure is a scorcher today." Dr. Hoffman removed his jacket, revealing large rings of sweat under his arms.

"I was just tired last night. I'm afraid Mother is wasting your time."

Dr. Hoffman opened his bag, peering inside. "Well, now. Your mother only wants to make sure that no harm has come to you."

"Wouldn't I know if harm had come to me?" Rumor asked. "I'm almost sixteen years old, and I'm telling you that nothing happened."

"I'm sure that you are telling the truth, dear, but your mother wants an expert opinion." He shifted the contents of his bag, pulling out a stethoscope that he looped around his neck, as well as a tongue depressor, a thermometer, and a flashlight. "I'll make it quick and be on my way."

Rumor climbed onto the bed, leaning back on the pillow.

Dr. Hoffman started his normal routine of listening to her heart and lungs, shining the flashlight at her pupils, and gagging her with the tongue depressor. It smelled as if he'd had fish for lunch, and it hadn't quite agreed with his stomach. His fingers seemed a bit short and clunky for a doctor, not really bending into angles at the joints, but merely arching in segments like a lobster tail.

He returned to his medical bag, dropping the stethoscope back into the depths. Rumor had no idea what his examination would reveal to her mother, but she was glad it was over. Outside, the neighborhood children chanted to the tap, tap, tap of a jump rope hitting the street: *Mimi had a boyfriend; his name was Michael Flynn.*

"Sit all the way up now, I need to check your head and back."

"You're not done?"

Whenever she was near him, his head began to spin.

"Almost." Dr. Hoffman burrowed through her tangled hair, fingering her scalp.

Rumor winced when he got to the lump on her head, but she didn't say a word.

He pressed harder on the exact spot, until she couldn't stand it. "Stop it." Rumor pulled away.

"How'd you get that?"

"I slipped and fell backward."

His arms started flapping, his knees began to quake.

"On what?"

"The children." Rumor waved her hand at the window, in the direction of the singsong. "I wasn't looking down and slipped on some marbles they'd left on the sidewalk."

The doctor rotated Rumor's arm, checking all sides. "And this bruise on your elbow?"

"Same thing."

"Lie back. I need to check your tummy."

Michael started twitching like a kooky rattlesnake.

The children started again with the same rhyme as Rumor scooted down, the lump on her head even more tender now that the doctor had irritated it.

He tried to dance the jitterbug but couldn't control his feet.

"I'm going to press down. Is that tender?"

"No."

"How about here?" he asked, digging his fingers into her muscles.

"No, but it will be if you don't stop pressing so hard."

Rumor felt Dr. Hoffman pulling up the bottom of her nightgown. "What are you doing?"

"I have one last place to check. Just relax. I won't hurt you."

"No!" Rumor kicked, sat up, and pulled her nightgown tight over her legs. "You're not touching me."

"Come now, I'm a doctor. I won't hurt you."

"Get out of my room and out of my house or I'm going to scream."

The door swung open. "What's going on in here?" Mother asked.

"Mother, he's trying to touch my privates. Tell him that he can't."

"Darling," Mother said. "You're a young lady now and you need to be checked there."

"Oh no, I don't."

"Yes, you do. You'll either do it nicely or we'll make you do it."

"Then, make me," Rumor said, cinching her nightgown tightly around her.

Mother advanced.

"No!" Rumor thrashed as her mother fought to grab her wrists.

Mother pushed her arms to the mattress, climbed onto Rumor's chest, and sat upon it, pinning her down like a butterfly in a display box. Dr. Hoffman pried her legs apart. Rumor brought up her knee and felt it hit something hard, guessing it to be Dr. Hoffman's jaw because he let out an angry "That is unnecessary; please hold still."

The entire thing took no longer than a few minutes, but it felt like an eternity, unable to breathe under her mother's weight and the doctor's fat hands prying her legs apart. He must have climbed up on the bed with them; she felt his forearms clamping her knees wide open, and his lobster fingers probing in her private parts.

The children outside chanted, *"Good-bye," said Miss Mimi, running down the street.*

When they'd finished and let her loose, Rumor pulled the covers over her head, wiping her tears on the edge of them.

"She has a small contusion to the back of her head and bruises on her left elbow and hip. I'd say that she fell onto something hard, but I didn't find any evidence of penetration. She is still intact."

"So, you don't think that . . . ?"

"No," Dr. Hoffman said, both of them talking as if Rumor weren't in the room with them. He gathered his bag and his hat, heading out the door. "I'll find my way out."

Her mother, just about to walk out of the room behind him, stopped in the doorway. With her back still to Rumor, she said, "I had to make sure."

Rumor pushed the covers back and sat up. "I told you nothing happened."

"I know," Mother said, turning around to face her. "But it's my obligation to protect you. I needed to make sure you weren't violated."

"The only people who violated me were you and Dr. Hoffman."

"We didn't violate you. He's a doctor."

"He's still a man."

"You and I are never going to get anywhere if you won't trust me, Rumor."

"Do you trust me?"

"No," Mother said. "Obviously not."

346

"Me, either," Rumor said, turning onto her side and pulling the covers over her head.

"I know you're trying to protect your papa, but are you sure he deserves it?"

Rumor didn't answer, and after several minutes of silence, she heard Mother walk out of the room. She didn't know if Papa deserved it or not, but her mother surely didn't deserve anything.

The children outside began a new rhyme. *Charlie Chaplin sat on a tack, how many feet did he jump back? One, two, three . . .* The rhythmic singing and tapping of the rope lulled Rumor to sleep. *Sally Rand waved her fan. Dance, dance, dance, as fast as you can.*

When she woke up, the children were gone, but their voices had mixed in with Rumor's dream of Ruby sitting on Papa's floor, with her bathing suit all cockeyed, exposing the tender flesh of her privates and the voices singing, *Ruby Anne, scary man, run, run, run, as fast as you can.* Rumor could make sure she was never alone with Papa again, but what about Ruby and all the little girls at the amusement center? Girls who thought of nothing but jump-rope rhymes and pretty seashells?

Rumor's wrists still hurt from Mother's bony hands pinning her to the bed, and her thighs felt bruised where Dr. Hoffman had pried them apart and clamped them down. How could Mother do that to her?

"Rumor?" Mother called into her room, her voice like nails on a chalkboard.

Rumor pulled the blanket over her head, wrapping herself in a cocoon like a silkworm, waiting for her own metamorphosis. She wished she could stay there until she was old enough to break free and flutter away.

"It's been two days. You cannot stay in bed forever."

Rumor rolled over, away from Mother, binding herself tight. Every breath she exhaled spread across her face, warm and moist.

"I'm sorry about the examination. Dr. Hoffman had to know that you were okay."

Rumor knew it wasn't the doctor who'd had to know. Mother wanted to know so she could have Papa locked away into some prison or loony bin. Poor Papa. He said he'd never do it again.

"You don't want me to love anyone . . ." Rumor paused, bit down on her lip, and then, through the fibers of the blankets, said, ". . . since I don't love you."

Mother tore off the blankets and rolled her around to face the light. She lay exposed and looking straight into her mother's red face. With her finger just inches from Rumor's nose, Mother hissed, "How dare you talk to me that way?"

"What other way do you deserve?"

Mother's face looked about to explode, and Rumor felt the sting and burn of Mother's hand across her cheek.

"Hit me again," Rumor said. "Do you think that will make me love you?"

Rumor lay wrapped in her blankets, listening to the muffled sounds outside. The rumble of cars, children singing jump-rope songs, her mother in the kitchen, and Mary coming home from work, tiptoeing into the room, and the sounds of her changing and the soft clink of coat hangers in their closet. Mary pressed her lips to the top of Rumor's bundle of blankets, and then she heard the door being quietly shut. Later, the door opened again, and she heard the sound of a plate on her night table and Mary's soft voice telling her that she should eat. She'd brought her a ham sandwich and glass of milk. The room went dim as the night snuck in along with the sounds of Mary and Mother mumbling from the living room and the radio creating a soft hum beneath their words. Later, she awoke to Mary coming in again, the scrape of a wooden drawer, and the soft sounds of her changing. The mattress sank as Mary sat on its edge, creating a slight rhythmic pitch to the surface as she brushed her hair. One hundred strokes. Rumor silently counted each one. The hairbrush clinked onto Mary's night table, and chilled air seeped beneath the covers as Mary lifted them and slid into her cocoon with her. Mary reached a cool hand over her, and groping beneath the covers, she found Rumor's and interlaced their fingers.

"Good night," Mary said, but Rumor didn't answer.

Mary's fingers warmed as they lay there, adjusting to the temperature of her nest.

"I'm sorry," Mary said.

Rumor poked her head out from the top of her blankets and listened for any sounds in the house. Mary breathed in and out, whistling deep and sleepy. Rumor didn't hear any footsteps, the ruffle of magazine pages, or the clink of dishes. The only sound was the deep tick, tick, tick of the old grandfather clock in the living room and the high spring-wound clicking of her own alarm clock. Rumor eased a leg out from beneath the covers, testing the air with her toes before slipping her entire body out into the dark room and padding in her bare feet to the bathroom.

Back in her room, the streetlight made the window glow, and a slice of bright light came in through the gap in the curtains, cutting diagonally across Mary's form—a bundle in the center of the bed, with silky strands of blond hair slipping from the top. The ham sandwich and milk still sat on her night table, the milk too warm to drink, probably sour and beginning to clot. The bread on the sandwich felt dry but edible. Rumor took a few bites, forcing herself to chew. The ham and mustard made a lump in her stomach, so she set it aside and looked out the window. Seeing only the yellow haze of streetlights and a dark and starless sky, she slipped back into bed with Mary.

"You need to tell," Mary said softly, her breath close and warm on Rumor's neck. "What about Ruby?"

It almost sounded as if Mary were talking in her sleep and had dozed back off, because she didn't say anything else.

"Scoot over," Rumor said. "You're on my side of the bed."

Mary moved, taking her warmth with her. Rumor pulled the blankets tight, waiting for her body heat to radiate and warm the inside of her cocoon. She remembered Papa's warm breath on the top of her head as he whispered for her to relax and lay still, murmuring, *Hey diddle diddle, the cat and the fiddle.* The sand on Papa's cot, his dry hand snagging across her stomach and breast, the queasiness, knowing it was wrong. Anger. Shoving back against him and toppling them to the floor. And the arc of the lightbulb swinging back and forth, and Papa saying he was sorry, promising never to do it again, and calling her love bug. She couldn't forget the image of Ruby, sitting on the floor, with her privates peeking out the side of her bathing suit and the sand of Papa's garage clinging to the insides of her thighs. Mary was right—what about Ruby? Rumor would never forget the sound of Papa walking away, his steps fading into the fog, and the white slices of light piercing through the gaps of the boards. And then the voice of Sergeant Darby come to take her home. What about Ruby? What about Papa? What would happen to her papa? She couldn't imagine him in a cell or locked into a room where he couldn't tinker with his inventions or pull scallop shells from behind children's ears. She couldn't imagine him not being able to gaze up at the stars. What would Papa do without the stars?

How long had the ham sandwich been sitting beside her bed? Her stomach churned and she felt it coming up her throat. Rumor ran for the bathroom and made it just in time to be sick. Kneeling on the cold tiles, her head over the toilet, she began to cry big tears that plunked into the bowl. Mary came up behind her, and with her soft and gentle hands, she gathered up Rumor's hair. The cool air felt good on her neck.

"Thank you," Rumor said.

But instead of Mary's voice answering, it was Mother's. "You're welcome."

Rumor swatted at the hand holding her hair. "Leave me alone. I don't need your help."

"I'm your mother and you do need my help, whether you know it or not."

Rumor stood up and turned on the spigot in the sink. Cupping her hand under the running water, she took a drink, then left her mother standing in the bathroom and slid back into her bed.

When morning came again, Rumor listened to Mary getting out of bed, the sounds of clinking dishes in the kitchen, and the low murmur of her voice and Mother's. Why was Mother home? It seemed as if she hadn't left the bungalow since Sergeant Darby had brought Rumor home. Dozing off and on, Rumor lost all track of time, gauging it only by the light, the sounds outside, the smell of fried eggs in the morning, tomato soup in the afternoon, and then Mary coming in to get dressed for work. Rumor imagined her in her uniform walking up and down the aisles of the theater, hawking her candy and cigarettes and throwing demure looks at the customers. She'd caught Mary practicing different faces in the mirror, in one instant looking innocent and surprised, just like little Shirley Temple, and in the next, transformed by the smoldering and sexy gaze of Claudette Colbert. After much tiptoeing around the room, sliding the drawers open and shut, and the clinking of hangers, she felt Mary's hand on her shoulder and her lips on top of her head.

"I'm going to work. I'll bring you back a treat. How about a Baby Ruth?"

"Thank you," Rumor said, poking her head out from beneath the blanket.

"Your hair is a wreck. You look like a heathen," Mary said. "When I get home, I'll brush it out for you."

Rumor nodded and Mary tiptoed out of the room, holding her heels by the buckles.

She wasn't sure how long it had been since Mary had left, but it was still light outside when Rumor heard a knock on the front door. Her heart jumped. Could it be Dr. Hoffman again? Or maybe Mother had called the orderlies from the loony bin to cart her away. Rumor wrapped the blankets tight around her. She wouldn't let anyone near her again, even if she had to kick and scream and run out of the house in her nightgown. But instead of a man's voice, she heard a woman's. Rumor uncovered her head to listen. It didn't sound like Ruth. She sat up. Aunt Addie? Rumor stepped as silently as she could to the door and pressed her ear to the crack. It was Aunt Addie.

"I'm sorry," her mother said. "I don't approve of your lifestyle."

"I'm not going away." Aunt Addie sounded strong and firm and sure.

"I'll call the police."

Rumor felt like jerking the door open and screaming at her mother, but something told her to wait and listen to see what Addie would do.

"I didn't mean right now. I'll leave your doorstep, but I'm not leaving San Diego. I'm looking for a job. A regular job. I'm leaving the colony as soon as I can get myself work and a place to live."

"Do as you please. It has nothing to do with me. Just stay away from my girls."

"I won't betray your wishes," Aunt Addie said, her voice quavering but resolute. "But I'm your sister. I hope you find it in your heart to get to know me for who I am. I'm not a bad person."

"You're here with a nudist colony."

"I know, but I'm leaving that behind. And if you knew the people, you'd see they're no different than anyone else. It's not like everyone thinks. I have been safer at the colony than I was at the orphan home or at Uncle Henry's. It was a sanctuary for me."

"I don't want to hear it," her mother said. "Please go away."

"Okay," Aunt Addie said. "But I'll be in San Diego for good, once I find a place."

"Suit yourself," Mother said, just before Rumor heard the door shut.

Hurrying to the window, Rumor wrenched it open and leaned out, hoping to spot Aunt Addie. Aunt Addie stepped out from the courtyard, her white dress brilliant against the orange stucco of the bungalows.

"Aunt Addie," Rumor yelled, "don't give up."

Aunt Addie turned toward her and waved, her white dress fluttering like the sail on a small skiff about to tack into the wind.

Rumor jumped at the sound of her bedroom door slamming against the wall.

"Shut that window," her mother yelled.

Rumor pressed her back to the sill, feeling the cool breeze seep through her nightgown and up her spine. "Are you going to beat me? Or call Dr. Hoffman so the two of you can molest me again?"

"Shut that window."

"No," Rumor said in the most firm and defiant voice she could manage. Mother stood still in the doorway, gripping both sides of the frame, her entire body shaking.

"Shut the window, or else."

"Or else what? You've thrown Papa out and you sent Aunt Addie away. There's nothing left."

It looked as if the doorframe was the only thing containing Mother. Rumor gripped the sill, bracing for an attack, ready for her mother to pull her away. Outside, the children started jump roping again and chanting their song. *Sally Rand lost her fan. Run, run, run, as fast as you can.* Rumor did not take her eyes from her mother. The rope hit the ground in time with the children's counting. *One, two, three, four, five, six.* And with each number, Mother began to cool. Her shoulders drooped, then her hands slid down until they hung by her sides. The last thing to drop was her head and then her voice. "Well, if that's how it's going to be," she said, turning and closing the door behind her.

The next day, when the room had fallen dark but the night still sounded young, Mother's and Mary's voices mingled together in the living room. Outside, cars rattled by, and Louis Armstrong crooned from a radio somewhere down the street. Rumor heard a knock on the door, then Sergeant Darby's deep rumble as he entered the house. After the door had shut, his murmurs combined with her mother's sounded harmonious—a male and a female, like most homes had. Like she used to have with her own mother and father. Rumor listened, trying to make out individual words. She heard "privacy" and "thank you" just before her bedroom door squeaked open and Mary stepped in.

"Is that Sergeant Darby?" Rumor asked.

"Yes, darling." Mary climbed up onto the bed with Rumor and sat cross-legged, tucking her dress into the diamond her legs had formed.

"What's he want?"

"Beats me."

They both listened, but only a few words made it through the wall. Rumor slid out from beneath her blankets and padded to the door in her bare feet. With her ear to the door, she heard Sergeant Darby say, "Yes, I'm sure."

"Where?" her mother asked.

"Los Angeles."

"How do you know for sure?"

"He checked in at my old precinct, just like I told him to."

"How do you know he won't turn right around and come back?"

"He's got to check in every day until he has a permanent place, then once he does, they'll keep an eye on him."

Until Rumor felt Mary's hand take hold of her own, she hadn't known she'd been listening too. They both rested their heads against the door.

"That's the best we can do for now," the sergeant said.

"How do you know he won't find other girls?"

Rumor's insides clenched, and she felt nauseous, picturing Ruby's tiny little body sitting on the floor of Papa's garage. Would there be another Ruby living in Los Angeles? Mary squeezed her hand, returning her tight grip.

"I made my point with him, and he knows we're watching. I'm sorry, but that's all we can do."

Rumor felt like pounding on the back of the door and sobbing for them to stop. The man they were discussing was her papa. Not some stranger in a police file. He was her papa and he was sorry. He liked doing magic tricks and taking them fishing and building bonfires on the beach. He invented things. He had a surfboard with a motor and he fixed radios and bought them candy apples and popcorn.

"It gives me peace of mind to know my girls—" Mother stopped in the middle of her sentence but then continued, "Rumor and Mary will be safe."

Mary tugged on Rumor's arm, leading her away from the door and back to the bed. They both climbed on, sitting face-to-face. Mary's hands had always been so thin and white, too useless to twist open jar lids or play Red Rover, but right then, holding them in her own, Rumor realized that no matter how weak Mary was or how much Mary's head was filled with fluffy dreams, she had been there for her. They were sisters, and that was something Mother hadn't taken from her.

"I can't believe that Papa's gone," Mary said. "None of this has felt real, and I keep thinking I'll wake up and we'll still take the streetcar on Sunday."

Rumor gasped, a sound that felt as if it had been trapped inside her for days and had just finally bubbled out. Sobs racked her shoulders and she couldn't stop. Mary pulled her closer, rubbing Rumor's back in small circles, without words, just holding her, trying to soothe something that couldn't be soothed.

They eventually climbed back beneath the covers and lay clinging to one another. Rumor's eyes felt puffy, like anemones when you poked your finger into them. She wondered if they'd ever see Papa again. As she listened to Mary's soft cries, Rumor realized that Mary had lost him too, and it was all her fault. If she'd stayed home that night, never going to the fair or taking the taxi to Mission Beach, they'd both still have Papa, and he wouldn't be lost somewhere in Los Angeles, without a place to live. She imagined his garage, the crates of wires and scraps of metal, and the sand on the floor. And his cot. Her stomach felt queasy, that guilty-conscience kind of sick—when you know you've done something wrong, but you can't take it back.

Rumor didn't know how long they'd been lying in bed before she heard the front door open and close and the sound of the sergeant's shoes on the walk, fading away down the courtyard steps. An engine turned over, strong and oiled. It shifted into gear and rumbled down the street.

The smell of gardenia crept into the open crack of window and, like soft, perfumed fingers, beckoned her outside. Rumor shimmied the sash up and swung one leg over the sill.

"Where are you going?" Mary asked.

"Outside. I need some air."

"Are you running away?"

"No. I'm not even wearing shoes," Rumor said, wiggling the foot she still had inside the room.

"Can I come with you?"

"If you like." Rumor dropped out the window and onto the grass, coarse and cold on her naked feet. The sea breeze pressed Rumor's nightgown against her skin, the thin rayon so cold it felt wet. Goose pimples ran across her shoulders.

Mary's head and arms poked out the window, emerging like a worm from its hole.

"You need to come out sideways, one leg at a time," Rumor said.

"Help me, darling," Mary whispered.

Mary wrapped her arms around Rumor's neck, and she pulled her through the window, sliding her out into the night.

They sat on the grass with their nightgowns pulled tight around their legs. The bay sparkled with the deck lights of the carriers and destroyers, and beyond them lay black ocean. Nothingness. There was a gap of dark water between the city and the horizon, where the stars began and then folded back, over their heads, covering them and the city.

Mary scooted close, looping her arm around Rumor's. "It's chilly out here, darling."

"You can go back in."

"And miss seeing the night with my dear sister? I wouldn't think of it. Remember when we threw my school notes into the bay? What do you think ever happened to them? You think they made it all the way to China?"

"Maybe," Rumor said, knowing they couldn't have possibly made it out of the bay. "Or maybe Hawaii or Japan."

Scorpio sat on the horizon, just about to drop into the nothingness, chasing Orion to the other side of the world. In a few hours, the seven sisters would appear behind them, on the eastern horizon, followed by Orion and his everlasting lust.

CHAPTER TWENTY-FIVE

ADDIE

Addie closed her eyes, languid in the sun and letting the distant noises from the fair lull her. She imagined herself floating on the jumble of voices, over the waves of music and distant screams of delight. Everything felt more intense, more meaningful, as if she had to soak it all in because it would soon be gone. She would no longer be a part of the colony. Whether Wavey took her in or not, she planned on finding a job in San Diego, come hell or high water. Even with her eyes closed, she knew where everyone was and what they were doing. She felt Clara and Yvette lying close to her on other cowhides. Frieda would be behind her easel; Joe and Lilly were either shooting at the target or sitting on a rock, with their bows propped next to them. Heinrich would be on the exercise ground waiting for cues from the customers as to when he should lift his barbell or rouse the women into action; the chickens would be by the brook, flirting with young customers, and Daisy would be either napping or rolling a ball for Hobbs to waddle after.

Maybe one day she'd have the feeling of being wanted somewhere. She had thought she'd found that at Sleepy Valley, and she had for fifteen years, but now she was no longer of any use to Heinrich. Deep down, she'd always known this was not a real family. Heinrich cared about them, but business was business. She loved the crazy nudists with all their quirks, gossip, and melodrama. Addie couldn't imagine what it would be like waking up each morning without Daisy in a bed or cot next to her. She'd especially miss Sal and the chickens. And even Joe giving his blasphemous sermons. She'd never again spend a morning at Sleepy Valley with the damp, freshly mowed grass sticking to her ankles and all the suntanned bodies lounging around, the nudists laughing and sharing meals. She'd never again float in the emerald lake or take a canoe into the center, away from the guests, drifting wherever it went, without a worry about where she'd end up. Maybe one day she could visit Sleepy Valley as a guest and stay in one of the rustic cabins, exercising, sweating in the sun, and bathing in the lake before breakfast.

Something hummed next to Addie's ear. Not the normal drone of fair noises or customers, but a close, buzzing sound. She opened her eyes to see a June bug with a metallic-green body and black wings, hovering just inches above the ground next to her. She reached out a hand, causing it to whir off on its drunken flight path, bumping off the trunk of a eucalyptus. The boys at the orphan asylum used to catch them and tie threads to their legs, then fling them around, scaring the girls, or walk their tiny droning kites down the street. They'd fly them for hours, until the bugs either died or their legs fell off, leaving the boys with nothing but fragile legs dangling at the bottom of their threads.

A shadow moved across the ground and over Addie. She turned her head to see Lilly's silhouette looming over her. "Sal said to give you a message."

Addie put her hand across her brows, blocking the sun from her eyes. Lilly had on her usual bleak expression. "He said that you have a visitor, and it isn't your troublemaking little niece."

Addie didn't know who it could be other than Rumor. Maybe Sergeant Darby or Mary? "Did he say who it was?"

"Yes."

Addie waited, but Lilly, in her normal melancholy way, didn't say.

"Who?"

"It's her mother."

"Wavey? My sister?"

"How the hell am I supposed to know? That's all he told me."

Addie jumped up so fast, the garden spun and tiny white prisms floated across her vision.

"Heinrich's not gonna be happy about this," Lilly said, not waiting for an answer and walking off, back toward Joe and the giant bull's-eye nailed to the tree.

Addie had worn her training suit to the garden that morning, but she couldn't possibly go into the fair in it, and she had no time to go to her tent to change. Who knew how long Wavey would wait for her? She noticed Clara's sailor-blue dress hanging on one of the pegs, with a pair of low heels below it. Clara wouldn't mind. Okay, yes she would, she was stingy about her stuff, but desperate times called for desperate actions. As Joe liked to say, *it's easier to beg for forgiveness than to get permission.*

She and Clara weren't exactly the same size, but the dress had a belt. Addie cinched it tight enough to look presentable. The shoes didn't fit, either, and with every step, she had to clench her toes to keep them on her feet. What did Wavey want? Addie doubted that she'd come all the way to the fair to be angry or to have Sergeant Darby arrest her for murder, but then again, what if Wavey wanted to get her away from her daughters once and for all? That would be the way to do it. What if she had come to reconcile? When Addie stepped around the corner, from the narrow path between the garden and the Palace of Better Housing, she didn't see Wavey. She'd expected to find her standing next to the ticket booth. She looked up and down the avenues but saw nothing but families and couples. There was no woman with curly brown hair walking alone. Had she left? Had Lilly taken her sweet time giving her the message? When Addie approached the ticket booth, Sal looked up from a newspaper, smiling when he saw her.

"Did she leave?" Addie asked.

"No." Sal shook his head. He gave an exasperated sigh and, aiming his thumb at the stockade fence, said, "The apple doesn't fall far."

And there she was, among all the Peeping Toms, with her eye to one of the knotholes.

"Thanks," Addie said, not sure if she should interrupt Wavey or wait until she backed away from the fence. Wavey wore a pink sundress, with white flowers, and a white hat, with her brown curls spiraling at the nape of her neck. She supported herself against the fence with one white-gloved hand while she clasped a tiny white purse under her other arm. The seams of her stockings curved inward just enough to give the illusion of a slight bow to her lower calves. Addie, mostly bare under Clara's sailor-blue dress, unstockinged, ungartered, ungirdled, and completely underdressed compared to everyone else, although thoroughly overdressed for a nudist, felt disheveled.

"Wavey," Addie called.

Wavey straightened up, turned, and faced her. "Oh. Uh, I was just seeing what all the hubbub was about."

Addie wondered if this woman who stood before her was anything like the Wavey she'd held in her heart all these years, suspended, locked, and unable to grow or change or mature.

"Do you know a place where we can sit and talk and have a drink?" Wavey asked.

"There's a restaurant, but I don't have my purse."

"My treat," Wavey said.

Addie took her toward the same restaurant she'd gone to with Frieda, El Cafe Solana, with its white adobe, red tile roof, and twisting iron bars on the windows. Walking down the avenue with Wavey at her side, neither of them saying a word, Addie felt stiff and unsure, afraid to say the wrong thing and lose her sister all over again. Wavey seemed so confident, so put together, and so modern.

A few people sat scattered in the cafe, a lull between the breakfast and lunch crowds. Addie asked for a spot in the back, telling the hostess that they needed a quiet table.

"I'll have a lemonade," Wavey said before the waitress had a chance to ask.

"Make it two," Addie said.

Glancing around, Wavey said, "They've really done things up for this fair. I hardly recognize the place."

"Is this your first time to the Expo?"

"Yes," Wavey said. "I've been meaning to go for a while but haven't been up to it." Wavey set her white clasp purse onto the bright tiles of the tabletop. The white rectangle was a complete contrast to the vivid blue, orange, and green geometric shapes.

"Is everything okay with your girls?" Addie asked. "It worried me when Sergeant Darby came looking for Rumor."

"She's home." Wavey pulled at her gloves, one finger at time, sliding them off and placing them on the table, limp and white and crossed, just like Aunt May's hands used to rest in her lap during church services.

Wavey dug in her purse, pulling out a silver case. She opened it and held it out to Addie. "Cigarette?"

"No, thanks," Addie said.

Wavey shrugged, plucked one out, and placed it between her bright red lips. To Addie's surprise, she saw that her hand was shaky.

The waitress approached, balancing the two lemonades on a small tray. Addie felt grateful for something to hold on to, something to sip. Wavey had changed. The sister she remembered had long, curly hair, just like Rumor's, but now it was cut short, just below her chin, modern and jazzy and fashionable under her white-brimmed hat. Wavey's features had taken on a sharper look too, her cheekbones more prominent, not as soft and round. And when had she started smoking? The color of her eyes hadn't changed, they were still the beautiful blue that reminded her of a pale summer sky, but the way she looked out of them had. They seemed even more fractured. Her eyelids, painted with makeup and perfectly lined, made her look as if she belonged on the cover of *McCall's*. Heinrich wouldn't let them wear makeup, at least not enough to show. They usually snuck a bit of mascara and tinted their lips with a light lipstick, but nothing like Wavey's vivid red lips. Heinrich said cosmetics took away from the natural spirit of the colony, turning them into nothing more than a girlie show.

"Why didn't you read my letters?"

"I couldn't." She took a deep drag from her cigarette. The ashes dropped into her lemonade, peppering the surface. "I didn't want to deal with it."

"I don't blame you," Addie said. "I made a mess of everything."

"You have no idea," Wavey said.

"I've always wondered what I left you with and what you went through," Addie said. "It eats away at me."

"I didn't come here to rehash the past."

Wavey had never been one to share her feelings, but it used to be more of a soft avoidance than a harsh reprimand spoken through a puff of cigarette smoke.

"Sometimes things need to be spoken before they can be forgotten. Or forgiven," Addie said.

Wavey pressed her hands together, put her thumbs to her lips, and closed her eyes. It looked as if she were praying over her lemonade, a long and silent prayer. A yellow jacket flew over their table, buzzing languidly, seeming already drunk on all the sugar from the fair. It circled Addie's lemonade, round and round, dropping one of its feet into the liquid. Addie watched it, afraid to shoo it away. They were aggressive and easily angered. Heinrich said that they sensed fear, and if you panicked, they'd sting you. Addie watched as it rose and dropped on an uncertain flight path. Its markings were beautiful, striped yellow-and-black with translucent wings. It dropped down again, hovered above her drink, and landed on one of the ice cubes. Moving slow and not taking her eyes off the wasp, Addie felt for her spoon, moved it over her glass, and scooped the yellow jacket out. She tipped the spoonful of lemonade and wasp onto the patio. She looked up to see Wavey's eyes on her.

"I didn't want to anger it," Addie said, wondering how long Wavey had been watching her.

Wavey took a deep breath, flicked her ashes to the ground, and said, "I've already told you that I've forgiven you. You were a child."

Addie knew that Wavey had something else on her mind, something that she had to say or she wouldn't have come to the fair, but the sooner Wavey got to the point, the sooner she'd leave. "I want to understand what you went through and to understand why you never sent for me."

The blue prisms of Wavey's eyes shifted and hardened. She put the lipstick-stained butt of her cigarette back in her mouth and took a long drag. "I already told you, I wanted to protect Mary."

"You knew I would never hurt Mary," Addie said. "I waited every day for a letter from you. At first I thought that Uncle Henry kept them from me. Until I wrote you and it came back 'return to sender' in your handwriting."

Wavey crushed her cigarette out in the ashtray with a resigned sigh. "After you left, Clyde—Officer Darby as you knew him—stopped by at the most perfect time. Do you remember him?"

"Yes," Addie said. "I recognized him when he came here the other night, looking for Rumor."

"He already knew all about Ty and his temper." Wavey paused. "And what Ty did to you. I'd been talking to Clyde, trying to figure a way to safely get you, Mary, and me away from Ty. I was afraid of Ty and what he'd do to us if I left. And I worried about losing Mary."

"I didn't know you were looking for a way out," Addie said. "I thought you felt as helpless as me. Why didn't you tell me?"

Wavey shrugged. "You were a child."

"I should've trusted you," Addie said. "You'd always taken care of me. I didn't know."

"Clyde arrived not long after you left. I didn't know what to do. Ty was dead and I'd sent you away. When Clyde first saw him, he thought it was the flu. So many people were dying of it. And Jack had thought it was the flu also."

"Jack?" Addie asked.

"Yes, Jack, the man who brought Ty home that afternoon. Do you remember?"

"The skinny man in the baggy suit?" Then it hit Addie, something that Rumor had said. "Is he the same Jack as Papa Jack?"

"Yes, Jack Donnelly."

Addie thought his name had sounded familiar when Rumor had told her, but she hadn't been able to place him. "You married him?"

"I'll get to that. It's a bit of a story.

"Clyde was training to be a detective at the time. I watched him run a finger along the counter and touch his tongue to it, then he looked into the trash at all the eggshells and bits of oleander blossoms. He looked up, and I knew he saw the can of rat poison. I felt as if I'd faint on the spot. I couldn't go to prison and lose Mary. Clyde asked Jack to wait out front, to flag down the ambulance when they arrived. I thought he was just trying to get rid of him and would interrogate me right then and there, but he didn't. Then he asked me where you were, and I told him you went to stay with family. He reached above the hutch and grabbed the canister. I guess we didn't figure how easy it was for someone taller than us to see it. I told him I'd done it, but somehow he knew I was lying and it was you. He dropped the poison into his pocket. I thought he was taking it for evidence until he told me to wipe the counter down and take the cut-up oleanders out of the trash. We hid them in the oatmeal canister, burying them beneath the oats and putting it back on the shelf."

Addie remembered the exact shelf where Wavey had kept the oatmeal, and could picture the dark stains of blossoms in the oats as clearly as if she were watching a moving picture show, except Wavey was talking about a real crime scene with real consequences, not one filled with actors and props.

"Shortly after that, the ambulance came. They took Ty off. Clyde told them he thought it was the flu, and with so many influenza deaths at the time, that was what everyone believed. Luckily, the symptoms of arsenic poisoning are similar to influenza, but Clyde told me that if the pathologist suspected anything and tested for arsenic, it was easily detectible. For months, I waited every day, expecting a knock on the door and the police to haul me away, but it never happened."

"I'm sorry," Addie said.

"You can stop apologizing. I know you're sorry." Wavey had a note of annoyance in her voice. "After that, Clyde came around more often. And so did Jack Donnelly, both checking on me, helping me with repairs around the house and getting my finances in order. I'd never handled money before and didn't know much about it. Ty didn't have life insurance, and most of our savings went toward burying him. When we first got married, Ty had told me he didn't believe in life insurance, because if he died, he didn't want some other man marrying me and cashing in on his death. Maybe he worried about me poisoning him for the money all along."

Addie let out a little laugh, but then felt guilty.

"Do you remember that neighbor, Miss Mabel?" Wavey asked. "The one always in everyone's business?"

"Yes, I remember she was furious that Ty had planted oleanders between the houses."

"Miss Mabel started getting suspicious about Ty's death and how you had suddenly disappeared. I think she thought Clyde and I had murdered the both of you. She told Clyde that she knew what was going on and she was keeping an eye on him. She even went to the station and filed a complaint that one of their officers was involved in a death. One of the detectives questioned him and started poking through Ty's file. Clyde said that if they exhumed Ty's body, the arsenic would still show up, and we'd all be in prison: him, me, and you. To protect us, he moved to Los Angeles. That put an end to the suspicions about Clyde and me. And an end to our future."

"But you were pregnant," Addie said.

A look of shock froze Wavey's face, but instead of saying anything, she reached for another cigarette and narrowed her eyes.

"They have the same smiles," Addie said.

Wavey closed her eyes, took a long drag from her cigarette, and blew the smoke into the air.

"Does Rumor know yet?" Addie asked.

"I don't think so, but she's not talking to me right now. It's all a mess."

"I should've stayed," Addie said. "They might have been lenient on me since I was so young."

"You would've been portrayed as a bad seed, a delinquent from an orphan asylum. What you did was wrong, but it was Ty's fault. And mine."

"How was it yours?"

"I should've told you what I was doing. I should've let you know that I was still looking out for you." Wavey ran her finger down the condensation on her glass. "When you first came to my house last month, you asked me for forgiveness. Like I told you, I forgave you before I sent you away."

"And what about Jack? You married Jack?"

"I'd lost everything. Almost. I still had Mary, but I lost you and I lost Clyde and I was expecting. I worried every day that I'd be arrested and then I'd lose Mary too. And there was Jack. Sweet and bumbling and completely in love with me, so I married him."

"But it didn't last?"

Wavey shook her head. "No. I tried to love him, but I loved Clyde. I could've stayed with Jack, though, until I realized he had a sexual perversion for little girls."

"Oh my God. Did he?" Addie couldn't speak the words.

"At first I thought I'd imagined it. The way he'd touch Mary and Rumor didn't seem quite right, but he loved them, and I dismissed it as innocent. Until he was arrested for touching a neighbor girl."

"You didn't tell your girls?"

"I couldn't. They both think he's their father. I never told them about Ty, either, so to Mary, he's her father too. I didn't want to shatter them. He agreed to move away and I thought that would solve it. But he didn't, and they've been sneaking over to see him every Sunday. I just found out."

"When Rumor went missing?"

"Yes, and I think he did something to her, but she won't speak to me."

"And that's why you've come to me?"

Wavey squeezed her lips together until they made one bright red line and nodded. "How'd you end up in a nudist colony?"

"It isn't as bad as everyone makes it out to be," Addie said. "After Daniel died, I couldn't bear to stay in Ohio, so I hopped on a train and ended up in San Francisco. I found myself sitting in the terminal, fighting the urge to jump on the next train and show up on your porch, when Heinrich, the founder of the colony, spotted me and offered me a place."

"Most people run off to join the circus."

"If the circus would've been there instead, I probably would've," Addie said. "I was pretty low."

"What're they like?"

"Who? The nudists? Just like anyone else, I suppose. Except Heinrich's very strict. We don't drink, smoke, or eat meat."

"Good God, that's a bit oppressive."

"They're good people. It's not what the papers make us out to be."

"That's what I've been told."

"By Clyde?"

She nodded.

"You're back with him?"

"We're gonna try. He got married a few years after I married Jack, but his wife was sickly and they never had children. She died last year, and with the fair here, he got back on with the San Diego PD."

"Did he know you and Jack had divorced?"

"Yep. He's kept track of us all along, mailing me money every single month since he left, to help me raise the girls and provide them with a home. Jack never did make much, and he had trouble holding on to jobs, so thank God for Clyde's check. It kept us going."

"Clyde didn't worry about the police tracking the money?"

"No, he sent it anonymously."

"Are you going to tell your girls that Jack's not their father now?"

"Oh God, I don't know. I don't know anything anymore."

"Your girls are old enough for the truth. And maybe the truth will give Clyde a chance to know his daughter."

Wavey hid her face, resting her forehead against her hands. Her glass of lemonade, still filled to the rim, had beads of condensation weeping down the side and pooling up on the table. Only one translucent sliver of ice still floated in it. Addie wanted to move to the other side of the table and put her arms around Wavey, but there seemed to be an ocean of time and trial between them.

"I'm leaving the colony," Addie said.

Wavey looked up from her hands, her eyes smeared with mascara. "So you said."

"You're not getting rid of me so easily this time."

"Easily?" Wavey snorted. "Nothing about this has been easy."

"My place is here with my family."

Wavey nodded, and her shoulders and face went slack, as if something gave way within her. "My girls need you. Rumor won't talk to me or get out of bed. I'm afraid something happened to her, and I don't know how to help. I'm terrified that she'll run off."

"Do you think she'll try to find her father?"

Wavey put her hand over her mouth, closed her eyes, and nodded. It looked as if she were afraid to speak the words for fear they'd come true.

"Then you need to tell her," Addie said. "Everything."

Wavey's eyes shot open. "Good Lord, not everything."

"It would probably be best to leave out the part about me poisoning Ty. You can say it was because of the flu."

"But then, how would I explain Clyde not staying around to raise his own child? She'd hold that against him. And what can I tell her about why I threw you out? And why I married Jack? And why I never told Mary she had a different father?"

"You're right; this is a mess."

"Sometimes it's easier to not say anything."

"That's all fine and good until the truth comes knocking at your door."

Wavey let out a resigned laugh. "Twice. Both you and Clyde."

"Seems like we've sure rocked your boat."

"Yes, you did. Now you have to help me fix it." She reached out and took one of Addie's hands. "Together this time?"

"Yes, together."

"To tell the truth," Wavey said, "my girls and I have been lost ever since I kicked Jack out. You and Clyde are just the two final straws."

"We're gonna have to figure out how to tell the truth without telling it all. Do you think Clyde would help us come up with something?"

"Yes," Wavey said. "He's got a lot at stake too. Seems like it's been the three of us ever since he dropped that canister into his pocket."

Addie picked up her glass of lemonade and put it to her lips.

"You're gonna drink that?" Wavey asked.

Addie remembered that the yellow jacket had landed in it. She shrugged, then smiled and lifted her glass in salute. Wavey looked down into her own glass. A few of the ashes still floated on top, but she raised it to Addie. They clinked their glasses, and both took a drink.

Addie left the fair by the west gate, crossing the Cabrillo Bridge to wait for Wavey and Clyde by the bowling green. Below the bridge, two boys sat with fishing poles, their lines dropped into a tiny lagoon at the bottom of the ravine. At the bowling green, old men in white shorts and ankle socks rolled black balls across a manicured lawn surrounded by palm and eucalyptus trees. It amused Addie that she was waiting for her sister and a cop—the same cop who, years before, had been sent to monitor her, the orphan delinquent. And the same cop who had fallen in love with her sister and covered up Addie's crime. What alignment of the cosmos caused Clyde to enter their lives, separate from them, and then years later be reunited with them by the one child who tied them all together?

Clyde and Wavey rolled up in a shiny black four-door sedan, all fashionable with Wavey's wrist out the open window and a cigarette pinched between two gloved fingers. If they could fix things with Rumor, maybe Wavey and Clyde would eventually marry. Why not? Third time's a charm.

Addie climbed in the backseat, and they rolled off, with cigarette smoke blowing back into the car and Wavey's image in the side mirror, watching her. Clyde turned down a side street and pulled to the curb. It all seemed so hush-hush, like something you'd expect in some Dashiell Hammett caper. Once they came to a stop, Clyde killed the engine. Both he and Wavey turned in their seats, facing Addie.

Clyde started the conversation. "We've been thinking about how to clear things up with Rumor."

Wavey sucked in the last puff of her cigarette before flicking it out the window. "With a bit of a spin," she said.

"I've been thinking too," Addie said. "I think I've come up with an idea."

"Good," Wavey said, "because we couldn't come up with anything but more lies."

"I think she trusts me," Addie said. "At least, I think she did until I refused to see her. Anyway, I'll confess to her and take the blame."

She noticed Clyde's brow wrinkle and his mustache shift over tightened lips.

"Oh no—" Wavey began to say.

"Hear me out," Addie said. "I'll tell her that I did something really terrible, but I can't tell her what it is. I'll ask her to trust me and not ask for the details. I'll tell her that I caused the entire chain of events that made you send me away and kept you and Clyde from being together. After that, the rest should make sense to her."

Clyde looked at Wavey. "Think it'll work?"

"It might," Wavey said. "But how the hell would I know? Everything I've tried with that child has blown up in my face."

"But you haven't tried the truth," Addie said. "She's a smart girl, and I'm thinking she has some of her father's intuition about reading people."

Clyde smiled, a look of pride on his face. Addie realized how much he'd missed not having the chance to see Rumor grow, to discover his own traits and likenesses in his daughter. She had a pang of longing for Daniel. She couldn't even picture what he'd look like as a young man, except to compare him to Mary.

"What if she doesn't buy it and wants the details?" Wavey asked. "She's a persistent child."

"I'll tell her that I fell in love with your husband, and you had to send me away, but then he died of the flu."

"But what about Clyde? Why did he leave us?"

"He didn't. You fell in love with Jack and married him instead, leaving Clyde out in the cold," Addie said.

On the slow ride to Wavey's bungalow, they decided that Clyde would wait in the living room, without Rumor knowing he was there. They would call for him or signal him to leave, depending on the outcome. They all felt that his introduction as her father would be the touchiest point in the entire conversation. Rumor would come face-to-face with the facts that her beloved Papa Jack was not blood related and that she'd been misled by everyone she cared about. Mary, on the other hand, was the wild card. None of them knew how she'd take the news. Rumor would explode, but Mary . . . would she faint or swoon or have a fit? Several times, Wavey changed her mind, wanting to tuck it all back under the carpet, but Addie and Clyde convinced her that the time had come; things were already at the breaking point. It had to be done. No backing out.

But when they came to a stop at the courtyard steps, all three of them stayed in the car, without talking or moving, just staring at the bungalow where the two girls, oblivious, waited. Clyde made the first move, stepping out and coming around to Wavey's door. He opened it and offered her his hand. Once Wavey took it and climbed out, Clyde opened Addie's. With Rumor's smile emerging beneath his mustache, he extended his hand to her and said, "Time to put it all back together."

Wavey's bungalow was dark and quiet and smelled of toast. Mary sat on the couch, reading a magazine, and when she looked up, her eyes went from her mother, to Clyde, and then, with a look of confusion, to Addie. She stood, as if she knew some bad news was on its way but didn't know how to react.

"Follow us," Wavey said, heading toward Rumor's closed door.

Clyde replaced Mary on the couch and picked up her magazine.

The three of them bunched together at the door. Wavey turned and looked at Addie, her blue eyes unsure. Addie nodded and Wavey turned the handle. The room wasn't as dim as Addie had imagined it would be. She'd expected it to be like a sickroom, all stuffy and shut in, but the curtains rippled in the breeze that blew in the window.

"Rumor," Wavey called to a bundled-up lump on the bed.

"Go away, Mother," she said.

"Rumor," Addie said, "it's me, Aunt Addie."

The shape popped up on the bed, flinging the covers off and revealing a mass of tangled brown hair. She looked as if she'd been marooned on an island for weeks without a bath or mirror or comb.

"What's wrong?" A look of panic washed across her face. "Has something happened to Papa Jack?"

"No," Wavey said. "He's fine."

"Then why's Aunt Addie here? If you're trying to get me to say something bad about my papa, you can forget it."

"That's not why I'm here," Addie said.

"It's time to come together as a family. You girls are old enough to know the truth." With a tender hand on Mary's shoulder and directing her toward the bed, Wavey said, "Have a seat."

"I've already figured it all out," Rumor said with a huff.

"You have, have you?" Wavey said, irritation coming into her voice.

"Yes, I have. Now, go away. Aunt Addie can stay if she likes, and Mary too, but you can go away."

"I'm not going anywhere, young lady. Now, you stop being so snippy and listen to what we have to say."

Addie intervened. "Rumor, there are some things we need to clear up."

"Like what? That Mary is really your daughter, but my mother took her from you because you were too young, and then she threw you out because she was afraid that Papa Jack would love you more than her?"

"Where in the hell . . . ?" Wavey's voice began to rise, but Addie put a soft hand on her back, and she stopped, her whole body quivering under Addie's touch.

Mary got up, peeked into the living room, and shut the bedroom door. "Keep your voice down," she said.

But before she had a chance to tell Rumor that Sergeant Darby was on the couch, Addie interrupted, "How did you ever come up with that?"

"She looks just like you."

"Your mother and I are sisters. You may have a daughter one day that looks like me too."

Rumor stared through narrow and unbelieving eyes.

"We're here to tell you the truth. Will you give us a chance and listen to what we have to say?" Addie said.

Rumor nodded but crossed her arms. Mary sat propped on the edge of the bed, looking stunned.

Addie started at the beginning, telling them about the death of their parents and how Wavey went to live with an aunt and an uncle in Ohio, but Addie was sent to an orphan asylum, and how Wavey sent for her once she was married and pregnant with Mary. "Your mother and her husband took me in."

"But . . ." Rumor said, "Papa Jack said he never met Aunt Addie."

"I was married before," Wavey said. "My first husband was Mary's father."

"You lied to us?" Rumor's voice began to rise. "Where is he now?"

"He died during the influenza epidemic when Mary was a baby," Wavey said.

Mary sat still, looking dazed and white, but Rumor flushed red, her temper obviously rising. "You didn't need to lie about that."

Addie put her hands in the air, as if she were a fugitive surrendering. "Hang on, can we get it all out first, and then you can get angry, if you still feel like it?" She hated seeing the looks on the two girls' faces.

Addie looked over at Wavey, who gave her an encouraging but disheartened smile.

"It all happened when I was your age, Rumor. Mary, you were born into my hands. I was the first person to ever lay eyes on you. Now, we are being honest, but there is something that I'm leaving out. I did something terrible and unforgivable, and it's not what you think, but please trust me and don't ask. Because of what I did, your mother had to send me away to protect me. When her husband died, she fell in love with a man and became pregnant with you, Rumor."

"Papa Jack?" Rumor asked, her voice questioning, as if she sensed another brick about to hit.

"No," Wavey said, causing a heartbreaking cry to escape from Rumor.

"He's not my father, either?"

"No," Wavey said again.

"Does he know that neither of us are his daughters?" She'd gone from red-hot to wounded, and Addie almost wished she'd start cursing them out.

"Yes, he knows," Wavey said, "but he's always loved you, the both of you, as if you were his."

Mary spoke for the first time. "Is it Sergeant Darby?"

All heads turned to Mary and her soft-spoken truth.

"You look like him," she said to Rumor. "I'm surprised you didn't notice."

"And you did?" Rumor seemed to have found an easier target. "What is it with this family and all the lies and secrets? You're just like Mother."

"No, I didn't keep it secret, darling," Mary said, regaining her composure. "I just now realized it. It makes sense why he's at this very moment sitting on our couch in the living room."

"So that's why you wanted to get rid of Papa Jack? That's why you divorced him? You used him? What kind of a father would go off and leave his baby? Or did he not know, and you lied to him too?" Rumor looked like a lunatic, ranting in her pajamas, with her wild hair and flushed face. "I bet you told Papa that I was his child. How do I know that you're telling the truth now? Maybe you're lying. How do I know? How do I know?"

The bedroom door opened, causing instantaneous silence in the room. Clyde stood in the frame, filling it with his large form. "You can believe it because it's true. Your mother did the best she could to protect you. I did not abandon you. I had to leave to protect all of us. I never forgot you and have not gone a single day without wondering how you were growing or wondering when you took your first step or went to your first day of school. I missed it all. Another man got to be there instead."

"It's my fault," Addie said. "If you're going to be mad at anyone, be mad at me. Your mother loves you, and whether you can see it or not, she has been the one left to take care of things she didn't cause."

Rumor sat on her bed, her arms crossed and her face in a defiant glare. When she finally spoke, her voice quivered. "So, what now? You're both going to leave us again?"

Clyde was the first to say anything. "I've transferred back here to San Diego, so even if you want me to leave, I'm not going to."

"Me, either," Addie said. "I'm leaving the colony and looking for work here."

"And what about Papa Jack?" Rumor addressed her question to Clyde.

"He's in Los Angeles."

"What's going to happen to him?"

"Nothing. They're monitoring him. That's all they can do."

She looked back at her mother. "Do you swear that he knows I'm not his child?"

"You are his child, just not by blood, and, yes, he knows it."

"I still love him," Rumor said. "And so does Mary."

"Nobody's asking you not to," Clyde said. "That would be mighty unfair."

Rumor sat, looking like a wild child, completely untamed.

"So, my father's dead?" Mary asked in a tiny voice threaded with a sadness that Addie hadn't expected. She'd been braced for Rumor's reaction.

"Oh, sweetie," Wavey said. "He loved you very much. You were barely over one year old."

"What was his name?"

"His name was Tyrone Fulton Briggs, and he worked construction with your papa Jack."

As it all began to soak in, Rumor's muscles relaxed and she uncrossed her arms, becoming limp and civilized. Addie wondered if Rumor was just realizing that she had a father, but Mary had none.

Rumor stood up, walked around the other side of the bed to Mary, and put her arm around her. When Rumor looked up, she met Addie's eyes, then her mother's, then Clyde's. "We'll be fine. Now that we have the truth, we'll get through it."

Wavey bent toward her girls, as if she wanted to wrap her arms around the two of them, but before she had a chance, Rumor said, "We'll be okay. Can we have some privacy?"

Clyde left first. Before Wavey pulled the door shut, Addie took a final look back. Mary and Rumor sat on the bed, clutching each other like two survivors adrift in a lifeboat.

And just like that, Addie's life at the colony was over. Done. *Fini,* as Giselle would say. She felt grateful it wasn't the same as Eleanor's end, being thrown out when nobody was looking. Addie's was a grand exit, with a party planned by Frieda and financed by Heinrich—and a swank one too. Right there in the Exposition, at the Cafe of the World, where waiters in black trousers and short white jackets wove through the maze of tables, and the hostesses, dressed in traditional costumes from around the globe, flirted with the male customers and occasionally received slaps on their rears. The tables surrounded a dance floor and orchestra in the cavernous restaurant, a replica of a Spanish courtyard, complete with pillars disguised as palm trees. The colony had come late, just catching the nine o'clock performance of Chiquita, the Mexican Nightingale, a dark-haired soprano singing like an angel, in Spanish.

Heinrich ordered for the entire table, choosing everything on the menu that didn't include meat: cantaloupe with fruit, sliced tomatoes, salad *fantasie,* cauliflower *persillé,* potato *garbure,* sautéed mushrooms, cheese enchiladas, and native beans. But he surprised them all by adding, almost as a second thought and catching the waiter just before he left, four bottles of champagne—bending his own decree of no alcohol.

They all looked like misfits, stuffed tight into their clothing and itching to be out of it. Once the silver ice buckets and champagne arrived at the table, Heinrich rose, clinking a spoon against his glass, which vibrated as high as the note Chiquita had just hit. "A toast," Heinrich said. "May we always part with regret and meet again with pleasure."

They all raised their glasses, chanting *hear, hear* and *cheers* and sipping the forbidden champagne.

Joe stood, stuffy and dignified, his shirt buttoned up and a white clerical collar cinched around his throat. "We cannot mourn your leaving, Sister Addie, for as the Good Book says in Ecclesiastes, chapter three, 'To everything there is a season, a time for every purpose under heaven: A time to be born, and a time to die; A time to plant and a time to pluck what is planted; A time to kill, and a time to heal; A time to break down, and a time to build up; A time to weep, and a time to laugh.' This is your time to leave, and this is your time to love. We wish you the best and thank you for all the blessings you have given us during your time at Sleepy Valley."

"Amen," everyone said in choral response. Joe looked every bit the part of a preacher at that moment. If only the people at the surrounding tables knew of his vices and sacrilegious sermons.

Daisy stood and raised her glass. "An Irish blessing—'May the sun shine all day long, everything go right, and nothing wrong. May those you love bring love back to you, and may all the wishes you wish come true.'"

Giselle remained seated, but raised her glass. "*Au revoir et que Dieu vous benisse.* Good-bye and may God bless you."

"We're on a roll," Ida said, standing and squaring her shoulders. "Here's one from the great state of Texas. 'May your trails be smooth and your saddle well greased.'"

Ida sat just as Chiquita finished her song and the audience erupted in applause. Perfect timing. The waiter appeared with trays of meatless food, spacing them out across the table and serving them family style, like Heinrich had requested. By the time they'd begun eating, the restaurant was emptying and Chiquita had taken her final bow, leaving the orchestra to play for the last of the customers.

"Time for gifts," Clara said, taking one from the pile they created on a table next to them. "I will play Santa's elf."

The waiter, not attempting to hide his frustration, looked at his watch and turned his back to the group. Clara handed her a package wrapped in brown paper without a tag. "It's from me," Lilly said. "Didn't have time to get a card."

"Socks," Addie said, holding them up in the air.

"I figured you didn't have many," Lilly said in her dour voice. "People on the outside rarely walk around in bare feet."

Giselle and Yvette gave her a set of four ceramic eggcups painted with delicate pink roses. Heinrich and Frieda gave her a cookbook called *Meatless Meals* and a card with fifty dollars inside. The chickens gave her a box wrapped in floral paper and tied with a yellow ribbon. Inside, a girdle with enough boning to hold a whale together lay buried beneath several sets of silk hose, two slips, a pair of bloomers, a scarf, two pairs of leather gloves, and a red silk kimono with cherry blossoms.

"Since you have to start wearing clothes, they may as well be slinky," Lucille said.

The next box, from Eva, had some sort of a cast-iron mallet, flat on one side and, on the other, a pattern of sharp, pointy teeth, like some medieval torture device.

"What is it?" Addie asked.

"The saleslady said it's a meat tenderizer. I figured even if you don't start cooking or eating meat, it'll still come in handy for any man who tries to get fresh with you."

Addie gave it a few flicks of the wrist. "Thanks, Eva. I'll keep it in my night table."

Clara gave her a box of stationery, asking her to stay in touch, and Joe had the quote he had given from Ecclesiastes written out in beautiful script on a scroll tied with a purple ribbon. Daisy gave her a card with twenty dollars in it. Addie told her that it was too much, but Daisy refused to take it back, telling her not to look a gift horse in the mouth.

They spent the rest of the evening finishing off the champagne and sharing stories from their escapades at the Chicago World's Fair and Sleepy Valley. The orchestra had packed up, and the tables were cleared. Most of the service staff had disappeared, but they remained until someone began turning off the lights, a not-so-subtle cue that they'd overstayed their welcome. Just as Eleanor had overstayed hers and was forced to leave. Addie felt relieved she would be moving away from the colony on her own terms.

Late that night, Addie heard the boards creak outside her tent. She was glad that Daisy had finally come back, but instead of a female voice, a deep male voice whispered through the tent flap, "Addie, are you awake?"

"Sal?"

"Can I come in?"

"Yes," Addie said, feeling around for the box of matches on top of her trunk. She found them, struck one, and held it out to the wick on the lantern. Sal stood inside next to Hobbs's cage and Daisy's empty cot.

"Your mother's not here. She said she didn't want to lay around with me all night, reminiscing and blubbering."

"I know," he said. "She's out with a new man from Gay's Lion Farm."

"What's behind your back?" Addie asked.

Sal held out a small and soft package wrapped in brown paper, tied with twine. "I didn't forget to get you a present. I just wanted to give it to you in private."

Sal stood there with his hands in his pockets, looking shy about his gift. Addie untied the string and opened the paper. Inside was a single pillowcase.

"Unfold it," Sal said.

Addie lifted it up by the edges, revealing an intricately embroidered frog sitting on a lily pad the shape of a heart.

"I had it specially made," Sal said. "To always remind you of the little boy who used to put frogs in your bed."

"Oh, Sal," Addie said. "This is the best gift I've ever received. Now look what you've gone and done; you've made me cry."

He sat down next to her on the cot. "I'm going to miss you, Addie. You've been like family to me."

"Do you know I had a son?"

"No."

"He would've been just a couple of years younger than you, but he died as an infant. I've loved watching you grow into the young man you are. I hope you don't mind, but I've loved you like you were my own."

Sal put his arm around Addie's shoulders. "I've always felt that. Thank you."

"I'm going to miss you the most," Addie said. "San Diego's not too far from Sleepy Valley. Promise you'll visit sometime."

"You can count on it," Sal said. "You sure you can trust me around your niece?"

"You should talk to her."

"I know," Sal said. "I need to straighten things out with her."

"I'll see what I can do to help you out."

"I can use all the help I can get with her. She's one live wire."

"Yes, she is," Addie said. "And I thank the Lord for it."

CHAPTER TWENTY-SIX
RUMOR

Mother had found work for Aunt Addie at Pinkie's Cafeteria, where she offered to train her herself. On moving day, they'd all planned on helping Aunt Addie move into the Parkers' old apartment, but she had only one trunk, and Sergeant Darby pulled it up the steps with a dolly in a single trip. That was it. A two-bedroom apartment and one trunk. It was hard to believe that a grown woman had so few belongings. Aunt Addie ordered some furniture with money she'd put aside, but the store said they couldn't get it delivered for two weeks—until the sergeant made a trip there, pulled a few strings, and said she'd have it the next day.

They all decided not to tell the neighbors about Aunt Addie's propensity toward nudism. Mother said it wasn't a lie, just none of their goddamn business. Ruth already knew, of course, and wasn't all too thrilled about it, but she treated Aunt Addie cordially to her face. Rumor figured it was more out of jealousy about losing her time with Mother than anything to do with Aunt Addie herself, so they'd all have to tolerate it. Mother said Ruth would get over herself soon enough.

Rumor decided to give Sergeant Darby a break, but she wasn't about to call him *Father* or *Dad*, and definitely not *Papa*, so both she and Mary settled on *Sergeant*. Aunt Addie's furniture did arrive the next day, packed in wooden crates that the workers pried open with crowbars. For weeks, Aunt Addie had boxes delivered to her porch. If she wasn't home, Rumor would take the extra key she'd left at their house and set them inside for her. When she got home, Rumor and Mary would follow her in to help open the cartons and see what she got. Sometimes they uncovered a toaster or cooking utensils or a set of dishes with pink roses. An entire new life was delivered box by box, for weeks, until they dwindled down and her place was filled.

One night, a couple of days after Aunt Addie had moved in, Rumor tapped on her window. When Aunt Addie's face appeared through the opening in the curtain, she looked scared, but then smiled when she realized it was Rumor. She shimmied the window up. "Why didn't you come to the door?"

"Windows have become a habit for me."

"Is everything okay?"

"Yes. Would you like to come out and stargaze with me?"

"Sure," Aunt Addie said. "Does it require me sneaking out my own window?"

"Of course."

Aunt Addie slipped a bare foot out the window, and for a moment, Rumor worried she'd caught her in the nude, but as more of her emerged, she saw she wore a white silky nightgown. Hand in hand, they walked to the corner. The city lights glowed to the south, and farther south, on the hills of Tijuana, a few tiny specks winked back at them. A ship moved in the harbor, its running lights gliding across the black water.

"I see the Big Dipper," Aunt Addie said.

"The Big Dipper is part of Ursa Major, the Great Bear. And right next to her is the Little Dipper, part of Ursa Minor, the little bear. See it?"

"Yes," Aunt Addie said. "I do."

"The story is that Ursa Major used to be a beautiful nymph named Callisto. The Greek god Zeus fell in love with her and fathered a son named Arcas. Zeus's wife was very jealous, so she turned Callisto into a bear. Her son, Arcas, became a great hunter and almost killed his own mother. Seeing this, Zeus turned Arcas into a bear, also, and set the two of them into the heavens as stars, where he can always gaze upon them and they can always be together."

Rumor glanced over at Aunt Addie and noticed tears in her eyes. "Are you okay?"

"Yes," Aunt Addie said. "That story just touched me is all. I had a son once, and maybe one day, he and I will be together again in the heavens. He died as a tiny baby."

"I'm sorry," Rumor said. "I didn't know. I didn't even know you'd been married."

"I haven't. Just like in the story, he had a wife."

"Was she jealous?"

Aunt Addie smiled, then let out a little laugh. "No, but she did turn me into a bear."

Rumor wanted to know everything about her aunt Addie but knew not to push it. She trusted Aunt Addie to tell her things when she was ready, a little at a time, and each time it would be like finding a shiny new coin. "See that constellation right overhead? The one that looks like a man? That's Hercules with his foot on the head of Draco the Dragon."

"You're a bona fide stargazer, now, aren't you? How'd you learn so much?"

"Papa Jack. We used to lie under the stars, and he'd point them out, telling Mary and me the stories."

"Which is your favorite?"

"It used to be Orion, the hunter, but not so much anymore."

"I think the story of Callisto will be my favorite," Aunt Addie said. "With her son for eternity."

"I'm getting cold," Rumor said. "Do you mind if we go in now?"

"Of course, sweetie. I'd love to hear more of the stories. Can we do this again?"

Rumor looped her arm around Aunt Addie's and put her head on her shoulder. "Yes, I'd like that very much."

"Go fetch your aunt for breakfast," Mother said. "I swear, how she never learned to cook is beyond me."

"She's working on it," Rumor said on her way toward the door. "Yesterday, she heated a can of soup and I showed her how to make a grilled cheese sandwich."

"I think it sounds marvelous," Mary said, "having someone to cook and clean for you and never having to get your hands dirty."

"Of course you do," Rumor said. "Maybe you should become a nudist. There's an opening now."

Rumor stepped out into the courtyard, shutting the door on Mary's shocked response and Mother's "now, girls" warning.

Dew beaded up on the grass, and the smells of breakfast filled the courtyard. Rumor knocked once, then tried the doorknob of Aunt Addie's bungalow. It was unlocked. "Hello," Rumor called before stepping in, then froze with one foot in and one still on the stoop.

Sal stood so fast, the kitchen chair he'd been sitting in tipped back. He caught it.

"Come in," Aunt Addie said, still seated, with a cup of coffee in front of her.

"No," Rumor said. "I just . . ."

"Don't be silly," Aunt Addie said. "Come in."

Rumor stepped in, closing the door and leaning her back against it. "Mother said to let you know breakfast is almost ready."

"Wonderful."

"Want me to tell her you'll be a while?"

"Nope. That won't do. I'm starving."

"But . . ."

"No buts about it. I'm famished, and Sal didn't come here for me anyway. Why don't you two take a spin around the block? I'll cover for you."

With that, Aunt Addie moved toward Rumor, scooted her out of the way, and opened the door. With the grand gesture of a doorman, Aunt Addie bowed them out. "After you two."

Rumor took a deep breath, wishing she had time to sort through her feelings and decide whether she'd slap Sal across the face or wait to hear what he had to say.

"Come on," Aunt Addie said. "I'm wasting away, and I can smell your mother's eggs from here."

As Rumor passed by, Aunt Addie whispered, "He's a nice boy. Give him a chance."

Rumor felt like heading straight home. Who cared what he had to say, and no, he wasn't such a nice boy, kissing her, then giving her money for a taxi—leaving her standing stark naked and embarrassed in the garden. And now he had the nerve to use Aunt Addie to get to her.

"Toodle-oo," Aunt Addie said. "Remember, kids, 'To err is human, to forgive divine.' And if you're going to bury the hatchet, make sure it's not in each other's skulls."

"I guess that's some good advice," Rumor said, speaking to Sal for the first time.

"They're words of wisdom from our resident priest."

"You have a priest?" Rumor asked.

"So to speak."

The two of them walked around the side of Aunt Addie's bungalow and onto the sidewalk. The street was quiet except for a milk delivery truck, probably empty and heading back to the dairy.

"Is your priest a nudist?"

"Nudist, exhibitionist, millionaire, and womanizer," Sal said, shrugging as if it were a common thing for a priest to be.

"Is any of that biblical?"

"It's all in there but certainly not encouraged." Sal smiled, his white teeth slightly crooked and bright against his tanned face.

But then Rumor remembered she was mad at him. He'd sent her away, and if he hadn't given her the money for the taxi, she'd never have gone to Papa's, and Papa wouldn't have been tempted by her story, and . . . And what? And Papa would have continued giving candy to Ruby, and Mother would've never gone to ask Aunt Addie for help? But he had left her standing there, one moment warm and flushed from his kiss, the next shivering in the cold, with nothing but a coin in her hand and pity on the faces of Ida, Dottie, and Lucille. "It figures. Are all the men at the colony womanizers?"

Sal appeared confused for a moment, then realization came to his face. "Is that what you think?"

"What else would I think?"

"I didn't mean to hurt you," Sal said. "You're a beautiful girl, and I lost my reason for a moment."

"And what made it come back?" Rumor stopped herself from asking if she wasn't good enough for him or sexy enough for him. Who was he anyway? What did his opinion matter?

"It came back when I reminded myself that you were Addie's niece and you're only fifteen years old and that I'll be gone as soon as the fair closes."

Rumor felt the tears rising, but she didn't want to give him the satisfaction of making her cry. She turned her head away. Down in the harbor, a battleship was leaving port, heading to deeper waters.

Sal pulled her to his chest. He smelled like Lifebuoy soap, and she remembered the feel of his lips and his scratchy face and his warm hand across her back. She tried to push away, but he held her against him.

"Let go of me. I hate you."

"No you don't. You're angry with me."

"You're damned right I am." Rumor pounded her fist against his chest; the thud reverberated, sounding dull and hollow. "You shouldn't have come here. I was fine until you showed up."

"I thought about that, but I can't leave things unfinished and unsaid." Sal took a step back but held Rumor by the arm, as if he were afraid she'd escape. "I should've explained it to you then, that night in the garden, but I couldn't think straight. I didn't understand it myself at that moment."

"Oh, but you've been enlightened since?"

"Yes," Sal said.

Rumor let out a sarcastic "Humph."

"It would be no good to start something and leave."

"Are you saying you've never spent time with girls at other fairs?"

"Not girls like you."

"What were they then? Prettier girls?"

"No. They were girls only out for a good time. You're not like that, and I'm not about to break your heart."

"You can't break it if you don't have it," Rumor said, pulling her arm free and turning back toward her bungalow. "You've had your say and it's finished. I'm going in to breakfast now."

"Rumor, please," he said, but she kept going. "I'd still like to be friends with you."

It felt good to be walking away from him. Much better than it had felt when he gave her cab fare. This time she had the choice. She knew she'd get over it and go see him at the fair before the summer ended, but for now, for that moment, it felt good to leave him standing there.

***

"Rise and shine, the sun is in the sky, get up, get up, drink sunshine from a cup," Mother's voice sang into their bedroom. "How about church this morning? I thought we'd go to First Methodist Church and then take your aunt Addie to the beach."

The smell of butter-fried eggs, toast, and coffee wafted in from the kitchen. "Since when do you want to go to church?" Rumor asked, her voice still groggy.

"Since last night, when Addie and I decided. Get up, you lazybones."

Mary sat up, her hair flattened on one side, and groaned, "Can't a working girl get some sleep?"

"Not on a beautiful Sunday when we all have the day off. Your aunt Addie wants to see Mission Beach, and she's determined to get me on a roller coaster."

"We're going to Mission Beach?" Rumor asked. "But what about Papa? It will be hard for us to go without him."

"Only at first," Wavey said. "When you keep a place tied to old memories, it will haunt you forever, but if you can make some new ones there, they'll dilute the pain."

Mary shrugged. "Why not? It should be a marvelous adventure."

Mother left the room, humming something that vaguely sounded like "It's Only a Paper Moon."

"Who was that woman?" Rumor asked.

"It looked like Mother and it smelled like Mother," Mary said.

"But it sure didn't sound like Mother," Rumor finished for her. She got out of bed and went to the closet. "I like the new Mother."

"Yes, darling, it's been magnificent, but I think it started when Sergeant Darby showed up. That's when she stopped going out drinking and dancing. Aunt Addie is like the icing on the cake."

The radio clicked on in the living room, filling the bungalow with the music of an orchestra and a man's voice crooning.

"Come on, girls. You're burning daylight," Mother called from the kitchen, accompanied by the sound of clinking plates and silverware. "And your eggs are getting cold."

"This new Mother is going to take some getting used to," Rumor said to Mary.

Rumor pushed the edge of her toast through the skin of her egg, and the yolk oozed out, spreading the yellow across the blue-and-white plate. The front door opened, and Aunt Addie walked in. Not too long ago, she'd stood on their porch afraid to knock, and now she had a permanent invitation to come and go as she pleased.

"How do you want your eggs?" Mother asked before Aunt Addie had a chance to shut the door behind her.

"I'm all egged out, but I'd love a piece of toast."

"Have I been making you too many?" Mother asked, dropping a piece of bread into the toaster and cracking an egg for herself on the edge of the pan.

"I just can't stomach another one at the moment. I've been practicing my cooking, trying to master over easy. I went through half a dozen last night and couldn't bear to waste them. I ate so many, I could hatch my own chick."

"Come here and practice on mine," Mother said, holding out the spatula.

"Morning, girls." Aunt Addie kissed the top of Rumor's head, did the same to Mary.

When the toast popped, Mother scraped off a chunk of butter and mushed it into the bread. She set the plate at Aunt Addie's spot, then dropped in another piece for herself. "There's peach marmalade in the refrigerator if you want any."

***

The four of them slid into a back pew at First Methodist. Funny that Mother chose First Methodist, since that was where Rumor had first heard that a nudist colony would be coming to the fair, before she knew that she had an aunt, much less a nudist aunt. All the women had been agitated that day, moving from pew to pew, whispering and wagging their fingers, but now they sat subdued in their ribbon-trimmed hats, divided into family groups, with hymnals on their laps. Rumor saw Mildred and her amazon mother at the end of a pew on the opposite side of the aisle. They stared forward with the same pursed lips and stiff backs. Rumor wondered if Mildred ever got to go to the fair, even though there were nudists. Wouldn't she be surprised to know that one of them sat right here, in a pew in her very own church.

Mildred must've felt Rumor's eyes on her, because she turned to look behind her. Rumor waved. Mildred returned the greeting with a fake smile, and her eyes moved across Rumor, Aunt Addie, Mary, and her mother.

A door to the left side of the pulpit opened, and the pastor stepped through, wearing the same black robe, with a long stole draped around his neck. Rumor wondered how often they washed those things, or if it had the same perspiration in it from the last time she was there. He approached the pulpit in the usual church stride, slow and dignified, a servant of the Lord approaching his own personal platform to deliver the Word.

The organist began and the congregation launched into "A Mighty Fortress Is Our God." Rumor mouthed the words, sparing the congregation from her singing voice but feeling the joy in her heart as her lips moved silently with the music. Aunt Addie sang beautifully, just like Mary, but she could hear Mother off-key on the other side of Mary, which reinforced her vow of hymnal silence.

The pastor's bald head glistened with sweat as he blessed the congregation, opened his Bible, and jabbed at its inner core with his finger. "In Paul's letter, First Corinthians 13:13, he emphasized that when all else was stripped away, the church must excel in three areas, which are: faith, hope, and love. 'And now abide faith, hope, and love, these three; but the greatest of these is love.'" The pastor paused, wiped his brow with a handkerchief, and continued. "And again in Romans 5:3 through 5:5, we can find the joy of faith, hope, and love even through troubling times. 'And not only that, but we also glory in tribulations, knowing that tribulation produces perseverance; and perseverance, character; and character, hope. Now hope does not disappoint, because the love of God had been poured out in our hearts by the Holy Spirit who was given to us.'"

Aunt Addie placed her hand on top of Rumor's, giving it a little pat. When Rumor turned to look at her, Aunt Addie offered her a smile and a wink, which Rumor took to mean that, through all their trials, they now had hope.

When the collection plate came around, Mother unearthed her change purse, twisted open the clasp, handed Rumor and Mary a nickel each, and took one out for herself. As the golden bowl moved past and they dropped the clinking money into it, Rumor smiled, realizing that it was the first time Mother's offerings had made it into the church.

Throughout the service, Mildred never looked back at them, but as soon as it was over, Rumor worked her way through the crowd until she came face-to-face with her. Mildred acted polite, as her mother would've expected her to, but Rumor thought she lacked sincerity.

"I haven't seen you in ages," Mildred said. "Church isn't something you do on a regular basis?"

"Of course it is," Rumor said. "This just isn't our primary church."

"Mother says it's best to stick to one church for the fellowship and—"

"Did you ever get a chance to go to the Exposition?"

Mildred's face drooped, but then she stiffened her shoulders. "No, Mother and Father wouldn't allow it, what with all the sin and wickedness allowed to fester there. Mother doesn't want me anywhere near any nudists." She put on a look of superiority. "It is beneath good Christians to be lulled into an unholy environment by advertising and cheap carnival tactics."

Rumor put her hand on the back of Mildred's arm. "Come and meet my aunt Addie. She came for a visit but decided to stay."

"Is the other woman your mother? I've never seen her come to church with you."

"Oh, yes, she usually has to work, but she has today off." Mother, Aunt Addie, and Mary all stood at the back of the church, waiting for Rumor, as parishioners milled around visiting, waited in line for cookies, or slowly disappeared out the doors and into the city. Guiding Mildred by the arm, Rumor brought her face-to-face with Aunt Addie, whose head barely came to Mildred's chin, making Mildred look like an ungainly giant. "Mildred, this is my aunt Addie."

Mildred put out one of her monstrous hands and shook Aunt Addie's. "Pleased to meet you. Welcome to our church."

"My pleasure," Aunt Addie said. "Are you a friend of Rumor's?"

Mildred hesitated, then put on one of her well-trained, junior-class secretary, and League of Women Voters smiles. "We're in the same class at school."

"It's nice to meet you, Mildred," Aunt Addie said. "You sure have a lovely church. I enjoyed the sermon."

That set Mildred off, and she went into elaborate detail about the reverend and his wife, and how her family was regularly invited to their home for dinner, and how she babysat the reverend's two children, four-year-old Teddy, and six-year-old Virginia, or Ginny, as they liked to call her. Blah, blah, blah, blah. Thankfully, Mother finally cut Mildred off, telling her that they had to be going. But to Rumor's deep satisfaction, Mildred told her how beautiful and sweet her aunt Addie was and how they'd just have to come back and hear more from Reverend Carlisle.

Once out of the church, Rumor headed straight for Third and Broadway, leading their little entourage to the Number 16 streetcar and their final destination of Mission Beach.

"What was that all about?" Mother asked Rumor once they'd paused at the window of the Owl Drug Company for Mary and Aunt Addie to ogle everything in the window display, with Mary pointing out all the perfumes and cosmetics.

"I don't know what you mean," Rumor said.

"Yes, you do. You sure went out of your way to bring that obnoxious girl over."

"I just wanted her to meet you and Aunt Addie."

Mother gave her a sidelong glance, narrowing her eyes and shaking her head. "You were up to something."

Rumor smiled and shrugged her shoulders. "Some people need to be put into their place, whether they realize it or not."

"I thought so." Mother smiled and slipped her arm around Rumor's. "That's my girl."

A bright sun in the cloudless sky shimmered over the city, glinting off the windows of the tall buildings and the streetcar lines crisscrossing the intersections. As usual, the transport stopped at the US Marines base, headed through the meadow, no longer filled with wildflowers, and then across the tidal marsh to Ocean Beach Junction, where the motormen unhitched the cars, sending them their separate ways.

Seeing the ragged men lined up on the sides of the bridge with their fishing poles dipped into the bay, and the breakers and beach, made Rumor feel the brief flutter of anticipation she'd always felt before seeing Papa, until she realized he was no longer there. No longer marooned on his Isle of Despair. Completely shipwrecked. Alone. A drowning man with no daughters. A man who probably thought she hated him. Did he have a beach? A place to build his inventions? Did he feel disgusted with himself? Was he racked with guilt? Rumor wished she could have said good-bye and that she forgave him. But did she? She loved him. How could he think it would be acceptable to touch her? When would that ever be? Had he been out of his mind? Had he been drinking? There seemed to be no logic in it; whether she was his daughter by blood or only in his heart, it didn't make sense.

Rumor automatically reached up and rang the bell for the motorman to stop at the amusement center. She had expected it to be different without Papa, but people in dresses and suits, sailor uniforms, and swimsuits still strolled along Ocean Walk as if his presence or absence meant nothing. The same red-and-white-striped tents and umbrellas crowded the sandy beach, and surfers rode the frothy waves, and children chased the surf. At the amusement center, the Giant Dipper still clanked and rattled on its track, rising and dipping like ocean swells. Lifeguards with sun-bleached hair still stood watch in their towers, and the smells of caramel and hot popcorn mingled with the ebb and flow of people and laughter—all unaware that Papa was gone.

"This is lovely," Aunt Addie said, stepping down onto the platform.

Mary surprised Rumor by slipping her hand into hers. Mary's nose was red. It always turned red, like a warning light, just before she broke into tears.

"Maybe you girls should take a walk," Mother said. "Addie and I can manage for an hour without you."

"Your mother's just putting off her roller coaster ride," Addie said.

"Go ahead," Mother said. "We'll be here when you get back."

Could Papa be back? Waiting in his garage? Did Mother arrange a surprise? Rumor and Mary mechanically headed toward the seawall, like they always had. "Do you think he's back?" Rumor asked Mary.

"No, darling. I think she's letting us go see for ourselves and letting us visit Mrs. Bailey."

"You could be wrong."

"I could be."

Rumor didn't know if she wanted to be right or not. The thought of seeing Papa thrilled her and terrified her. What would she say? Would it ever be the same? Would she feel trapped in his bear hug, unable to move?

Rosa sat in her usual spot, weaving her palm fronds. A menagerie of fish, birds, and dolls lay arranged around her, the new ones still a soft and vibrant green, but the older ones faded and stiff. She sat alone, no tall and lanky Papa squatting on a crate next to her. Esmeralda and the baby were nowhere in sight, probably hunkering in the little bit of shade on the other side of the seawall.

"Should we stop and say hello?" Rumor asked Mary.

"On the way back."

The cockeyed doors to Papa's garage, or his castle, as he liked to call it, were shut and latched but not locked. Rumor swung one open, and the familiar smell of motor oil and dust washed across her. In the light of the single window, she saw his workbench, now empty except for the oil stains and dirt. His army cot, folded up and bound, stood against the wall, surrounded by crates and crates of his scrap metal, wood, and wire. In one box, the jar of Tootsie Rolls leaned against some sort of an engine part coated in dust. The motorized surfboard, with blue wires still reaching out like the tentacles of a sea anemone, lay on its side, leaning against the bare studs of the wall.

"Not to boast or anything, darling, but it looks like I was right. He's long gone." Mary bent over one of his crates. "You think he's coming back for this junk, or do you think Mrs. Bailey's having it hauled to the dump?"

Rumor looked into one of the cartons filled with Papa's clothes. His red-and-white-striped vest lay neatly folded on top. "Without his belongings, how will he make a living?"

Papa's lone lightbulb hung down from the ceiling, not looped to another hanger, but long and dangling a foot from the floor. Rumor remembered it swinging like a pendulum, back and forth, back and forth, lighting one wall and then the other that horrible night. She took the wire and looped it on the hook over his workbench.

Rumor found an old notepad, yellowed and curling at the edges, sticking up from one of the crates. She leafed through pages and pages of Papa's diagrams and sketches and his distinct handwriting that Mother called chicken scratches. He had labeled his inventions: Automatic Toast Butterer, Popcorn Sorter, Motorized Surfboard, Shoe Mop, Radio Hat, Portable Extension Bridge, Bread and Pie Cooler, and on and on. All of Papa's plans. She found a blank page toward the back. "You got a pen or pencil?"

Mary dug around in her purse and pulled one out.

In her best handwriting, Rumor left a note for Papa in case he ever came for his crates. "Dear Papa, I still love you and I forgive you, just please never do it again. I know you don't want to hurt anyone, but that is a terrible thing. Sincerely, Rumor." She flipped all his notes and diagrams back over the top of her message. He'd find it as soon as he had another idea.

"Hello?" They heard Mrs. Bailey's voice call from outside. "Who's there?"

"It's only us, Mrs. Bailey. Rumor and Mary."

Mrs. Bailey appeared in the doorway, in her housedress, with a scarf tied over her hair. "Oh, dear, dear. Sweet girls. Your papa has gone. Didn't he tell you?"

"Yes, we knew," Rumor said. "We only wanted to stop by."

"What a terrible thing," she said. "Having to move away from you girls to find work. If you ask me, there is more to it than that. He wouldn't leave you unless he had no choice, and by the look of his black eye before he left, I can tell you that he had no other choice. I think he got into a row with one of the local boys, and you know what a pacifist your papa is, I don't think he could do business here anymore."

Rumor looked back at the crates. "Is he coming back for his things?"

"Unfortunately not, dear. A nice sergeant from the police department arranged for them to be shipped to your papa in Los Angeles. A man will be here this coming week to put them into shipping containers.

I'm wondering if the police are hiding your papa to protect him. Maybe he witnessed a crime. Would you girls like to come in for a glass of milk? I got some Ovaltine from the market."

"Thank you, Mrs. Bailey," Mary said. "That would be marvelous, except that our mother and aunt are waiting for us."

"Oh, how wonderful. You girls run off and enjoy your day now. Don't be strangers. I do love your visits."

Rumor gave Mrs. Bailey a hug and wondered who'd look after her now that Papa was gone.

"That looks like Ruby," Rumor said, pointing to a tiny figure sitting on the edge of the sidewalk planks with her bare feet in the sand and her hands covering her face. Rumor and Mary sat on either side of her, and she peeked out at them but then closed her fingers back over her eyes.

"Hi, Ruby," Rumor said, placing her hand on Ruby's back, feeling the thin bones beneath her blouse, as tiny and fragile as a sandpiper.

Ruby raised her head but kept her eyes closed. "Shhh," she said. "I'm counting. One thousand eleven, one thousand twelve, one thousand thirteen . . ."

Rumor and Mary sat on either side of her, watching the tiny face with eyes squinted tight and her little lips forming the numbers.

"One thousand twenty," she shouted, jumping to her feet. "Ready or not, here I come."

And without a word of good-bye, she skipped down the lane, peeking around bushes, on the other side of fences, and behind garbage bins until she came to the corner of a garage, and another girl leapt out, running in the opposite direction, with Ruby hot on her heels, both giggling until they disappeared around the corner and down another lane.

Mary took Rumor's hand, and the two of them headed off toward Ocean Walk. Instead of heading down the crowded walkway, they removed their shoes to walk along the surf. Two kites snapped in the breeze, pulling tight against the string that held them to the earth.

Mary found an unbroken sand dollar. "Why do you think God put doves inside sand dollars?" she asked as she broke away the outer shell, dropping the pieces into the sand. "Look, there's five. Always five," she said, cupping the tiny white doves in her palm.

Rumor looked down at the broken pieces, already half-sunken in the sand.

"You have to break it, darling . . ." Mary began to say.

Rumor held her hand out. Mary, looking unsure for a moment, dropped the five white doves into her palm.

"I know," Rumor said. "Some things need to be broken in order to free what's inside."

ACKNOWLEDGMENTS

Nothing in life is done in isolation, and this novel would not be possible without all the love, support, instruction, and feedback from the people in my life.

Thanks to my biggest supporters—my children: Brittany Romo, Brennan Romo, and Ryan Romo; my mother, Sandy Folk; my siblings, John J. Folk III and Kristy Oliver; and to my father, John J. Folk II, who left this earth far too early but always encouraged me to do what I love in life. Much appreciation to my sweet buns, who provided many hours of love and laughter as we made our way through Pacific University's MFA program: Kim Flugga-Ciha, Sarah Potok, Jane Stark, and Joyce Tomlinson. I'm also blessed by the rest of my big and loving family, my friends, and all of my students, past and present, who have believed that I would succeed no matter how many years went by.

I am grateful to the San Diego Historical Society and the dedicated archivists who so thoroughly preserve the history of San Diego and make it available to the public.

Thank you to my agent, Larry Kirshbaum, and my editors, Jodi Warshaw, Kristin Mehus-Roe, and Jerri Corgiat Gallagher. I appreciate the feedback from my readers: Diane Peters, Kim Flugga-Ciha, and Jane

Stark; and all the instruction from Pacific University's MFA program, especially my advisors: Craig Lesley, Pete Fromm, Ann Hood, and Mary Helen Stafaniak.

A special thanks to Deborah Reed for giving me the jump-start on my career—there are just not enough words; and to my daughter, Brittany Romo, who has spent countless hours sitting with me in coffee shops from the time she was in elementary school till now as a professional woman, meeting me in San Diego to research and create beautiful artwork for me.

ABOUT THE AUTHOR

 Kelly Romo currently lives in Oregon with her three children, where she teaches writing, literature, and social studies. She loves the outdoors: hiking, kayaking, and camping. Kelly grew up in California running around with all her thrill-seeking cousins and siblings, jumping off cliffs into the Colorado River, exploring caves on the beaches of Mexico, riding dirt bikes, water skiing, and snow skiing.

Made in the USA
Monee, IL
21 June 2023

35986284R00246